PRAISE FOR *Neurotically Yours*

"*Neurotically Yours* had me hooked instantly, offering laugh-out-loud moments, brilliant lines, and a realistic portrait of all kinds of human emotion. I particularly adored the vibrant and colorful characters—including a reiki-dispensing feline! Brilliant reading and great entertainment skillfully delivered."

—Nicky Wells, author of *Sophie's Turn*

"This novel is a roller coaster ride of emotions and you are with Dara all the way, getting mad, having fun, getting confused and more than a little neurotic, shedding a tear, and then falling madly and terrifyingly in love with 'The One.' I absolutely loved this story and once I started reading it I found it hard to put down."

—Janice Horton, author of *Reaching for the Stars*

"What's not to love about *Neurotically Yours*? Dara is the perfect flawed heroine—quirky, relentless, and ultimately, completely loveable."

—Kaira Rouda, award-winning author of *Here, Home, Hope*

"Back with a second novel that's both giggle-out-loud funny and at times touching, Trachtenberg gives readers a sneak peek into the Los Angeles dating scene. Featuring a great main character, snappy dialogue, and an engrossing storyline, *Neurotically Yours* is hard to put down!"

—Jessica Strassner, bestselling author of *The One Who Got Away*

"Witty, sharp, and emotional—a perfect tale of love, loss and the dating game."

—Mandy Baggot, author of *Strings Attached*

"I loved *Neurotically Yours*! It features a dazzling set of characters. Each page is full of clever banter and charming references to the nonsense we pet owners say on a daily basis to our furry children. Prepare to laugh, fume, and finally swoon with this endearing story."

—Christine Cunningham, bestselling author of *First Snow*

"Hilarious, moving, and completely entertaining, this is a novel you can devour in one bite…With *Neurotically Yours*, Ms. Trachtenberg has hit another home run!"

—*The Long Island Tribune*

"Bonnie Trachtenberg brings such life to her characters in *Neurotically Yours* that I imagined them as real people, and this actually happening to someone I knew personally. I honestly couldn't put this book down! I wanted to keep reading until I knew the ending, and then I wanted to read more!"

—Emerald Barnes, author of *Read Me Dead*

PRAISE FOR *Wedlocked: A Novel*

"*Wedlocked* speaks to so many people...Trachtenberg's appealing wit and ability to create characters that jump off the page and into our hearts has a lot to do with it...I highly recommend this book."

—*The Long Island Tribune*

"I laughed out loud at this story. Got a tad teary here and there and I also loved every page I read. Ms. Trachtenberg is a hoot! If you're looking for a gift novel, here it is—give it to yourself first!!"

—Nancy Erickson, *Cheryl's Book Nook*

"*Wedlocked* is a wonderful, amusing escape...you will find yourself laughing throughout the book...Don't miss the read....it is splendid!!! You will love it....I certainly did." **Five Stars**

—*Silver's Reviews*

"Trachtenberg's story is not only moving, but inspiring...a beautiful story about friends, family, dreams and most importantly second chances in love and life...I thoroughly enjoyed reading *Wedlocked*...
I highly recommend this novel." **Five Stars**

—*Boekie's Book Reviews*

"Bonnie Trachtenberg is T-A-L-E-N-T-E-D! WOW! LOVED this one! This is a story that will have you smiling, frowning and everything in between!..DEFINITELY highly recommend with 5 Books and two thumbs up! I can't wait to see what Ms. Trachtenberg has in store next for her new found fans!"

—*ReviewsbyMolly.com*

"*Wedlocked* is a transformational novel, filled with family, friends, love, heartache, and redemption, just like real life—only much, much funnier! Enjoy!"

—*PopcornReads.com*

"This book has everything – drama, humor, sadness and even some adventure tossed in. *Wedlocked* is a fast-paced book that makes you giggle and cry at the same time…I didn't want this book to end."—**Five Stars (Kitties)**

—*Socrates Book Reviews*

"I can't quite put my finger on what makes *Wedlocked* so special. Is it the strong characters…or is it the universal story of trying to live up to others' expectations while staying true to your own dreams? Whatever it is, *Wedlocked* is a fun, emotional and intensely satisfying read that I would highly recommend."

—*Hands and Home*

"*Wedlocked* is Iris Rainer Dart meets Jennifer Weiner with a few zany plot twists added in. It was such a compelling story with well-developed characters and plot and fun Jewish humor. It had the feel of a chick flick without even being on the big screen…I really enjoyed *Wedlocked* and can't stop thinking about it. I've been recommending it to all my friends and want to recommend it here, as well! I think Ms. Trachtenberg has a real winner on her hands and I wish her tons of success with it."

—Melissa Amster, *Chick Lit Central*

"*Wedlocked* showcases an author that has grasped the importance of sinking her readers into the unfolding inner lives of her characters, particularly that of her strong central character, Rebecca, who does things that most of us would only dream about. And this is what makes this novel a worthwhile read, leaving us with a lasting impression and impact."

—*American Chronicle*

"*Wedlocked* is a perfect late summer escape from reality. Fast-paced, full of eclectic supporting characters...a romantic romp with both heart and a message about self-worth and not allowing oneself to be swept along by others' expectations and hopes for us. It is a well-crafted first novel and I look forward to reading more of Trachtenberg's work."

—Janie H. Siess, *Colloquium*

"This hilarious take on love and marriage will captivate readers and have them laughing out loud. The easy, flowing pace and genuine, easy to love characters make this book hard to put down. The entertaining and well thought out plot bring everything together to make this a truly great read."

—Nicole Mahoney, *Review the Book*

Also by Bonnie Trachtenberg

Wedlocked: A Novel

Sony Wonder adaptations:
Snow White
The Night before Christmas
The Swan Princess
The New Adventures of Peter Rabbit
The Prince and the Pauper
The Christmas Elves
Noah's Ark

Neurotically Yours

A Novel

Bonnie Trachtenberg

THAT'S AMORE PUBLISHING

Neurotically Yours
A Novel

That's Amore Publishing
25 West 43rd Street
Suite 711
New York, N.Y. 10036

Cover art by Laura Grace Montaruli
www.LauraGMontaruli.com

Author photo by Jennifer LoRe Muller
www.photosbyjlm.com

ISBN: 978-0-9849985-0-0 (sc)

Printed in the United States of America

Library of Congress Control Number: 2012901067

Release date: 4/2012

For Mitchell, who rescued me from it all.

Neurotically Yours

Prologue

Stamford, Connecticut, 1973

AT JUST SIX YEARS OLD, Dara Lynn Harrison confronted her romantic destiny. It happened the evening of her sister's ninth birthday, when Amanda slipped off the top to her most coveted gift, a hand-me-down game from their older cousin, Beth, called Mystery Date. Amanda had been privileged to play it only once with the "big girls," and afterward begged her mother to buy it, to no avail. Instead, her frugal mother secured a promise from Aunt Jean that Amanda would receive the game as soon as Beth outgrew it.

As the yellow and white floral wrapping paper drifted to the floor at Amanda's feet, the gift emerged—still perfect, despite two missing cards and a pizza stain on the corner of the board. Amanda, after much badgering from Dara Lynn and some scolding by their mother, deigned to let her little sister enter the inner sanctum of her bedroom. There, Dara Lynn joined her and her friends Angela and Ivy, and experienced for the first time the thrilling and precarious world of dating.

A girlie-girl's paradise, the room featured frilly pink and white curtains that matched the linens on Amanda's canopy bed. The shag carpet was also pink and white, with a small burn mark where an Easy Bake Oven had once sat. That April day, the rain beat against the double-hung windows, and the harmonized voices of the Partridge Family emanated softly from Amanda's turntable.

The object of the game, Amanda explained, was to draw the cards that would make up one complete outfit. Then you would turn the knob of the mysterious white door at the center of the board and pull it open. If you twisted it just right, you'd find the man who perfectly coordinated with your ensemble.

Amanda reached for the Magic Knob and opened the door with a flourish to present the men.

"The one you'll want the most is the prom date," she advised, revealing a suavely handsome young man dressed in a tux and bearing flowers. "Then there's the skier, the bowler, and the beach date," she continued, introducing each one. "But whatever you do, you don't want to get *this* guy."

Dara Lynn looked at the slovenly dressed man Amanda called the Dud. She didn't say that he looked kind of cute despite his disheveled clothing, for fear of ridicule—but she thought it just the same.

As the girls played, giggles, groans, and excitement filled the room. Amanda, fixated on her prom date, sought to win him with a single-minded approach, and grew more perturbed with every superfluous card she drew. Dara Lynn, on the other hand, thought the object of Amanda's affections to be a rather boring prospect.

Ivy announced that her dreamboat was the beach man and made a fervent plea to God, half under her breath, each time she grabbed the tiny blue plastic knob between her little fingers. On the third try, Ivy's prayers were answered, and from her reaction, anyone would have sworn Frankie Avalon himself was about to sweep her off for a game of Beach Blanket Bingo. Amanda tried to hide her jealousy, but with each turn of the knob her frustration grew.

Then came Dara Lynn's moment of truth. She would relive it for many years to come, that tingly, anxious, excited feeling of knowing her dream man could be standing just beyond the threshold. She took a shaky breath and opened the plastic door. There he stood, trousers four sizes too big, dirty, scruffy, and utterly hopeless—except he was cute, really cute. He just needed a makeover. She thought about her paper dolls and the array of clothing she pinned on them. She could do the same for him. Dara Lynn smiled for an instant—

"Yuck! You got the Dud!" yelled Amanda. She laughed, and Ivy and Angela joined in.

"He's not so bad," Dara Lynn said meekly.

"Okay, turn in your cards," Amanda ordered.

"What if I want to keep him?"

"Keep him? You can't keep him. You lost!"

"But why?"

"Now you see why I told Mom I didn't want to play with you? You don't even know how to follow rules."

"Well, I like him!"

"He's a bum, Dara Lynn. Look at him. Do you want a bum or a dream date? He's probably a grease monkey like Dad," Amanda said disdainfully.

"So?"

"And he'd probably leave you, just like Dad left Mom."

Dara Lynn ran crying from Amanda's room down the hall to her own, as her sister's harsh words rang in her ears. She slammed her door shut, flung herself onto her bed, and bawled into her pillow. After a few minutes, she took a breath and grabbed a tissue from her nightstand to wipe her nose. Still sniffling, she slid open the top drawer, reached into the back, and pulled out a photograph. A man wearing baggy pants and an undershirt looked back at her. He had a streak of grease on his face, a hammer hanging from his belt loop, and was holding a baby girl in his arms. She touched his face with her finger as a tear wound its way down

3

her cheek. It wasn't her fault that he'd left, or so her mother had told her again and again—but deep down, she still wondered. Dara Lynn laid her head on the photograph and cried herself to sleep.

One

Los Angeles, Thirty Years Later

Navigating Dating

Dear Dara,

I've read your column for three years and you always give really smart advice, so I thought I'd give you a shot. My boyfriend of six months has been distancing himself from me this month and when I ask him why, he just denies it and tells me I'm crazy. He doesn't want to see me as often, doesn't call me back sometimes for a day or two, and I'm afraid he may be dating someone else even though we said we'd be exclusive. Also, a friend told me he was out with his friends last Friday night even though he told me he was working. What do you think I should do to get him back the way I want him? He used to be so attentive.

Signed,

Troubled in Tarzana

Dear Troubled,

As I see it, you can narrow your problem down to one of two scenarios. Only time will tell which you are facing. Either: A) Your boyfriend may be going through a period of relationship claustro-

phobia, which typically happens around the six-month mark. If so, back off and get busy with your life, as he will find his way back to you when he feels less panicked, OR B) Your boyfriend is a slithering coward who is no longer interested in you but can't bring himself to break up. It might be he's afraid of confrontation and/or hurting you. At least that would afford him the excuse of having a conscience. However, he might just be keeping you in the wings until something better/prettier/younger/richer/bitchier comes along to entice him.

Either way, you have only one mode of action: Let him go! Now the thought of doing this is, to some women, about as daunting as skydiving, but it's a must. Forget about him and act as if you've broken up. Go out with your girlfriends, flirt with other men, get busy with your hobbies, and, whatever you do, don't call him or act like a sappy-eyed wimp if you run into him unexpectedly. If he calls and asks to see you for a date, tell him you've been so busy and will call him back when you're in front of your calendar. Then, if you so choose, you may see him once more to determine if his attitude has changed for the better—but, remember, he needs to know he could be on the verge of losing you forever (and he is!) unless he gets his ass in gear and wises up.

Now, being the optimistic person I am, my advice is to assume you are dealing with scenario A and act accordingly. Within a month or so you will know if he is responding, or sense that scenario B is a more apt diagnosis. If that's the case, then the actions I suggest will afford you some dignity and respect, while letting him know you are just fine—even better—without him darkening your door.

Reggie Dayton leaned back in the office chair of his cubicle and folded his Bruno Magli shoes left over right on his desktop as he read Dara's latest column. He had milk chocolate skin, sea green eyes, a finely chiseled jaw, and was dressed elegantly enough to be featured in *Gentlemen's Quarterly*, despite the less than extravagant salary he earned from their weekly paper, *LA Entertains*. Although only five foot nine, he had the broad shoulders and strapping physique of a man who spent an inordinate amount of time at the gym.

Dara tapped her tan high-heeled pumps in a manic beat while gnawing a pink pencil and eyeing the poster on the wall behind him. A mostly nude and very fetching man rippled his muscles while luxuriating on a tropical beach, his delectable body showered by a bottle of Stone Cold Vodka. When the new editor, otherwise known as The Beast, had first spotted it, he asked Reggie to take it down—until he learned that the vodka model was none other than Reggie's longtime flame, Vincenzo. He backed off more out of shock than anything else.

When Reggie finished reading, he placed the column on his Mac's keyboard and looked at Dara with a knowing smirk.

"So, what do you think?" she asked impatiently, now playing with a button on her indigo Dolce and Gabbana suit jacket.

"I have a theory," he replied. "You know why you're so popular, Harri?"

Dara shot him a confident grin. "Yes, because I give great advice."

Reggie scratched his head and thought for a moment. "No, that's not it."

Dara rolled her large azure eyes and leaned back in Reggie's guest chair, realizing a compliment would not be forthcoming.

"It's because people looking for love are so desperate they become masochistic, and you, Harri dear, are the only columnist in town who gives them what they want."

Dara fidgeted in her chair and tossed her blonde hair, which hung in chic layers to the top of her shoulders.

"Are you calling me a sadist, Reggie?"

He shrugged and raised his eyebrows. "If the stiletto fits…"

"Really? Well that's a fascinating observation, Reginald," she said as she stood up and grabbed the column off his keyboard. "I'm the guest speaker at the Christian Singles Annual Gala tonight. Maybe I should begin by crucifying a volunteer from the audience."

"Don't get pissy. You know I mean it affectionately."

"What did you mean affectionately?" asked Barb, the nosy arts critic who happened to be passing by at just the wrong moment. She had a slightly turned-up nose, long strawberry blonde hair, and wore a skin-tight dress, despite her chunky midsection.

"Apparently Reggie thinks I'm a sadist."

"Oh, that's not true," said Barb, coming to Dara's defense.

Dara poked her tongue in Reggie's direction.

"Look at her. She's the cutest woman I know," Barb said. "She's just a little rough around the edges. If we can just get her laid again sometime this century, I'm sure she'd soften up a little."

"Shut up, Barb!" Dara said, bristling, as Reggie laughed heartily.

"How long has it been now?" Barb continued.

"None of your damn business."

"That long, huh?" said Reggie. "I told you not to break it off with Tony until you found another booty caller to replace him."

Dara shot him a death laser glare.

"Well, it's true. Your elusive mystery man that nobody's ever met was good for *something*, wasn't he?" asked Reggie. "Besides, he survived four years' worth of your PMS. He should have been awarded a Purple Heart as his parting gift."

Before Dara could retort, Barb cut in, "You know, honey, wearing that ring on your finger isn't exactly an invitation to Mr. Right."

"I have a lecture tonight," Dara replied. She had initially taken to wearing the fake engagement ring as a deterrent to any prying questions from audience members, although now she found herself wearing it even when she had no booking. "And besides, Tony threatened to buy me one many times, so it's not that far removed from reality."

"Not unless you realize you've been broken up for over a year and haven't had a date since," said Reggie.

"Oh, really? And how do you know?" Dara demanded.

"Because you haven't complained about any. You forget how well I know you, Harri."

"Then you should know why I'm sparing myself the misery. I remember vividly just how pathetic dating can be."

"Well, it might be a little less pathetic if you didn't make everyone take you to IHOP on the first date," noted Reggie.

"IHOP? You mean the International House of Pancakes?" asked Barb with surprise. "Not exactly the height of sophistication. Why there?"

"Because I wouldn't ever go there in my real life and therefore wouldn't be introducing possible maniacs to my favorite haunts."

Barb thought it over. "Actually, that sounds kind of brilliant."

"And besides, no date who pays for your silver dollar pancake special is going to think he's getting lucky after," added Reggie with a laugh.

"So whatever happened to that nice guy you met at the farmers' market?" asked Barb. "You seemed to really like him."

That had been two years ago, during one of her countless breakups with Tony.

"The guy talked in his sleep," replied Reggie with a widening grin.

"Is that such a crime?" asked Barb.

"It is if he says, 'I'll chop you up in little pieces, and no one will ever find you,'" Reggie informed her, "and on the first night they made whoopee!"

"No!" she exclaimed, turning to Dara. "Is it true?"

Dara miserably shrugged her agreement.

"Oh, my! Well, you still got to get back in the game, sweetie," Barb said as she headed for the copy machine.

"I dated for almost two decades. Don't you think I've earned a little vacation?" she asked Reggie.

"A vacation, yes; a sabbatical, no," he said. "We are so going for drinks Friday night and talking this nonsense out. This celibacy thing is getting very boring."

"There's nothing to talk about. I'm perfectly happy with my life—and to tell you the truth, I love being alone. It's being *with* someone that poses a challenge for me. Besides, I have the three Cs of contentment: my career, my condo, and my cat."

"And that's another thing. You are way too attached to that cat!" said Reggie, removing his feet from his desk and sitting upright. "Didn't you write a column once about cozy attachments standing in the way of relationships?"

"Mallory is not coming between me and anyone. I just find her better company than the vast population of Los Angeles."

Reggie considered her words. "Understandable," he concurred, "but you're missing an important point."

"And what is that?"

"You can't give good advice to the lovelorn when you're more hard-up than they are."

"I am not hard-up!" Dara whispered angrily. "And do you think you could keep your voice down? You-know-who is in his office—"

"Fine," he interrupted in a loud whisper, "but one day you're going to have to face your fear of falling in love again."

Dara, caught off guard, had no retort. She just leaned her head back for a moment and sighed before changing the subject.

"So getting back to my column—"

"Nice duck," said Reggie.

"Wasn't it?"

"As usual, your column is pure brilliance, darling. Confucius would be proud."

She smirked at him. "Thanks for nothing."

"Happy to not help," he said with satisfied smile, turning back to his own work.

Dara huffed her way back to her cubicle, which was situated on the next aisle in the paper's newsroom. To the left of her computer stood the *Merriam-Webster Dictionary, Roget's Thesaurus, The Elements of Style,* and *The Chicago Manual of Style,* all held upright by the overstuffed rolodex she refused to computerize. To the right sat a heart-shaped frame with a picture of Mallory in it, a pink stuffed bunny, and her World's Best Advice Columnist mug filled with a bouquet of colorful pencils, which upon closer examination appeared to have been assaulted by a colony of termites. She used them to color code edits to her columns before making any permanent changes, a habit from fourth grade she couldn't seem to shake.

Dara knew that Reggie, the paper's fashion editor, had made a small—albeit overstated—point, and since he was usually on the money, this irked her. Reggie had worked at the paper for four years; she had ten under her belt. Being the resourceful woman that she was, she'd used her popular column and the paper's prestigious reputation to promote herself as L.A.'s mating maven and had become one of the busiest and most requested guest lecturers in the singles' arena. She had even begun pitching her idea for a book to some local publishers. So who needed an angst-ridden relationship to stand in her way?

Two

I T HAD BEEN FOURTEEN MONTHS since Dara had broken it off for good with Tony, yet he still called her at least once a week to see if she'd changed her mind. Tony was a walking contradiction. He couldn't commit, yet could never let go either. It was enough to drive a woman crazy, and Dara had come close.

This week's call came as she entered her front door at nine-thirty, after her lecture. She hadn't eaten dinner since food tended to squirm in her stomach before a public performance. She dropped her purse and grabbed the cordless phone that sat on her kitchen counter. Before clicking Talk, she glanced at the ID and saw Tony's number. Although she knew she should stop taking his calls, something impelled her to keep answering.

Like it or not, Tony Remini had become somewhat of a fixture in her life. She knew he loved her on some remedial level, but he was often inconsiderate, self-absorbed, and had a history of unavailability when she needed him most. Besides that, his frugality made sure that their dating life was less than eventful. Their four-year on-again, off-again relationship never took a more serious turn, and ironically, estrangements brought out the best in him.

"Hi, Tony. I just got home, can I call you back? I'm starving and I have to feed Mallory," she said while removing her three-and-a-half-inch heels. She let out a groan of relief as she shrank to her normal five foot one size.

"Mallory? You always cared more about that cat than me," he joked.

"That's 'cause she's always been nicer to me than you were."

"Oh, that's not true."

"Like hell it isn't."

"Okay, I can see where this is going. Anyway, don't forget to call me back...like you did last week."

"I won't," she sang with annoyance. "Bye."

"Brrrrrp," Mallory called up to her while weaving her way though Dara's legs.

"Oh, my poor baby's hungry!" she crooned apologetically.

Dara put a dish of Fancy Feast on the floor and filled another dish with fresh cold water. She picked up the long-haired Siamese mix whose eyes were even bluer than her own and kissed her several times on the head before placing her in front of her dinner.

"How was your day, cutie?" she asked.

Mallory lifted her head briefly to look at her, and then turned her attention back to the Savory Salmon. Dara pulled a Lean Cuisine from the freezer, pierced it with a fork, and popped it in the microwave. Five minutes later, she stood eating fettuccini at the black and white granite counter, bachelor style. She could have eaten at her lovely French country dining room table but figured it wasn't worth the effort, since her so-called gourmet dinner would be gone in half the time it took to cook it.

Dara had bought the Marina Del Rey condominium when the market was right—or as right as it could get in Marina Del Rey—but had never made the changes she'd planned when she first moved in. Her career had always taken precedence and ate up most of her free time.

The condo had a terrace with a side view of the Pacific. Her neighbors were a hodgepodge of mostly transplanted East Coasters seeking the good life on the shores of the West. She had left Connecticut to attend UCLA, her alma mater, and had been a California girl ever since.

She undressed, showered, and plopped onto her queen-sized bed next to Mallory, who had curled up between two pillows. After grabbing a Granny Smith apple from her nightstand, she dialed Tony's number.

"Hi."

"All settled in?"

"Yes," she answered, taking a hefty bite.

"Guess what?"

"What?" she asked, chewing noisily.

"I sold six boats today."

"Good for you!"

"One I had to send to Iceland. Where the hell is Iceland?"

"Near Greenland. Didn't you ever play Risk?"

"No."

She took another bite.

"What are you eating?"

"An apple."

"It's a very loud apple. Can you turn it down?"

"I'll try," she said, swallowing. "Glad you're doing well, Ton. I guess more people can afford your inflatables than fiberglass, huh?"

"Looks like. I just got back from a show in Maine. Nice place. I could live there."

"Yeah? You moving?"

"Maybe. You like Maine?"

"What difference does that make?"

"Just wondering."

"We're not getting back together, Tony. You're free to move wherever you want."

"You say that now, but you'd miss me."

"Why? You can call me just the same from there."

"I miss you."

Dara sighed. "I know."

She took another zesty bite.

"But I know you don't miss me," Tony said matter-of-factly.

"Oh? And how do you know that?"

"Because you never would have chomped in my ear when we were a couple."

"That's silly."

"I know."

"I was thinking today how good you are at staying in touch and whispering sweet nothings now that we've been apart for all this time. How come you were such a lousy boyfriend?"

"Lousy? Was I really lousy? I don't think I was *lousy*."

"Well, a good boyfriend doesn't yell at you when you accidentally burn his crappy old frying pan."

"I did that?"

"Or give you a hard time when you get mascara on his pillow because you've been having a hormonal breakdown."

"I'm a proud survivor of more than a few of those—"

"Or not come meet your parents when they're in town because you suddenly have to be in San Diego for a boat show you never mentioned."

"There *was* a boat show. I showed you the brochures."

"Anyway, it doesn't matter what *you* think. You weren't dating you, *I* was."

"True. Hey, I know it's kinda late, but I'm sorry for all the things I did wrong."

"Don't worry. I already forgave you."

"You did? So does that mean you want me to come over and show my gratitude?" he asked mischievously.

"That won't be necessary."

"I was afraid of that. Well, ya can't say I didn't try. 'Night, Dara."

"'Night, Tony."

Dara turned out her light. She felt one of her headaches coming on but was too exhausted to get up and find her migraine medication. The caffeine in it would have given her an uneasy sleep anyway. She'd been no stranger to headaches for most of her life, though they had become more manageable and infrequent since she'd brought Mallory home from the shelter.

The little rescue cat came to Dara's rescue now, climbing onto her pillow and wrapping her warm, furry body around Dara's head like a Russian *czapka*. She knew it was weird, even crazy to think it, but deep down, she was convinced Mallory had Healing Paws. Whether Dara hurt herself or just felt under the weather, the cat instinctively came to her aid. At first, Dara figured it was just her writer's imagination in over-drive, but whenever the cat laid her paws on the problem, within a few minutes, the pounding headache, the gastritis, the sprained finger inexplicably felt worlds better.

Dara lay in the dark as Mallory purred. She could feel the soft furry heat of them, the smooth little under pads, gently working their magic. She thought that most people would just chalk it up to coincidence—or think her mad—but she knew better. That furry little feline was a reiki master in disguise.

❧ *Three* ❦

"**H**EY NOW, YOU'RE AN ALL STAR, *get your game on—go play! Hey now, you're a rock star, get the show on—get paid ...*" A tinny Smash Mouth emanating from Dara's cell phone alarm jarred her awake at six A.M. She kissed Mallory good morning and jumped out of bed to feed her. After washing up, she pulled on her running shorts, bra and tee, laced up her sneakers, grabbed her trusty ten-year-old walkman, and for the hundredth time thought about upgrading to an iPod. As she fumbled to lock up, her next-door neighbor Jesse poked his curler-bedecked head out of his door, pinching the white ruffles of his nightgown collar together.

"Morning, Dara Doll," he said, startling her a bit. "How's the best advice columnist in the U.S.A. doing today?"

"Fine," she said. "What are you doing up?"

"I didn't sleep a wink last night!"

"What's wrong?"

"I have the most painful ingrown toenail," he complained, sticking his left foot out the door and wiggling his blue painted toenails. "Those damn pedicurists do it to me all the time. I'd come out, but I'm in my jammies," he whispered.

"Sorry to hear it, Jess. Maybe you should see a doctor."

"Doctor, shmoctor. All they want to do is operate. I was wondering if I could come by later and have Mallory work on it."

Jesse was the only one she had confided in about Mallory's "gift." She knew he wouldn't laugh in her face or offer to call the local funny farm. In fact, he had the polar opposite response, taking the news so seriously that he now counted on the little feline's attention when he had so much as a paper cut.

"Sure. I'll be home early tonight. I'll call you when I get in," she said.

"Thanks, honey. Kiss kiss."

Dara flew down two flights of stairs and pushed open the heavy metal door. Another sun-drenched California day greeted her. She stretched her legs against a cement half wall and then began to jog down the quiet beach road.

Leaning back in her office chair, still feeling rejuvenated from her workout, Dara spoke on the phone, while glancing at what she'd just written on her computer screen:

Ten Questions to Ask a Man on Your First Date
(Assume Nothing!)

1. *Are you married?*
2. *Do you have a steady girlfriend?*
3. *Do you live with any females (including your mother)?*
4. *Are there any women with whom you are sleeping and would call a "close friend"?*
5. *Are there any female relationships in your life that you would classify as "complicated"?*
6. *Do you have any reason to hate your mother?*
7. *How many children are you supporting?*
8. *How many children might come looking for you in the future?*
9. *Are you wanted in any of the fifty states or abroad?*
10. *Is there any reason your fingerprints might be on file with the FBI?*

"I'd be delighted to speak at the seminar, Ms. Randolph," Dara said, dragging her attention back to the phone. "How much time is allotted for each speaker? Great, I'll make sure to prepare enough material. You know, you should really put an ad in our paper if you want to increase your attendance." She laughed charmingly. "Of course you can use my name. I'd be flattered."

Dara noticed Reggie standing over her shoulder and motioned that she was almost done. "Okay, terrific. Bye now."

Dara sat up and looked at him with excitement.

"I just got my first full seminar," she sang.

"I'm impressed," he told her.

"Now, what can I do for you, my darling Reginald?"

"For me? Nothing," he said, then lowered his voice to an ominous whisper, "but The Beast wants to see you."

Dara's high spirits began to deflate. "Oh, what now?" she asked with exasperation.

Over the last month, since Bob "The Beast" Bastley had taken over the job of editor-in-chief, she'd been chewed out for several new company violations, most notably: contaminating the refrigerator with outdated half and half; eating a grilled cheese sandwich at her desk instead of in the newly christened Corporate Dining Area (a makeshift four-by-four kitchen); and using Valuable Company Time to schedule a dentist appointment.

"I don't know," said Reggie. "Did you flush something other than toilet paper down the toilet?"

"I'm going to flush his K-Mart tie down the toilet," she whispered angrily, "after I strangle him with it."

"Now, now," Reggie whispered back, "he's only trying to 'ensure a safe and hospitable work environment for everyone.' Remember?"

Reggie flashed his stunningly white teeth.

"Hospitable, my ass," she retorted, rolling her chair back on the plastic carpet saver and heading toward the editor's office.

Dara took a cleansing breath and knocked on the half open door. The Beast glanced up from his computer with barely disguised annoyance, his diminutive figure eclipsed by his oversized desk. He had brown wavy hair combed neatly to one side, wore an ill-fitting bargain basement suit, and looked to be in his late twenties. She wondered how someone so young could secure an editor-in-chief position at a reputable entertainment newspaper. Smitty, the previous editor, had been with the paper for twenty years until his retirement, an announcement that had brought tears to Dara's eyes. She knew that work relationships like theirs came few and far between.

"You wanted to see me?" she asked.

"Yes. Please close the door and have a seat."

Something in his formal tone told her this had nothing to do with outdated dairy products. She waited for him to open his mouth and breathe some fire her way, but instead, he opened a folder on his desk and shuffled through the stack of papers inside. It didn't take long for Dara to realize the folder contained a collection of her columns. He pursed his flaky lips and narrowed his eyes as he looked at her.

"I've read over your columns, Dara, and I'm very concerned."

"Really? Why would they concern you?"

"I've never seen an advice columnist let loose on her readers the way you do. You've been writing this column for, what, almost eight years?"

Dara nodded slowly.

"I understand that a column will progress along with the columnist over a period of time. It's only natural—but in your case…"

"Yes?"

"Well, I find the *progression* quite disturbing."

"Disturbing?" she echoed with surprise.

"Well," he said, "early on, your column was more like a pep talk, more hopeful. That's good. That's what people want to hear, but lately..."

The Beast tapped his bony fingers on his desk while sighing.

"You can get to the point, Bob," she said with some irreverence. The change in tone brought out the editor she was starting to know and hate.

"Telling people they're better off on their own is not the best romantic advice."

"It is if they're dating a creep."

"Last month you suggested that a forty-eight-year-old woman—" he shuffled through the file so he could quote her accurately, "'would be better off with goldfish for company than the pathetic stream of misfits polluting her dating waters.'"

"Well, it's true," Dara replied.

He pulled out another page. "And in March, you told Stymied in Santa Monica that, and I quote again, 'Couples therapy would be a waste of time considering your fiancé's obvious obsession with killing small, defenseless animals.'"

Bob looked sternly at Dara. "So he's a hunter," he said with annoyance. "Lots of people are hunters. That doesn't disqualify such a person from couples therapy—or good relationships."

"It does when the person does it every weekend instead of paying some modicum of attention to his fiancée. My God, they're not even married yet, and he's totally ignoring her, not to mention murdering innocent wildlife."

"Well," Bob added as he pulled Exhibit C from the pile, "at least you're an equal opportunity offender. You told this man that his girlfriend was 'clearly a narcissist who will play nice until she sinks her claws deep enough into your skin to hold you down and eat you alive.' Then you quoted lyrics from a Hall and Oates song, 'Maneater.'"

"Yes," Dara commented coolly, "I've seen it happen many times with women like that."

"You told him to 'get over his hard-on for bitches unless he wants a life of pain and misery.'"

She nodded with assuredness. "Sound advice."

The Beast huffed at her and began to raise his voice, "First of all, you can't diagnose someone with a personality disorder when you've never even met her."

"Oh, come on, it's so obvious though—" she started.

"And, second, if he breaks up with her after reading this, we could have a lawsuit on our hands!"

"We have a disclaimer, remember? This is only for entertainment purposes, blah, blah, blah—"

"That doesn't mean someone won't start trouble anyway! We live in a very litigious state." The Beast tried to calm himself with a deep breath. "Dara, your column is way too...depressing."

"Depressing?" she repeated with indignation. "Then why is it more popular than ever? I'll tell you why," she added before he could interrupt. "Because people know it's the truth. I'm not dolling up my advice with bull and phony platitudes. I tell it like it is, and my readers appreciate it. There's a hunger for practicality and realism out there. Many of my readers are older and wiser and more cynical because of it. They'd see right through a fairy tale answer."

"And what about the hopeful younger readers?" he asked.

She folded her arms across her chest. "They'd do well to get their heads out of the clouds and learn the lessons early so they don't have to become cynical older readers," she proclaimed.

"Dara, it's not the readers who are cynical, it's you. And as editor of this paper, it's up to me to decide its tone."

He looked intently at her, but she didn't shrink from the gaze.

"No offense, but if your advice works so well, I imagine it would have worked for you by now. That ring isn't fooling anyone around here."

The remark hit her like a kick in the stomach. She swallowed and felt her cheeks burn. "Excuse me, Bob," she said venomously, "but what does or does not happen in my private life is none of your business and does not affect my job in any way."

"You're right. It is none of my business, but you have to admit this fact might give some people...pause," he said leaning back in his chair. "Anyway, getting back to the subject at hand, I don't like cynicism. I've decided to go with another, more cheerful columnist. I'm sorry."

At first his words didn't compute.

"Excuse me?" she managed with a slight laugh. The thought that she was being fired was so unbelievable that her brain couldn't comprehend it.

"I've arranged for a severance package for you. HR will lay out the details."

The no-nonsense tone coming from a man who could have been her annoying little brother made the reality even more difficult to accept. She leaned forward.

"Do you have any idea how popular my column is? How many thank you letters I get? That I have actual fans?!"

When The Beast shook his head and said nothing, Dara couldn't seem to choke out any more words.

"You have until tomorrow to clear out your things—and that includes anything you might be...*storing* in the company refrigerator."

❦ *Four* ❦

DARA'S PHONE HAD BEEN RINGING off the hook since she'd entered her apartment an hour earlier. The persistence of the ringing told her it was probably Reggie. He'd been speechless after hearing the news. She'd fled the office in shock, unable to talk until her brain stopped spinning and the pain shooting through the back of her head subsided. She'd immediately run for her medicine chest, downed two migraine tablets and prayed they'd make a dent in the pain. Then she stripped down, cocooned into her fuzzy robe, and climbed into bed.

After a few minutes, she heard a loud knocking at her front door. With the comforter pulled over her head and a quickly diminishing box of Kleenex clutched in her arms, she tried to ignore it, but the knocking became more adamant. Reluctantly, she dragged herself to the door and peeked through the keyhole. Jesse was standing outside with a look of concern on his face. His highlighted hair was pulled into a high ponytail and his pink cat-eye glasses sat slightly askew on his nose. She suddenly remembered his appointment with Mallory.

"I'm not feeling very well, Jess," she called through the door. "Can you come back tomorrow?"

"But, honey, I can barely even walk. I need to see the little Mallomar."

Dara sighed, knowing she couldn't dissuade him. She opened the door. He flounced in wearing a poodle skirt and pink sweater.

"What do you think? Sandra Dee?" he asked with his hand on his hip.

"Spittin' image," Dara replied cheerlessly.

"Now what's wrong with you? You look terrible, girlfriend."

"Don't ask," she said, sniffling her way to the Tuscan-inspired sofa, a lovely floral with carved cherry wood frame. They sat down together.

"Bad cold?"

"Not exactly." Her eyes spoke volumes.

"What happened?!" he asked, suddenly grabbing her hands.

"I...was fired today," she squeaked out.

Jesse gasped as if it were his last lungful of air. "Oh. My. God!" he exclaimed. "No!"

Dara nodded.

"That horrible little man had it in for you from the beginning! He can't do this to you!"

"Unfortunately, he can, and...he did. Said my column was too depressing. Can you believe it?"

"Depressing? Your column is the bible to L.A. singles. Is he a complete dingbat?"

"Said he wants someone more optimistic to appeal to his younger readers."

Jesse sniffed the air suspiciously. "Does anyone besides me smell ageism?" he asked.

"You think that's bad, he also told me if my advice was so good, it would have worked for me by now. I...I don't know, maybe he's right."

"Nonsense!"

"I don't know what to do with myself. I'm in shock. This column isn't just a job, it's who I am. I mean, I'm the one who birthed it, nurtured it, cultivated it into the success it is today. I'm booked for lectures—and a seminar—because of it. I was going to write a book—and he's going to bring in some inexperienced...Pollyanna to replace me?"

"This is just terrible. What are we going to do?" he said.

"It's not your problem, Jesse."

"Like hell it isn't. I'm not only your best friend, I'm your biggest fan!"

"Well, as of five P.M. tomorrow, I'm officially a nobody."

Jesse gasped again and cupped his hand over Dara's mouth. "You hush your mouth, hear? You are *not* a nobody. You are a star! You will persevere and be even bigger and better without that lousy rag."

"I thought you loved the paper."

"Only because of you. Besides, there's nobody I know who's more capable or self-sufficient than you are. You don't need them! You don't need anyone—well, maybe a friend right now, and I'm very glad to be here."

"Thanks, Jess. I'm sorry. I know you need to see Mallory. I'll go get her."

"Don't trouble yourself," he told her. "I have a special way of calling her. She always comes to me."

Jesse raised his voice a couple of octaves.

"Mal-o-mal-o-Mallory," he yodeled. "Where's my little pal-o-ry?"

Sure enough, Mallory came trotting in from the bedroom and jumped up on the couch between them. Jesse began to fawn over her, petting and kissing her.

"Who's the best little kitty in the Golden State?"

Dara smiled in spite of her mood. Jesse could always get her to smile by just being Jesse. He pulled his foot out of a pink house slipper and lifted it up to the cat.

"It's an ingrown toenail, baby," he told her. "Can you help?"

As Mallory began to inspect his foot, the phone rang again. Dara ignored it.

"Aren't you going to answer it? It could be important."

"It's probably just Reggie checking up on me."

"Well, don't keep him worrying, go talk to him."

Dara stood up and went to the kitchen phone. The ID showed Reggie's home phone number.

"I'm okay, Reg."

"Where have you been? I've been trying to reach you."

"Under the covers."

"I'm in shock. Everyone is just in shock, and we're all wondering who's next. I mean if you're dispensable, so are the rest of us."

"I'm sure you'll be fine. After all, *you're* not *depressing*. Jesse thinks Bob fired me because he thinks I'm too old," she complained, checking out her reflection in the oven door.

"Jesse? Oh, you mean that nutty neighbor of yours?"

"He's right here," she said uncomfortably, looking over to see Mallory now lying on his foot.

"You're only thirty-seven. That's not exactly ancient."

"Who are you kidding? Fifty years ago, I'd have been deemed an old maid."

"With your sexual history? I doubt it."

"Thanks a lot."

"Are you coming in tomorrow?"

"Just to clean out my things. Oh, God, how am I going to face everyone?" she cried, covering her forehead with her free hand.

"That should be the last thing on your mind."

"You're right, I need to worry about how I'm going to pay my mortgage and feed and clothe myself. Thanks for reminding me."

"You will find another job easily. I wouldn't be surprised if other publications start clamoring for you when they hear—"

"—that I was fired?"

"I'm not cheering you up, am I?"

"No, but that would be an impossible task anyway. I'll see you in the morning."

"Call if you need me."

"Yup," she said sadly, hanging up.

Jesse patted the cushion next to him and she joined him on the couch again. She blew her nose into a tissue as he placed his arm around her shoulder. Then they both gazed at Mallory, now lounging on her back under Jesse's bad foot.

"My toe feels better already."

"She's pretty amazing, isn't she?"

"You both are, honey."

The following day, Dara showed up at her office in jeans, sneakers, and a T-shirt for the first time. She was accosted by coworkers expressing their disbelief and condolences. The Beast avoided her and she him, making the whole nightmarish event just a little more bearable. Reggie promised to "get on the horn" and help her put out feelers. Barb looked at her with pity and said, "I can't believe it. I just can't believe it."

Dara packed a box with her things and grabbed her precious rolodex filled with the names and numbers of ten years' worth of business acquaintances. Then she hugged her colleagues and blinked away the tears.

She knew a full court press was the best way to handle the situation, and back in her apartment, she unleashed a torrent of calls to every influential person in or closely associated with the publishing businesses of Los Angeles. She did not say she was fired but instead began with some variation of, "I've left *LA Entertains* and I'm looking for a new home for my advice column." She made calls from noon until five P.M. that day and for the better part of nine to five for the next two days, garnering words of encouragement, promises to keep eyes and ears open for her, and wishes of good luck, but unfortunately, no offers.

When she had neared the end of her prospects on Friday evening, reality began to settle in. By Sunday, it had overtaken her and began draining away any enthusiasm she had managed to muster. For the first time, she started second-guessing her column, her abilities, her philosophy, her life.

She began to wonder if there was any validity to what The Beast had said. Pretending to be engaged? What did that say about her? It said she was a fraud. Worst of all, she now doubted that she would ever bounce back from this blow. Suddenly, the dreaded Sunday blues of her childhood reared its head. Little did she know it hadn't just come for a weekly visit but had packed a trunk and would be staying awhile.

Five

AFTER THREE WEEKS, DARA FOUND herself spiraling down an emotional vortex. She slept fitfully and had no appetite—which was fortuitous, since she had also stopped her daily runs. She had no visitors except for Jesse, who brought gifts to cheer her, starting out with comfort foods such as homemade oatmeal cookies and chocolate brownies, then shifting to more therapeutic offerings like a DVD of *Norma Rae*, the CD *Silver Lining* by Bonnie Raitt, and Gloria Steinem's book *Revolution from Within*. But Dara put them aside in favor of brooding. Her cat followed her around the apartment, barely ever leaving her side. She was grateful for the support.

Dara rarely answered the phone and went out only for necessities—to the drug store for more sleep aids, or the supermarket to replenish her supply of bottled water, Lean Cuisines, and cat food. She waited until late in the evening to make the trips in hopes she'd avoid seeing anyone. After warding off depression for nearly two decades, she suddenly found herself drowning in a dark pool of melancholy.

Spending her days swathed in her robe and sipping a stunning variety of herbal teas, Dara kept the shades drawn tight to block out the annoyingly pleasant L.A. weather, which refused to dovetail with her state of mind. When her bottle of Tylenol PM ran out, she downed melatonin and valerian nightly like some sort of New Age junkie.

Reggie called at least twice a day to beg her to come out for a drink or some dinner. She declined every time. Tony rang several times before she finally called him back. She didn't tell him she'd been fired, for fear he'd take advantage of her vulnerability and maneuver his way back into her life. Instead, she finally put her foot down, insisting they no longer speak. She blamed his ongoing calls for the romantic stagnancy in her life. He finally relented.

The shrill ringing of her phone pulled Dara from an afternoon snooze. Too dazed to check the ID, she grabbed the receiver. It was her mother, who had already threatened several times to hop a plane to California. Dara's assurances that she was minutes away from a job offer had begun to wear thin. Realizing she could not worm her way out of the call, she sandwiched the phone between her ear and pillow and curled up in a fetal position. Her mother was calling from the Stamford, Connecticut hardware store she and her husband had owned for nearly twenty-five years.

"Hello, dear. I was beginning to worry when I didn't hear back from you."

"Nothing to worry about, Mom. I told you that."

"Do you need any money?"

"No, I told you, I'm fine. I have savings, remember?"

"I know, but I don't want you to go through your savings account. You may need it for a rainy day."

"Well, what do you call this, Mom?"

Her mother thought for a moment. "Yes, I guess you're right—but if you need any—"

"I'm fine, really."

"I just wish you had someone looking out for you all the ways over there. I feel so helpless knowing you're three thousand miles away."

"There *is* someone looking out for me. Her name is Dara Harrison."

"I know you're a smart, independent woman, but at times like these, it's a Godsend if you have a partner. I just wish—"

"I know what you wish, Mom. We've been all through this before—"

"And?"

"—and I have to get ready for another interview, so I'll speak to you soon, okay?"

"Okay, dear," she said. "But Bill just wants to say hello."

Dara tried not to sigh into the phone. She didn't think she could manage any more fibbing.

"Hi, Dara," Bill said, "how come no Skype this week?"

Bill, her stepfather, was a gadget enthusiast. He had set her up with the software program the minute it had hit the market, hoping it would help them all feel closer despite the miles between them.

"Uh, my camera fell and broke," she lied. "I have to get a new one."

All she needed was for them to see the dark circles under her eyes, the unkempt hair, the sloppy sweatsuit.

"Don't forget. We like to see your pretty face once in a while, you know."

"I won't."

"So I hear you have some good prospects. Glad to hear it."

"Yes, I'll let you guys know which one comes through."

"Mom says you have an interview. What's this one?"

"Another local paper," Dara lied again. It wasn't getting any easier. "You haven't heard of it."

"Okay, we're wishing you lots of luck."

"Thanks, Bill."

"Maybe now's a good time to do some of those home improvements you talked about. Remember, it doesn't cost much when you do it yourself."

"I know," she replied.

"You were always my little fix-it girl, remember?"

"Yes."

"Well if you need anything, just holler."

"Will do! Thanks, Bill. Gotta go, okay?"

"Okay. We'll speak to you soon."

"Right," she said and placed the phone in its cradle. Then she pulled her maroon-colored comforter over her head once again.

Two days later, a large, heavy box arrived from Federal Express. Dara signed for it and lugged it inside. She saw the return address in Connecticut and figured it was a food basket from her mother, who probably assumed she was starving herself to death. After ripping open the box, though, she discovered a large metal chest.

Inside was everything from a set of hammers to pliers to several sizes of nails and screws. It also contained an electric drill, an electric jigsaw, a sander, a ratchet set, assorted screwdrivers, and everything else a do-it-yourselfer could need, including a big picture book with instructions for home improvements. She shook her head and smiled, proud of Bill for not thinking of women as the weaker (or less handy) sex. She dragged the box into the kitchen and unloaded it onto her counter.

Bill had joined her family a couple of years after her father had abandoned them. Before Bill, her mother, devastated by the desertion, had fallen into a long depression that she and her sister Amanda would later refer to as Mom's Bad Time.

Dara remembered climbing into bed with her mother on several occasions and sleeping in her father's spot, keeping it warm for him. She also recalled her mother's muffled sobs late in the night after she'd assumed her daughter was fast asleep. Dara never acknowledged this for fear it would upset her mother further, but she became fiercely protective of her, trying to keep her remaining parent from running off the rails. She tucked her own grief away in the outskirts of her mind where it had languished ever since.

Once her mother had pulled herself together, she'd found a job at a nearby clothing store and, with some financial help from Dara's grandparents, managed to keep the family afloat. Then luck finally shone on their home.

Dara was only eight when her mother married Bill. She was thrilled when he came to her mother's rescue, proving himself to be a sturdy, loving presence in their house. Bill referred to her and Amanda as his daughters, but for some reason, calling him Dad had been too difficult for her. It felt fraudulent, knowing her real father was probably still alive somewhere in the world. Nevertheless, Bill had taught her to ride a bike, dance the waltz, make banana-blueberry pancakes, and handle fresh men. He sang her to sleep with Beatles songs. Her favorite was "In My Life."

At Dara's urging, Bill taught her how to repair household fixtures and appliances and build things like breadboxes and decorative shelving. It was all part of the pact she'd made with herself during her mother's depression. She would learn to do everything for herself so that when she grew up, she would never be as helpless and fragile as her mother.

During her early years and even through college, Dara secretly harbored the wish her father would return to his senses—and to his family. Somewhere in her mid-twenties, she finally let go of that fantasy. She had a good relationship with Bill and that would have to sustain her, though sometimes she wondered if he sensed her disappointment or was wounded by the friendly little wedge she had lodged between them so long ago. She picked up the note he had put inside the box.

Dear Dara,

For the remaining few days you may have some time to spare, I thought I'd send you some things to help keep you busy and productive. Hint: Did you hang those living room curtains yet? And do you still have the chainsaw we bought you last time we were

there? If you need any more tools or advice (ha, ha) don't hesitate to
call.
Love,
Bill

After calling to thank him, she sat down in front of her television set with a bowl of tuna fish and channel surfed until she found the home improvement channel. Then she watched as a young woman expertly wallpapered her own dining room.

Six

THE NEXT DAY, DARA AWOKE with a craving she only indulged once a month. She tried to ignore it, but it stayed with her all day long—as she fixed a lamp that had been broken for months and hung the curtains that had been in a box under her bed for nearly a year. She played the Bonnie Raitt CD that Jesse had bought her, listening to the poignant lyrics while stroking Mallory's silky fur.

At about four-thirty, she finally gave in and got dressed. She drove down Washington Boulevard, made the familiar right turn on Via Marina, and pulled her silver Lexus into the parking lot of her favorite neighborhood haunt.

The valet gave her a ticket and she headed inside. She remembered it was Saturday, and hoped the place wouldn't be a madhouse. Although the restaurant was quite full, she breathed a sigh of relief when she spied the almost empty bar, and waved to the bartender, a tall, attractive man of about forty with lush dark hair, a sinewy physique, and a gold wedding band on his left ring finger. Dara had come to know him fairly well over the last year's worth of monthly excursions.

"Hey, Hal," she called as she slid onto an empty barstool.

"Hey, how're you doing?" he asked.

"Oh, I've been better," she told him with a sigh. "I'll have the usual."

He offered a quick look of concern. "You got it," he said, before turning to call in her order. Then he looked back at her and squinted suspiciously. "What's going on? You look more—*disturbed* than usual."

"Nothing good."

"And have you lost weight?"

"Stress diet."

"Sorry to hear it."

After a couple of minutes, Hal picked up a plate from the other end of the bar. He placed it in front of Dara with a large glass of ice water. "One White Chocolate Raspberry Truffle cheesecake for the lady," he said with a flourish.

"Thanks, Hal."

He leaned on the bar as she dug into the dense and decadent dessert.

"So, want to talk about it?"

She shook her head while licking the cream off her fork.

"You sure? You know I know you at your hormonal worst. Who could be better to confide in? At least there's not mascara dripping down your cheeks this month—and I don't see that crazed look in your baby blues."

"That's 'cause I got all my tears and agony out early."

"Okay, now you have to tell me."

Dara sighed and put down her fork. She let the creamy mouthful slide down her throat and then looked him straight in the eye. "This isn't for publication, but...I lost my job."

"What?" he said with surprise. "How the heck did that happen?"

"All it takes is one moronic, out-of-touch editor."

"I'm so sorry!" he said, still in shock. "Bizarre. You're like an L.A. institution already."

"Yeah, and now I'm just about ready for one," she said picking up her fork again.

"What an idiot this guy must be. You know, I had a bad feeling about him when you first mentioned him."

"Really? What gave it away? Was it the beady eyes, the nasty sneer, or the insufferable temperament?"

Hal smiled. "I'm sure you'll have no problem finding a better situation."

"Don't be so sure."

"Why?"

"Well I haven't had any luck yet," she complained, gulping down some water.

"It'll happen, don't worry."

"I hope so. My cat keeps looking at me like she's thinking, 'You still here?'"

Hal chuckled as she dug in to her cake again. "Okay, let's change the subject," he said.

"Good idea."

"So, you still managing to avoid your ex?"

She'd shared some stories with him about the relentlessly disappointing Tony.

"I've been a good girl," she replied.

"Any new men on the horizon?"

"Hardly."

"Now how can that be? You're a gorgeous, smart, sexy dating expert with a good head on your shoulders. You should have men knocking down your door."

"They can't. I put up a barricade."

He smiled and shook his head. "If I were single…"

"I know, I know."

"Tony cause this nonsense?"

"No. In fact, he's a prince compared to the revolving door of cretins out there, and he knows it. That's why he lurks in the wings, hoping I'll just finally give in already and settle for him."

"Cretins, huh?"

She nodded while shoveling in another mouthful.

"Example?"

Dara drew in a deep breath and swallowed before speaking.

"Okay. I once went out on a blind date, an accountant with one of those big fancy firms, I forget which one. He asked me out to Jerry's Pub for a seven-thirty reservation. I assumed it was for dinner, but when I got there he told me he'd already eaten, so we would just have appetizers instead. He ordered a shrimp cocktail and I ordered the vegetable soup. But I had a hankering for French fries and when I mentioned it, he said, 'No, we have enough food.' Can you imagine begrudging someone a side order of fries? What kind of person does that? At first I thought he just didn't like me and was too cheap to be a gentleman, but after paying the check, he asked if I would go out with him again."

"What did you tell him?"

"No, of course! I also informed him that in the future, he should really consider springing for the fries."

Hal laughed. "See? At least he got a lesson in dating etiquette."

"That's nothing," she continued. "I once went out with a guy named Artie I met online. I knew on the first date that he was definitely not for me. He kind of freaked out when I told him this the next time he called, but I stood strong. A couple of weeks later I got an email, supposedly from his twin brother, Andy, telling me that Artie had lost his life in a helicopter accident helping tsunami victims in Thailand."

"Yikes!"

"I felt bad for a few days—until I saw Artie online again trying to pick up women."

Hal laughed even harder this time. "No wonder my wife loves me so much."

Another customer sat down, and Hal went to wait on him. Dara watched as he expertly mixed a Martini with olives, placed it on a coaster in front of the man, and made change from a twenty dollar bill. Then he returned to Dara, who was scraping the last bit of cake and raspberry sauce from her plate.

"Well, I'm getting ready. I have two girls, thirteen and fifteen. It must be hell for your father to watch you go through all this."

Dara's eyes welled. Now she knew her hormones *must* be raging. With all the time that had passed, she usually didn't flinch after a reference to him.

"My father left us when I was five. He was spared the agony."

"Man, sorry I said that," said Hal, looking painfully contrite. "I thought you once spoke about—"

"I have a stepfather."

"Oh, the one with the hardware store?"

"Yup."

"Can I ask a personal question?"

She shrugged. "Sure, why not."

"Did you ever hear from him? Your birth father, I mean."

"Nope. Never," she said, turning her attention to her purse in search of her lip gloss.

"That sucks! No wonder."

"No wonder what?" she said, plucking the vial out and unscrewing the cap.

"No wonder you have so many man issues. You've got emotional baggage."

"Believe me; I'm completely over it, Hal. It's been a long time," she said as she applied the gloss to her lips.

"Nobody gets over something like that. Not really."

"I did."

"But you never got closure. That can weigh on you for a lifetime. Have you ever tried to find him?"

"Hal, you're supposed to be cheering me up, not depressing me more," she said with a laugh.

"Sorry. It's just that talking with him might clear so many things up for you. I could just never imagine leaving my...anyway, you're right. We were discussing your love life—and I use the term very loosely. You know we bartenders are frustrated psychologists, right?"

"Apparently," she said, smiling.

"So would you like a little free advice?"

Dara relished the thought of someone else doing the problem solving for once. She dropped her gloss back in her purse and motioned with her hands to bring it on.

"Okay, you've obviously had more than your share of crap," he told her. "But hiding away isn't the answer. I mean, there's got to be a prince for you out there...somewhere...I'm sure," he said, "and maybe, just maybe, he's looking for a princess like you. The only problem is, you've built a moat for him to drown in. Now, a wise prince might just save himself some trouble and move on to the next castle. See what I mean?"

Dara gave him an inscrutable look. After a moment she responded. "Are you sure you're a bartender? You're beginning to sound like my freaking fairy godmother."

Hal laughed heartily.

"I'm not one for fairy tales or Cinderella complexes," Dara admitted, "but I catch your drift, and if my prince really exists and one day attempts to cross my moat, I promise I'll throw him a life jacket."

"Well, that's a start. So tell me what you want in a man. I meet a lot of people."

"What I want? What most women want, I guess, cute, warm, giving, sane."

"Can you be more specific?"

"Well, it's mandatory that he be good with kids."

"Oh, you want kids?"

"Not necessarily. It's just a very important quality to have. You know, it says a lot about a man—about what he's made of."

Hal nodded, making the connection. "Anything else?"

"Yeah," she said, breaking the mood with a smile. "A cute butt."

"I'll see what I can do. In the meantime, can I get you another one?" he asked indicating her empty plate.

"No, thanks. The sugar's going to my head."

"Hmm, drunk on cheesecake. That's a first. Should I call you a cab?"

"Nope. Got my golden coach parked out front." She pulled some money from her purse.

"Okay. I see I'm never going to live this one down."

"Thanks, Hal," she said, offering him the money.

"Hey, today is on me."

"Thanks!" she said, leaving him a large tip. "Your wife's one of the lucky ones."

"See you next month," he said with a wink, "and good luck with the job hunt."

That night, after hammering together the beginnings of a spice rack for her kitchen, Dara climbed into bed at about ten o'clock and pulled her comforter up to her neck. She leaned her head back on her pillow and stared at a ridge in the white ceiling paint. It had been so long since she'd given her father much thought. Years before, she used to run the few cherished memories she had of him over and over in her mind: a trip to Adventureland; a piggy-back ride down the block; her fifth birthday party in their backyard with chocolate pudding cake; watching "The Honey-mooners" with him when she couldn't sleep; holding his rough, raw hand as they walked in the park; the smell of Barbasol when he lifted her in his arms to kiss her good night.

Now, she wistfully wondered which of those memories were real and which were merely dreams or fantasies created by her deep and abiding hunger. Was this phantom father still wreaking havoc on her life? Did she still long for him? She wondered if she'd ever find the closure Hal spoke of—or a partner she could truly love.

Dara woke the following morning feeling surprisingly lighter than she had in a while. Before she could change her mind, she donned her running clothes and forced herself to jog. It felt good to be out again, and she berated herself for having ceased her daily routine. Soon, she could feel that wonderful endorphin rush. She mulled over her thoughts from the night before, and suddenly, she knew what she needed to do.

Instead of waiting for the elevator, she ran up the three flights of stairs to her unit two by two. She unlocked the door, went into the kitchen, and opened the refrigerator, twisting open a cold bottle of water and chugging half of it down. While drying her face and neck with a paper towel, she grabbed her cell phone and pressed a few buttons.

"Hello?"

"Hi, Claire. It's Dara."

"Hey. How are you doing? Haven't heard from you in a while."

"I know, things have been crazy. How have you been?"

"I'm doing well. I'm actually on a stake-out."

Dara laughed and mopped her forehead again. "Who's cheating now?"

"Oh, some twenty-something tramp with a rich, jealous husband—the usual."

Dara and Claire had been friends ever since the kick boxing class they had taken together two years earlier. Claire worked at Jennings, Inc., a private detective firm in West L.A. specializing in cheating spouses, grifters, and other sordid cases. Dara had always enjoyed talking with her because her work stories were as bizarre and colorful as her own.

"That's some job you have," Dara told her.

"Pays the bills," she laughed.

"Look, I called because I wanted to hire you for something," Dara said, pacing back and forth on the terra cotta tiles of her kitchen.

"Really? What?" Claire asked, sounding genuinely surprised.

"You ever get missing persons cases?"

"Sure, once in a while."

"Well, I was hoping..." Dara had difficulty even saying the words.

"Spit it out, girl."

Dara took a deep breath and stopped pacing. "I'd like you to find my father."

❧ Seven ❧

DARA, FEELING MORE RELAXED than she'd felt in weeks, sat in her living room surrounded by her rolodex, a notebook, a telephone, and her laptop. She began writing down every possible job she felt she was qualified for and wouldn't mind doing. Then she did a search of websites and jotted down any pertinent listings. One link led to another, and the next time she checked her watch it was already past lunchtime. Her stomach growled as if on cue, and as she padded into her kitchen for a look-see in the fridge, her phone buzzed. The ID showed Reggie's cell number. He'd been checking on her regularly. She picked up the receiver, glad she finally had something positive to share.

"Hey, Reg, what's up?"

Instead of his usual teasing tone, she was surprised to hear panic in his voice.

"Reggie? What's wrong?"

"I...I can't believe it—"

"Can't believe what? Did The Beast—"

"I...I just went over to Vincenzo's place," he stuttered. "I used my key. I was going to surprise him with a picnic lunch...I'm such an idiot."

"Reggie, what happened?!"

"He wasn't...alone."

"Are you telling me he was—"

"On the couch...the one that I just had reupholstered for him...with—"

45

"—another man!"

"Not exactly."

"Huh?"

"A woman. It was a woman!"

"What?" Dara asked, suddenly more confused than alarmed.

"A model. I recognized her from a Gucci ad."

"Are you sure they were—"

"What else do two people do buck naked? I just can't believe it!"

"Where are you?"

"Driving around."

"What town?"

"West Hollywood."

"Okay," she said and thought for a moment. "I'll meet you at that Cuban restaurant on Melrose. Remember the one?"

"I think so."

"We went there for drinks last summer?"

"Yeah."

"Drive over there, then call the office and tell them you're not feeling well. I'll be there in less than a half hour."

"Okay," he said and disconnected.

Dara had never witnessed this side of Reggie. He was always so confident and in control—the go-to person if you ever needed a cool head to steady you. She slipped into her black mules, grabbed her purse, and ran out the door.

Twenty-five minutes later, at around two-thirty P.M., Dara found Reggie on the far side of the large, round bar sipping a frozen piña colada. She slipped onto the leather barstool to his left and began to rub his back sympathetically. He said nothing, but his eyes were bloodshot.

"Since when do you drink piña coladas?" she asked, trying to break the ice.

"Since today. I never allowed myself the calories. Who cares now?"

The bartender came by and Dara ordered the same.

"I know it seems like the end of the world, but you're only thirty-two. You're gorgeous, bright, talented—you have everything going for you. You'll realize that when you get past the pain."

"I just can't believe he did this."

"Italian men aren't exactly known for their monogamy."

"I mean, we were an item. I figured there were a few other men who might wage some competition—but a woman? He told me he'd never been with a woman. I checked, you know, like you always say you're supposed to do, and it didn't even matter. I thought he was *it*."

The bartender slid the frothy drink in front of Dara and she took a sip.

"What did he do when he saw you?"

"Just…sighed and put his head in his hands, as if he was annoyed that I caught him. My God, I worshipped that man."

"I know you did," she said, rubbing his back again, "but maybe that's the problem."

"What's that supposed to mean?"

"It means you were always trying so hard, first to win him, then to keep him, and always to please him. My God, Reggie, aren't you exhausted? Love isn't supposed to be *that* much work, and it's not like he made the same efforts. He knew he could always count on you for everything. He didn't have to lift a finger to keep the relationship going. You did it all."

Reggie put his elbows on the bar and began to cry into his hands. Dara looked at him with a pained expression.

"Come on, Reg. You can't cry into a piña colada. That's a happy drink, a vacation drink."

"Then order me something stronger. Anything but Stone Cold Vodka!"

"You got it. Excuse me," Dara said, raising her hand for the bartender to see. "My friend will have a Ketel One cosmopolitan—not too sweet. Better yet, make it two."

The bartender nodded and went to grab a shaker.

"Ketel One, that'll fix him," she said to Reggie with a little smile.

"Some revenge."

"Oh, I can do better than that. I just have to marinate my brain a little bit." She took another sip of her piña colada and munched on the pineapple slice that had been balancing on the tip of the glass. "Although you know the best thing you can do is grieve and move on."

"Don't be the voice of reason, not today, okay?" he pleaded.

Dara nodded and took his hand. "Okay, Reg."

By the time five P.M. rolled around and the bar began filling with its usual chic clientele, Dara and Reggie, not exactly seasoned drinkers, were well on their way to sloshed. They didn't notice as people took the barstools around them and an energetic din filled the room.

"Maybe we should get something to eat." Dara looked around. "Want to get a booth? There's a good one in the corner over there."

"I dunno," he said, his eyes half closed.

"Come on, I haven't eaten in weeks," she told him. "Bartenner," she slurred, "can you please move our tab to that table? We're hungry."

Dara placed a twenty-dollar tip on the bar, took Reggie's hand, and helped him off his stool. They walked gingerly to the booth and slid in across from each other.

"Now isn't this more comfy?" she asked with a tilt of her head.

"I guess so," he answered with a pronounced hiccup. "I haven't even asked about you."

"You ask all the time. I'm okay; feeling much better. Guess what I did today? Forget it, you'll never guess."

"What?"

"I hired my private detective friend to find my father."

"You're kidding! Why?"

"Closure. I just want to rule him out as the cause of my pathetic track record with men."

"Wow. That's big news," said Reggie, raising his eyebrows and attempting to lean an elbow on the table, but missing.

"I know, and I figured another thing, too."

"What?"

"I decided the worst thing I could do is let The Beast ruin my career. I mean, who the hell is he? I was counseling daters before that twerp was born, right?"

"Right," Reggie agreed. Then he scratched his head. "Wait a minute. How old are you again?"

"I bet I could mop the floor with his new little chippy girl. What's she, like sixteen or something?"

"I don't know. But I don't like her."

"Of course you don't. 'Cause you're a loyal friend," she said with a pat of his hand.

A waiter brought them menus and a busboy slid two glasses of ice water in front of them. They both opened their menus and studied them. Dara squinted and sighed.

"It's all written in Cuban. What's Camarones al Ajillo?" she said, mangling the words.

"I dunno."

"Let's ask the waiter. Hey, waiter," she called, trying to flag him down with two waving arms. The man approached.

"You've got to translate this menu for us, we're *starving* to death!"

The waiter recommended a few dishes and Reggie and Dara ordered.

"You know," Reggie said thoughtfully, "it's weird, but I'm not just jealous that he was with somebody else. I'm jealous 'cause I wish *I* could get hot for women. They're so much easier to deal with—much more manageable."

"Manageable? What's that supposed to mean?" she said, wondering if she should take offense.

"They have more self control."

"Yeah, I think you're right. Sometimes I wish I liked women, too. At least I understand them better. They're more...emotionally verbal."

"True!"

"They communicate their feelings and that's so-o-o important, you know?"

"Yeah," Reggie agreed, finishing the last triangle of pink liquid at the bottom of his martini glass.

"Wouldn't it be so cool if there was a way to get both sexes to communicate better? You know, really lay all their crap on the line? What a time saver that'd be, huh?"

"Sure would. That's why everyone in L.A. is going to miss your column, Harri. You taught them how to do it and now the world is going to be...b-bereft of your wisdom."

Dara smiled at him with a tilt of her head. "I love you, Reg. You're a great guy."

"I know, right?"

They both started laughing and, drunk as she was, Dara felt some relief at seeing his face morph from morose to almost cheerful for just a minute. The waiter placed three dishes in front of them, and they dove into the food with gusto.

"Reggie," Dara said when they were half finished, "wouldn't it be cool if there was a dating service that cut away the whole tiresome sham of getting to know people? I mean, really force you to lay everything on the line: no ten-year-old pictures, no lying about age, income, weight, a place where everyone could speak freely and was encouraged to totally be themselves, warts and all."

"Wow, I know a whole lot of people who would love that. You know, some of them don't even date anymore 'cause they don't have the patience for all the nonsense. Hey, wait a minute. You're one of those people."

"I know! And what about those even older singles who just keep dating and dating and dating and never understand why nothing ever works out for them. This service could help them figure out what the hell's wrong with them!"

"That's a fabulous idea! I mean it. You always said you wanted to own your own business. You should do it. You should open a dating service for chronically single people. Teach them what they've been doing wrong and finally get them paired off with someone who knows all their faults, and still wants to be with them for some reason."

Dara thought about it and the more she did, the more excited she became.

"I could call it MateSearch, the online dating service for prener... perener... perennially single people," she said, finally spitting it out. "People could post reviews and analyses after their dates. Instead of wondering why someone hasn't called you back, or doesn't want to see you again, you can find out in the...the...Rate-a-Mate section!"

"Rate-a-Mate!" Reggie shouted. "That's brilliant!"

"But I'd need your help if I ever did something like that. Are you in?"

"You mean I'd have to tell The Beast I quit? Sounds sublime," he laughed.

"Great! Now all we need is a big bunch of money," Dara announced. "I got about seventeen thou saved in the bank and I can take a second mortgage out on my condo. Still don't think that'll cut it. Whatchu got, partner?"

"Plenty."

"Really?" she said, mocking him.

"Yeah."

She laughed and said, "You forget I know what you make…and you have rent to pay."

"No, I don't."

"What do you mean, you don't? That rich family doesn't charge you for the guest house?" she asked with surprise and envy.

"Nope."

"Holy moly, how'd you get a deal like that? You putting out or something?"

He laughed. "I know people on the inside."

"What people?"

"All of them, actually."

"Reg, what the hell are you talking about?"

"They're my family."

"Your family?"

"Yup."

Dara blinked her eyes a bunch of times trying to comprehend past the alcohol haze. "Your family has an estate?"

"Uh-huh."

Then her face broke into a smile. "You're kidding me, right?"

"What's so difficult to believe?"

"I've worked with you for four years. You never told me your family was rich."

"It's not something you just announce—unless you're an asshole or something—and I don't like to talk about it. Makes me uncomfortable. Nana always said we should keep our finances a private issue."

"Nana?"

"Nana Hannah."

"Your Nana is Nana Hannah? As in Nana Hannah's Creamy Cupcakes?"

"That's the one."

"I don't believe it."

"You want me to get her on the phone?"

"Geez! You're not kidding, are you?"

"Not kidding."

"So what does that mean, you've got a trust fund and everything?"

"Yeah."

"I'm so fucking jealous!"

Reggie laughed.

"Well, then, we've got nothing to worry about. You have the money, I have the expertise. We're set!"

Dara called a cab for each of them. On the way home, she mulled over her brainchild. When she entered her condo, she put down some food for Mallory. Then she went into the living room and, in a semi-drunken scrawl, wrote down every detail she could remember about MateSearch. She hoped it would seem as brilliant an idea in the morning light. She shuffled into her bedroom, stripped down, and passed out peacefully in her bed.

The next thing Dara felt was Mallory gently licking her eyelids. She only did this when Dara slept through her breakfast feeding. Dara slowly opened her eyes, finding her upper and lower lashes crusted together with remnants of yesterday's mascara. She moaned and pulled Mallory closer.

She turned her head to glance at the clock—it was nine-fifteen—and grunted at the thunderous throbbing in her head. She dragged herself out of bed, wrapped herself in her robe, and staggered into the bathroom to down three aspirin and a glass of water. Then she stumbled into the kitchen, opened a can of cat food, and spooned it into a plate, trying not to gag at the smell. After placing it on the floor, she headed into the living room and sat on the couch.

Her eye caught sight of the notes she'd written the previous evening, and the events of the previous day rushed back. *The bar, Reggie's boyfriend's new girlfriend, the idea for the dating service, Nana Hannah's Creamy Cupcakes?!* Did she dream it or was Reggie really the heir to a cupcake fortune? She rubbed her head and tried to shake off the haze. She picked up her notes and began to peruse them.

Either her brain was still pickled, or this was the greatest idea she'd ever had! She wondered if it was the answer to the question: "What the hell am I going to do with the rest of my life?" Owning her own business had always been her dream. She knew she could make it a reality— something she'd never let anyone take away from her. She picked up her cell phone and dialed Reggie's office number. He wasn't at work. She waited an hour and then called his cell.

"Hello," he grumbled.

"Still asleep?" she asked.

"Mmm."

"Sorry. Wanted to see how you were doing."

"I was okay 'til you woke me and made me remember my life sucks."

"No, it doesn't. In fact, you're on the cusp of a new life—and so am I."

"If you say so."

"Listen, I need to know something."

"What?"

"I may have had a wild dream that your grandmother was that cupcake woman and you were a trust fund baby."

Reggie sighed. "You weren't dreaming."

"Really?" she said excitedly. "What a relief! And were you serious about going into business with me or was it the cosmopolitans talking?"

"I think I was serious."

"Are you sure?"

"As sure as you can be when you're hung over and half asleep."

"Well, wake up, 'cause I want to do this thing. It's fresh, original, and could be big...the next big thing to hit L.A.! So come on over here so we can figure it all out."

"Okay, I'm getting up," he growled, "but you come here. Remember, I'm deathly allergic to cats."

"Oh, stop being such a wuss."

"It's true."

"Fine," she said with resignation. "I'll be there in an hour."

Eight

Ten Months Later

LA Post Style Section

LA Singles Discover a Surprising New Way to Date

LOS ANGELES-Remember when going out on a date meant donning your best outfit—and your best attitude? Not anymore. Combining the advantages of traditional matchmaking agencies with the convenience of online dating, MateSearch has emerged on the Los Angeles scene—and dating may never be the same. The tony new dating service located in West Hollywood opened only three months ago, but owners Dara Harrison and Reggie Dayton are already changing the ways we think about dating.

The folks at MateSearch claim to take the anxiety out of making that first impression by encouraging clients to immediately reveal their true selves instead of striving to be someone they think will impress their dates. Dating through MateSearch is not about putting on airs or even putting your best foot forward. There are no outdated pictures, and lying about your age, weight, or marital status is not tolerated.

Each prospective client fills out an extensive profile and is encouraged to tell the truth, the whole truth, and nothing but the truth. Unlike most other online dating services, background checks are completed before a client is allowed to join—and fork over the substantial fee. But Harrison believes that if someone is serious about finding a significant other whom they can spend the rest of their life with, it is worth every penny.

"I believe all singles, whether just starting out, or long on the dating scene, will find our timesaving shortcuts refreshing and of great assistance in figuring out if someone is a viable mate," she says. "We call it 'Souldating.'"

Most notably, Harrison cites her trademark Rate-a-Mate Wall, where singles can post reviews and analyses of their recent dates, letting others make more informed decisions about whether someone may be compatible with them.

For those who think this may be a rather harsh process, Harrison insists it's been a great help to many, and even more important, "It's a way for longtime daters to see themselves more objectively and make positive changes. It is tough love, but we promise when you find the right person at MateSearch, they are going to love you for you. All you have to do is check your delusions, your pretense, and your ego at the door."

"I love it!" Dara said, grabbing scissors and cutting the article out of the paper. "They even used our picture, and Claire called to say she caught me on *Good Morning LA* and *PM Magazine* and I was 'fab'! Practically every single person she knows wants to sign up. Who knew you were such a whiz at PR, Reg?"

"I have many talents, Harri, and don't forget it," said Reggie as he leaned back on a nearby loveseat, his arms behind his head.

Dara grabbed some push pins and tacked the latest article onto the cork board next to four others with headlines that read:

Getting to Know You—Getting to Know ALL About You!
LA Singles Let It All Hang Out!
Southland's New Cupid Takes Aim at Longtime Singles
Longtime Singles' Last Great Hope?

She stared at the board and said, "I'm going to have to get someone to frame these before they start to yellow. I told you this thing was going to be big, didn't I?"

She twisted in her office chair, an expression of glee on her face.

"You did," he admitted.

All the long hours and lost weekends over the past ten months were finally paying off. She and Reggie had hired an office crew and pulled out all the stops with a massive computer system, an aggressive sales force, and an innovative public relations campaign. They'd also managed to find the patience and dedication it took to work out all the kinks.

Their office was in a professional building on Santa Monica Boulevard. It had three private offices, a general seating area for the sales and administrative staff, a conference room, and a lobby. The floors were covered in plush blue carpet and the walls were painted "Antique Lace."

Dara's office had a large mahogany desk, something she'd always yearned for, and a view of the boulevard through three large windows. The seascape paintings she'd hung lent a serene ambiance, and with the curtain pulled back, sunshine washed through the room. She was so glad they were able to swing the rent on this place and the business overhead, thanks to Reggie, her own nest egg, a second mortgage, and her stepfather's insistence on making what he called "a sure shot investment in business innovation."

"Who you working on now?" she asked Reggie.

"It's a surprise," he teased.

"Oh, come on, you can tell me."

"I don't want to jinx it."

"Okay," she reluctantly agreed, grinding a blue pencil between her molars. "We signed four new clients today. That makes almost two thousand in less than three months. Whatever we are doing, we are doing it right!"

"Let's not get too self-congratulatory. Did you see that complaint yet?"

"No, what's it about?"

"Hard to explain. You kind of have to read it for yourself."

"Did you forward it to me?" she asked, turning to her computer.

"Yup."

Dara scanned down her email inbox and found one titled "RE: Complaint." She double-clicked and began to read aloud.

"'Dear Complaint Department.' I guess that's us," Dara said wryly. "I recently went out on a date with Mark D. No. 0897 and thought I was having a pretty good time. He took me to the movies and out for ice cream. But this morning, when I checked my post board, he wrote what I believe is an inappropriate and cruel review of me and our time together. I am sorry to say that I thought enough of him to confide in him one of my "shortcomings" as you encourage us to, but he used it to mock me. I thought posts were supposed to offer helpful hints, not poke fun. After all, it isn't my fault I'm sometimes—"

Dara stopped to make sure she was reading the words correctly.

"—possessed by a vampire?!" Dara looked up at Reggie incredulously and then continued. "I know some people may find that hard to believe, but I have the scratch marks on my arms to prove it. I didn't know he was anti-vampire when I accepted a date with him, and I think it would be the politically correct thing to force him to take down his unseemly post. Can you please help me?"

Dara turned to Reggie, her jaw slack. He just stared at the email over her shoulder.

"No offense, honey, but I think you may be beyond help," he diagnosed.

"Possessed by a vampire? Is she for real?"

"I called her to make sure. She is. For real, I mean."

"And how did she avoid mentioning this in her interview?"

"My best guess is she was on medication then."

"Did you speak to this Mark guy?"

"Not yet, I thought we should discuss it first. Figure out how to handle it."

"Yeah, I'd say so," said Dara, leaning back in her leather chair. "First I think we should take a look at his post."

"I read it. It is a bit snide, but can you blame him?"

"I guess not, but maybe you can get him to rewrite it in a more respectful tone."

"And what about her?" asked Reggie, indicating the computer screen.

"She signed a contract to accept even critical posts, but I think we should preach some kind of courteous protocol. I'll include a paragraph or two on civility in my next newsletter. There's no need to be purposefully hurtful. You can stick with the facts and everyone will get the picture."

"So I guess this means we've got to get her to add vampirism to her profile. That'll go over well," said Reggie.

Dara nodded and sighed. "Eternally alive—and eternally dateless."

 Nine

NICK WYATT MOANED AND THRASHED in his bed, his forehead moist with perspiration. How many times would he have to relive it? It had been over a year since that devastating motorcycle jump. Until then he'd been on top of the world: a hit television series, a spacious home in the Hollywood hills, and a beautiful starlet in his bed. One goddamn leap had obliterated them all.

The nightmares plagued him a few times a week: his heart thumping in his chest; his motorcycle hitting the ramp; the awkward twist that set the bike off its intended trajectory and careening toward a cement wall. But the dreams didn't end the way the accident had, with Kenny, his stunt coordinator, desperately calling his name in an ambulance as he fell in and out of consciousness. In the dream, death was imminent, just as it had been for Matt Everhart. Matt, one of the show's handsome young stars, had perished in a completely different kind of on-set accident just a few months earlier. Matt didn't appear in the dreams, but Nick felt him nonetheless—felt him quietly watching and waiting for Nick to join him in the cosmic void. Upon awakening, that feeling would haunt him well into his day.

Somehow, Nick had suffered only a broken leg, sprained ligaments, and tears in his right rotator cuff, left hamstring, and meniscus, along with assorted cuts and bruises. The injuries took forever to heal, but they would heal. He'd been lucky—that is, if you consider losing your livelihood, your home, and your girl lucky.

After a moment, he took a long breath and ran his hand over his moist forehead. When the pounding in his chest slowed, he sat up in bed and took a swig from a water bottle on his nightstand. He grabbed his cane, which he now needed mainly for morning stiffness, and slowly maneuvered his six-foot, still-muscular frame off his bed and toward the bathroom.

Flushing his face with cool water, he stared at himself in the medicine chest mirror. The rugged stuntman with the killer smile was long gone. In his place he observed a forty-year-old wreck of a man with bloodshot eyes and rows of deepening lines crisscrossing his forehead. He wondered if the creases had materialized over the preceding months, or if they'd been long in the making, and he'd just been too busy living life to notice.

Nick's sister, Annie, had left three messages over the course of the week, but he hadn't been in the mood for one of her cross-examinations. Ever since he'd made the mistake of accepting the very extravagant gift she and her husband had sprung on him for his birthday, he'd been regretting it.

Ever the hopeful romantic, Annie had believed her brother's accident was a sign for him to change the course of his life, find a good woman, and settle down. She and her husband, Ralph, had been married for a dozen years, had two perfect children, and lived in a bedroom community outside Portland, Oregon. Unlike Nick, she had managed to eke out a relatively normal life despite their unconventional upbringing.

After their mother's untimely death from an ectopic pregnancy, they'd lived with their father in the Los Feliz section of Los Angeles. Their dad, Cliff Wyatt, was celebrated in the Hollywood stunt world, having worked with such heavyweights as John Wayne, Sean Connery, and Burt Lancaster. He'd been known for his innovation, expertise, machismo, and charisma, but his career didn't leave him much time to raise children. He relied on the services of their live-in nanny, a warm-hearted woman named Aretha.

When Nick turned ten, his father began bringing him to the sets of some of the shows and movies he worked on. He introduced him to mega-stars and legendary directors like Sidney Lumet and Francis Ford Coppola. While Cliff was off performing stunts, he let hired hands look after his son. Nick absorbed the action on the set like a thirsty sponge, and it was during these special days that the stunt life made its indelible impression on him. He watched as his father commandeered a Bell helicopter after scuffling with the pilot; witnessed his high-speed car chases, usually resulting in spectacular crashes; and rooted for him as he slugged it out with "goons" while hanging by one arm from a scaffold. When Nick turned sixteen, his father began to educate and train him, for he knew his son was fated to follow in his precarious footsteps.

As much as Nick had excelled at stunt work, and as many film and television sets as he'd graced, he never expected to escape the shadow of his celebrated father, and so he never tried. Instead, he cashed in on his nepotistic success with stunning starlets, glamorous nightlife, and the slice of fame he'd garnered.

Then, after years of death defying stunts, Cliff Wyatt ironically died of lung cancer, and something shifted deep inside Nick's psyche. As he mourned the death of the father he'd idolized, he also began to grasp a mind-blowing new reality. He was finally free from the shadow that his father had cast over his professional life. He saw a huge opportunity. He would prove himself worthy of the Wyatt name by earning his own stripes. The way to do this, he decided, was by proving to the stunt world that he was their biggest daredevil ever.

Nick forced himself to pick up his telephone and dial his younger sister. "Hey. It's me," he said.

"It's about time!" she reprimanded. "What's wrong with you?"

"Where do you want me to begin?"

"Nick, you don't sound good. I know it's early, but Ralph and I have been thinking, why don't you plan to come up here for Christmas?"

After the accident, Annie had taken over the roles of mother and father to her ailing older brother, much to his chagrin.

"Not this year. Plane travel is a pain…literally."

"I don't think you should be alone for the holidays."

"I won't be alone," he assured her.

"Really? Who are you spending them with?"

"Some old friends—Rudolph, Charlie Brown, and Frosty."

"Not funny. I have Ralph's parents coming this year or we'd fly down to you."

"Annie, it's not such a big deal, really."

"Is your shoulder still hurting you?"

"Yeah."

"What did the new doctor say?"

"He agreed that the surgery could have made it worse. That it was probably a botch job. Needed that like a hole in the head. I filed a suit against the bastard."

"Good."

"Relax now, okay?"

"So what have you been doing with yourself?" she asked.

"Well, in between doctor appointments, I enjoy crosswords, eating in, and the Fishing Channel."

"I hope that's not what you put in your profile."

"What do you mean? You're the one who filled it out."

"I thought you were going to…you know, put it in your own words."

"What's the diff? You bought the membership and did most of the work. Too bad you can't go on the dates for me, too."

"Well, someone had to do something to get you off that couch."

"You could have just gotten me a gift certificate to The Palm or something. I'd have gotten off the couch for some surf and turf."

"An expensive dinner is not going to fix your life."

"What makes you think a dating service will?"

"Because they specialize in people like you who want to figure out why they're still single."

"You're the one who wants to figure that out, not me."

"I know why. Should I tell you?" She didn't wait for an answer. "For one thing, you just got too used to years of dating Hollywood bimbos. You need to find out what a normal, decent girl is like, one who's looking for a meaningful relationship, not just sleeping her way through a film crew."

Nick rubbed his eyes. "Adriana wasn't a bim," he said unconvincingly.

"A nice girl doesn't leave her ailing boyfriend a week after he almost kills himself and jump into bed with his director."

He sighed uneasily. "You got me there."

"Have you gone out again with that girl you mentioned?"

"Palulah? We went out three times. That was enough for me."

"Palulah? What, did you find the only airhead wannabe actress registered at the service?"

"She's a performance artist."

"God, that's even worse! So Palulah's her stage name?"

"She says her parents named her that."

"What kind of parents name their daughter Palulah?"

"Who cares? I'm not going out with her anymore. She seemed okay at first, kind of aggressive, but that's par for the course in L.A. Then it all surfaced."

"What did?"

"That she's a total nutcase. First, she insisted I watch her perform at this little dive theatre in Hollywood. It was *insane*. She was nude, covered in grease paint, and reciting some kind of gibberish while doing a bizarre interpretive dance and hurling raw sausages at passersby."

"Get out!"

"And as if that wasn't bad enough, that night after the show, she told me we were destined to be together forever."

"No way! After three dates? What did you say?"

"Nothing. I was speechless—but my life flashed before my eyes. I saw myself old and gray, still out of work, and confined to my couch while she flung sausages at me."

Annie laughed. "Then what happened?"

"She asked me to come over that weekend. I told her I had a fishing trip planned with my friends."

"That was quick thinking."

"Then she told me I'd have to choose between my friends and her."

"Oh, man! And what did you say?"

"I told her that was the easiest decision I ever had to make. Shortly after that conversation, she started calling me obsessively."

"I hope she's not a stalker," said Annie with a note of concern.

"I'm just glad she spilled her loony beans before...you know."

"What?"

"Guess."

"You mean you didn't jump into bed on the first date?"

"Or the second...or the third. See? Your dirty-minded, preconceived ideas about me need an adjustment."

"I'm shocked."

So am I, he thought. It wasn't like him to hold out if a pretty lady was willing, and this one had bordered on demanding! However, not only was Nick out of sorts—he was out of practice. There had been no hanky-panky for him since Adriana, and their last encounter had been the night before his accident.

Until then, he and Adriana had enjoyed a steady diet of steamy, imaginative, and sometimes outrageous sexual escapades. She wasn't just extraordinarily beautiful; she possessed something else—a fatal attraction of sorts—that made his sex drive take flight, and his good sense take a hike. They had fought like tigers—and mated like them, too. The things Adriana dreamed up could make a dominatrix blush. She transformed Nick—and, he was willing to bet, every other man she'd seduced—into some kind of ravenous, irrepressible sex zombie. It wasn't until they'd broken up that he realized they shared no friendship, no warmth, no foundation—but whatever it was that did exist between them had been powerful enough to make Nick do something he would forever regret.

"Promise me you're not going to stop using the service because of one ditsy dingbat. You know we spent a fortune on it!" she said, pouring on the guilt.

"I know, and I'm not happy about that. Look, I appreciate your concern, but this just isn't my style. I've been doing things my own way for a long time."

"Yes, and look where it's gotten you. Please, do this for me, Nick. Please?"

"Okay, all right. I'll give it another try."

"Good, because it's only been a couple of weeks and your profile is going to be up there for six months, like it or not. It's their policy."

"You kidding?"

"No, and I think it's smart. It forces people like you to not give up so easily!"

"They think of everything, don't they?" he said with futility.

"So are you okay with money?"

"Yes, I have disability and a bank account, remember? I sold the house for cash."

"And when they run out?"

"I'm sure I'll be back to work by then. Or I can just take to the streets of Hollywood with my cane and a tin cup," he said. "Too bad Grady isn't around anymore. Nobody could refuse him a few bucks."

This off-the-cuff remark had more of an effect on Nick than he cared to admit. His black lab had died only a few months after the accident, just when Nick was home and able to spend some quality time with his aging dog. Although he had never admitted it to anyone, Grady was the real reason he sold his home. He just couldn't bear to rattle around in the three-bedroom ranch without him. Looking out his back window, he'd kept remembering their Frisbee catches and wrestling matches. In fact, he'd rarely ventured into his own backyard again.

Annie sighed, knowing how hard her brother had taken Grady's death. "Maybe it's time to adopt again, Nick."

"Nah. Wouldn't be fair to the dog. I can't play with him, run with him—"

"Do me a favor. As soon as we hang up, log in to the service and take a good look around. There are beautiful new women joining every day.

"Okay, Annie," he said, trying to placate her.

"Promise?"

"Yes, I promise."

"You better not be crossing your fingers."

Nick hung up, and to appease his only sister, logged on to the MateSearch website. He typed in his client number and password. A blinking icon read, "A Rate-a-Mate post has been added to your profile."

Man! Despite how little he cared about this dating service, he still felt anxious. He reluctantly double-clicked and found a review that, according to the company pamphlet, would be inextricably tied to his name and profile for the life of his membership. He took a deep breath and began to read.

By the time Nick finished, his eyes were wide with anger and his jaw slack with disbelief. He tried to swallow, but his throat was so dry he could barely summon the saliva. He choked out the only three words he could muster.

"What the fuck?!"

❧ Ten ❧

"**L**INE TWO FOR YOU, Ms. Harrison. Says he's a member, a Nick Wyatt?"

Dara finished the sentence she was typing and took a sip of her French vanilla-flavored coffee. Then she pushed the button on her intercom. "Okay, Maxine. I'll take it," she said, picking up the receiver.

"Dara Harrison. May I help you?" she said cheerfully.

"Ms. Harrison?"

"Yes."

"My name is Nick Wyatt. I'm a...member of MateSearch and I have an urgent problem."

"I'm sorry to hear that. What is it?"

"I went out with a woman named Palulah—"

"Yes, that name rings a bell."

"And, well, things didn't work out. She was definitely...not for me."

"Okay, that happens."

"But this morning when I logged on, I found a post from her."

"Yes?"

"She wrote some blatantly false things about me," he said, trying to remain calm.

"I see. Well, I realize that sometimes people on dates don't see things the same way—"

"This is not about different...interpretations—"

70

"—and I know getting to know somebody can be challenging—" she continued.

"The woman is a lying lunatic!" Nick blurted out.

"Mr. Wyatt, please let's not get uncivil about this."

"Uncivil? I'm not the one getting uncivil," he said, his voice gaining steam. "Why don't you take a look at her post? Read it for yourself."

"Well, I know sometimes 'he said, she said' things can get a bit heated," Dara told him, purposefully keeping her voice calm.

"Yes," Nick said testily, "especially when what 'she said' is total bullshit. You've got to take it down."

"I understand your feelings, but you know postings aren't always going to be favorable. You have to toughen up. That's what you signed up for, remember? Part of what makes the service a help to our members is frankness."

"She was not being frank!" Nick bellowed. "She was being vindictive because I didn't want to go out with her anymore. When I didn't answer her obsessive calls, she played her trump card...Rate-a-Mate revenge!"

"I'm sorry you're upset and I'll look into the matter right away and get back to you. Can you please give me your member ID and telephone number?"

Dara wrote down the information on a legal pad next to her computer, laid the phone down, and sighed. No one said owning your own business would be a piece of cake. As she began to pull up Nick's profile, Reggie entered her office, out of breath.

"I did it! I did it!!" he yelled with glee, doing a little end-zone dance in front of her desk.

"Did what?"

"Got you booked on the biggest, the best, the most popular daytime talk show in the nation!"

"The nation? Not the *Ophelia Show*!"

"Yup!"

"Oh, my God! How did you do that? Reggie, you are absolutely amazing!" Dara stood and threw her arms around him and together they jumped up and down while squealing with delight.

"You tape in three days!"

"Three days? How am I going to do that? I need to prepare for this. It has to be just right! How come only three days?"

"There was a cancellation and I managed to snatch it for you."

"Wow. Okay. I can do this," she said, beginning to pace nervously. "I'll get started now, but I need your help."

"What do you want me to do?"

"Well, first help me come up with something exciting to talk about. We need to make some kind of memorable splash!"

"Right."

"And…clothes…I need clothes! I have to look hot and exciting and current and fabulous and you are just the guy to make that happen!"

"Aw, shucks," he said as he kicked his left shoe against the right one bashfully.

Dara fell back into her chair and twirled herself around. "Thank you, Ophelia!" she yelled into the air. "You won't regret it!"

❧ Eleven ❧

"AND NOW I'D LIKE YOU TO PLEASE welcome my next guest," said Ophelia. "You may not recognize her name, but everyone in Los Angeles is talking about her innovative brainchild, a new company called MateSearch, which is quickly becoming the hottest dating service in California. I'll let her explain what makes this place so special. Please give a nice round of applause for Dara Harrison!"

As the audience applauded, Ophelia, a tall, skinny blonde with a face like a Barbie doll and enough energy to eclipse the sun, stood and clapped heartily. Dara, clad in a chic pink Chanel suit and Prada shoes glided onto the set, shook Ophelia's hand, and sat down on the plush love seat. She crossed her legs, scanning the audience with a smile.

"Welcome!" the hostess said.

"Thank you so much, Ophelia. I'm so excited to be here!"

"My very reliable sources tell me that your dating service, MateSearch, is the talk of the town these days, so we brought in an audience filled with L.A. singles today to learn all about it! Tell us what makes it unlike other dating services."

"Well, MateSearch is especially geared for longtime singles who want to figure out why their relationships don't work out, and who would like helpful feedback on what they can do to improve themselves and their dating life. It's also geared for anyone who doesn't have the time or the patience for what we call 'the dating charade.'"

"You mean all the deceptions and exaggerations that people start out with?"

"Absolutely."

"And how do you ensure that?"

"First, we take great pains to make sure that people are laying it all on the line. We call it Souldating. Our extensive profile questionnaire encourages people to reveal not only their good points but their foibles, too—and then there's Rate-a-Mate!"

"Yes! That's the part that everyone's talking about! Please explain."

Dara smiled and continued. "Rate-a-Mate is a very effective dating tool. After you've dated someone, you have the opportunity to post a review of how it went and what you learned about the individual. Basically, it's designed to help members see what they're doing right and what they may be doing wrong! It's posted to the member's profile and made available to other members for consideration before choosing to go out with the individual."

"So it's kind of like when you want to know if a restaurant or hotel is worth going to—or even if a book is worth reading—by getting opinions from others. That's ingenious!" raved Ophelia with wide eyes and an enthusiastic smile. "Tell us how you came up with the idea."

"Well, it was born from my almost two decades on the dating scene and from the experiences of many, many others. You see, I used to be an advice columnist for *LA Entertains*."

"Yes, I saw that in your credentials. Very exciting! How's the success rate at MateSearch?"

"We've only been open for about three months, and already we've made almost a hundred successful matches! In fact, Ophelia, I'm excited to announce some wonderful news. I've arranged for complimentary memberships for three people from your studio audience, and I want to extend a challenge to them." Dara took a deep breath and smiled confidently while looking out over the audience. "I'm willing to bet that each of those three people will find a wonderful partner within six short months!"

The studio audience clapped uproariously and so did Ophelia.

"What a fabulous idea! And then the three members can come back on my show and tell us all about their experiences!"

Dara clapped now, too. That was exactly the plan her brilliant public relations sidekick, a.k.a. Reggie, had hatched in order to continue the coverage and perpetuate the excitement about MateSearch.

When the audience settled down, Ophelia asked one of her show's assistants to come on stage and spin the number wheel she used to pick audience members by seat number. A woman in her thirties, and a man and woman in their early forties were chosen. After coming on stage and giving their names, they were escorted backstage.

"Okay," Ophelia said to Dara. "I have to ask. Are you married or are you single, too?"

"I'm single right now," she said, trying to hide her discomfort.

"Now how can that be? Someone as pretty and successful as you with a dating service at her fingertips!"

"Well, I've been spending all my time planning and building up the service. Unfortunately, I don't have much time to date. Right now, my focus is bringing the philosophy of MateSearch to as many people as possible."

"So you're a woman with a mission! Well, I've just had an idea and my audience knows what that means!" Shouts of "look out" and "uh-oh" emanated from the crowd as Ophelia continued. "I have a challenge of my own," she said with a devious smile.

Dara's smile wavered.

"I want Dara to take the MateSearch Challenge, too!"

As Ophelia yelled this to the audience, they roared with applause and whistles. Dara smiled coyly and put out her hand as if to politely refuse, but Ophelia stood up and started clapping again.

"Yes! It's time to turn the tables on this beautiful matchmaker and make *her* a match this time! What do you say, people?" she yelled.

Dara's stomach flipped over, and her cheeks burned like fire. She saw no way to wheedle her way out of this one, not with three hundred people and a relentless talk show host snapping at her heels. She reluctantly nodded her head as the audience began to cheer again.

It was only three o'clock when the taping ended. Dara drove from Studio City back to her office in West Hollywood, stupefied by what had transpired. Her day had only gotten worse when, backstage, Ophelia told her she was planning to send cameras to document some of her dates for the follow-up show. What had she gotten herself into? More accurately, what had Reggie gotten her into? Yes, this was all his fault and he would have to figure out what she was supposed to do now. She climbed the stairs that led to the MateSearch offices and entered the reception area.

"How'd it go?" asked Maxine, the receptionist, with excitement. She was in her early twenties, tall and wholesome looking with lush brown hair that she wore in a ponytail. A transplant from Utah, she hadn't yet lost her starry eyes about Hollywood. "What's Ophelia like? Is she as great as they say?"

Dara forced a smile and between clenched teeth said, "It was great. Ophelia was great. Everything's just…great!"

She strode through the lobby quickly and stormed directly into Reggie's office. Reclining behind his desk, talking on the phone, Reggie immediately excused himself and hung up when he spotted her.

"You were amazing!" he said, standing up.

"How do you know? It wasn't live!"

"I just know. You're always amazing."

"Don't butter me up!"

"Why would I have to butter you up?"

"Because I'm about to bite your head off!"

"What? Why? What happened? Didn't it go well?"

"Oh, yes, it went very well—too well!"

"What's that supposed to mean?"

"It means Ophelia loved the MateSearch Challenge so much she challenged me to my own challenge!"

Reggie stopped talking, his eyes widened. "You've got to be kidding. *You?*"

Then he broke into raucous laughter while Dara stood in front of him with her hands planted on her hips. "I have six months to find Mr. Right! This is all *your* fault!" she said, pointing at him.

"How's it my fault?" he said, trying to catch his breath.

"Because it was your idea!"

"Oh, come on. You couldn't expect me to foresee something like that!"

"Why not? It's your job to foresee things."

"I'm a public relations executive, not a psychic."

"So how am I going to get out of this? She wants me back on the show with the three winners in six months!"

"Who says you have to get out of it? Why not take her challenge? What are you so afraid of? You could use some male companionship."

"I have male companionship."

"Yeah, but I'm gay and that nutty neighbor of yours isn't exactly...male, even if he registered here as one. I still can't believe you let him in!"

"How could I say no? He's a good friend."

"This ain't no gay dating service."

"He never said he was gay."

"Oh, right. So what, bisexual?...Asexual?...Post-sexual?"

"Come on."

"I just want to know if anyone has actually gone out with him yet, and if so, of which sex?"

"To tell you the truth, Reg, I'd really rather not know. Unlike you, I try not to be nosy about my friends."

"Uh-huh," he responded dubiously. "Just tell me one thing. He did list cross-dressing on his profile, right?"

"We insist on honesty."

"Anyway, aside from Jesse, it wouldn't kill you to date some of our members. Who knows, maybe you'd actually meet someone nice."

"I'm not dating any of our members," she said, folding her arms across her chest.

"Then what are you going to do?"

She looked intently at Reggie with narrowed eyes. "I don't know, but you'll think of something!"

Then she stormed out of his office and back to her own.

"Ms. Harrison?" said Maxine, whose conservative upbringing made it difficult for her to use Dara's first name. She stood in the office doorway holding a bunch of pink message slips. "I almost forgot. This man has left a bunch of messages since you've been out of the office. There were a few other calls, too."

Maxine handed her the slips and left. Dara shuffled through them. Five were from Nick Wyatt. *Crap*. With all the excitement of the *Ophelia Show*, she had never gotten around to checking out his Rate-a-Mate post. Then she spotted a message from Claire James requesting that she call.

After Claire's ten months of searching yielded few leads, Dara had all but given up hope of finding her father. She dialed her number expecting more discouraging news. What if he were dead? How would she feel?

"Hi, Dara," said Claire. "How are you doing?"

"I'm okay. What's up?"

"I just wanted to let you know that I got a lead from one of your father's old friends, a man named Henry Volker?"

"Don't know him."

"He said he thinks your dad moved somewhere outside London about fifteen years ago."

"London, England?" she said with surprise.

"That's right. So I contacted a firm we once collaborated with in London, and the owner said he'd see what he could find out."

"Wow," Dara replied, growing a bit nervous.

"Yeah. See? I told you not to give up."

"You did."

"Anyway, I'll be in touch when he completes his investigation."

"Okay, Claire. Thanks."

After they disconnected, Dara ruminated on the promising news. She was not inclined to get her hopes up. When it came to her father, high hopes were never a good idea. She sighed and picked up one of the messages from Nick. She typed his member ID into her computer and his profile appeared on her screen. When she saw his photo, she raised her eyebrows. *Wow, what a looker.* He was kind of a cross between George Clooney and Zachary Grovener, the man she'd been mad for in college. Dara floated off for a moment in a daydream—or was it more like a nightmare?—recalling that intense year-long romance with the film major who aspired to produce movies.

She and Zach had been joined at the hip—and a few other places—during that time, and they had planned an idyllic future together. He'd seemed to understand her like no man ever had. She could tell him anything—and she did, including the depth of her feelings about her father's abandonment. Then one awful night, the love of her life did a sudden about-face, shattering her heart like a hammer on hand-blown glass. He told her he was no longer in love with her, that there was someone else. It was the second most devastating desertion of her life—and one she had promised herself would be the last.

She should have known from all his flirtations at the industry "networking" parties that she had deemed harmless and from his growing tendency to put his own ambitions above their relationship that he would eventually explore his abundant options without her. Beautiful women ogled the handsome, charismatic guy who seemed destined for success. Why had she hidden her head in the sand?

After the breakup, Dara had been unable to study, eat, sleep, or practically breathe on her own. Her 3.8 average plummeted and she didn't care; she no longer wanted to live with the pain inside her. With nothing else available, she'd swallowed a bottle of buffered aspirin. Her last thought before the whiteness enveloped her was that at least she'd die without stomach upset. She was wrong on both counts. She had awakened in the emergency room at UCLA Medical Center to the pain of a stomach pump, thanks to Vicki, her quick-thinking roommate.

For the next two years, Dara had refused to date, determined instead to immerse herself in her studies. She majored in journalism, graduated with honors, and focused on her career. When she eventually began to go out with men again, she felt markedly different; there was a thick layer of scar tissue to protect her now. She sometimes wondered if Zach had "made it" in Hollywood. No matter how great his ambition, it was still an inordinately tough road, she knew. But she did her best not to read film credits, gossip magazines, or watch award shows—just in case.

Despite the years that had passed, memories of Zach still quickened her heartbeat and gave her a sickening feeling in her solar plexus. She shook off the mood as best she could, picking up a cup of orange blossom tea and taking a cleansing sip. She continued to scan Nick's profile: a

Hollywood stuntman who had worked on the set of *Stormcats*. Even she had heard of that show, although she'd never watched it. How had Reggie described it? *Baywatch* meets *CHiPS*? Not exactly her taste. They'd only discussed it because of the shocking news story a couple of years back about the tragic death of one of the show's hunky stars, who had accidentally shot himself in the head with a prop gun blank. The whole town had been in shock. Dara read further and realized that Nick had been the stuntman who'd had a motorcycle accident just months later. She vaguely recalled a female commentator on *E! News* posing the question, "Is *Stormcats* cursed?"

Dara sized up Nick's picture again—Mr. Hollywood—just like Zach. She pulled up the lone Rate-a-Mate wall post.

Posted by Palulah, No. 0436

I went out with Nick three times. He used to be a stuntman. Now he's just an out-of-work braggart who sits around his condo watching television. Productive, huh? Although he turns on a kind of devilish charm in the beginning, don't let it fool you. He's not the lover he thinks he is. He has a callous disregard for a woman's pleasure. And then there's that other small problem. Two inches worth, girls. Talk about exposing your "shortcomings"! Thank goodness he finally caught on and stopped hounding me with phone calls. A word to the wise: Steer clear of this loser.

By the time Dara finished reading, her eyes were wide and her right hand cupped her mouth. She remembered Nick saying the woman had lied about him, but would anyone make up something like that even if she were miffed? How was she supposed to mediate this one? She buzzed Reggie on the intercom.

"I haven't thought of anything yet," he answered abruptly.

"That's not why I'm calling. Come in here. There's something you've got to see."

The sound of her voice brought Reggie to her door in seconds. She motioned him over and let him read the post for himself.

"Holy bed sheets, Batgirl, this one's a doozy!" Reggie said. "Do you remember her?"

"Not really. Ginger interviewed her."

"No wonder. I warned you, Ginger's not the best judge of character. She really needs to stick to the admin end of the business," Reggie advised. "Wow, this chick makes Vampire Woman look downright attractive. What do you think we should do?"

"Well, first of all, we should stop calling our members chicks; and second, Nick Wyatt called me a few days ago and gave me an earful about the post. We have to do some research and find out how much of this is true."

Reggie bounced his eyebrows up and down. "Which one of us is the lucky girl?" he asked.

"Come on, I'm serious. You know we can't just take the whole thing down. It's against our policy. We have to verify her claims." She glared at Reggie. "Except for *that* one—and have this Palulah woman delete the sarcasm."

"And what about *that* one?" he asked, picking up the pink bunny from her desk and tossing it in the air.

Dara stood up to rescue it. "Don't throw Pinkie around. She gets nauseous," she admonished, putting the stuffed animal back in its spot as Reggie elevated one eyebrow at her. "I don't know. I never imagined something like this. What if it's the truth? I mean, I know it's very personal."

"I'd say so," he offered sarcastically.

"But we urge people writing reviews to be forthcoming about everything. It'll make us look like hypocrites if we just take it down."

"You kidding? You're going to leave it up there for everyone to see? Poor guy!"

"I didn't say that, I have to think about what to do."

"Yeah, and meanwhile, he's becoming the MateSearch leper."

"Not every woman cares about...you know."

"Oh, bullshit."

"It's true. Sexual things aren't a priority for everyone."

"Speak for yourself," Reggie told her.

"We need to brainstorm about this."

"We? I have enough on my plate now that you left the whole Challenge Debacle to me."

Dara barely heard him as her brain shifted into overdrive. "I have an idea. I'm going to meet with Palulah, feel out the situation. Then I'll know what to do."

"And in the meantime, what are you going to tell *him*?" he asked, indicating her computer screen.

"I'm going to practice what I preach and tell him the truth!"

Reggie smiled, nodded, and, while exiting her office, glanced over his shoulder and said, "Yeah, good luck with that."

Nick slammed his telephone into its base and pounded a sofa cushion with his good arm. She needed to investigate? What the hell was that supposed to mean? And why couldn't she take the post down in the meantime? He didn't accept her claims of company policy—and wasn't consoled by her promise to resolve the situation quickly. He was probably the laughingstock of Los Angeles by now. What if anyone he knew saw it? He'd be informally blacklisted, or at least humiliated for life. Who was this Harrison woman? She must be nuts. Only a lunatic would come up with an idea like Rate-a-Mate!

In his anger, Nick forgot his aches and pains and jumped off the sofa to look for his MateSearch paperwork. Unfortunately, his body didn't forget and he winced and groaned, cursing the dating service and the sadistic woman who ran it. Rubbing his bad leg, he limped frantically around his apartment in search of the forms. He didn't even remember signing a contract although he figured that was probably because his sister had wisely presented the gift only after pumping him full of very dry vodka martinis. He rummaged through his drawers and closets but could not locate any MateSearch material. For all he knew, it could have been lost in his recent move.

Twenty minutes later, Nick sighed and raked his hand through his hair. He headed to the refrigerator, grabbed a Samuel Adams, and pried off the cap. Taking a long pull, he leaned on the kitchen counter and looked at the phone. He knew he had to take action—though of what sort was still a mystery.

That evening, as Dara was washing pots and pans, she heard a quiet knocking. She shut off the water, dried her hands in a dish towel, and stepped to the front door. Through the peephole, she spotted Jesse, wearing large, red plastic-framed glasses and a conservative women's suit. She opened the door with a smile.

"Hey there," Dara said.

Jesse struck a pose. "Do these glasses make me look like Sally Jesse Raphael?"

Dara laughed. "You remembered I taped today, huh?" she said, inviting him in with a wave.

"Of course I remembered! How could I forget something like my best friend appearing on the number-one-rated talk show in the country for

God sakes? Come here!" Jesse stretched out his arms to give her a big hug. "So how did it go?"

"I'll tell you, but first, I keep meaning to ask how you like MateSearch," she said, with apprehension. "What's it been, like a month now?"

"Almost—and I'm having a great time at the service. Meeting so many nice people!"

"Really?" she asked with surprise. "I'm so glad!"

"You sound shocked. Don't you know your agency is the toast of L.A.?"

"Have you met someone special?"

"Not *the one*...yet! But I'm sure it'll happen!"

"I hope so," she replied, wondering which of her adventurous members had been dating Jesse. She walked toward the living room and Jesse followed.

"I told you that you were still a star! Although you look wiped out, honey."

"It's been a long day!"

"Tell me all about it! Leave nothing out!"

"Well take a seat, 'cause you're not going to believe this one."

❧ *Twelve* ❧

A FTER A FEW ANXIETY-FILLED NIGHTS tossing and turning with worry about The Challenge, Dara entered the lobby of MateSearch, greeted Maxine, and picked up her messages. She headed down the hall reading them. As she passed Reggie's office he poked his head out and exclaimed, "I've got it!"

Dara jerked backward in surprise and dropped her messages, which floated to the floor. She gave an exasperated sigh as she bent to pick them up. "What's wrong with you? Are you trying to give me a heart attack?"

Reggie grabbed her and pulled her into his office. Then he gave a furtive look down the hall in each direction and closed the door. "I figured it out!"

"What?" she asked, letting her briefcase slide to the floor. "And what's with the cloak and dagger routine?"

"This is top secret stuff. We have to be discreet."

"Reggie, what's going on?"

"Okay, so I know what you should do about the MateSearch Challenge."

Dara folded her arms across her chest and shot him a look of skepticism. "Yeah?"

"We hire someone we can trust and pay him to play the role."

"What? Are you crazy?"

"One of your exes perhaps? One you still talk to?"

"You and I both know that the only ex I've ever talked to is Tony—or at least I used to."

"Okay, so he owes you for all the grief. I'm sure he'd do this favor for you. He still loves you, right?"

"I don't know, but if he does then it's a good reason not to start trouble. I'm finally keeping him at arm's length for the first time and you want to go get us all...*involved* again?"

"Come on, it's just for show."

"Not to mention how completely unethical it is."

"Maybe, but as long as no one finds out, who cares? It's a victimless crime. Nobody gets hurt—"

"Except maybe for Tony."

"He'll get over it, and if the nation thinks you've found someone, imagine how awesome the publicity would be for MateSearch!"

Dara ran the idea over in her mind, then came to her senses and shook her head vigorously. "Is this the best you could come up with? Forget it. I won't lie. I promised myself I would live up to the MateSearch standard of truth in all things."

"Well, then I'm out of ideas, Harri, and you're going to have to dust off your dating duds and get cracking. It's not so bad once you get your feet wet again. Took me a while, but Cole took the sting out of it," he said, referring to his new boyfriend, a stockbroker he'd been fixed up with a month earlier. "Remember our ad: 'Someone special is waiting to meet you!'" Reggie patted her lightly on the side of her face.

Twisting her face into a smirk she said, "Yeah, sure he is."

Dara moped her way back to her office, sat down and dialed Palulah's number again. The phone rang four times before a machine picked up.

"Hi, it's Palulah! Tell me what's going on!"

Dara left a message in her most cheerful, professional voice, requesting that Palulah call her back as soon as possible. Then she took a deep breath and pulled a MateSearch profile form from a folder inside her desk. It was ten pages long and she stared at the cover sheet with misery apparent. Reluctantly, she picked up her pen and began writing.

Dara was on page three pondering a question about whether she practiced any behaviors others might refer to as bad habits. She had begun her confessional with knuckle cracking and pencil chewing, when a nervous Maxine appeared at her door. Dara casually hid the form under another folder and asked Maxine what she could do for her.

"There's someone in the lobby who wants to see you. I told him he needs an appointment, but he insisted."

"Who is it?"

"Nick Wyatt," Maxine mouthed in a loud whisper. "He's that member who's been calling—"

"Shit," said Dara, half under her breath.

"What should I do?"

Dara looked at her watch. "Tell him I can see him only briefly because I have a meeting in five minutes."

"Okay," the receptionist said, and scurried back to find him.

Dara fluffed her hair and checked her reflection in her darkened monitor. A few seconds later, Maxine and Nick appeared at her office door. Maxine introduced them, made a face that seemed to wish her good luck, and disappeared.

Nick was dressed in jeans, a T-shirt, and work boots. Although he looked more weathered than his photos, the lines added an appealing, rakish edge to his persona—like that of her long-lost Zachary. Her stomach tightened at this jarring bit of sensory recall, but she motioned him in, shook his hand, and offered him a seat opposite her desk. He sat down uneasily, and folded his arms across his chest.

"I hope you've been receiving my messages, Mr. Wyatt. Palulah is a very difficult person to get a hold of," she said, picking up a pink-colored pencil from her desk and rolling it between her fingers.

"Ms. Harrison, do you really think it's fair that I sit around and wait for you to meet with someone who, knowing what I know about her, is obviously dodging your calls?"

Dara squirmed a little in her seat and resisted the urge to lift the pencil to her lips. "What makes you so certain of that?"

"Oh, I don't know, common sense?" he said coldly.

She glared at him.

"Don't you think she knows why you're trying to get in touch?" he continued. "She knows that what she wrote about me is all lies and she doesn't want to be called out on it."

"I understand you believe her claims to be spurious—"

"Spurious?" he repeated, seemingly mystified by the term.

"—and I plan to investigate, but some people just have hectic lives, Mr. Wyatt," she said coolly. "Look, I know it's written insensitively, and I assure you that at the very least, that aspect will be modified."

"What do you mean, 'that aspect'?" he asked, unfurling his arms and leaning forward in his chair. "Have you been listening to what I'm telling you? Everything she wrote is a lie. We never had sex, and she harassed me for weeks after I ended things. She's crazy! Now I insist...no, I *demand* that post be taken down immediately! If it's not, I want my entire profile pulled off line and my membership terminated!"

"You know about our six-month policy, don't you Mr. Wyatt?"

"I don't care what the policy is. These are extreme circumstances!"

"Well, I can't break the MateSearch rules for you or for anyone. They're in the contract you signed. They're set in stone."

"I don't give a crap about the contract! I want it down, now!"

Dara tapped her pencil nervously against her legal pad, trying to keep her head. "I really don't think it's appropriate that you come into my office and make demands you have no right to make."

He took a breath to calm himself and spoke again. "Look, I work in the entertainment industry, Ms. Harrison."

"Yes, I know," she answered.

"So I'm not exactly anonymous. I have a reputation—and I'm not going to let that vindictive bitch...or some high-tech...yenta on a power trip destroy it."

Dara stared into Nick's eyes. She couldn't wait to reveal her endgame. "Have you examined your contract lately?" she asked in a measured tone.

"Why?"

"Well, to elucidate," she began, "according to your contract, you consented to abide by our Rate-a-Mate clause. You joined MateSearch, in part, for the constructive criticism we provi—"

"You call what she wrote constructive?" he asked, his voice practically cracking with rage. "Not only wasn't it constructive, it was all bull, as I keep telling you over and over, although it seems to be going in one ear and out the other!"

Dara took a deep breath. "Why don't we read over your contract together," she said with false politeness. She stood up and walked to the adjoining room. A minute later she returned with a blue folder, sat down, and shuffled through the pages.

"Is that my file?" asked Nick.

"Yes, it is."

"Can I have a look?"

Dara turned to the section labeled Liability Release and handed the contract to him. As he read the fine print, she felt her confidence grow. She'd be damned if she let some guy who just ambushed her in her own office get the better of her. MateSearch was her baby—the one she put her heart, her soul and all her money into—and no disgruntled date, especially one that looked like Zachary Grovener, was going to tell her how to run it.

Nick read the clause carefully.

Member hereby agrees to waive any and all claims against MateSearch, Inc. or co-members of MateSearch, Inc. from any Rate-a-Mate posts made during the term of the agreement.

Member hereby acknowledges, agrees, and understands that there is the risk that posts by members can be factually incorrect, nevertheless, agrees to waive all legal rights relating to any such factually incorrect posts and further agrees that member's sole recourse shall be through the policies and procedures of MateSearch, Inc. in resolving such disputes.

By the time he finished reading, he realized he was screwed. He wasn't a lawyer, but it did sound pretty ironclad. He took a breath and looked up at Dara whose subdued smile screamed, *Checkmate!*

"I told you I'm trying to resolve this issue, Mr. Wyatt. I'm sorry if it's not occurring fast enough for you."

Nick leaned forward in his chair, his intense chestnut eyes boring into hers.

"How would you feel?" he asked.

"Excuse me?"

"How would you feel if someone wrote something scathing about you that you knew had no basis in fact?"

"I understand this is frustrating for you, but you have to realize there are certain rules and protocols here at MateSearch that must apply to everyone."

Nick sighed unevenly and looked back at the contract, remembering his concern about the signature page. He flipped to the last page to see if he had in fact provided his John Hancock. What he found allayed his worries, and after thinking a moment, he smiled for the first time. "I see," he said, suddenly more agreeable.

"I'm glad."

"Could I trouble you for a copy of this? It would save me from having to turn my condo upside down."

"Indubitably," she answered with pleasant professionalism.

Indubitably? Nick mouthed, furrowing his eyebrows as she walked back into the file room. He could hear the sound of a copier as he tapped his good foot in a steady beat.

When Dara returned, she handed him a copy of the contract and crossed her arms over her chest. He stood up, nodded, and walked out the door. Dara took a deep breath and blew the air out. Why was she letting this guy get under her skin? She shrugged and sat back down at her desk. Then, she continued to spill the guts of her personal life onto the pages before her.

By the following afternoon, MateSearch members could find the profile and photograph of Dara, Member ID 2013, on their list of potential dates. Reggie had looked it over before posting it, and sent it back to her with the following comment:

Dear Harri,

You sound maaahvelous…but this is MateSearch. You may recall that we are the dating service that encourages its members to reveal their dirty little secrets. The following is a list of things I've learned about you over the years that I'm sure would be immensely helpful for the edification of your future dates:

You morph into Cujo if you forget to take your Mydol.

You think stuffed animals have feelings.

You grammatically edited the notes your grade school friends passed you in class.
You now do the same to neighborhood signs and restaurant menus.
You've never forgiven Nancy (the Holy) Grail for beating you out as valedictorian of your High School.
The people at IHOP think you're a slut.
You use big vocabulary words when you're feeling flustered.
You think your cat has magical healing powers (Jesse told me).
You gnaw at colored pencils all day like a little blonde rat.
You damn other motorists to hell if they drive too slowly.
You think you don't need anyone...ever...for anything.
You're harboring a chainsaw in your coat closet.
Your real name is Dara Lynn (Adorable!).
Hope these observations help you in your quest to find Mr. Right.
Your devoted Reggie

After cursing him in absentia, Dara added a few of his suggestions to prove she could stand the heat of her own company's kitchen; however, seeing her personal life splayed out in front of her and now available to so many strangers made her feel inordinately vulnerable. This feeling was magnified tenfold by the fact that every humiliating detail of her dating life would soon be pumped into the living rooms of every Ophelia fan in the country. How did she let this happen? Just last week her life was a thing of beauty—completely under control, just the way she liked it.

Finding it difficult to focus on work, she scanned the profiles of some MateSearch men in hopes that one or two might appeal to her. By lunchtime, she had found one, and by three o'clock, she had picked two more. The first, an electrician from Brentwood, liked cooking and comedy and his worst admitted problem was attention deficit disorder. The second, the owner of a vitamin store in Venice, liked travel and working out but confessed to having a fear of squirrels. The third, a pediatrician from Agoura Hills, was a native Californian and Dodgers fan who disclosed his inability to swim and his inconvenient but understandable germ phobia. Being newbies, the three men had yet to garner any Rate-a-Mate posts.

Dara sent them each a request to meet and now had to wait for them to check out her profile and reply. She pondered how she would explain the Ophelia factor. She would have to warn them that their dates with her might include a TV crew as chaperones. With luck, these particular men harbored a secret wish to star in a reality show.

Her nerves still frayed, she headed to the kitchen and made herself a cup of Tension Tamer tea. Her body, however, craved something more along the lines of a Valium or two.

"Ms. Harrison, Shelby Gerard, a segment producer at the *Ophelia Show*, is on line two for you!" Maxine announced.

Dara's stomach lurched. "Okay, I'll take it," she replied through the intercom. She picked up the phone and smiled, hoping it would somehow help mask her anxiety. "Dara Harrison," she said, trying to sound confident.

"Hello, Ms. Harrison, this is Shelby Gerard, from the *Ophelia Show*? We met—"

"Oh, yes, hello, Ms. Gerard."

"Call me Shelby."

"Sure, and please call me Dara."

"I hope you've recuperated from all the hubbub by now," Shelby said.

"Well, almost."

"I'm calling to coordinate a shooting schedule with you. As you know, we want to send our cameras out to document snippets of your upcoming dates for the show, and we have to work around everyone's busy schedules with the holidays right around the corner."

"I understand," Dara said with a pang of guilt for skipping Christmas in Connecticut this year. Her family had been disappointed, but they knew how difficult it would be for her to get away with a new business and the whole Ophelia circus. Her mother and Bill decided they'd fly to L.A. in March for Bill's sixty-fifth birthday instead.

"So, how have you been doing on the dating front?"

"Well, just getting started. Got to get back into the swing of things."

"Of course. So you don't have any dates planned yet?"

"Not yet. May I get back to you on that?"

"Of course, but don't wait too long. You're on a production schedule now!" she said with a giggle. "I'll give you my number so you can let me know when you've set some up—and make sure they'll allow for interesting viewing, if you know what I mean."

"Not...really."

"You know, Disneyland, rock climbing, maybe a nice balloon ride—fun stuff that people will want to see."

"I'm not much of an adventurer, but I'll see what I can do," she answered unenthusiastically.

"Oh," Shelby replied with barely disguised disappointment. "Okay, well, we'll work on you!"

Dara hung up the phone and stared out the window. *A balloon ride?* This was getting more appalling by the minute.

❧ Thirteen ❧

J OSIE'S HAD EARNED ITSELF A REPUTATION as one of the best Asian fusion restaurants on the West Side and a popular dating spot— which is why Dara tried to suggest a more low-key Middle Eastern restaurant instead. Her attempts were futile. Rob did not like Middle Eastern food—and worse, Shelby insisted on an elegant backdrop and beautiful people if she was going to have to film "a dull dinner date" as she called it. The compromise was Josie's.

Setting up the date had been relatively quick and easy. Rob, the electrician with ADHD and she had a brief conversation and exchanged two emails before meeting. He seemed almost eager to have his dinner with her documented for posterity. Dara glided into the restaurant wearing a graceful black Michael Kors dress and her three-inch black and silver Jimmy Choo sandals, both of which had been collecting dust in her closet for almost a year. Rob and the cameras were waiting at the hostess's podium. After greeting Shelby, a slender woman with thick, curly hair and eyes that looked permanently surprised, Dara shook hands with Rob. He was an attractive man of about forty with a jovial face and easy manner. He wore black slacks, an elegant striped shirt, and a sports jacket. After being told by Shelby to "just act natural," the two followed their escort to a table in the corner, cameras in tow. Dara's face flushed with embarrassment as she noted the full-to-capacity crowd, some of whom craned their necks at the production crew as they set up.

Rob held Dara's chair for her as she sat down, then removed his jacket and slung it over the back of his chair before taking his seat. Dara tried desperately to ignore the cameras and act normal. Rob, on the other hand, seemed to relish the spotlight and exuded confidence as they scanned their menus. A waiter approached, welcomed them, and requested their drink order.

"Would you like to start with a glass of wine, Dara?" asked Rob.

"Yes, that would be nice, maybe a Cabernet."

The waiter nodded and wrote down her order. Then he looked toward her dinner companion. Rob grimaced, shrugged, and flipped his head over to the left, his ear meeting his shoulder. The waiter stared uncomfortably at him for a moment. "And for you, sir?" he asked.

Rob repeated the movements two more times before asking, "What kind of beer do you have?"

Dara glanced anxiously around the room then back at Rob as the waiter spoke.

"Sapporo, Sam Adams, Bass, Blue Moon, Heineken, Bud, Guinness—"

Suddenly, Rob sniffed and grunted loudly, startling Dara, the waiter, who almost dropped his notepad, and the film crew who peered over their cameras curiously. The waiter tried to continue his beer listing but was interrupted again by a grunt, now followed by the head and shoulder routine.

Tourette's? thought Dara. *How could he have left that out of his profile without the interviewer noticing?*

"I'll have a Sapporo," Rob said as if nothing strange had just happened. The waiter nodded and fled the table. Dara forced a smile at Rob as she white-knuckled her menu and glanced at Shelby, who by now seemed completely fascinated.

"So what looks good to you?" asked Rob, opening his menu. He tossed his head to the left again and suddenly blurted out "Bitch!" Dara winced and dropped her jaw in shock. Rob looked at her for about five seconds with a straight face and then fell into hysterical laughter.

"Wha—?" Dara began.

"I was just kidding! I came up with this bit as an ice breaker. First dates are always so...somber! You know? I figured they'd get a kick out of it, too," he said, cocking his head at the cameras. "Funny stuff, huh?"

Dara sat in her chair, stupefied. "Hilarious," she finally replied, her expression like stone. She could hear the crew still chuckling. Dara figured thrill-seeking Shelby must be in her glory right about now.

"I dare them to edit that out!" he whispered to her conspiratorially.

My God, she thought. *I knew the man had attention issues, I just never imagined what kind.*

"Aw, come on, lighten up. You knew I was a jokester, right?"

"Why would I know that?"

"It said it right there in my profile. *Secret desire to be a standup comedian*?"

"Must have missed that line."

"So what's *your* secret desire, Dara?"

Dara shot a fleeting glance around the room, at the film crew, and reluctantly back at her date.

"You don't want to know, Rob," she said. "You don't want to know."

After that escapade, Dara realized no place was actually safe when it came to dating, so she decided to be more physically adventurous with bachelor number two. Edmund, the owner of the VitaLife vitamin store, suggested rollerblading on the Venice bike path, an activity he undertook every Saturday afternoon. Figuring this would be less life threatening than, say, scaling the side of a mountain, Dara agreed.

Unfortunately, the Venice bike path on a Saturday afternoon, with the bikers, skaters, painters, volleyball players, artisans, palm readers, and tourists, was too hectic an atmosphere for Shelby and her crew. She insisted on moving their date to Elysian Park. Edmund looked disturbed and quite uncomfortable with the change. After debating Shelby unsuccessfully, the six-foot-two body builder finally confessed his embarrassing phobia.

"Are you kidding?" asked Shelby, genuinely amazed.

"No," Edmund replied. "I'm not kidding. Why would I kid about something like that?"

"Sorry I just can't imagine why—" Shelby began.

"—anyone would be afraid of squirrels?" he said, finishing her sentence with his arms crossed defiantly across his chest.

"But they're so cute with those fluffy tails—and they run from you when you get close."

"Well they don't run from me. In fact, I was stalked and attacked by one when I was eight."

Shelby stared at Edmund's strong, chiseled face, her head tilted as if trying to visualize such an unlikely scenario. Then she assumed her professional stance again. "Okay, but what are the chances that lightning is going to strike twice? Really, Edmund, you have to face your fear sometime—and I already got the shooting permit. We don't have a choice."

Still flushed with trepidation, Edmund looked at Dara, who shrugged her shoulders as if to say it was out of her hands. With pressure all around, Edmund relented.

The couple, clad in biking duds, grabbed their helmets and skates and drove together in Edmund's car with one of the cameramen in the back seat. In an effort to calm him, Dara asked about his store. He commenced a detailed lecture on how he cared for his customers like patients, helping to treat them with natural prescriptions from the shelves of his shop.

Apparently, he fancied himself a modern-day medicine man on a crusade to heal Los Angelenos of their ills. He claimed to have cured one man of asthma with licorice root, and a woman of diabetes with basil leaves and turmeric powder. Dara felt skeptical, but who was she to judge? She had a cat that cured migraines with her paws.

They also discussed his vitamin intake, which sounded excessive enough to choke ten horses. Dara asked what a fruitarian was, as he'd listed it in his profile under eating habits. When she found out his diet consisted only of organic fruits, nuts, and seeds, she found it strangely ironic, given that his furry nemeses enjoyed the same nutritional regimen. Soon, the conversation turned to skating.

"You know, this is the first time I'm trying this," Dara admitted. "I'm a little nervous."

"Skating's a breeze if you know the ropes. I'll show you, and you'll be surprised at what you can accomplish on your first try. Just do what I do."

When they arrived at the park, Edmund took a long, slow look around the grounds like a Secret Service agent casing a risky venue. Satisfied that he was relatively safe, he found a bench, and they proceeded to don their skates and helmets. He taught Dara how to stop on a dime and showed her some tricks for keeping her balance. Then they skated down a path that would have been serene, had it not been for Dara's squeals of terror and comedic arm gesticulations, all caught on tape by the cameras that rolled behind them.

"Don't look down," he called over his shoulder. "Look ahead and be confident."

Dara made a valiant attempt at gliding but veered off the path and landed, bum first, on a patch of grass.

"Ouch!"

"You okay?" asked Edmund.

"Yeah. You're not going to use that, I hope," Dara called to the crew as Edmund helped lift her back onto the path.

Five minutes later, Dara again tumbled onto the grass—and then again, and again. She could tell she was trying Edmund's patience.

"You okay?" he called to her once again, his voice revealing annoyance.

"Yeah, yeah," she said, wishing the date could come to a quick end and she could go home and nurse her black and blue body.

Instead, they continued on. After about a half hour, she finally got the hang of it. Edmund called to her with relief. "By George, I think she's got it!"

Soon after, they skated through a double row of trees, with Edmund nervously twisting his head in all directions. Suddenly he sped up and raced ahead, abandoning Dara.

"Hey, wait up," she called, but he didn't slow down until he'd cleared the trees by about a hundred feet. *Geez*, Dara thought. When she caught up, she could see he was sweating, trembling, and on the verge of some sort of anxiety attack.

"What's wrong?" she asked him, trying to catch her breath.

"They hang out in trees," he said.

"And nothing happened to you, did it?"

"I guess not," he replied, although he was clearly still shaken.

"Okay, one more time around," Shelby called to them.

Edmund drew a deep breath. Dara took his right hand and coaxed him along the path. "Good, good!" called Shelby as they approached a long bench. Perched atop of its back railing, a plump little squirrel was nibbling on an acorn. Before Dara could warn Edmund, he spotted it and let out the kind of bone-chilling scream a person might give if he'd run into Jack the Ripper wielding a knife.

The squirrel, offended by the shrieking, dove off the bench and onto the path in front of them, causing Edmund to leap in fear and knock Dara, once again, onto the grass. Dara and the crew watched in shock as Edmund, fighting to regain his footing, flailed his arms and legs wildly in all direction before spilling onto the asphalt, his right leg splayed at an alarming angle. "Goddamn squirrels!" he shouted. "Get me out of here! I told you I was Sciurophobic!"

"Skioohrahwhat?" asked Shelby.

"There's actually a name for it?" Dara added in amazement.

"Help him up!" said one of the cameramen.

"No, don't move me. I think I broke something. Shit. I'm a sitting duck. He's probably gathering his friends so they can gang up and gnaw me to death. You!" he yelled to the cameraman. "Stand guard and don't let any of those ratty little monsters near me!"

The cameraman tried to hold back his smirk while assuring Edmund he was on the case.

"I think somebody better call an ambulance," said Dara when she got a gander at her date's leg.

Twenty minutes later, an ambulance carted off Edmund, but not before Shelby secured a promise that he would post a review of the date as soon as possible. Meanwhile, Dara, battered, achy, and exhausted, hitched a ride home with the crew.

❧ *Fourteen* ❧

"BOY, YOU SURE CAN PICK 'EM!" said Reggie, laughing as Dara shifted uncomfortably in her seat across the table from him at a West Hollywood deli. She was still feeling the bruises on her lower extremities.

It was the Monday after her skating fiasco. She had refused to discuss it at the office—especially after reading Edmund's post. Writing from his hospital bed, where he nursed a broken ankle, a slipped disc, and numerous contusions, Edmund had referred to Dara as "insensitive," "inconsiderate," and "a lousy skater"—and that was *after* she sent him a gift basket.

"Okay, I can forgive you the first guy and his Tourette's Surprise, but how could you pick a full-grown man with a fear of squirrels?"

"Leave me alone," Dara replied wearily, her head in her hands.

The waiter placed a corned beef sandwich on rye in front of Reggie and a spinach and cheese omelet and fries in front of Dara.

She began playing with her eggs. "The fun continues. Tonight I have to go out with a germophobic pediatrician."

"Are you kidding?"

Dara shook her head and slid a forkful of eggs into her mouth. "You can't make this shit up," she mumbled.

"With or without a television entourage?"

"Happily, this guy refused to be on camera—doesn't want to lose credibility with his patients or something. Guess I can't blame him."

"Lucky break."

"Shelby didn't think so. She's insisting on a full report anyway."

"Well, I've got to give these guys credit. They're copping to all kinds of embarrassing crap, just like we encouraged them to do." Reggie sank his teeth into his sandwich as a hostess seated a couple at the table beside them. "Where are you taking the Doc on a Monday night?"

"Starbucks."

"Starbucks?" he asked with surprise.

"Yup."

"Cheap date."

"Short date."

"Gotcha."

"And I'm feeling a bout of PMS on the horizon."

Reggie held his palm out. "Say no more!"

"Don't worry. I've been popping Mydol like M&Ms today."

Reggie winked and gave her the thumbs up while chewing a large mouthful of sandwich with gusto. "God, I love not dieting," he said. "Always had to be perfect for You Know Who. What a difference a new man can make. Cole likes me just the way I am."

"I don't know why you ever bothered dieting. Food doesn't even show on you."

"Pfff. You haven't seen my love handles," he said, beginning to pull up his shirt.

"Nor do I want to!" she said sternly. "God, haven't I been through enough?"

Reggie pulled his shirt back down. "You're such a prude these days! It's not like I was pulling down my pants...hey, speaking of which, whatever happened to that guy with the tiny—"

"Shhh!" Dara said, indicating the people next to them.

"Did you ever hear from him after that visit?"

"It's only been about a week, but no."

"I'm surprised."

"I'm not. I showed him that legally he didn't have a leg to stand on."

"And Pa-loo-lah?" Reggie said, enunciating each syllable comically.

"Still giving me the brush off."

At eight o'clock that night, Dara sat at a table nursing a grande decaf cappuccino with a shot of vanilla syrup when Dr. Sam Steiner walked through the door. He had a handsome face with strong features and a square jaw and he smiled when he saw her. She gave a little wave as he made his way through a small crowd to her table.

"Dara?" he said, offering his hand.

"Yes, hi," she replied, shaking it as she lifted slightly out of her seat.

"I'm going to grab a coffee. Can I get you anything else?" he asked.

"No, thanks."

Sam got in line, giving Dara a few minutes to discreetly run her eyes over him. He had dirty blond hair in a long crew cut, stood about five foot ten, and, from what she could tell, had an adorable butt. He was wearing brown slacks and a beige shirt open at the collar. After a minute, he returned with a grande coffee and a lemon poppy seed muffin.

"Dessert," he said, holding up the muffin.

She smiled and nodded.

"So you're the owner of MateSearch, huh?"

"In the flesh."

"I did get a call from Shelby Gerard like you said."

"And?"

"She tried to change my mind about the cameras. Sorry, I had to stick to my guns."

"You don't have to apologize to me. I welcome the break."

"I promised her I'd fully cooperate otherwise."

"Oh…good," she replied halfheartedly.

"So I'm curious how you came up with an idea like MateSearch," he asked, sipping gingerly from his cup.

Dara realized she was sitting stiffly and tried to relax into her chair. "I had a lot of on-the-job training when I gave advice at *LA Entertains*." She went into some detail about the types of people she had counseled and shared some of their stories.

He listened intently as she spoke and when she was done, he said, "I thought maybe it had to do with something more personal in nature."

"Personal?" she asked. "Why would you think that?"

"Well, seeing as you're not married, I thought maybe you channeled your frustrations into a lucrative business or something. You know, that you're one of us—'perennially single' like your brochure says."

Dara wasn't sure why she felt offended. Her idea was something she was proud of. Why should it bother her to be included in the ranks of her clientele? Being single was nothing to be ashamed of—especially when you chose that path wittingly.

"I think it was more about applying the message I'd been advocating for so many years at the paper—and it was also time that I headed out on my own. I tend to be a pretty independent person."

Sam nodded his head while chewing a bite of muffin. It was as if he were digesting this bit of information. "So things are going well for you?"

"Outstanding. We have over two thousand clients already." Then she launched into an almost automatic pitch for her business, describing all the coverage it had gotten over the previous few months.

"No wonder you made it to Ophelia. That's pretty impressive. So how did you feel when she turned the tables on you?" he asked.

Dara sighed. "Between you and me? I wasn't exactly pleased. You know, having your personal life on display can be uncomfortable to say the least."

"I know. That's what gave me pause about joining, but I figured it was worth a try. I look at it as a new adventure. When does the first show air?"

"In a couple of weeks."

"I'll set my recorder."

"Please don't," she replied, only half kidding. "So anyway," she said, "how did you hear about us?"

"I read an article. Believe it or not, my mother still nags me about when I'm going to find a nice wife and give her grandchildren. I think I finally decided it's time to settle down with someone who doesn't have dust for brains." He took another sip of his coffee and swallowed. "So with all your looks, charm, and experience, how is it you're still single?"

Dara fidgeted in her chair, interpreting his words as a backhanded compliment. "Well, it's really been a conscious decision lately. Starting up a big dating service, ironically, doesn't leave one much time for dating."

"I could say the same thing about my career."

"Yes, I'm sure there's never any shortage of germy kids!" she said. Then she caught herself and looked up at him to see if she'd made a faux pas. "Sorry, I know that's one of your...issues."

"That's okay. It's an occupational hazard. I've devised ways of coping."

"Glad to hear it," she said, pleased he'd learned to handle germs better than Edmund did squirrels.

"So your profile says you're a runner."

"Yup. Crack of dawn and all that."

"Crack of dawn, huh? I haven't seen that time of day since my residency. Frankly, I don't miss it!"

"If I don't run in the morning, I feel like a slug."

"Don't you ever sleep in?"

Dara thought about the weeks she had all but tied herself to her bed after the firing.

"Not really, but on the weekends, I run at eight o'clock instead of six."

Sam took a deep breath, and she noticed his eyes traveling around the room behind her. Was she boring him? She hoped not. This was the first decent date she'd been on in what seemed like centuries. She searched her brain for something interesting or clever to say as he finished his muffin and downed the remainder of his coffee, but her mind had gone blank.

"Do you like to do anything just for fun?" he asked.

"Me? Sure."

"What? I didn't really see anything much listed on your profile."

"Well, you know, the business doesn't leave me much time for socializing."

"You have to make time, I learned that early on."

Dara took a sip of her coffee while scanning her brain to remember the last time she really had any fun. He took the lull as an opportunity to check his watch.

"Gotta catch a train?" she joked.

"No, just have some paperwork I've got to get to tonight. Want to make sure I leave some time."

"Well I've finished my coffee, so...I'll let you go..." she said a bit awkwardly.

With that he stood up, threw out their cups and wrappers and walked her to her car. She held out her hand.

"Well, very nice to meet you, Sam."

He took it for a brief shake and before heading to his car said, "Good luck with Ophelia."

Dara lay in bed, running the evening over in her mind. Dr. Sam Stein seemed like a polite and decent man. He was the right age, available, attractive, socially adept, and looking for The One—the kind of man she imagined any woman would be eager to date, but something had felt off about their time together. Why didn't they click? Was she just not his type? More out of practice than she realized? She took a deep breath, dreading Shelby's cross-examination, especially since she herself didn't have a handle on what had transpired that night.

As she drifted into slumber, her worries faded away. It's not like she was looking for a mate anyway. She was dating for a show, nothing more. So who cared why Dr. Stein seemed eager to end their time together. For all she knew, he really did have a night's work awaiting him at home. If not, she was sure she could count on Shelby to let her, and the rest of America, know the truth.

Dara didn't have to wait for Shelby. At four o'clock the following day, after the company Christmas party and just as her hormones began to seethe, she made the mistake of signing on to her website to see if any new men had requested to meet her. There were no requests waiting, but a Rate-a-Mate review icon blinked at her tauntingly.

"Uh-oh," she said. She took a deep breath and double-clicked it. Up sprang a review from Dr. Sam Stein. She began reading it to herself.

Posted by Sam, No. 1422

I met Dara for coffee. My first impression was that she was very cute, stylish, and pleasant.

Dara breathed a small sigh of relief.

As her profile states, she is the owner of MateSearch and is now being featured on the Ophelia Show. I didn't get the feeling that I knew a great deal about her after reading her profile, so I was interested to meet her in person. Unfortunately, our face to face meeting didn't reveal much more. Dara seems a bit rigid and very reluctant to let her guard down. Kind of ironic given the fact that MateSearch is her brainchild.

Dara felt her pulse rate quickening and a queasy feeling in her stomach, but she kept reading.

The conversation was mainly about business. Anything else I broached caused the dialogue to become stilted, probably because of her reluctance to relax and be open and frank about her feelings. In other words, Dara's a nice woman, but she really needs to practice what she preaches!

Dara massaged her forehead with her fingers as she stared miserably at the computer screen.

Shit, she thought.

She looked over the post again. How dare he accuse her of being closed off. Wasn't she out there every day putting her philosophy of life and love on the line for the world to see? Sam was clearly just another pompous doctor with a propensity for misdiagnosis. She briefly flirted with the idea of removing the post but knew that would be an abuse of power, one that would come back to haunt her. Instead, she buzzed Reggie and requested that he come to her office. A minute later he appeared, still wearing the red and white hat he'd worn to play Santa at lunch.

"Hey," she said, "I need your opinion on something."

Reggie stepped behind her desk to see what had her attention. He smelled like candy canes.

"That germophobic doctor just posted a review of me and our date last night," she said heatedly. "Get a load of this."

Dara slid her chair over so Reggie could move closer to the screen. Halfway through reading, he glanced sideways at her. When he finished, he blew air through his lips but said nothing.

110

"So?"

"Hmm," he replied still staring at the screen.

"So?" she asked again more fervently, this time whacking his arm with the back of her hand.

"Huh? Oh, yeah. Not the best advertisement for our company, is it?"

"Is that all you can say?"

"What do you want me to say?"

"What do you think? I want you to tell me this guy's a jerk," Dara demanded.

"This guy's a jerk."

"And maybe you should get him to soften his comments."

"They're already civil, Harri."

"But they're wrong. He totally mischaracterized me."

"Uh-huh."

"What do you mean, uh-huh?"

"As your friend, I empathize. As your business partner, I'm suggesting you forget it and move on. And as Santa Claus, I'm telling you to relax and smile 'cause it's almost Christmas Eve. Are you sure you don't want to come over for dinner tomorrow night?"

Dara disregarded the invitation. She was still fully engrossed in her outrage. "He's totally wrong and you know it!"

"Look sweetie, you're not closed off with me, but apparently he has a different perspective."

"Meaning?"

"Meaning, he's entitled to his opinion."

"Excuse me, but this is a man who *microwaves* his *toothbrush!*"

"He's still entitled to his opinion," Reggie said, folding his hands across his chest.

Dara looked up at him, squinting her eyes suspiciously. "You think he's right, don't you?"

"Wha...what? I told you what I think."

"You were just trying to spare my feelings. You agree with him!"

"I wasn't even there! How can I agree with him?"

"Because...because you always insinuate that I'm closed off to relationships."

Reggie backed away from her desk, his hands raised in the air. "I am not having this argument. I'm too smart to fall into that trap!"

"Well, am I right or am I right?" she shouted at him.

"That depends."

"On what?"

"You take your Mydol today?"

"You value your life today?" she said angrily, grabbing her letter opener and holding it up like a dagger.

"Well, what do you expect when you go on an extended dating hiatus?"

Dara dropped the letter opener and pointed accusingly at Reggie. "Aha! See? I knew you agreed with him!"

"I'm getting out of here before your head starts spinning or something," Reggie said as he hurried toward the door.

"Well you're both wrong! I am a very open person. I have nothing to hide. So take your commentary and go!" she yelled.

But he was already gone.

When Dara got home that night, the post from Sam was still weighing on her mind. She sat on her couch, eating Chunky Monkey straight from the carton, as Frosty yelled "Happy Birthday" from her television set. She muted the TV and focused on finding a way to get out of the MateSearch Challenge, but she couldn't come up with a workable alternative. Reggie's secret plot to hire Tony began to look like the only game in town—and her only way of ending this extreme unpleasantness. As she scratched Mallory behind her ears, she wondered how she could make the scheme work.

She hadn't talked to Tony in over a year, ever since she had insisted that they stop speaking in order to form a more perfect disunion. She felt she was betraying both of them by reaching for the telephone, but rationalized it away. Maybe she was just calling to wish him a Merry Christmas for old time's sake? Dara punched in the digits she still knew by heart and heard two rings before he picked up.

"Can't live without me, can you?" he answered, a smile in his voice.

"Apparently not, but it's not what you think."

"I know. You were just calling to say Merry Christmas like you do every year, even when we're on the outs."

"Yes. Merry Christmas, Ton."

"To you, too. Thought you'd be in Connecticut."

"Couldn't make it this year. There's too much going on."

"Oh, yeah? Like what?"

"Well, something in particular I can actually use your help with."

"Me?" he asked with surprise. "What? You want to buy a boat or something?" "No, but I am interested in buying something else."

He paused before answering. "Aw babe, you know I give you freebies."

"Shut up. This is a real business proposition, and it's top secret."

"Ooh, sounds intriguing."

"We'll see if you still feel that way after you hear what it is," she said, covering her forehead with her palm.

"You're beginning to scare me."

"I started a dating service, Tony. It's called MateSearch."

"I know. I've read all about you. Who knew you were an entrepreneur? I was going to call to congratulate you but didn't want to break my promise."

"Thanks," she said, now feeling even more guilt for calling him. "Anyway, I want you to help me win the MateSearch Challenge."

"The what?"

"I made an appearance on the *Ophelia Show* a few weeks ago—"

"Ophelia? Hittin' the big time, huh?"

"To promote the service, I offered three people from the audience free memberships with a challenge to find a mate within six months."

"Catchy."

"And then Ophelia challenged me to the same challenge, and she wants me to come back with Mr. Right in a few months to prove my service works."

"Are you kidding?"

"No, I'm sorry to say I'm not. So I need your help."

"And what exactly does that mean?" he asked cautiously.

"Join the service, date me in front of the cameras, and say we're an item when we appear on the *Ophelia Show*—that we're on the verge of getting engaged."

"What? How do you expect to pull that off? We dated for four years."

"On and off."

"So?"

"So it's not like any of my friends ever met you, not even Jesse, since you almost always made me come to your apartment."

"What can I say? I'm a homebody."

"Yeah, well, to them, you're just my mystery man booty caller."

"I'm your what?"

"My mystery man who makes booty calls."

"Me? You just said you always came to my place. Hate to tell you this, but that makes you the booty caller."

"Never mind. The only thing we'd have to lie about is your first name. They know Tony."

"Well that's not really a problem."

"Why not?"

"Because that's my middle name. I told you that."

"Oh, my God! I totally forgot," she said as it came back to her. "You hate your first name, right? What is it? You never did tell me."

"None of your business."

"Oh, come on. You're not going to let a little embarrassment come between us after everything we've been through."

"I'm not?"

"This is important, Tony—or whatever your name is."

"How do you really expect to pull this off?" he asked dubiously.

"Easily. We'll just break up a few months after the show appearance, when all the publicity dies down. We can even let people think we're still together. I mean, what's the diff? I'm on hiatus from the dating scene anyway—or at least I was until recently," she said. "And you're not dating anyone, are you?"

"You sound so sure."

"Well, are you?"

"No one serious."

"So?" Dara heard silence on the other end of the line. "Tony? You there?"

"I'm here."

"So what do you think? I'll pay you back for everything. Won't cost you a dime. On top of that, I'll pay you a fee. I just need you to do me this favor."

"Why? You can get legitimate dates left and right."

"I can't take it anymore. It's humiliating! I don't want to date my own clients. I don't like them," she whined, "and I'm on the verge of punching the segment producer in the face. Do you know she encourages my dates to post mean things about me?"

"Like what?" he said with a laugh.

"I don't want to talk about it. Anyway, are you in?"

"Do I get to think about it?"

115

"No! I won't sleep a wink until I know."

Tony sighed.

"What's the problem?" she asked. "You hassled me to go out with you for a year. Now you're getting your wish. What is there to think about?"

"Oh, I don't know. The lying? The cameras? The national television appearance?"

"It could mean big publicity for your boats. I bet Ophelia will let you plug your company," she said, dangling a carrot.

Tony took another deep breath. "Okay."

"Oh, thank you, Tony!" she squealed with delight. "You're a life saver! I'm so relieved!"

"Yeah, yeah, I'm a real saint...Saint Aloysius."

"Who?"

"That's who I'm named after. I come from a long line of Aloysiuses— but you can call me Al."

Fifteen

THREE DAYS LATER, Reggie finally met the man he'd only heard about through Dara's vague and unenthusiastic answers to his probing questions. Tony was cleaner cut than he had imagined, having created some sort of subversive bad boy in his head. His dark, wavy hair was thinning, and his face featured an aquiline nose and intense tortoise-shell brown eyes. He was about Reggie's height and weight, but a lot less dapper. He wore jeans, cowboy boots, and a blue striped Van Heusen button-down shirt. Reggie snapped photos of him and handed him a profile to fill out. He would be the only other person who knew this man's true identity.

Two hours later, Aloysius "Al" Remini became MateSearch client number 2111. Soon after, he went to the online site and requested a date with Dara. He did the same with two other women, in an effort to quell any future suspicions. Dara waited until that evening to accept. The next morning, she was happy to call Shelby to report her upcoming date. At Tony's suggestion, they would go out New Year's Eve. He had arranged for them to take a gondola ride through the waterways of Venice. The camera crew met them at the docks.

After being fitted with tiny microphones, Dara and Al, as he introduced himself to the crew, climbed into their gondola. They sipped red wine and nibbled olive bread and cheese as the gondolier poled them through the canals under an almost full moon. The soft evening breeze fluttered Dara's hair. An occasional sparkler burst in the distance. Tony impressed Dara with his ability to plan such a romantic night, since their past New Year's Eve dates had always involved a television set, a couch, and takeout.

Shelby and the TV crew followed the couple in two large row boats, showing extreme vigilance in order to keep their expensive equipment from toppling overboard into the somewhat murky waters. Dara made small talk with Tony, careful to keep the conversation first-date appropriate. He spoke openly about his family for the first time, revealing that his married brother had found out years before that he had another son in New Mexico, and that their mother had a beautiful singing voice and had performed on stage until she was forty. Dara also learned that in his youth, Tony had planned to be a fireman like his favorite uncle, Dave, until he was tragically killed in the line of duty.

Stunned, Dara wondered how she could have known so little about a man she'd dated for so long. Who was this Aloysius person, and where had he been hiding while she'd wasted all that time with Tony? Dara couldn't help but glance over at Shelby, who had been watching them interact with an excited smile on her face. Did she sense their rapport? Dara said a silent prayer. Maybe it wouldn't be impossible to pull off her crazy scheme after all.

"Hello?" Dara croaked into the phone. She had one eye open and the clock told her it was two in the morning.

"Hey, it's me," Tony whispered.

"Hi, what's wrong?"

"Sorry to wake you. Just wanted to see if you had a good time tonight."

"I told you I did."

"But that was for the cameras. I wanted to know if you meant it."

"Yes, Tony. I meant it. Now can I go back to sleep?"

"In a minute. I also wanted to know if you thought everything went well, you know, with that Shelby woman. She fall for it?"

"Far as I know."

"That's good."

"Yeah."

"You know how hard it was not to kiss you passionately after you gave me that peck on the cheek at midnight?"

"Good thing you didn't. It would've given us away."

"I guess. So am I safe in assuming you want to go out again?"

Dara yawned loudly into the phone before she could muffle herself. "Yes."

"Don't get *too* excited about it."

"Sorry, that's what happens when you ask me out in the middle of the night."

"How about Saturday? Shelby thinks we should go for a hot air balloon ride."

"Really?" Dara replied with annoyance. "What a coincidence. I think Shelby should go for a balloon ride, too—under an open power line perhaps?"

"I'll think of something else."

"Good idea."

"I'm posting a review about you tonight."

"Don't you dare!"

"Only good things, babe, only good things."

Dara smiled. Perhaps it really would be a happy new year.

❧ Sixteen ❧

DARA TRIED TO FOCUS ON WORK despite the fact that the long-awaited *Ophelia Show* episode was scheduled to air that afternoon. Reggie had set up the conference room VCR to record mode. A few minutes before four o'clock, Reggie walked into Dara's office. She was typing an article on L.A. dating hotspots for the newsletter and didn't notice him.

"It's show time!" he yelled, flailing jazz hands in the air.

Dara squealed and held her heart. "I thought I told you not to scare me like that."

"Sorry, but you want to watch it in real time, don't you?"

"Yeah, yeah. I'm coming," she complained. She finished typing her sentence, saved the document, and stood up.

"Maxine brought snacks," Reggie informed her as they walked to the conference room. "She bribed the intern to watch the phone so she could join us."

"Who else did you invite to witness my coast-to-coast humiliation?"

"Just a handful of MateSearch's essential employees. We have to offer some perks at this job."

When they entered the conference room, they were greeted by the scent of buttered microwave popcorn and their excited crew, including Robin, Jenna, Fred the computer guy, Gabby, the head of sales, and an overly keyed-up Maxine, who ushered Dara to the chair with the best view of the TV.

"Madame," she said with a flourish, pulling the chair out for her.

"You're over there," she told Reggie, "at the head of the table."

"Assigned seating? Who died and made you party hostess?" asked Reggie.

Maxine just shrugged.

"I won't be able to see from there," he whined. "Hey, Fred," he called out, "switch with me."

Fred, a chubby man of about twenty-eight, dutifully forfeited his seat.

"That's better," said Reggie, plopping into the chair next to Dara and grabbing one of the bowls of popcorn. "Want some?" he asked her.

"No, I don't want some," she replied, annoyed.

"It's on, it's on!" said Maxine, pointing at the television as a montage of the famous hostess graced the screen along with her well-known musical theme.

"Here we go," Dara moaned.

Reggie mussed her hair. "Stop being so uptight! It's not like you don't know what's going to happen. Besides, if all of America doesn't fall in love with you, you know you'll always have us."

"Oh, shut up and hand me that bowl."

At about the same time, Nick was sitting on his couch eating trail mix and watching *Jaws* for the umpteenth time. He had spent the holidays just the way he told his sister he would—on the couch in front of his television. Considering the way he'd been feeling both physically and mentally, that's exactly where he wanted to be. Just as the clueless mayor declared the beaches safe for swimming, Nick's phone rang. He reached to answer it, but before he could speak, he heard his sister's voice brimming with urgency.

"Turn on ABC!"

"Why?"

"Just do it, quick!"

Nick picked up his remote and turned the channel to find the MateSearch Madwoman sitting, legs crossed, on a couch while Ophelia questioned her about her dating service.

"It's about MateSearch! I told you it was hot!" Annie shouted.

"Dara Harrison?" he said, dismayed at seeing her on the electronic box that, until now, had been a source of happy escape.

"You met her?" Annie asked.

"Unfortunately."

"Wait, I want to hear this," said Annie.

"...*we take great pains to make sure that people are laying it all on the line. We call it Souldating. Our extensive profile questionnaire encourages people to reveal not only their good points but their foibles, too—and then there's Rate-a-Mate!*" Dara was saying.

"Aw, geez!" Nick bellowed as he listened to her describe the "brilliant idea" that had given rise to his current misery. A minute later Ophelia offered her analogy.

"*So it's kind of like when you want to know if a restaurant or hotel is worth going to—or even if a book is worth reading—by getting opinions from others. That's ingenious!*"

"Ingenious?" Nick shouted at the television. "Treating a human being like a restaurant or a hotel is ingenious?"

"Shhh!" said Annie.

"I know how you came up with the idea!" he roared at the television. "You were probably high on hallucinogens—or drunk off your ass!"

"Nick! Stop shouting! What's wrong with you?"

Nick and Annie listened as Dara presented the MateSearch Challenge to three audience members.

"Hope you know what you're in for!" Nick said to the three sitting ducks on his television.

"What's going on? Why are you so hostile?"

"Nothing," said Nick. He was too embarrassed to even talk about the post with his own sister. He turned his attention back to the TV set when he heard the audience shouting and cheering.

"I have a challenge of my own," Ophelia announced. *"I want Dara to take the MateSearch Challenge, too! It's time to turn the tables on this beautiful matchmaker and make her a match this time! What do you say, people?"*

Hearing this unexpected development had a sudden, sanguine affect on Nick's grumpy mood. "That's an awesome idea!" he said as a smile spread across his face. Then he laughed heartily. "Ever heard of divine justice, Annie?"

"Huh?" his sister replied.

Nick leaned back on his couch and put his feet up on the coffee table. "Looks like there is such a thing!"

Watching her appearance on national television turned out to be a lot less painful than Dara had imagined. She was proud of the way she promoted her company and how diplomatically she'd handled the bombshell that Ophelia had hurled her way.

She returned home that evening to find Jesse lurking outside her door dressed in a poodle skirt, sweater, bobby socks, and saddle shoes. He held out a MateSearch pamphlet and a pink feather pen as he bounced on the balls of his feet, his ponytail swinging. "Ms. Harrison, Ms. Harrison! May I have your autograph?" he fawned.

She laughed as she took the pen and began to write. "Whom should I make it out to?" she said with wide eyes.

"Your bestest friend, Jesse, of course."

When she finished signing, she handed the pamphlet and pen back to him, and he gave her a big hug that barely let her breathe.

"I am soooo proud of you! That was the most amazing *Ophelia Show* ever!"

"Thank you, Jesse, but you may be a little biased."

"Oh, who cares?" he said, laughing. "I just wish we could have watched it together so I could see your face!"

"You can always ask Reggie. I'm sure he'd love to dish the details to anyone who cares to know."

"You're a natural, Dara Doll—and what a great way to start off the new year!" Jesse said, following her inside. He picked Mallory up off the floor and kissed her furry head. Then he asked Dara questions about the show while she fed the cat and surveyed her fridge for something to eat.

"By the way, honey, there's something I've been bursting to tell you."

"Really? What?" asked Dara, turning her attention to him.

"I met someone!" he said with an excited little jump.

"You met someone?"

"Someone special."

"Where?"

He furrowed his eyebrows. "At MateSearch of course. We've been out on four dates, and it's getting hot and heavy!" he sang.

"You're kidding!" said Dara nervously. The friend in her longed to know who in the world it could be, but the professional business owner panicked a little at the thought. If it was a man, it would throw a monkey wrench into the business plan, something she didn't have the energy for right now. Ever since Jesse had joined, she'd gone out of her way to give him complete privacy. She'd even reprimanded Reggie when he'd suggested they check out his ratings, because she didn't want to do anything to affect their friendship and good neighbor status.

"So let me tell you—" began Jesse.

"No, Jess!" she said before he could continue.

Jesse looked at her, perplexed. "Huh?" he asked, pushing his cat eye glasses further up his nose, which set them slightly off kilter.

"As much as I'm dying to know, it would be unprofessional of me. I mean, what if I know the person? Things could get sticky. I don't want to influence you in any way. This is your life, your romance. It shouldn't be marred by any outside influences. It would be unfair to both of you."

"But you're my best friend!"

"I know, but I'm also the owner of MateSearch. I don't want there to be any...conflict of interest."

"Oh," said Jesse, thinking it over. "Maybe you're right—but I can't be held responsible if you get a gander one day outside your door!"

"I guess I'll just have to take my chances," she said, making a mental note to avert her eyes in the hallway.

"Okay, but if this turns out to be *the one*, and things get serious—"

"Then, of course, that would be different," she said as her phone rang. "That's probably my mom."

"Okay, honey. You go talk to her and I'll speak to you later." Jesse kissed her goodbye and left. Dara answered the phone.

"You never called us back!" said Bill. "You were great!"

"Amanda thought so, too," said her mother, who was also on the line. "She's going to call you later."

"Sorry, I got so busy!"

"Dara Lynn," her mother said, "I'm so proud of you! I never thought I'd see my daughter on the most popular talk show in the country!"

"Yeah, me neither," Dara replied.

"And the best part," said her mother, "is now you can take a little break from playing matchmaker for everyone else and work some magic for yourself."

"Yeah," Dara replied, lackluster. Her mother hadn't been privy to the dating disasters she'd just weathered.

"Now don't go in with a bad attitude. You have to be positive and put your best foot forward," her mother stated firmly.

"Jackie, she knows what to do," Bill piped in. "She's the dating expert, remember?"

"Listen," said Dara, "I just walked in a few minutes ago, and I haven't eaten anything but popcorn all day, so—"

"Oh! Well then go eat, of course!" said her mother.

"You did an awesome job, honey," added Bill.

"Thanks. I'll call you tomorrow when I can talk," she told them.

"Bye, sweetie."

❧ Seventeen ❧

ON HER WAY TO WORK the next morning, Dara found herself singing Madonna's "Crazy for You" along with the car radio. She pulled into the outdoor parking lot and drove up the first row toward her reserved spot. She had driven two parking spots too far before realizing a gray Toyota Corolla had snagged her space.

"What the hell?" she said aloud, lowering the radio. She backed up and saw a man sitting in the driver's seat. He wore wire-rimmed glasses and a denim jacket. She put her car in park, opened the door, and got out. The man exited his car holding an envelope. He pointed to the sign that read "Reserved for Dara Harrison."

"Excuse me, are you Dara Harrison?" he asked politely.

"Yes, why are you parked in my spot?"

"I'm sorry. I'll get out of your way right now. I just wanted to make sure you received this," he said, handing her the envelope.

"What is it?"

"You've been served," he said and got back in his car.

"What?" she asked. But he was already in reverse, pulling out of the spot as she stepped out of his way.

Dara looked at the envelope. The return address said, "Woodbine, Rivers, and Johnson, Attorneys at Law. Her heart skipped a beat. She got back in her car, pulled into her spot, and shut off the motor. With shaking hands, she opened the envelope to find a legal document that read Nick

Wyatt vs. MateSearch, Incorporated and Dara Harrison, Summons and Complaint.

"That bastard!" she yelled, after slamming Reggie's office door. He jumped in his seat.

"What's wrong?" he asked with alarm.

Dara threw the envelope down in front of him.

"What is it?" he asked.

"Open it and see."

Dara waited, her arms crossed, her lips pursed in anger, as Reggie pulled out the document.

"Aw, man," he murmured, studying the first page and then thumbing through the others.

"Can you believe that creep? Who does he think he is?"

"I warned you, Harri. Men don't like to be accused of," he held his thumb and forefinger about two inches apart, "especially not macho stuntmen."

"It's not like I haven't been trying to get in touch with Palulah. I call her all the time!"

"Well, maybe he was right. Maybe she is jerking you around. Look, just take out the part about his size and—"

"Oh, read on. That's not good enough anymore. He also wants his whole profile taken down, his money refunded—and he's seeking damages of three million dollars!"

"What? Shit!" he said, shuffling through the papers for the page that confirmed this information.

"This is just what we need right now while I'm under a goddamn microscope."

"We'll keep it under wraps. First, go and take down his profile, then we'll figure out what to do. I'll call Mike Blum and tell him what's going on," he said, flipping through his rolodex for their attorney's number.

Dara stood there, her arms still crossed, not moving.

"What are you waiting for? Go take it down," Reggie told her.

She didn't budge.

"Dara?" he asked nervously. "Why are you not leaving my office?"

"I'm not taking it down."

"What?"

"He's not going to get his way just because he gets some legal muscle to fight his battles."

"Oh, yes, he is—at least when it comes to getting him off of our website."

"Have you forgotten he signed a legal contract and release that he would accept the criticism of the women he dated? Remember that? We can't be sued for libel. Mike made sure of it."

Reggie began to enter Mike's number into his phone as he spoke. "Why are you looking for trouble? What's the big deal? If we take him down and give him his money back, maybe we can get out of this cheaply."

"I am not admitting to doing something wrong when we clearly did not do anything wrong. I am leaving your office, and I'll be in mine," she said pointedly.

"Doing what?" he asked, still holding the receiver.

"Figuring out how to find Palulah and doing a little research on our friend Mr. Wyatt." She picked up her briefcase, turned, and walked out the door.

Something about knowing that the cold-hearted, power-wielding businesswoman had been legally served that day gave Nick a sense of satisfaction he hadn't felt in eons. This was despite the fact that he had dreamt about his crash three times that week and was on the verge of pulling his hair out from the dearth of recuperative sleep. He had decided, while watching *Scrooge,* that ghostly visits notwithstanding, a lawsuit would be the best way to handle a hardhearted woman like Dara. He found solace knowing Drew Johnson, Esquire would now be his advocate. In order to prove damages, Drew advised him to continue searching for dates for as long as his profile remained active.

Nick was also pleased to run into his old riding buddy, Gary Lighter, at the attorney's office. Gary had been in the waiting room reading a magazine while awaiting an appointment with another lawyer when Nick entered the room. Although on the shorter side, about five foot seven, Gary exuded virility. He looked up when Nick called his name.

The two men hugged and pounded each others' backs with affection. Nick hadn't spoken to Gary in ten years, around the time Nick's career had taken off like a rocket. Gary had gotten married soon after, his life veering in a very different direction.

"Hey, man, I read about your accident," Gary confessed. "I actually tried to call one time but couldn't find a number for you. How's it going?"

"It's been rough, you know, but I'm getting there. How've you been?"

Gary said that he'd recently opened his own motorcycle shop in Venice and was making a success of it. Now he needed a lawyer to help him keep his assets in order. Nick, reluctant to go into details about his own legal meeting, managed to avoid the topic until Drew Johnson's assistant beckoned him into his office. The two men hastily exchanged telephone numbers with the promise to meet for a beer very soon.

A Google search of Nick Wyatt yielded some new information. Dara found three articles featuring his accident in detail. She pulled up the *Los Angeles Times* piece first. His injuries didn't seem to be life threateningly bad, but he was still out of work. Dara needed to know more. She dialed the phone. After two rings, a woman answered.

"Claire? It's Dara. I need your help."

Eighteen

WHILE NICK WATCHED an old man on TV struggling to reel in the biggest marlin he'd ever seen, he had the sudden urge to get in touch with Gary. It had been a long time since he'd felt the desire to get out socially with a buddy, and he wondered why he'd so easily traded in his old neighborhood friends for the Hollywood crowd. He'd never really developed the same kind of camaraderie at work. Everyone had focused so intently on doing their jobs, or securing their next ones, that true friendships were few and far between—if they existed at all.

Gary sounded genuinely glad to hear from him. They shot the breeze and set up a meeting at an English pub in Santa Monica for the following evening. When Nick hung up, he felt elated. It amazed him that something as mundane as meeting a friend for a beer could raise his spirits. He recalled old times with Gary for a few minutes, but then his MateSearch humiliation intruded on his thoughts and he cursed aloud. Curiosity got the better of him. He sat down in front of his computer, typed his password, and saw that not only was he still a MateSearch member with a profile, but Palulah's post was still glaringly evident to anyone who cared to look.

Nick took the opportunity to document evidence as his lawyer had suggested. Since the post had gone up, there had not been one request by a woman to meet him. A stark contrast to the dozen or so per week he had garnered initially. Still irked by Dara's impertinence, he reminded himself that it was just a matter of time before the walls of Jericho crumbled around her. He reveled in the thought of it.

Nick shut off the Fishing Channel, slipped an Allman Brothers CD into his stereo, and stretched his sore muscles as Gregg started singing: *Nobody left to run with anymore.*

Dara left her office and drove into Hollywood. She pulled onto a narrow street and sat anxiously behind the wheel, rechecking the address she'd written on a scrap of paper. She looked up at the little house. The numbers matched. She backed her car into a spot in front of a neighbor's house. It was six o'clock in the evening, which, she surmised from Palulah's profile, was a good time to catch her. Aside from her performance art, she worked as a dental hygienist in Beverly Hills, and the office, Dara learned, closed at six. If she came straight home, Dara would be in luck.

As she sat watching the house and the people who passed by on the street, a conversation she'd had with Reggie flitted through her mind. In the past month, four more members had complained about their Rate-a-Mate postings. The restlessness of the natives weighed on Dara's mind, especially in light of the lawsuit and, of course, the national exposure she would be getting from Ophelia.

It was ten to seven before a woman matching Palulah's profile picture pulled into the driveway of the house and emerged from her BMW with a brown grocery bag. She had long brown hair pulled back into a ponytail and stood about five foot eight. She wore a beautifully fitted light blue suit and had striking features, despite the dramatic makeup that gave her look a hard edge.

Dara grabbed her purse and quickly slid out of the car. She hurried to the house and caught up with the woman just before she entered the front door.

"Palulah?" she said with a pleasant smile.

"Yes," she answered, a little apprehensively.

"I'm Dara Harrison—from MateSearch? I've been trying to reach you."

"Oh, yes," Palulah replied. "Sorry we haven't spoken yet."

"Well, it's become really urgent that I speak with you, so I hope it's okay that I took the liberty of coming over. Do you have a minute or two to talk?"

Palulah seemed edgy, but mustered politeness. "Sure. Won't you come inside?"

Dara breathed a sigh of relief. "Thank you," she said as she entered Palulah's home, closing the door behind her.

"Have a seat," said Palulah, indicating her living room couch. "I just need to put this in the fridge."

Dara took a seat and looked around. It was a pleasant room with white-on-white striped furniture adorned with afghans and a verde-colored wrought iron coffee table displaying a picture book about Greece. In sharp contrast to the room's conventional decor, on the sage-colored walls hung enlarged black and white photos of what she assumed must be Palulah's so-called art. The first featured a naked woman pulling a long, skinny scroll or something out of her vagina. The second, a scratchy, overexposed shot of a woman straddling a man during sex, caused Dara to wince. The third photo portrayed a bunch of semi-naked people rolling around in paint and what looked like raw fish, chickens, and sausages. On the opposite wall hung three photos of Palulah in the same vein—nude, painted, dancing. The photos featured props like sausages, metal chains, and hoops of fire.

"Would you like something to drink?" Palulah called from the kitchen.

"No, thank you. I'm fine," said Dara, trying to wipe the look of shock and distaste off her face.

A minute later, Palulah returned and sat down in an armchair across from Dara.

"That's a very interesting art collection," Dara commented.

"Yes, that's me on the wall behind you, and the goddess, Carolee Schneemann, over here," she said, indicating the wall behind her. "She's my artistic inspiration. I love that her art focuses on women's sexual expression and liberation rather than their victimization. Are you a fan, too?"

"Actually, I've never heard of her."

"You're kidding! You've never heard of *Meat Joy*?" she said, pointing at the orgy-like photo. "Or *Interior Scroll*?" she asked, indicating the first bizarre photograph.

"Can't say I have," said Dara with an apologetic shrug.

Palulah shot her a look that mixed disbelief and disdain.

"Anyway," said Dara, changing the subject, "the reason I'm here—"

Palulah cut her off. "I'm so sorry it's taken so long for us to hook up," she said. "There's just so much going on in my life right now with the new show and everything."

"I understand," Dara assured her. "I'm glad you're able to give me a few minutes now. You see, one of your posts has caused quite a stir at MateSearch. One of the men you dated is very upset by what you wrote about him."

"Really?" she responded coolly.

"Yes, his name is Nick."

Palulah rolled her eyes while taking a deep breath. "I was under the impression that brutal honesty was encouraged at the service," she said.

"Honesty is very important, of course, but the tone of the post could be perceived as rather...mean-spirited? And he says you harassed him via telephone."

"Oh, that's a lie! I never call men. Men call me."

"Well, getting back to the post, we encourage our members to be constructive without being offensive."

"It's quite a challenge to be...*kind* when you only have negative things to report about someone. Just like in my art, I can't be deceitful. I live in truth," she declared as if reciting poetry.

Dara leaned forward in her seat. "I understand, but just the same, we'd like you to rewrite the post, sticking only to...the facts. It seems Nick feels that what you wrote was not factually...correct," she explained, choosing her words carefully.

"Oh, really? Well I can assure you *every* word is true," she said defiantly, crossing her arms across her chest while her eyes darted in all directions.

"I see." Dara paused before asking for clarification. "*Every* word?"

"I know what you're getting at here. Look, if you don't want to take my word for it, why don't you ask him to prove otherwise?"

Dara took an uneven breath. "I think you know that would be very inappropriate, not to mention an invasion of privacy. MateSearch could never request such a thing."

"I don't see why not. You're all about getting people to open up."

"Their hearts and minds, not their zippers," she said as gently as she could.

Palulah shrugged. "Well, if you insist, I'll modify the post. I don't want to cause you any trouble, of course."

"Well, I appreciate that, and any commentary you have should be couched as your opinion and be respectful in manner. Please email it to me personally so that I can check it over and post it back up for you," she said, handing her a business card. "And please, as soon as possible so as to avoid any more unnecessary...ill will?"

"Of course," Palulah said, but with a note of reluctance.

Dara took a deep breath. "I certainly appreciate your time and your cooperation, Palulah, and I hope your future dates are a vast improvement."

"So do I. Thank you, Dara."

"Okay," Reggie said as he entered her office first thing the next morning. "I spoke with Mike, and here's the deal."

Dara had just gotten in, removed her suit jacket, and slipped it over the back of her office chair. "Yes?" she said, barely looking up.

Reggie closed her door and sat down in the guest chair. "He looked at the documents, took down the details, and he's already writing an Answer to the Summons. I told him we want this thing wrapped up yesterday! He just has a few questions for you, so call him today."

"What was his general comment?" Dara asked, swinging from side to side in her chair.

"Actually, shockingly, he agrees with you. The contract is ironclad, and even if it weren't, Mr. Wyatt is going to have to prove some sort of damages if he's going to have a case. Mike says we aren't required to take down the post or the profile right now."

"Told ya," Dara sang with a self-satisfied smirk.

"Though I still think we're just making things more contentious by leaving it up."

"We're also admitting guilt by taking it down."

"Yes, he mentioned that possibility."

"I see," she said, tapping her index finger against her lips, "so basically your business partner's a lot smarter than you thought."

Reggie lowered his chin and raised his eyebrows as he stared into her eyes. "I always thought you were smart, Harri. Humble—not so much."

"Anyway, I met with the lovely Palulah yesterday evening."

"You did, huh? The stakeout worked?"

"It did."

"Well, if Nick takes the agency down, at least you have a backup career."

"Don't even joke about that!"

"Don't get so touchy. I was just kidding. Anyway, did you get the feeling she's full of crap?"

"Not necessarily. She probably just couldn't stand the guy. After meeting him myself, I certainly understand why."

"And what else?"

"She's going to rewrite the post despite the fact she swears it's all true," she replied, firing up her computer. "I told her to email it to me for a look-see."

"Okay, so that's a positive step forward. Maybe we can nip this in the bud before it gets to court. By the way, what was the mysterious Palulah like?"

"Well, aside from a bunch of nude, crude photos hanging on her living room wall, she seems offbeat, but reasonable."

"What photos?"

"She's a performance artist by night, remember?"

"Oh, yeah. That shit scares me. Don't they use skeletons and cadavers and stuff?"

"I don't know. I just saw a lot of naked people and raw meat, but this is L.A. If you want to be scary and naked, I guess you're in the right place."

Reggie thought for a moment before responding. "True dat."

❧ *Nineteen* ❧

DARA HEARD HER TELEPHONE RINGING as she walked in the door after her Saturday morning run. She ran for the kitchen phone and picked it up on the third ring to find Tony on the other end of the line.

"Getting all dolled up for our date?"

Sweating and out of breath, she looked down at her perspiration-soaked jogging suit. "Dolled up? Not exactly. And who are you, my grandmother?"

Tony chuckled. "Well, come on, it's nine o'clock. I'm picking you up in less than four hours," he said.

"Four? You know it takes me a good six hours to look decent," she replied sardonically.

"Hey, I'm sure you look hot right now."

"You're right about that," she said, fanning herself with a department store flyer as rivulets of sweat trickled down the sides of her face.

"Shelby wants us to meet her at the place by two sharp, so I'll pick you up at a quarter to one."

"'The place?' You're still not going to tell me where we're going?"

"It's a surprise."

"You don't do surprises."

"That was the old me. The new me is totally into them."

"Yeah? What else is the new you into?"

"You'll have to find out on your own. That's what dating is for, right?"

"We're not really dating, Ton, remember?"

"You told me to be convincing."

"To them, not to me."

"Well, it's still a surprise."

"Then you'll have to tell me what to wear."

"How about a mini skirt, halter top, and fuck-me heels?"

"How about a black eye for the cameras?"

"It's dressy casual. I called and asked," he said, trying to behave. "And bring a sweater."

"Dressy casual? Isn't that an oxymoron?"

"A what?"

"Nothing. I'll figure it out."

"And just kidding about the fuck-me heels. Wear shoes you can walk in. You can wear the others when we get to your place."

"Dream on."

At twelve-fifty P.M., Dara and Tony climbed into his Land Rover and headed toward the 405 freeway south.

"Well, we're not dressed for the beach, so I guess that leaves out Manhattan, Hermosa, or Redondo," she said, trying to solve the mystery.

"I'd say that's a wise deduction," he concurred.

She gave it another minute of thought. "We're not going to Disneyland, I hope."

"What do you have against Disneyland?"

"Nothing, except every time I have out-of-town guests, they drag me there, and that's enough times for a lifetime."

"Don't worry. We're not going to Disneyland."

"Or Sea World, right?"

"Right."

"Thank God! Wait a minute. The San Diego Zoo?"

"What part of 'it's a surprise' do you not understand?"

"Fine." She turned on the radio, and they continued through the Saturday afternoon traffic until Tony veered off to I-710 toward Long Beach.

"Long Beach? Isn't there an aquarium there, too?" she asked with distaste.

"What have you got against fish?"

"Is that where we're going?"

"No, I'm just wondering."

"I don't have anything against fish. I'm just not interested in watching them swim around in their tanks all day. It's boring." Then Dara saw the freeway sign leading them to the Queen Mary. "Hey, the Queen Mary! That's it, right?"

"If you must know, which obviously you must, yes, that's it. Happy now?"

"Yes. I always wanted to see it."

"I know."

"How did you know?"

"You once mentioned it."

"And you were actually listening?"

"Believe it or not."

Dara was stunned into silence for a moment. "I think I'm starting to kind of like the new you," she admitted. She glanced over to find him smiling as he watched the road ahead.

When they got to the ship, Dara looked around for the TV crew but saw no sign of them. She looked at her watch, which read two o'clock.

"I guess we beat them here," she told Tony, "unless they're inside already."

"They're not."

"How do you know?"

"Because there's still one surprise you didn't guess."

"Huh?" she asked, looking baffled.

"We have the whole afternoon to ourselves."

"Why? What do you mean?"

"I only told Shelby about our evening plans, so we'd have some time to relax and enjoy the ship."

A look of genuine, happy surprise spread across Dara's face. "Really?"

"Really," he answered, smiling down at her with pride for thinking of such a great plan.

"Ton...I mean, Al, that is so sweet!"

Dara, wearing sensible flats, stood up on her tippy toes to kiss him on the cheek.

"The cheek again, huh?"

He took her hand and led her to the Observation Bar. It was a lovely art deco room with a big curved bar, cocktail tables, historic art work, and panoramic views. Afterward, they enjoyed a light lunch and then embarked on a tour of the famous ship, learning about its history, including its key role during World War II. Finally, they attended the Ghosts and Legends Show, where they were regaled with stories about some of the longtime spirits haunting the ship.

When six o'clock rolled around, Dara was beginning to tire, but she'd had a wonderful day. Being with Tony seemed so familiar, yet so different—almost surreal. She couldn't put her finger on how it made her feel, so she decided not to try.

"Okay, so when and where are we meeting the crew?" she finally asked.

"In fifteen minutes and very close by."

They drove for about three minutes before turning onto a street called Aquarium Way.

"Don't tell me there's another aquarium around here."

"Okay, I won't tell you," he said as he pulled into the parking lot next to the Aquarium of the Pacific.

"Are you sure it's open at night?" she asked, hoping for an out.

"You are something else, babe," he said as he got out of the car and started to walk around to her side.

"Okay, enough with the chivalry. You're freaking me out. I'm perfectly capable of opening a car door by myself," she said, pushing it open and climbing out.

At that moment, Tony's phone rang. He pulled it from his waist band and spoke. "Hey, Shelby, how are you doing? We're just arriving now...what? You're kidding. That sucks. So what should we do? Okay. Okay. Okay, sounds like a plan—or a backup plan anyway. Speak to you later."

Dara looked at Tony as he hung up. "What is it?"

"They're stuck on the 405 behind a bad accident. They're not going to make it here in time, so she's cancelling for tonight. They're going to cover one of the other challengers instead."

"Too bad," Dara said with a smile as Tony took her hand and walked her toward the aquarium. Then he turned sharply and guided her in another direction. They ended up on a dock where a riverboat sat. Dara felt thrilled that her evening would not be spent watching fish swim in circles. "You and your boats," she said.

He took her to the upper deck where Dara spotted a sign that read Murder Mystery Dinner Show.

"What's this?" she asked.

"My friend Jimmy told me about it. Says it's a fun night. Dinner and a murder mystery. What do you think?"

A smile slowly spread across her face. "I think it sounds great," she said, taking his hand again and walking toward the theater. "So tell me, who the hell are you and what did you do with my ex-boyfriend?"

❧ Twenty ❧

I T TOOK THE WEEKEND, but by monday morning, Dara had received Palulah's revised post. She took a sip of her morning java as she anxiously opened the email and began reading.

I went out with Nick three times. He used to be a stuntman. I wasn't impressed. Now he isn't working and mainly just watches television every day. Although he's obviously attractive, I didn't think much of his bedroom prowess. In my opinion, he has a low regard for a woman's pleasure. And then there's another small problem. Two inches worth. Needless to say, I don't recommend dating Nick.

Oy, Dara thought when she finished. Palulah had done exactly as asked, but it was not going to appease Nick in the slightest; however, she believed her petulant adversary would now have even less of a prayer in court. She would have her lawyer tell Nick about the rewritten post pursuant to their policy against incivility. Just then, Reggie appeared in her office.

"Hey, I got some good news," he announced.

"Well, come on in and share. I could use it."

"It's about the MateSearch Challenge. I think we got one."

"What do you mean?"

144

"Stella, one of the women from the Ophelia audience, has met, as she put it, 'the love of her life.'"

"Really?" Dara asked, her eyes widening. "That's wonderful! Which one is she?"

"The forty-two-year-old from the Palisades."

"And who's the lucky guy?"

"His name's Eric, a forty-eight-year-old contractor from Playa del Rey. I spoke with him, and the feelings are mutual," Reggie said excitedly.

"Well, thank God for that. Okay, so hopefully that's one down. Any word from the others?"

"The man, his name's Ken, has been dating up a storm and seems pretty content, but the third, Serena, didn't sound enthused when I checked in on her. Nice lady, but a little on the inhibited side. I wish we could figure out a way to jump start her love life."

"How old is she?"

"Early thirties, I think," Reggie replied.

"Maybe we could send her some suggestions."

"That would be favoritism. No can do."

Dara sat back in her chair, twisting back and forth as she thought. "Unless we offer it to all our members as a sort of elective incentive. If there's a substantial fee, we don't have to worry about playing cupid for two thousand people, and since the Ophelia guests are free, she won't have to pay a dime."

"Yeah, okay," Reggie said, thinking it through. "I think that's a good idea. Only who's going to wade through a thousand men for her Mr. Right?"

"Get Jenna and Robin on it. Have them run a general mate search for her, appropriate ages, locations, etc., read through them, narrow the field, and send the best prospects to me. I'm swamped, but I will make time in my schedule to pick out a few good men for her."

"What are *you* so swamped by these days?" he asked. "I'm the one counseling all the thin-skinned Rate-a-Mate victims. Maybe we should rethink things—"

"Rethink things?" Dara interrupted. "Rate-a-Mate is what makes us original, what's gotten us all this amazing publicity."

"Well, I like to think I may have helped in that regard."

"You know what I mean. Anyway, I forgot how time-consuming dating can be."

"Speaking of which..." he said, fishing.

"It's going fine. We're actually having a good time for once."

"Really? How...interesting. Maybe we can double date sometime. You still haven't met Cole."

"I'll meet him when I have a real date. This is strictly a business deal, remember?"

"I remember. Do you?"

"Yes, Reginald, I do."

But in her heart, she knew it was beginning to mean a lot more to the man called Aloysius Anthony Remini.

Nick sat in a round, red banquette at the King's Head drinking Bass Ale on tap from a frosty glass mug. It was five-thirty in the evening, and the after-work crowd lent a boisterous atmosphere to the place. Nick thought about the message he'd received from MateSearch regarding the rewriting of Palulah's post. He'd wanted to ignore it but couldn't, and had quickly pulled up his profile once more to see the supposedly toned down version of the venomous tirade.

They call this civility? He felt a surge in his blood pressure just thinking about it but calmed himself with the thought that his lawyer was calling hers with a shattering development. Too bad he couldn't be a fly on the wall when Dara's little blonde skull exploded from the news!

Gary entered the bar dressed in jeans, work boots, and a Guinness T-shirt. He slid into the seat across from Nick. A gruff looking waiter of about sixty immediately approached their table.

"What can I get you?" he asked with an English accent.

"Fullers," Gary replied. Then he looked Nick over with approval. "You know, all things considered, you're looking pretty damn good."

"You think?" Nick asked dubiously.

"Sure. Especially for a guy who's been out of commission for a year. Do you at least get out for recreational riding?"

"Nah."

"Man, you were always like a caged tiger if you didn't get out for your evening ride. Hey, I know the accident threw you for a loop—no pun intended—but the Nick Wyatt I knew would have been climbing the walls by now."

"Probably would be if my leg didn't hurt so much."

"How could you just give it up cold turkey?"

"How? I nearly killed myself, that's how. Besides, it's not forever."

"So now your bikes are sitting in a garage somewhere collecting dust?"

"Nope. Sold 'em."

"All of them?" Gary said, a look of disbelief on his face.

"All but one."

"No! All the vintage bikes are gone?"

"Yup," Nick said. "Made a pretty penny, too," he added, sounding less than enthused.

"Why'd you do it?"

Nick shrugged. "I was moving. Didn't have the space anymore."

"So which one did you keep?"

"The Dyna Glide, custom designed and built by moi. Too much blood, sweat, and tears went into that one to let it go."

"So what do you do with it? Visit it? Dust it? Stare longingly into its headlights?"

"Pretty much," Nick replied.

Nick and Gary had been riding motorcycles since they bought their first Harleys at the age of seventeen. When they weren't riding, they restored old bikes and talked shop. Through the years, they'd taken many trips together—Sturgis, South Dakota; Daytona, Florida; and even a two-week-long bike trip to Alaska, one of the highlights of Nick's life. Of course, once he started working regularly in Hollywood, the trips grew fewer and further between, but as the *Stormcats'* resident motorcycle expert, he was rarely far from a bike, be it a Harley, Yamaha, Ducati, or just about any other type of motorcycle in creation.

"Okay, that was a year ago. Time to get back on the horse."

"The doc says no, not yet anyway."

"So get a second opinion."

"I'm just getting around without a cane these days. Believe me, there's nothing I want more than getting my life back." As he said the words, a sudden vision of his nightmare flickered through his head. Nick shifted uncomfortably in his seat, reminded of his bad leg. He decided to change the subject. "So how's Nancy?"

Gary took a short breath. "We're divorced. Four years."

"Shit."

"I know."

"Kids?"

"Two girls. Every other weekend."

"Sorry, man."

"I'm used to it. How about you? Seeing anyone new? I saw some pictures in one of those tabloids. Adriana Norris moved on, huh?"

"Don't tell me you read that crap."

"Only when I want to live vicariously through you," he replied with a wink. "Was she really sleeping with your producer when you were in the goddamn hospital?"

"Director," Nick grudgingly corrected. "He's number three, I think. Poor devil."

"Number three?"

"Yeah, Adriana seems to have some sort of obsession with conquering and destroying the lives of *Stormcat* men," Nick said. A knot formed in his gut when he thought about her first victim.

Matt Everhart had possessed a salt-of-the-earth quality that seemed unlikely given his appearance. He had been a tall, inordinately handsome man of twenty-five, with cropped, light brown hair and mesmerizing light aqua eyes. Despite his muscular frame, he'd been soft-spoken, and had exhibited the innocence and wonder of an Oklahoma farm boy who'd gone to sleep one night and awakened on the set of one of television's highest rated shows—as its star, no less. Nick had admired Matt's good nature and stunning lack of ego, and they had often hung out in Matt's trailer discussing the show and, at Matt's urging, the latest upcoming stunts. A person might think that being one of the stars of a hit television show would have had Matt dizzy with success, but in actuality, he'd envied Nick and the other stuntmen. He found their work much more stimulating.

Then, Adriana Norris had been hired to play Matt's leading lady. Soon she'd charmed her way into Matt's life—and into the single bed that sat against the far wall of his trailer. It wasn't long before Nick's friendship with Matt had been marginalized. Adriana, Nick knew, was like a brilliant sun that could blind a man to everything else—and every*one* else—in his midst.

"Damn. Nice to get kicked when you're down, huh?"

Nick took a swig of beer instead of answering, which said more to Gary than any words could have.

"Her loss, man," Gary told him. "You'll do just fine. You always did. Hey, remember Barb Stafford?"

"How could I not? She was the only thing we ever fought over."

"Man, she was hot! And boy was I pissed! The chicks always went for you over me. Hell, you over everyone else."

"Come on," Nick said with embarrassment.

"It's true. I was always jealous, but you were too cool about it all to hate your guts."

"Thanks—I think."

The men shared a laugh. Nick took another sip of his beer and swallowed with a faraway look in his eyes. He was still thinking of Adriana. His sister was right. He had been blinded by glamour and lust. He'd never loved her—and he'd never felt compelled to lie to her about it either. In fact, he'd never uttered those words to any woman. To him, holding his tongue where emotions were concerned made him feel like he had the moral high ground. How many men had said the words without really meaning them, and in the process, set women up for inevitable heartbreak? He knew Adriana was immune. But now he wondered if never having spoken those words said something truly pathetic about his ability to love at all.

"So when do you think you'll be getting back to work?"

Nick had answered the question countless times and always evasively. "I don't know. My shoulder's still a mess," he said while rubbing it, "and the leg's kind of stiff, so—"

"You should come round my shop. Check it out. You'll love it. Maybe even teach my restoration expert a thing or two."

"I'd love to see it, Gar," Nick replied brightly.

"Good. Come down on Sunday morning. We're a stop on the Harley Ride for Muscular Dystrophy."

"Cool. I'll be there—on four wheels, but I'll be there."

❧ *Twenty-one* ❧

C LAIRE JAMES LOOKED MORE like a soccer mom than a private investigator. That fact had only helped her in her undercover career. Now, however, the thirty-something, dishwater blonde had donned the more professional demeanor of a business woman. She wore a gray suit and pumps, and placed her briefcase on the dark polished wood of Dara's desk. She clicked it open and handed Dara a small pile of papers.

MateSearch was now Claire's biggest client, the one that made it possible for her to head out on her own professionally. Instead of working for an agency stalking cheating spouses with a camouflaged camera, she had become a reputable corporate operation with four other employees who spent their days running computer searches and typing up reports. Her daily professional life may have been less stimulating, but it was certainly more lucrative—and less anxiety provoking, than her old job. She was still working Dara's missing person's case, but even with the help of the London firm, they'd still had no luck in finding the man Dara had once called Dad.

Claire had been eager to take on this recent assignment, Nick Wyatt, despite Dara's fervent request to have the report back "as soon as humanly possible." That meant working practically round the clock for a few days, but Claire had hoped the former stuntman would help spice up her now-routine life with a little Hollywood glamour and excitement. Unfortunately, investigating Nick Wyatt proved to be a lot less entertaining than she had imagined. Claire's general summary of the case focused, in large part, on Nick's post-accident life, which was quite uneventful. In fact, it seemed that Nick didn't have much of a life at all these days. He had sold his home and was living off disability and his savings account. He went out mainly to food shop and attend doctors' appointments, and for the most part kept to himself.

Before the crash was another story entirely. Claire reported that he had been performing stunts for *Stormcats* for four years and had often traveled on location. She included a list of women to which Nick was known to have been romantically linked. One stood out: Adriana Norris, the captivating star of *Stormcats*. Claire had attached a publicity shot of the raven-haired beauty and a tabloid photo of her shopping in Beverly Hills with a man who was holding the leash of a black dog—a man who, despite his dark aviators, was clearly Nick Wyatt.

"Adriana Norris, huh?" said Dara. "So what happened?"

"A short time after the accident, she started dating Jim Tanner, a *Stormcats* director, and she recently became a hot item with Chris Leeds, the *Stormcats* set designer."

"Geez, she really needs to get out more."

"Yeah, and that's not all. Remember the show's star, Matt Everhart? The one who died on the set?"

"Sure."

"She was hot and heavy with him for a while, too—right before she and Nick became a thing."

"Really! So how come when you're a Hollywood starlet who sleeps around, nobody calls you a slut? What is it, part of the job description or something?"

Claire smiled as Dara perused the long list of Nick's former girlfriends.

"He's just as bad," she said with distaste, gnawing on a blue pencil.

"Looks like," Claire agreed.

"I could've guessed that. He has that cocky attitude that gets under my skin."

"But that prolific list suggests to me that at least *one* of Palulah's claims may not be on the level, if you know what I mean."

Dara tapped her pencil against her desk as she continued reading. "Or it could be an indication that he's less than a satisfying lover and has to keep moving on. I mean, we don't know who dumped whom, do we?"

"No, I suppose that's possible, too."

Dara flipped to the next page, which described three civil lawsuits: the one filed against MateSearch; a malpractice suit against the surgeon who performed Nick's shoulder surgery; and a personal injury suit against the studio producing *Stormcats*. "Are we feeling a bit litigious this year?" Dara asked. She looked up at Claire with a victorious look in her eyes. "Now I see why he doesn't have a job. He thinks he can sue his way back to solvency. Well, he ain't gonna use MateSearch to do it. I promise you that!"

"The suit against the surgeon seems to have merit. I spoke with a medical malpractice attorney and, from the information I gave him, he thinks the doctor screwed up his rotator cuff surgery."

"Uh-huh," Dara said, distracted.

"As far as the studio lawsuit, the whole thing seems convoluted. The rest of the report is pretty routine stuff," Claire said, seeing that Dara had found the raw meat she had hoped for. "Look it over, and if you have any questions, call me."

"Thanks for everything. This is a big help."

Claire left as Dara stared into space, the wheels in her head revolving. There was only one thing on her mind now: proving Nick Wyatt was a lying, parasitic bum!

It was almost nine in the evening, and Dara was still at work. Before he'd left, Reggie had handed her the list of names and profiles that Jenna and Robin had compiled as good matches for challenger Serena. She read over the twenty-eight-year-old woman's profile and eyed her pictures. Serena was attractive in an unassuming way. She was five foot four, had shoulder length brunette hair, almond-shaped brown eyes, and an athletic physique. Raised in the Midwest, she'd been living in West Los Angeles for ten years, working as manager of a sporting goods store in El Segundo. According to her profile, she didn't like dating (that was obvious) and considered herself more of a homebody who also enjoyed volleyball, biking, and water sports.

Dara thumbed through the printed-out profiles one by one. Robin and Jenna had narrowed the field to ten men. As she turned the first few pages, she nodded her head at the first-rate matchmaking skills of her two employees, making a mental note to use them for future projects.

She continued reading the profiles until she came face to face with a picture of Al, a.k.a. Tony Remini. Her stomach flipped over. The women obviously hadn't heard she was "dating" him. *Tony?* she thought with surprise. *Really?* She shook her head and was about to pull him from the file when something stopped her. Instead, she began to read over his profile again and objectively compared it with Serena's. She had to admit that on paper they seemed a pretty good match: water sports/boating; homebody/couch potato; didn't like dating/didn't like paying for dates. She might just put up with him nicely.

Dara put Al's profile at the top of the pile and picked up her phone.

"You want me to date who?" a perplexed Tony asked.

"A very nice woman named Serena. She's one of my challengers and she's, well, let's just say she needs a little push," Dara explained, twisting the telephone cord nervously.

"Why do *I* have to push her?"

"Because I asked you to."

"But I'm already dating someone. In fact, we have a date Saturday night."

"Well, your date is hereby giving you her blessing to take Serena out on Friday night."

"That's very magnanimous of her. Unfortunately, I don't want to date anyone else."

"Don't worry, you'll still be on my expense account."

"That's not the problem."

"I thought you wanted to help me."

"I thought I *was* helping you."

"Well this would help me even more."

"How are you going to explain to Shelby that I want to see other people?" he asked. "She'll think we're not hitting it off."

"I'll just tell her that you're new to the agency, so I encouraged you to make the rounds, so to speak. I wouldn't want you to feel you missed out later when we're, you know, going steady."

"Going steady?" he asked in a mocking tone. "Are you going to wear my fraternity ring around your neck, too?"

"I mean dating exclusively."

"I see. So how many times do I have to take her out?"

"I don't know. Start with once, and we'll see from there."

"What's she like?"

"I think you'll like her. She likes water sports."

"Oh, she likes water sports. Well why didn't you say so? That changes everything!"

"Your sarcasm isn't helping matters."

Tony sighed. "So what's she look like?"

"She's pretty. Would I fix you up with a troll?"

"I don't know. Would you?"

"No. Now sign on and ask the poor woman out if you know what's good for you. I have a court case to prepare for, and you're keeping me from it."

"What court case?"

"I'm being sued by some ass who didn't like his member review."

"Really? We can sue? I'll have to make a note of that."

"I'm hanging up now."

"Ms. Harrison, Mike Blum is on the line," Maxine announced. Dara looked up from Claire's report on Nick, which she'd been examining with a fine-toothed comb. "Okay, put him through." She picked up her phone and leaned back in her chair. "Hi, Mike, how's it going?"

"Hello, Dara. Do you want to call Reggie in so we can conference?"

"Sure," she said, putting him on hold and buzzing Reggie.

"Mike Blum's on the line. Can you come into my office?"

Reggie immediately appeared, and Dara motioned him to close her door. He sat down as she put their lawyer on speakerphone.

"Well, I have some news you're not going to be happy about," Mike said.

"Why? What happened?" Dara asked nervously.

"I spoke with Mr. Wyatt's attorney."

"And?" she asked.

"Did you know that Nick never signed your contract?"

"What?" Dara looked over at Reggie. He seemed just as perplexed. "Of course he did. We check for signatures as a regular rule. Reg, pull his file, please."

Reggie headed quickly for the records room as Mike continued talking. "Well, whoever was checking failed to notice that the signature on his contract did not belong to Nick Wyatt."

"How's that possible?" she asked.

"Apparently his sister signed it for him. Seems it was a present from her."

Reggie appeared with the file and held up the signature page for Dara to see. Sure enough, it read *Annie Crawford*.

"How could this have happened?" Dara asked with alarm.

"The sales crew looks for signatures, but I guess we better tell them to look closer," Reggie said.

"Uggggh!" Dara yelled, throwing her pencil down. Then she caught herself and continued. "I'm sorry, Mike. I just can't believe this!"

"So what do we do now?" Reggie asked him.

"Well, first, I'd advise you take down Mr. Wyatt's profile, especially that post of his."

Reggie shot her his best I-told-you-so look. Dara glared back.

"And since he's not withdrawing his complaint, I suggest we talk to Ms. Palulah James right away and hope she'll be of some help to us down the line. If we're lucky, Wyatt will see reason and agree to settlement talks."

"Settlement talks? But we can rip him a new one in court. I told you he's lawsuit crazy. Judges hate that, don't they?" asked Dara with desperation.

"That's not a defense. Don't hang your hat on it," said Mike.

"Especially after the judge gets an eyeful of his member review," added Reggie.

Dara shook her head and said nothing.

"Look, his lawyer is a reasonable man. I'm sure we'll work this out to everyone's satisfaction. We just have to be sensible in our negotiations,"

Mike advised. "I've filed the Answer and I'm going to push for immediate depositions. I know you want this over with as soon as possible."

Dara stopped listening at that point and let Reggie take the wheel until they brought the call to an end. After they disconnected, Dara looked at Reggie defiantly. "I'm not negotiating with that jerk!"

"Come on, Harri, you heard the man. Instead of fighting, why not let me try to smooth things over. Maybe he'll settle for an apology."

"Are you kidding? He doesn't want an apology. He wants our money."

"You don't know that."

"Oh, really? Well, three lawsuits in one year speaks volumes."

"So what do you plan on doing?" asked Reggie apprehensively.

Dara narrowed her eyes. "I plan on giving Litigious Louie a nice long run for his money!"

Twenty-two

A FTER SHADOWING THEM AROUND L.A. all evening, Shelby and her camera crew packed into the elevator along with Dara and Tony, now insisting on filming their good night kiss. "You don't really have to say good night on our account," she joked. "Seeing you both go in together would be a pretty juicy development, especially after meeting Serena last night."

"I told you we're taking things slowly," Dara told her. "I want...Al here to date around a little. He's new and shouldn't be tied down so fast."

"I know, I know," Shelby replied.

That night, the couple ate sushi at a hot spot in Santa Monica and saw a comedy show in West Hollywood, followed by a nightcap at the Ritz Carlton in Marina Del Rey. Unfortunately, Dara was still smarting about Nick's missing signature and couldn't enjoy the evening. She tried to appear enthusiastic for the cameras, but the thought of the lawsuit filled her with anger and dismay.

Shelby and the crew had managed double duty that night, shooting portions of challenger Ken's fourth date with an attractive young woman named Constance in a restaurant a few blocks from the club. During the crew's welcome—albeit brief—absence Dara grilled Tony about his date the previous night.

"So what'd you think of Serena?"

"She's nice."

159

"Told you she wasn't a troll."

"Not a troll," he agreed.

"Where did you take her?"

"She likes steak, so we went to The Palm," said Tony nonchalantly.

"The Palm? What am I, made of money?"

"You wanted me to show her a good time, didn't you?"

"Sure," she replied, "but maybe you can do it without bankrupting me."

Tony smiled, probably sensing this was less about money and more about a certain green-eyed monster.

"And then where did you go?" she inquired.

"Just had a drink at this piano bar she knew about."

"Oh," Dara replied, trying to picture him in a dimly lit room, old standards emanating from the keys of a baby grand, while another woman canoodled him in a leather banquette.

"And then home," said Tony with an assuring tone in his voice.

"Your place or hers?"

"You're funny."

"Wasn't trying to be."

"I dropped her off and was home by midnight."

"Are you going to go out with her again?"

"That depends."

"On what?"

"On you."

The emcee's return to the stage to introduce the next standup comic brought an end to their conversation.

Huddled together in the condo elevator, everyone looked a bit weary from the evening's escapades—especially Dara, who now had a jabbing pain over her right eye. She couldn't wait to slip off her heels, exchange her snug pants and top for a loose nightshirt, and climb into bed with Mallory.

The elevator doors opened and they all piled out. As Tony followed Dara to the door, Garrett, one of the cameramen walked behind them, filming the scene. Shelby, wanting a better view, pushed through the crew, inadvertently knocking over a tripod that was leaning against the wall. The crash echoed through the hallway. They scrambled to right the tripod, but as the cameras rolled, Jesse's door opened a crack. Dara saw her friend eyeing the men suspiciously.

"It's okay, Jess, just me and the film crew."

"Dara Doll? That you?"

Suddenly, his door opened a little wider and Jesse stuck his head out while sliding on his cat eye glasses and smoothing his wavy hair behind his ears. "Hi, honey!" Jesse said to her with excitement. "Wait just a sec."

Jesse stepped back, wrapped a floral robe around his baby doll pajamas, slipped on his fluffy pink slippers and opened his door wider. Dara observed the puzzled expressions on the faces of Tony, Shelby, and the crew.

"Well, aren't you going to introduce me?" he asked Dara.

"Of course," she replied. "This is my date, Al. Remember, I told you about him?"

"Well sure, honey."

"This is my friend, Jesse," she said to Tony.

Jesse extended his hand to Tony as if he expected it to be kissed. Tony shook it firmly, forced a smile, and replied, "Nice to meet you."

"And this is the *Ophelia Show* segment producer Shelby Gerard and Lance, Rodney, and Garrett, production crew."

They each shook Jesse's hand, except for Garrett, who continued filming the scene, much to Dara's chagrin.

"Isn't Dara just the most adorable, wonderful, and brilliant woman you've ever met?" Jesse gushed. "I'm her biggest fan. Have been since she was L.A.'s hottest advice columnist."

"Thanks, Jess," Dara said, "Sorry we woke you."

"Oh, honey, you didn't. I'm so glad to meet everyone. I was just up watching an old Frank Capra with a cup of hot cocoa anyway. Couldn't sleep." Jesse turned his attention back to the crew. "You tell Ophelia how lucky she is to have Dara on her show," he said while shuffling over to Dara and putting his arm around her. "This woman is a born star. I mean it—a born star!—and MateSearch is the greatest dating service in the country. I should know. I'm a member, too," he said with pride, "and it's because of Dara that I met my new honey!" Jesse turned excitedly to face Dara. "And another news flash, Dara Doll, we're taking a trip to Hawaii together!"

"That's great, Jesse!" said Dara, trying to sound enthusiastic and hoping to end things there, but Jesse wasn't finished.

"I am so happy to call Dara my very best friend," he said, squeezing her around the shoulders for the camera. Dara smiled weakly and gave him a squeeze back.

"Well, it's late, so I'm going to skedaddle," said Jesse. "So nice to meet all of you. Oh, and Al," Jesse said, turning his attention to Tony, who appeared completely bemused by the situation, "you take good care of our girl, ya hear?"

"Sure thing," Tony replied.

Jesse tightened his robe and waved enthusiastically for the camera before ducking back into his apartment. Dara used the opportunity to wrap up the date. "Well, good night, Al," she said, taking his hand. "Thanks for a wonderful night."

"My pleasure," he replied. Then suddenly he pulled her close and planted a passionate kiss on her lips. It was their first kiss in ages, and Tony gave it everything he had despite the crew and cameras. Already on emotional overload, Dara could not process any feelings she might have still had for her old beau. All she knew was that she had to get away from both him and the crew as fast as she could. She pulled back from the embrace while faking a smile of pleasure. Then she backed into her apartment with a wave and closed the door.

Bikers' Heaven impressed Nick. It was much larger than he had expected, housing a garage, a detailing area, a showroom, and offices. Motorcycles packed the showroom: some for sale, some in the process of being custom painted, others under restoration or repair. The customers ranged from beach vagabonds to hard-core bikers, yuppie joy riders to L.A. posers, all wandering around awestruck.

Gary was conversing with some prospective buyers when he spotted Nick across the showroom. After a moment, he strolled across the white tile floor. "Hey, you made it!" Gary said, grabbing his right hand for their old buddy handshake.

"I did! This is some place you got here. Is it always this busy?" asked Nick.

"Weekends? Sure. Especially when there's a Harley ride coming through! Come here, I want to show you something."

Gary led Nick into the paint and detailing area and pointed out a crystal blue Softail drying in the corner. "Check these out," said Gary, pointing to the tanks. "Careful, still wet."

Nick stepped up to take a closer look at the custom paint and saw that on the right side was a hologram of the Grand Canyon, and on the left, a hologram of Niagara Falls.

"Pretty wild, huh?" asked Gary. "If you hit the light right you can see the water falling."

"Who did the work?" asked Nick, obviously impressed.

"Jerry. He's taking a break. I'll introduce you later. I've been doing a lot of restorations lately. I just got a Manx Norton, a couple of Triumph Speed

Twins over there waiting for work, and a Ducati Desmo I bought from a guy up in Santa Barbara."

"How many guys you got on restoration?"

"Two, but like I told you, one ain't up to par. I gave him the day off, so we could talk freely. Nice guy but just not the caliber we need."

Nick followed Gary into his private office, which looked out on the showroom. As they walked through the door, a dog that looked like a mix of lab, Dalmatian, and a touch of shepherd got up from his bed and ran to greet them, tail waving wildly.

"Hey, Ziggy, hey bud," said Gary, vigorously rubbing the dog's head. "This is an old friend of mine. Say hi to Nick."

Ziggy sat down in front of Nick and offered his paw. Surprised, Nick took it and gave him a head rub, too. "Wow, you know your stuff."

"I found a great trainer. He only works with mutts, though. Ziggy was his best student."

Nick looked down at the dog, feeling pangs for Grady. Maybe it was time to hit the shelter.

"Have a seat," said Gary as he sat down behind his desk.

Nick sat and looked around. The walls were covered with framed photographs of every kind of motorcycle, many adorned with scantily-clad biker models sporting lots of tattooed flesh.

"I know restoring bikes may seem a little dull next to stunts, but even if you can help me out short term, I'd appreciate it. When you're ready to get back to Hollywood I'll understand. I promise, no hard feelings."

"You know it's been years since I did this kind of work. I gave up all my hobbies when I started working those crazy hours on the set."

"So you just need some time to get back into the swing of things. From what you told me, that's something you got plenty of right now."

"Yeah, I guess," Nick replied.

"Come in a few days a week, get your feet wet. You may be out of practice, but if there's one thing I know, it's that you got talent. I've seen enough of your work to know that."

Nick smiled. The sparkle was back in his eyes. "Maybe I will," he said, nodding. "Maybe I will."

❧ *Twenty-three* ❧

"**T**HANKS FOR MEETING WITH US," said Dara as Maxine ushered Palulah into the MateSearch conference room. "I know you have plans, so we won't take up much of your time."

Mike Blum sat next to Dara. He was in his mid-fifties, wore a fine suit, and smelled like expensive cologne. Salt and pepper hair framed his face, which looked unusually kind for a lawyer. He stood up to shake Palulah's hand and introduced himself. Palulah took a seat across the table from them. She had come straight from her day job and was in sensible office attire, although her hair was a tumble of waves and her makeup looked recently touched up.

"So the rat is suing you, huh?" Palulah said.

"We're hoping to settle the case, Ms. James," said Mike. "You haven't been named in the lawsuit, which surprises me, but if we can't settle this, you're going to end up as a defendant one way or another. I'm going to be serving you later today with a notice to take your deposition as a non-party witness. As long as the facts of your post bear out, we shouldn't have a problem."

"Deposition? Do I need a lawyer?"

"That's your prerogative, but I'd advise it."

"Well that stinks. I have to pay for a lawyer now? I'm a struggling artist, you know," she said, as if dental hygiene were just a hobby.

"Entirely up to you, Ms. James," he said. He took a sip from the paper coffee cup in front of him.

"Would you like some coffee or water?" Dara asked her.

"No, thanks."

"I just have a few questions to ask you right now," Mike told her as he flipped over a page on his legal pad.

"How many times did you go out with Nick Wyatt?"

"Three times."

"Can you remember where you went on those dates?"

"The first night he took me to dinner at Remy's in Santa Monica. The second date we went to hear jazz in Hollywood, and the last date he came to see my performance of Meat in Art and then we went for coffee and dessert."

Mike scrawled down the information and looked back up at Palulah. "Okay, now you indicated in your review that you had sexual relations with Mr. Wyatt."

"Yes."

"How many times?"

"Just once. That was enough for me."

"And when did this occur?" asked Mike.

"It happened on the third date when I invited him in for a nightcap."

"I see," he said, taking notes. "And the two of you engaged in...intercourse?" Mike asked with the dead-pan expression they must teach in law school.

Palulah sighed uncomfortably. "Yes, though very inadequately so."

"You wrote in your post that his penis was two inches long. When exactly did you make that estimation?"

"Just before we had sex, when he had taken off his pants."

"So the room was light enough to see?"

"Yes."

"Did you notice any other distinguishing marks on his body that would normally be hidden by clothing?"

"Huh? No, I don't think so."

"And did he sleep over?"

"No, I told him I had to get up early, and he took the hint and left that night."

"And you never spoke to him after that?"

"No, but he kept calling me to ask me out, leaving messages on my machine at all hours even though I never returned the calls."

"Did you save those messages?"

"No."

"So you never called him after that."

"No, I just said, no," she answered, getting defensive.

"Okay. I just needed to clarify that," he told her. "Thank you, Palulah."

"Yes, thanks so much for coming in," added Dara.

"Is that all?" Palulah asked with surprise.

"I told you we wouldn't take up too much of your time!" Dara said.

Mike stood and extended his hand to Palulah. She shook it and then Dara's, picked up her purse, and left the office.

"So, what do you think?" asked Dara with hope.

"Well there may be a bit of a glitch here."

"What do you mean?"

"When I spoke with Drew Johnson, he made a remark that concerned me."

"What was it?"

"It's the reason I asked Palulah if she noticed any distinguishing marks on Mr. Wyatt's body."

"She said she didn't notice any."

"Right, but don't you think if a woman takes the time to visually measure a man's penis, she might also have taken note of the fact that, just below it, on his left leg, is a nasty scar from his motorcycle accident?"

Dara felt her stomach drop.

"If she's making all this up, we haven't got a snowball's chance in hell," said Mike, as he placed a folder back in his briefcase and locked it. He stood up and looked at Dara. "I'll be in touch."

Dara reclined in her chair and blew a long shot of air through her pursed lips.

Later that day, Dara was in her office when Maxine buzzed her.

"Someone named Amy Landry is on the line for you. She says she's a member and wants to talk to you about an article she's writing."

"Oh," said Dara with surprise. "Okay, I'll take it."

Maxine patched the call through.

"Dara Harrison."

"Hello, Ms. Harrison. My name is Amy Landry, and I'm a member of MateSearch. I also happen to work for the *LA Times*, and I'm writing a follow-up story on your company."

"I see," Dara said, picking up a yellow pencil and tapping it against her desk anxiously.

"I'm calling to see if you'd like to respond to some of the comments and complaints of members I've interviewed."

Dara felt panic rising inside her. "You've been interviewing members? What about?" she asked, trying not to sound nervous.

"About how the service has or hasn't been working for them, what their experiences have been with regard to your 'lay it on the line' policy, how they feel about rating and being rated by their dates—"

"Well, I can tell you that we have many, many success stories already. From what I hear, our members are finding all the honesty quite refreshing."

"I see. Well, I've spoken to several people who have complained that they've found some of the postings about them to be kind of cruel. One woman told me her self-esteem has taken a hit since becoming a member of the service, and another characterized the posting feature as her 'wall of shame.'"

"Well, I'm sorry to hear they felt that way, I've written several articles in my newsletter on Rate-a-Mate etiquette, and I'm finding that most of our members write very civil and helpful reviews. Of course, there are always thin-skinned types, but we at MateSearch think that accepting constructive criticism is a crucial way to improve relationships."

"Okay," she said. "Thank you for your time."

"You're welcome. Now, may I ask *you* one question?"

"Yes," Amy said apprehensively.

"Did you join the service to meet someone special, or did you join so you could write this story?"

The awkward silence that followed did more to answer the question than the answer Amy finally offered: "Well, I am still single and looking."

❧ *Twenty-four* ❧

A T SEVEN IN THE MORNING, the ring of the telephone pulled Dara out of a disjointed dream. She released her right arm from the confines of her comforter and blindly reached for the receiver.

"Hello?" she mumbled.

"Don't tell me you're still asleep," Tony said.

"So?"

"It's seven o'clock. Past your running time."

"I'm sleeping in today. I need a break."

"From what?"

"Consciousness."

"Oh."

"What did you want?" she asked as Mallory stretched her legs and climbed on top of Dara's chest for her morning affection fix.

"Just wanted to talk. I'll call back later."

"No, no. I'm getting up. Mallory's hungry anyway."

"Okay."

Dara pushed herself up to a sitting position and placed a pillow between her head and the carved oak headboard as Mallory pushed her whiskered face against Dara's fingers.

"So I just thought we had some things to discuss about this whole...situation. Basically, I'm confused."

"About what?" Dara said through a yawn.

"You're joking, right?"

"Tony, I'm still groggy. Spell it out for me, okay?"

"I want to know if you've been having a good time with me."

"Sure, I have. I told you that."

"I mean a really good time. I want to know if you still...you know...have feelings for me."

"Wow."

"Wow, what?"

"Remember how you used to always give me grief for—how did you put it?—'Taking the emotional temperature of our relationship?'"

Tony sighed, "I guess the tables have turned a bit, huh?"

"Look, I'll always care for you. You know that," she said.

"I think you were a little jealous that I had a good time with Serena."

"We were together a long time, Ton. Of course, hearing about another woman is going to make me a little...uncomfortable."

"Just thought you should know we're going out again."

"Really?"

"What do you think about that?"

"I think that's fine as long as you're not just doing it to make me jealous."

"Not everything is about you, you know."

"I know."

"So what about our kiss last night? How'd you feel about that?"

"I don't know. After the whole Jesse thing—"

"Yeah, speaking of which, in all the time I've known you, you never once mentioned that your friend Jesse was—"

"What?" Dara asked innocently.

"You know…"

"Colorful?"

"Is that how you describe him?"

"Yes."

"Anyway, getting back to the kiss—"

"Tony, when the cameras are rolling, nothing is real to me."

"Then maybe we need to spend some time together away from the cameras. You know, I still love you."

Dara felt the pain she was inflicting on her former lover. It pushed her already gloomy state of mind a few notches south. "I know, and I'm sorry I opened up the wound again. I wanted to believe you'd moved beyond it."

Tony got very quiet, and for a moment she wondered if they'd been disconnected.

"Tony? You there?"

"So you're over it and you wish I'd be too," he said sadly.

"I…I'm sorry. I don't think I can go back—"

"How do you explain how well we've been getting along?"

Dara put her hand on her head. "Well, in part, I explain it by realizing that we set up this fantasy together. You coordinate it, I finance it, but it's still a fantasy."

"I knew I should have paid for the dates myself."

"It's not the money, Ton."

"Don't you think I've changed? Don't things seem different now?"

"You were always pretty set in your ways. Can you honestly tell me that if this whole Ophelia mess didn't exist you'd be spending all this quality time with me? That you'd still be making the efforts you've been making? I guess I don't believe that you—or anyone for that matter—can change that drastically without a lightning bolt—or years of therapy. If I came back, I'm pretty sure things would slowly but surely go back to the way they were."

"Dara, stop being the relationship expert for once."

"I can't help it. I can't pretend to not know what I know. It's who I am. It's what I do. There was never real *intimacy* between us—not the lasting kind."

"I don't know, I thought we were pretty intimate!"

"That was sex, not intimacy, and I'm not blaming you. Neither of us could do it. It was actually quite convenient," she said.

Tony didn't respond. Dara had never heard him even come close to tears, but the dejection she sensed through the phone line overwhelmed her.

"So I guess I have just one more question," he said.

"What?"

"Why did you stay with me for so long if that's what you were thinking?"

Dara took a minute to give it honest thought. She owed him that much.

"The truth?"

"Yes."

"I think it's because you were safe."

"Safe? Why?"

"Because you disappointed me all the time," she said.

"Huh?"

"When someone disappoints you a lot, it kind of takes the fear out of losing him. See, if you ever did leave, I could always convince myself it was for the best."

Tony groaned. "Remind me not to ask for the truth anymore."

"I'm sorry I got you into this," she said. "If you want out of the deal, that's fine. I don't want to cause you any more pain."

He said nothing.

"Tony? I'm serious. Why don't we just end this...arrangement? You keep the membership for as long as you like, and I'll figure something else out."

There was more silence before he finally spoke. "I think that's probably a good idea."

Dara felt that old familiar pang, the one she'd experienced every time she'd said goodbye to Tony, only this time there was a distinctive tone to his voice—was it resignation?—that made her believe it really was over for good.

Twenty-five

"DON'T YOU THINK YOU'VE HAD enough caffeine for one morning?" asked Reggie as Dara refilled her cup for the fourth time from the coffeemaker on the conference room credenza. "I don't want to have to retrieve you from the ceiling—or from Nick's esophagus when you jump down his throat."

"Shut up," she said.

"Excuse me? At your pleading I agree to depositions on *my people's* holiday and that's the thanks I get?" Reggie said with false indignation.

"Sorry, I just need to be at the top of my game. This is a very critical day for us," said Dara. She looked at the clock as she paced the carpet: 10:06 A.M. "We have things to discuss before the meeting. Mike is late."

"Only six minutes. Give the man a break, will ya?" said Reggie.

Mike had arranged the meeting on Martin Luther King, Jr.'s birthday, because Palulah had bitched relentlessly about not wanting to miss a day of work "for this nonsense." He set it up at MateSearch due to its central location. The office was empty except for Maxine who'd volunteered to help. Just as Dara finally sat down, much to Reggie's relief, the conference room door opened and Maxine ushered Mike in.

"Sorry I'm late."

"No worries," Reggie replied.

"Well, maybe a few," Dara corrected as she pointed Mike to the chair at the head of the table.

"Would you like some coffee?" asked Reggie. "If there's any left," he added, glancing in Dara's direction.

"No, I'm good," answered Mike as he sat down. Clicking open the buckles of his briefcase, he pulled out some files and looked up to find Dara watching him anxiously.

"Okay, so what's troubling you?"

For the next fifteen minutes, Mike listened patiently as Dara rattled off her concerns about the case, everything from Palulah's credibility to the opposition's true objectives to her own fear of financial ruin at the hands of her new nemesis. To add insult to injury, she also informed him of the unfavorable article about to run in the *Times*, written by a member/undercover reporter. Mike's response did little to quell her caffeine-jolted nerves.

"Look," he said with a grim expression, "Nick Wyatt never signed the contract, and I don't have much faith in our friend Ms. James. If she didn't notice a four-inch scar, I'm doubtful of what she did see. We have to hope the opposition wants to settle this case. I'm telling you right now, if the opportunity arises today, I'm going to attempt to talk settlement with Drew—and I suggest you both be as amenable to it as possible."

There was a knock on the door. Maxine escorted in Drew Johnson, Nick, and Ms. Flanagan, the court reporter. Nick, dressed sharply in a dark gray suit, exuded confidence as he greeted everyone. Dara noticed Reggie giving him an approving once- and twice-over. She kicked him under the table, and he yelped. Everyone looked at him.

"Sorry, banged my knee on the table leg," Reggie said while glaring at Dara. She had donned her best professional comportment, though beneath the surface she was still angling for a fight. She firmly believed that Nick had no intention or interest in striking a deal that did not include a substantial monetary award—something, as far as she was concerned, he'd get over her dead body.

After everyone got situated, Mike Blum took the reins with an amiable smile. "Okay, Ms. Flanagan, I think we're all ready," he announced, cuing the court reporter, a middle-aged woman with a Cleopatra bob and a stodgy blue suit.

"Before we get started, can everybody please pass me their business cards or names so I can note who is in attendance?" she said.

Nick's lawyer, Drew, had a moon-shaped face, thick curly hair, and a serious demeanor. He took a card out of his wallet and handed it to her. Everyone followed suit except for Nick, who had no card and no paper to write on. Reggie ripped a piece from his legal pad and handed it to him with a pen.

"Thanks," Nick said.

"No problem."

Nick wrote his name and passed it to the court reporter as Dara seethed.

"Who will be deposed first?" the woman asked.

"My client, ma'am, Nick Wyatt," said Drew.

After Nick was sworn in by Ms. Flanagan, Mike proceeded, asking basic questions including his name, age, profession, etc., working his way up to his involvement with MateSearch.

"Did you purchase your membership at MateSearch?" asked Mike.

"No, I did not," he answered.

"Then how did you come upon this membership?"

"It was a gift from my sister and her husband."

"What are their names?"

"Annie and Ralph Crawford."

"Who filled out your membership paperwork?"

"My sister, Annie."

"Who signed the contract for your membership with MateSearch?"

"Annie did."

"Did you realize that it was her name on the contract during your time at MateSearch?"

"No. Not until I paid a visit to Ms. Harrison, and she showed me the contract."

Dara's eyes narrowed at Nick. *That little sneak,* she thought. *Didn't even let on. No wonder he'd left so hastily.*

"Can you please tell us how you could not have been aware that your sister, Annie, had signed the contract?"

"She gave me the membership after getting me drunk on martinis."

Drew smiled.

"And why was that?" continued Mike.

"Because she knew I normally wouldn't be caught dead at a dating service."

Dara sniffed with annoyance.

"And when you were sober the next day, did you think about the fact that you hadn't signed the contract?"

"No."

"Why not?"

"Because it was the last thing on my mind. I had just moved into my condo and was still busy unpacking. I wasn't thinking about MateSearch."

"So when was it that you started using the dating service?"

"Soon after I settled in."

"And what made you participate in something you normally wouldn't 'be caught dead at'?"

"I wanted to appease my sister. She spent a lot of money on the membership and wanted me to use it."

"How many women did you date there?"

"Four."

"Did you date Palulah James?"

"Yes."

"How many times did you go out with Ms. James?"

"Three times."

"And why did you stop dating her?"

"Because I knew she wasn't right for me," he said, with some diplomacy.

"Why was that?"

"Honestly? Because I thought she was completely nuts."

"And why was that?"

"For one, she's very into performance art. She invited me to see her perform on stage."

"And why did you find that...nutty?" asked Mike.

"Well, if you were on a third date with a girl, and she showed up on stage nude, painted in grease, and throwing sausages around, wouldn't you find that a little odd?"

Mike raised his eyebrows but didn't comment.

"Any other reasons?"

"The things she said, the way she acted...it's hard to explain. She's just...bizarre."

Dara picked up a blue pencil and began to chew on it.

"So how and when did you tell her you no longer wanted to see her?" asked Mike.

"A couple of days after our date she called me to ask why I hadn't called her. I told her I didn't think we were right for each other."

"And what did she say?"

"She freaked out on me, started calling me names. Then she started harassing me with phone calls, trying to get me to see her."

"When you say harassing, what do you mean exactly?"

"I mean calling my house about a dozen times a day."

"How long did this go on?"

"A couple of weeks."

"And then she stopped?"

"Yes. And that's when I found that nasty post on my MateSearch profile."

"This is a copy of the original post," Mike said, handing a copy to Nick and Drew. "Can you tell me specifically what in that post you knew to be a lie?"

Nick sighed and picked up the paper in front of him, reading it over again.

"I see three lies: one, that we had sex; two, the size of my...penis," he said with some difficulty, "and three, that it was *me* who was harassing *her* with phone calls."

"So what did you do when you read the post?"

"I called Dara Harrison, the owner of MateSearch, and complained."

"And what did she tell you?"

"She basically told me to toughen up," he said, finally acknowledging her with a disdainful glance.

Dara squirmed and exchanged looks with a disapproving Reggie, who discreetly pulled the pencil out of her mouth and placed it on the table.

"Anything else?"

"She didn't seem to believe me but told me that she'd talk to Palulah about it."

"And did this satisfy you?"

"Not at all."

"Why is that?"

"Because she didn't take the post down. I have a name, a public persona, a career on television, and she wasn't in the least bit concerned about my reputation."

"Note my objection," said Mike. "Mr. Wyatt doesn't know that to be a fact."

"And she didn't say the lies would be taken out," Nick added.

"So what did you do?"

"I waited for her to take down the post, and when she didn't I called her again and left messages. I had to leave several before she finally called me back."

"And when she called you back, what did she say?"

"She told me she was investigating the situation and I should be patient."

"She was in touch with you after that, correct?"

"Yes, she left me a couple of messages that she was having trouble connecting with Palulah."

"So what did you do?"

"I went to her office and met with her in person," he replied.

"Did you have an appointment?"

"No."

"But she met with you anyway?"

"Yes."

"And what happened at that meeting?"

"She told me she still hadn't met with Palulah but was expecting to soon."

"And what was your response?"

"I told her that from what I knew about Palulah, she was most likely avoiding Ms. Harrison so as not to deal with what she'd done."

"Did Ms. Harrison say anything else to you?"

"She agreed that the post was uncivil and told me that she'd have Palulah rewrite it to make it more civil," he said. "She also told me I joined MateSearch for the constructive criticism," he added with sarcasm, "and that there were certain rules at MateSearch that I had to follow, including having my post up for six months."

"And what did you say?"

"I told her how it made me feel to have these lies up where everyone could read them, and I told her to take the post down immediately."

"Her response?"

"She told me that my signature on the contract bound me to accept the criticism from Palulah. She pointed out the Rate-a-Mate clause and I read it."

"And did this convince you?"

"Well, it did until I saw my name wasn't on the signature page."

"Why didn't you say anything?"

"I wasn't sure how I should handle it, so I decided to think it over before I acted."

"Pffff," Dara commented, unable to control herself. "Told you it was all about the money," she whispered to Reggie as Nick gave her a sideways glance.

"Has Palulah James's post affected your life in any way?"

"Yes, it has."

"How?"

"For one thing, I was getting at least ten requests from women a week at MateSearch before it was posted. Since then, I haven't gotten any. I've also asked out about two dozen women since the post and not one has agreed to even meet me. In fact, two of the women wrote very demeaning notes back."

Mike gave a barely audible sigh but continued.

"Anything else?"

"Since my motorcycle accident, I've been going through a very rough time and a lot of negative changes in my life. I was trying to pull myself out of a funk, and this knocked me right back into it. I'm humiliated, afraid that people outside MateSearch will also get wind of these lies, and that I might become the laughingstock of Hollywood before I get a chance to go back to work."

"Why would you think your colleagues at work would find out about the post?"

"Because I was contacted by another member of MateSearch who's writing a story on it for the *Times*. She saw Palulah's post and wanted me to comment."

Dara laid her forehead in her hand at this.

"Did you?"

"No. I told her I didn't want to be quoted in the article and I didn't want my story used, but she never assured me that it wouldn't be."

Reggie tapped Dara as if to say, *See, he isn't so bad.*

"Thank you, Mr. Wyatt," Mike said.

When it was Dara's turn, she practically leapt at the invitation to be sworn in and took her oath with an overzealous mix of conviction and enthusiasm.

Dara's deposition, conducted by Drew Johnson, gave her version of her run-ins with Nick. Her alleged lack of concern for his plight became professional consideration for all involved parties. She conveyed how he'd been demanding and rude, quite unlike the wounded victim he portrayed.

What kind of woman was Palulah James? By Dara's account, a perfect-ly nice woman who was trying to do what MateSearch had encouraged her to do: be forthcoming about her dates. When Dara had requested she rewrite the post for civility concerns in keeping with MateSearch rules and regulations, Palulah had done so without objection. This was, for all intents and purposes, a "he said, she said" situation and beyond the scope of what MateSearch could determine as true or false one way or another.

"And what was your impression of Mr. Wyatt when you met him?"

I thought he resembled my ex-boyfriend, the heartless cad otherwise known as Zach Grovener, she thought. "I don't like to make rash judgments," she said, "but I found him impudent."

"Impotent?" asked Drew, befuddled.

"Im-pu-dent," she corrected.

"And what the hell does that mean, Professor?" asked Nick angrily. Drew placed his hand on Nick's arm to quiet him.

"No pun intended," Dara told him, "but it means cocky."

Both lawyers and Reggie tried to hold back smiles. Nick rolled his eyes.

"He also seemed like a disgruntled member who may have had an axe to grind," added Dara. "It was important to do a certain amount of investigation before I flagrantly ignored the rules of my own dating service."

"Why would you think he would make the claims he made if they weren't true?"

"When I met Mr. Wyatt, he seemed very dour, and people like that try to bring everyone else down to their level of misery," she diagnosed.

Dara couldn't keep her eyes from traveling across the table to Nick's face: a stony glare. This only emboldened her. Drew, sensing her rigidity, had one question he knew would set her off kilter.

"Ms. Harrison, Mr. Wyatt has stated that there were three blatant lies in the post from Palulah on his profile page. Do you know whether any of these claims are true?"

Dara didn't respond.

"If you want, Ms. Flanagan can read back Nick's answer from the transcript to refresh your memory."

Dara looked over at Mike, who nodded. "Yes, please," she replied.

Ms. Flanagan reviewed her script and began reading aloud.

"Mr. Blum: 'Can you tell me specifically what in that post you knew to be a lie?'" Ms. Flanagan read, "Mr. Wyatt: 'I see three lies; one, that we had sex; two, the size of my penis; and three, that it was me who was harassing her with phone calls.'"

Drew looked at Dara once more. "Ms. Harrison, I'll repeat the question. Do you know any of these claims to be true?"

"No, how could I?"

"Then shouldn't the burden of truth be with Ms. James, the party making these claims?"

"No, I don't think—"

"And don't you think your company should be responsible for making sure that no malicious lies are posted to your members' personal profiles?"

"Our contract clearly states—" she began.

"You mean the contract Mr. Wyatt never signed?" Drew interjected.

Dara sighed. "Yes," she said reluctantly. "But I had no reason to think any of Palulah's claims were lies."

"What if you were to find out that one of her claims was false? Would you be likely to think all of them were?"

"I don't know."

"Well," Drew said, pulling some papers from the file in front of him, "we subpoenaed Ms. James's telephone records and received them this morning." He handed a copy of the papers to both Mike and Dara. "As you can see, from September the third, three days after Nick and Palulah's last date, through September eighteenth, there were a plethora of calls made from her home and her cell phone to Nick Wyatt's home telephone. I've highlighted them. You don't have to do the math, I already did. There are one hundred and eighty-two calls made by Palulah James to Nick Wyatt during that period of time."

Mike covered his mouth with his fist, his brows knitted together. Reggie shook his head at Dara. She refused to give Nick the satisfaction of seeing her distress and did not meet his eyes, although she felt them fixed on her triumphantly.

"Does this information change your mind Ms. Harrison?"

"Mr. Johnson," Dara said, her voice a bit shaky, "even if Palulah did make all those calls, that doesn't mean she was lying about the other two claims."

"Are you kidding?" Nick said. He hit the top of the table with his open hand. "You've got to be kidding!"

"Please, no outbursts," said Mike calmly.

"I can't believe this crap!" said Nick to his lawyer, who tried to quiet him with a hand on his arm.

Just then, the conference room phone buzzed. Dara looked at the clock and saw it was noon. She answered the phone.

"Yes, Maxine?"

"Palulah James is here for her deposition," said Maxine, "and you had a call from Claire James. She says it's important."

"Okay," said Dara, her mind now reeling. That was the first time Claire had attached any urgency to a message.

"We'll be with Ms. James in a few minutes," added Mike.

Dara's deposition ended about ten minutes later with no further revelations. Mike suggested everyone take a quick break before continuing with Palulah. Dara used the opportunity to run to her office and call Claire.

"Hi, what's so important?" she asked.

"Dara, we found him."

"You what?"

"We found him living in a town called Banstead. It's south of London."

"Oh, my God," Dara whispered, her hands beginning to shake.

"As far as we can tell, he lives alone and works nearby, managing a supermarket. I have the names, addresses, phone numbers and some other information here. I just wanted to know if you want me to fax them over or what."

Dara was silent for a few moments.

"Dara, you there?"

"Huh? Yes."

"I know it's a shock."

"Yeah," she said, taking a breath.

"I'll fax it over, that okay?"

"I'll tell Maxine to look for it. I'm in the deposition."

"Oh, right! Forgot it was today. Okay, I'll fax now and we'll talk later."

"All right—and Claire?"

"Yes?"

"Thanks for everything."

"You got it."

After giving Maxine a head's up about the fax, Dara headed back to the meeting. Everyone else was already seated. Within seconds, Maxine ushered in Palulah, who looked more primed for a strut down a runway than a legal deposition. Her hair in long billowy waves, her makeup befitting a *Vogue* fashion shoot, and her form-fitting white suit clinging to her curves, Palulah had clearly dressed to show her former date—and every other male who crossed her path that day—what he was missing.

Nick avoided looking at either her or Dara, but both of them now glowered at him.

Mike greeted Palulah and introduced her to Reggie and Drew.

"You know Ms. Harrison," he said, indicating Dara.

Palulah gave a little wave in Dara's direction. Mike seated her at the far end of the table next to the court reporter.

"Ms. James," Mike began, "we'll give your lawyer a few more minutes to get here and then—"

"Oh, I didn't hire one," said Palulah, removing her suit jacket to reveal a silky camisole top. "You said I didn't have to."

"Yes," said Mike with some concern, "but I did recommend—"

"Mr. Blum, I really don't see the need to waste my money on an attorney. I'm a big girl and perfectly capable of handling this on my own."

A look of doubt passed over Mike's face. "All right, then. Ms. Flanagan will swear you in."

"Swear me in? We're not in court."

"I know, but this is considered the same as if we were."

"No one told me that," she said, half under her breath.

"Is there a problem?" asked Drew.

"No, of course not," she replied.

The court reporter instructed Palulah to raise her right hand.

"Do you swear to tell the truth, the whole truth, and nothing but the truth, so help you God?" she said.

"Yes," replied Palulah.

"Please state your full name for the record," said Mike.

"Palulah Contessa James."

"Ma'am, my name is Drew Johnson. I'm an attorney and represent Nick Wyatt in a case that's currently pending in the Superior Court of Los Angeles County against MateSearch, Inc. and Dara Harrison. Have you ever had a deposition taken before?"

"No."

"I just want to review some of the rules. The court reporter is taking down your testimony. The court reporter can't take down a nod or a shake of the head, so I'd ask that all your responses be verbal, and if there's a question that I ask you that you don't understand, just stop me and say, 'Mr. Johnson, I don't understand,' and I'll try to rephrase it so you do understand it. If at any time during the deposition you need to take a break, just let me know."

"Okay," Palulah said more quietly.

Drew requested her address, age, and employment information. She stated her jobs as dental hygienist to Dr. Larry Lederberg and performance artist with a troupe called Feminymphs.

"Ms. James, how long have you been a member of MateSearch?"

"Seven months, I think."

"And did you date a man named Nick Wyatt through the service?"

"Yes," she said with distaste.

"How many times did you go out with Mr. Wyatt?"

"Three times."

"Did you have sexual relations with Mr. Wyatt during that time?"

"Yes."

"How many times?"

"Just once, on the third date."

Nick shook his head as he watched her.

"Why did you stop seeing Mr. Wyatt?"

Palulah sighed and flipped her mane over her right shoulder. "Let's just say he was a disappointment."

"I'd ask you why, Ms. James, but I suppose I don't need to, since you posted a very descriptive review of Mr. Wyatt on his profile at MateSearch that seems to explain why. True?"

"I guess you could say that."

"Here is a copy of the original post," Drew said, sliding the page in front of her on the table. "Is that the post you wrote?"

"Yes."

"You claimed he hounded you via telephone. Is that true?"

"Yes."

"You also claimed his penis was two inches long. Is that correct?"

"Yes."

"How did you determine this?"

"Well, it's not like I got out a ruler," she said, causing Reggie to smirk, "but that's sure what it looked like—and felt like—to me."

"What a liar!" Nick blurted out. "She's perjuring herself!"

Palulah stared at him indignantly as Drew put his hand on Nick's arm again.

"We subpoenaed copies of your phone bills," Drew informed her as he slid a page in front of her. "Can you confirm this is your telephone number and your telephone bill?"

Palulah looked it over, color rising in her cheeks. "Yes," she said reluctantly.

"Whose number is this?" he asked, pointing to a listing.

"My mother's."

"And this?"

"My friend Ginny."

"And what about this one?"

Palulah didn't say anything.

"Ms. James?"

"I'm not sure."

"Let me help you out. It belongs to Nick Wyatt."

"So?"

"It's posted three days after you allegedly broke up with him, at a time you said you never called him."

"So maybe I hit redial by accident or something," she said.

"Ms. James, we have a record of calls from both your home and cell phone to Mr. Wyatt's home phone beginning on that day and continuing for over two weeks," he said, putting the rest of the pages in front of her.

She stared at them, swallowing hard.

"We counted one hundred and eighty-two calls between September third and September eighteenth of last year. To most observers it would seem that you were doing the harassing, not Mr. Wyatt."

"Well, I left my earrings at his condo, and I was trying to get them back. They were diamonds—"

"What?" Nick squealed.

"It's true. He wouldn't give me back my diamond earrings. He still hasn't!"

"This is ridiculous!" yelled Nick. "She was in my home for about a half hour and she never took off any earrings."

"Yes, I did! They were my grandmother's," she said wistfully.

Nick grunted and put his head in his hand, trying to control his anger.

"You never mentioned them in the post. Why not?" asked Drew.

"I…I didn't think suggesting he was a thief would be a couth thing to do. I mean, what if I got them back?"

"Meaning you thought advertising his purported penis size *was* a couth thing to do?" said Drew.

"Well, it's certainly something a woman wants to know about, even if she doesn't admit it."

"We're going around in circles here," interjected Mike, trying to lift Palulah from the hole she had dug. "No matter what, we have no real way of knowing if the other claims are true or false."

"Well, there is one way!" announced Nick, now unable to contain himself.

"And what is that?" asked Mike.

"What do you think?" Nick replied, now irate.

"He's not saying what I think he's saying, is he?" Reggie whispered to Dara out of the side of his mouth.

A look of alarm came over Dara's face.

"Apparently it's the only way to settle this nonsense once and for all!" Nick said. "Is there a ruler in here?" he asked Reggie pointedly.

"You've got to be kidding," Dara muttered.

"There's one right in there!" announced Reggie as he ran to the credenza and began shuffling through a center drawer.

"Reggie! What are you doing? Are you crazy?" Dara exclaimed.

The lawyers began to argue as Palulah squirmed, and the court reporter looked all around, unable to decide which part, if any, of the current discourse should be documented for posterity.

"Nick, calm down," said Drew. "This isn't necessary."

"Found it!" Reggie cried, holding up a wooden ruler.

Mike tried to quell the outburst. "I object to Mr. Wyatt engaging in this display and demand that you control your client," he yelled to Drew.

"Nick, now's not the time," his lawyer pleaded. "We'll prove it in a more civilized manner!"

Nick ignored both lawyers as he stood and began to unbuckle his leather belt. The room erupted again. Reggie stood next to Nick holding the ruler expectantly.

"Reggie, sit down!" cried Dara.

"I don't have to sit through this vulgar exhibition!" yelled Palulah, standing up.

"Why not? I sat through yours!" Nick yelled, referring to the flying sausages.

Palulah grabbed her suit jacket off her chair and bounded for the door. Reggie, inspired by the passion in the room, began to orate.

"I have a dream," he roared, his voice deep and booming amid the cacophony. "I have a dream that someday man will not be judged by the size of his penis—but by the content of his character...I have a dream today!"

Dara observed the absurd spectacle unfolding before her eyes like a zany Hollywood film. Her case was about to fall off the proverbial cliff, her hard won business success going south as Nick's blue striped boxers came into full view. Suddenly, the intercom buzzer brought her back to reality, and mercifully deterred Nick from his big reveal. She pressed the button.

"Not now, Maxine," she yelled.

"But it's your mother."

"Tell her I'm still in the meeting."

"Dara, she says it's an emergency."

Twenty-six

"WOULD YOU LIKE SOMETHING to drink?" asked the pretty brunette flight attendant as she smiled down at Dara and the middle-aged woman next to her.

"I'll have a diet Coke," the woman replied, pulling down her folding tray. The order pulled Dara from her haze. She briefly considered a Bloody Mary before a little voice in her head warned, *alcohol is a depressant.* Besides, it would only aggravate her already pounding head. She opted for a diet Sprite and pulled down her tray table, too.

The attendant placed a bag of pretzels in front of each woman and poured their drinks.

"Would you like my pretzels?" asked Dara's seatmate. She had short, reddish brown hair and was dressed for comfort in a gray sweat suit. "I'm trying to be good."

Dara nodded, and the woman placed the pretzels on her tray table.

"Thanks," Dara said.

"I hope the movie's good. It always makes the trip go faster."

"Hmm?"

"You okay?" asked the woman.

"Yes."

The woman picked up her drink and took a sip. "This is my first trip to New York. I always wanted to visit, but my husband never wanted to. Says it's just a big, expensive hassle. But now that my friend Stacy moved there, I have someone to visit," she said cheerfully. She looked at Dara, who was staring into space. She took it as her cue to shut up and turned her attention out the window instead.

Dara ripped open one of the bags of pretzels before realizing she had no appetite. She put them back on her tray table. Then, for some reason, she felt compelled to confide in the stranger sitting next to her.

"My stepdad died," she said.

The woman turned her head back to Dara, unsure if she'd heard her correctly.

"Oh, I'm sorry! That's terrible!"

"I'm on my way back home for the funeral."

"Was it sudden?"

"Yes, a heart attack. Happened at his store," she explained in a dazed voice. "He was gone before the ambulance arrived."

The woman put her hand on Dara's arm in a gesture of comfort. "Both my parents are gone, too. When they go suddenly, it may be better for them, but it's very hard on us." Seeing that she wasn't helping to cheer her seatmate up, the woman smiled and put out her hand. "I'm Nancy."

"Dara," she said, taking it for a shake.

"I have some magazines if you want to read something light."

"No thanks. I've been up all night. I should probably try to take a nap."

Nancy nodded.

Dara took another gulp of soda, leaned back, and closed her eyes. The events of the last twenty-four hours were now a jumbled, sickening mess, clouding her mind and upsetting her stomach. How could Bill be gone? It was unfathomable. He was the one man who'd been there—as solid and reliable as the giant oak tree in their backyard—ever since the first day her mother introduced him to her and Amanda. Bill became everything to her mother. They'd run the business together, raised a family together, and even had the same hobbies. He was only sixty-four, her mom, sixty-two. What would she do now?

As she drifted in and out of sleep, she relived the moments just after finding out. Her mother's shaky voice, breaking the news. Dara's shock as she told the room full of people what had happened. Reggie hugging her; the lawyers rendered silent; and most surprisingly, Nick's genuine, empathetic response. He had told her how sorry he was, that he'd been through it himself. That he hoped she'd be okay. At least for a few moments, the fight between them had been rendered insignificant. To her, he seemed to transform from ogre to human being in the span of a single phone call. Pretty good for the man who seemed hell bent on destroying her livelihood. Then Maxine, handing her the once all-important and now ironic fax on her way out the door. She had folded it up and shoved it in her purse.

Reggie had followed her home and helped her pack and make reservations while sneezing up a storm from the cat dander. He expected her to break down after everyone had gone, but she never did. She told him that Jesse was vacationing in Hawaii with his mystery flame, so Reggie reluctantly took Mallory home with him along with her food, litter box, and a two-week supply of antihistamines. The next morning he came back to drive her to LAX

"Take good care of my little Mallomar," she told him when they reached the airport.

"Take good care of *you*," he replied, giving her a bear hug.

It took a little while, but Dara finally fell into a much-needed slumber as the 747 soared over the Southwest.

At La Guardia Airport, Amanda was waiting for Dara at the baggage claim while her husband Andy circled the airport in their Honda Accord. They lived only fifteen minutes from their mother, which was a comfort to Dara. She spotted her older sister, who looked pale and distraught, her eyes

swollen and red rimmed. She wore no makeup and her light brown hair was pulled back in a messy chignon. Clad in a pair of old jeans and a sweatshirt, she held her purse and her down ski jacket in her arms. Dara took one look at her and knew that she was going to have to be the glue that held everyone together for the next few weeks.

They walked quickly toward each other. Dara dropped her carry-on and hugged her sister tightly. Amanda pulled some tissues from her pocket and blew her nose as they waited by the conveyer belt that had just started revolving.

"How's Mom doing?"

"She's a mess. I didn't want to leave her alone at the house, so Aunt Jean came over. Mom's so glad you're here. So am I," she said, giving her a squeeze. "This is a nightmare."

"I know. Everything seems so surreal to me."

"Me, too."

"What time is the funeral?"

"Tomorrow morning at ten."

Dara took a deep, shaky breath.

After they collected her bag, they waited at the curb for Andy. Dara shivered in her black pea coat and tied her chenille scarf more tightly around her neck. According to the pilot, it was thirty-five degrees and cloudy, but now that her blood had thinned out in sunny L.A., it felt more like thirty-five below. The dreariness made her thankful she no longer lived in the land of dark, wintry days, although this weather perfectly reflected the gloom and doom in her life.

After about five minutes, they spotted Andy and flagged him down. Tall, thin, and attractive, he rushed out of the car to hug Dara. Then he loaded her bags into the trunk as both sisters climbed into the back seat together. The heat was on high and Dara tried to absorb as much of it as possible. In less than a minute, they were headed toward the Grand Central Parkway and back home to Connecticut.

Amanda had been right about their mother. When they entered the spacious colonial home, they found her sitting on the couch with Aunt Jean, her head on her shoulder like a lost child. She wore sweat pants and a worn, oversized sweater; her blonde hair tied back with an old scrunchie; her pretty face ravaged by grief. Dara walked over and bent down by her knee. Her mother leaned over to hold her.

"Thank God you're here."

"Where else would I be?" asked Dara.

"You must be exhausted."

"I slept a little on the plane. I'm fine."

Aunt Jean stroked her sister's hair as Amanda and Andy took off their coats and sat down on a nearby loveseat.

"Mom, what can I do for you?" asked Dara.

"Just hug me tighter," she said, tears spilling down her face.

Dara squeezed her mother harder and scooted up next to her on the couch. "Have you eaten?"

"She had a quarter of an English muffin with some butter," answered Aunt Jean with disapproval.

"That's it?"

"I can't eat."

"You need some food in your stomach or you'll feel even worse," said Dara.

"She's right, Jackie," said Aunt Jean.

"It's almost six o'clock. I'll go see what you have inside and maybe I'll just whip us up some dinner," said Dara.

"You?" asked Amanda dubiously. "You don't cook."

"Just because I don't cook doesn't mean I can't if I want to. I promise I won't poison you."

She stood up, took off her coat, draped her scarf around her shoulders, and headed into the kitchen to explore. Although weary, she knew that if she put in the effort of making a meal, her mother would be more likely to eat. She opened the freezer and pulled a large tin halfway out. *Lasagna,* she thought. *Bill's famous turkey lasagna.* She closed her eyes and imagined him preparing it on a Sunday afternoon, a pot of tomato sauce on the stove, a baseball game on the tiny kitchen television set. She took a deep breath and swallowed the lump in her throat. Then she pushed the tin back into the freezer and extracted a box of chicken cutlets instead.

Twenty-seven

REGGIE SAT IN HIS OFFICE devising a plan. He was determined to use Dara's unfortunate state of affairs to her advantage—whether she liked it or not. He would strike while the empathy iron was hot and contact Nick at home. Reggie debated whether to consult their attorney first, but decided against it. This was a delicate matter, and he didn't want to hear all the impersonal legal reasons he shouldn't do it. He leaned forward, pulled the phone closer, and punched in the number at the top of Nick's paperwork. He took a deep breath and leaned back in his brown leather chair.

Nick was fixing tri-color fusilli doused in store-bought pesto sauce when the telephone rang. The number on his caller ID seemed familiar, but it wasn't until he picked up the phone that he remembered why.

"Hello?"

"Nick?" said a friendly male voice.

"Yes," he answered.

"This is Reggie Dayton from MateSearch."

"Yeah, hi," Nick replied with surprise, placing the empty glass jar in the sink for a rinse.

"I'm sorry to bother you at home, and I know this is a bit unorthodox, but I was wondering if I could talk to you for a few minutes."

"What's this about? I was just having lunch."

"Oh, sorry about that. Do you think we can meet for coffee later?"

Nick grew suspicious. *Is this guy asking me out? Is the theatre of the absurd taking another curtain call?* "Can you tell me what's on your mind?"

"It's about the case. You know Dara went home to Connecticut for the funeral, and I was hoping that in her absence I might be able to...work a few kinks out with you to ease things along here."

"Shouldn't this be left to our lawyers?"

"Well, you know lawyers, always making mountains out of mole hills. I wanted to keep things friendly."

"Hey, I know your case is in the toilet, but I don't see any logical reason we should get together without counsel present. I mean—"

"Look," Reggie said, dropping all pretenses, "I can tell you're a good guy who wasn't out looking for trouble. I'm sorry you found some. I know my partner's a little rough around the edges, but Dara's a good friend of mine, and now with her father dying—"

"I thought it was her stepfather."

"Yes, well, he raised her. She never really knew her father, and besides that, her company is under threat and there's just an awful lot on her plate. Deep down, I promise, she really isn't the bitch you think she is."

"Really? How deep down?"

Reggie laughed. "Come on, meet me for coffee. A half hour. Hear me out. Please?"

"I don't drink coffee at night. I'll meet you for a beer—a quick beer at about six."

"Great!" said Reggie with relief.

"Do you know Murphy's Bar and Grill on Wilshire?" asked Nick.

"That's perfect. I'll see you at the bar."

As they disconnected, Nick thought, *I hope I don't live to regret this.*

With dinner over and the dishes cleared, Dara climbed the stairs to her old bedroom, her head in a dark fog. From her doorway, she took in the almond lacquer headboard and dresser, and the mauve carpet, noting the circa-1986 décor. The curtains had, thankfully, been replaced by almond-colored cloth blinds, and the walls were covered in light green and pink floral wallpaper. Andy had already brought up her suitcase and carry-on bag. Dara unpacked. She hung up her sensible black dress; she'd never worn it and, until now, had never found a use for it.

After showering and pulling a long nightshirt over her shivering torso, she went to check on her mother. She found her sitting up in bed, leaning against her powder blue tufted headboard. Amanda lay next to her on her side, staring into space.

"Hi," Dara said. She picked up the bottom edge of the queen comforter and slipped her legs under it to join them.

"Mom was wondering if you were going to speak tomorrow," said Amanda.

"I...I guess so," she said reluctantly. "I hadn't even thought of it." Dara eyed her mother who looked almost too weary to cry anymore.

"Are *you* going to speak?" she asked her sister.

"I'm going to try—no promises."

"I'll write something before I go to sleep," Dara assured them, accepting her painful duty.

"How long can you stay in town?" her mother asked.

"I made reservations to go back in two weeks, but I can change them. We'll see how things go."

"We're keeping the store closed for a week. Then Nelson said he'd be able to hold down the fort until I was ready to go back," Jackie said. Dara nodded. Thank goodness for Nelson, a loyal and competent worker Bill had hired eight years earlier so they could take an occasional much-needed vacation. Jackie added, "*If* I'm able to go back."

"Don't think about that now, Mom. You have things under control in the meantime," Amanda assured her.

"We were thinking we'd try to sell the store in a year or two," said Jackie, her eyes welling up again. "We were going to retire and go see all the places we've never had a chance to see because the business held us down...Bill always wanted to see the Orient."

Jackie began crying again, and Dara reached out to touch her mother's ankle. Jackie wiped her face with a tissue and tried to compose herself. The image stirred a flashback for Dara, whisking her back to when she was only six years old, when she would lie in bed with her mother during her Bad Time. The hopelessness and fear she had felt watching her mother's inability to cope after her father left flooded through her again. She took a deep breath and waited for it to slip away, but it wouldn't budge.

"Do you know what one of our last conversations was?" Jackie asked her daughters.

"What?" asked Amanda.

"He wanted to plan a family vacation to Peru. Take you girls, Andy, and the kids."

"Peru? Why?" asked Amanda, perplexed.

"That's what I asked him. He said he was reading a Shirley MacLaine book where she went to Peru and had all these mystical experiences. He thought since you were into yoga," she said, looking at Amanda, "you'd appreciate it, and since you love animals, Dara," she said, turning her head toward her, "we could visit the Amazon jungle while we were there."

The girls both looked at their mother with the same befuddled expression on their faces, which had the unexpected effect of making Jackie smile between tears.

"Bill read Shirley MacLaine books?" asked Dara.

"Just this one, I think. Not sure why he picked it up. Anyway, he said we could go swimming in the hot springs and visit Machu Picchu."

"Actually, that doesn't sound too bad," said Amanda.

"Well, I told him it was a crazy idea, but he just told me to read the book."

Dara smiled. That was so like Bill—thinking outside the proverbial box. Who wanted to cruise the Caribbean or see the Grand Canyon like normal families anyway?

"Maybe we should all read the book," said Dara.

The moment of lightness passed, and the three of them sat on the bed, melancholy thickening the air again.

"He loved you girls very much, you know," said Jackie.

Amanda took her mother's hand and nodded while Dara looked at Bill's night table. A photograph of Dara and Amanda as teens sat under the lamp in a porcelain frame. They had just finished washing the family Oldsmobile with a hose and bucket. A wave of emotion rose in Dara's throat. She swallowed hard, and her head began to throb.

"Well, I better go write something up. I'll see you in the morning," Dara said. She climbed out from under the covers and kissed them both good night.

When Nick arrived at Murphy's, the bar was bustling. Taking a stool at the far end, away from the happy hour crowd, he ordered a Bass Ale. The businesspeople drank, laughed, and discussed the goings-on at their offices as U2's "Pride" played over the jukebox speakers. It was a scene so common, yet so foreign to Nick. Working in an office? He wouldn't have lasted more than a week in their world. Clock-watching would have become a blood sport for the man who loved the open road and the feel of wind in his hair. Of course, killing time on a movie set between stunts didn't send his pulse racing either, but as long as you stayed in earshot, you could pretty much do as you wanted.

He'd had some really good times on the *Stormcats* set, horsing around with the stunt team, playing practical jokes on unsuspecting cast members, and sometimes just sitting around shooting the breeze. Nick's mind traveled back to the day he wished he could forget. He had been setting up a stunt with Kenny when Ralph, a production assistant, ran onto the set screaming for someone to call an ambulance. When Nick heard him say Matt's name, he ran to the young star's trailer. There was already a crowd of actors and crew blocking Nick's view, but he heard them murmuring about a prop gun that had gone off, lodging a blank into the right side of Matt's skull. It wasn't until the next day that Nick pieced together all the gruesome details.

At exactly six o'clock, Nick spotted Reggie and motioned him over. Reggie shook his hand and grabbed the stool next him.

"Good to see you, man," said Reggie. "I'll have a Bud Light," he told the bartender.

"So," said Nick, "what's on your mind?"

The bartender opened the bottle of beer and began pouring it into a frosty glass mug. Reggie took a sip. "Thanks for meeting me," he said. "Since Dara left town, I've been doing a lot of thinking, and I think this whole legal debacle we're in is completely absurd and totally unnecessary."

"You do, huh?"

"Yes, and I thought if you understood where Dara was coming from, we might be able to work things out to everybody's satisfaction. I know her like a book. We worked together for four years before we even decided to go into business together. She's one of my closest friends."

Nick shot him a skeptical look but motioned with his left hand to continue talking, while lifting the cold mug to his lips with his right.

"First of all, I apologize for not insisting she take down the post immediately. Sometimes Dara lets her so-called principles get in the way of doing what's right. But understand this: The philosophy behind MateSearch is what Dara's been preaching and promoting for years—it's her credo. Having her own business was her lifelong dream. Put those two things together and add a perceived threat and, well, the girl just couldn't see the forest for the trees." Reggie took a gulp of beer. "She did the wrong thing by leaving that post up, and when you rightly demanded she take it down, it just got her dander up even more. She's really her own worst enemy. She just doesn't know it."

"So what's her problem?"

"When it comes right down to it, she has a hard time trusting men."

"You're a man and you're her partner."

"I'm gay. I'm safe."

"Does anybody really trust anybody these days?"

Reggie thought about Vincenzo for a moment. "I know what you mean," he replied, "but when you're abandoned by your father and then by the only man you ever loved, it's kind of understandable, don't you think?" asked Reggie, unabashedly playing the sympathy card.

Nick rested his elbow on the granite bar and leaned the side of his head into his palm. "You come here to tell me about her hard-knock life?"

Reggie shrugged. "In part, I guess. Knowing what makes people tick can sometimes help you let go of a grudge."

"This isn't a grudge. It's a lawsuit."

"Sometimes they're the same thing."

Nick sighed and rubbed his five o'clock shadow between his thumb and fingers.

"Look, you had every right to file in this case," said Reggie. "I don't be-grudge you that, but this is a new company, with all the problems and pitfalls of a new company. Three million dollars…well…that could very well put an end to it."

"This was never about the money."

"I know that. It's Dara who thinks you're looking to milk her, and with the lawyers involved, it could very well happen. Now me," he said, pointing at his own chest, "I could move on just fine from that point if I had to, but Dara, well, you should have seen her before MateSearch," Reggie said, rolling his eyes. "It wasn't pretty! This company means everything to her. It's all she has."

"Yeah…"

"So now that your profile is down and you're no longer a member, how about if we printed a retraction of some sort for all the members to read? And maybe institute a new set of rules to make sure what happened to you never happens again?"

"It'd be a good start."

"And we could pay your legal fees and maybe fork over a reasonable sum for your pain and suffering? It would save you any further invasions of your privacy," said Reggie.

Nick shook his head slowly while smiling. He motioned for another beer. "You want another one?"

"Sure," Reggie replied even though his glass was half full and he was watching his weight again.

"Him, too," said Nick to the bartender. Then he turned his attention back to Reggie. "I have a question."

"Shoot."

"Does Dara know how lucky she is to have you around?"

Reggie smiled. "You don't know the half of it. I'm babysitting her cat."

"That's nice of you."

"I'm deathly allergic."

"That's *really* nice of you!"

"Yeah!"

"I don't know about cats. I'm a dog person."

"What kind do you have?"

"Had," he corrected. "A black lab." The bartender slid them another round. "Thinking of adopting again," said Nick wistfully.

"That's nice."

Then Nick switched gears. "Look, I don't know what to tell you right now."

"Hey, I'm not asking you to make any decisions today. Just think about it. Sleep on it. Let me know when you decide."

"Okay," Nick replied, taking a deep breath.

"Good, thanks," said Reggie with some relief. "Want to order some appetizers?"

One shrimp cocktail and a basket of chicken wings later, the two men found that aside from their unfortunate legal drama, they got along quite well. Reggie listened intently to Nick's description of his accident, the stunt life, and his new position restoring motorcycles. Reggie told him about how he and Dara had come up with the idea for MateSearch after finding Vincenzo in bed with a woman. He also shared some of the cool publicity he had secured for the company.

"Yes, I caught her on the *Ophelia Show*," Nick admitted.

"Pretty cool, huh? I arranged that," he announced proudly.

"So how's she doing with *The Challenge*?" he said in an ominous, baritone voice.

"Let's not go there," said Reggie.

The half-hour meeting turned into two hours before Nick finally looked at his watch. "Wow. It's eight o'clock already," he said. He looked around. The happy hour crowd had thinned out.

"Really?" asked Reggie, checking his Rolex. "Sorry, didn't mean to keep you this long."

"Don't worry about it," he said, pulling his wallet out of his jeans pocket.

"Hey, don't even think about it. This is on me," said Reggie, motioning for the bartender to bring the check.

"Thanks."

"No. Thank *you* for coming. You're a good man, Nick Wyatt. In fact, I'm going to take your picture down from Dara's dartboard."

Nick caught Reggie's eye.

"Kidding," said Reggie, breaking into a winsome smile.

Twenty-eight

THE FUNERAL WAS A BLUR OF MISERY, a societal ritual that Dara had always dreaded. Stuck on autopilot, she greeted family and friends, and tended to her mother. She'd been lucky before this, only having to come to terms with the deaths of her mother's parents, who had both followed a natural progression, living to a reasonably old age.

She couldn't come to grips with this loss, however. Bill shouldn't have been on *that* list yet. He'd had too much life left in him, something she explained in detail to the amazingly large audience before her, as if she were pleading his case to God. She shared memories of Bill throughout her childhood: how he'd taught her to fix her own toys; patiently tutored her in trigonometry when she'd risked failing the course; took her shopping for her prom dress when her mother had the flu; how he'd always offered an ear and a hug when needed. She wanted to say so much more, but couldn't form the words. She looked out at the front pew and saw her mother and sister crying. Amanda motioned to her through tears that she could not come on stage, so Dara finished by including Amanda's thoughts as well.

"Mom, Amanda, and I have been so lucky to have Bill in our lives. I can't imagine another stepdad who we could have loved more than him," she said, choking up. "We'll love and miss you forever, Bill."

After the interment, their black limousine headed back home. Aunt Jean had arranged for a caterer, and the house quickly filled up with family

211

and friends. Amanda kept a watchful eye on her two children, a girl, age six and a boy, age eight, whom she feared would be scarred by their first funeral. Dara made small talk, but only after downing some valerian root in her bathroom. She hoped it might make the next few hours more bearable. Jackie sat on the couch, zombie-like, her eyes swollen and glazed, as a steady stream of well-wishers paid their respects.

Dara could hear the phone ringing and for a moment thought, *Bill will get it*, as if he were in the kitchen coordinating the wait staff. Then came the punch in the stomach she felt every time she remembered he was no longer with them. She ran into the kitchen and grabbed the phone after the fourth ring.

"Hello?"

"Yes, is...Dara there?"

"Maxine?"

"Yes! Hi!"

"Hi."

"How are you?" asked her receptionist.

"We're just back from the cemetery," Dara said, figuring that would say it all.

"I didn't have a chance to tell you how sorry I am for your loss," she said.

"Thanks, Maxine. It was nice of you to call—"

"That's not the only reason I called, though."

"Is something wrong?"

"Well, I hate to bother you at a time like this, but—"

"It's okay," Dara said. "Tell me."

"Well, Reggie's in the hospital."

"What?" she said, panic in her voice. "Why?"

"Seems he had an asthma attack. It's your cat."

"Oh, my God!"

"He's okay now, and we're holding down the fort here, so don't worry."

"Are you sure?"

"I'm positive. I saw him myself today and got the key to his apartment, so I'll go feed Mallory until he gets released."

"Do you know when?"

"Not long. A day or two."

"Thank you, Maxine," she said. "Where can I reach him?"

"He's at Cedars Sinai. I'll give you the number."

Dara excused herself and ran up to the relative quiet of her room. She closed the door, picked up her pink princess phone, and called Reggie's hospital room. After three rings, he picked up, his voice raspy.

"Hello?"

"Reggie?"

"Told you I was deathly allergic."

"You did. I'm so sorry! Are you feeling better?"

"Yeah, yeah. They took good care of me. Gave me some new medication."

"That's good."

"But they told me I've gotta get Mallory out of my house."

"Damn."

"Don't worry. Maxine and I are on it. We'll figure out a backup plan. Do you have any idea when Jesse is due back from Hawaii?"

"I honestly don't remember. Look, I'll try to make some more phone calls, too."

"Hey, you got enough going on. Let us handle it. Cole's got a Doberman so he's out, and Maxine would take her, but she doesn't want World War III in her apartment," he said, referring to Maxine's three cats. Reggie took a breath. "You make it through the funeral okay?"

"I guess. We got your flowers, thanks."

"Sure."

"Did they say yet when you'll be getting out of the hospital?"

"Tomorrow. So we kind of have to act quickly on the cat situation."

"How's Mallory doing?"

"She's fine. Tried to sleep with me last night, and I didn't have the heart to kick her out of the bedroom."

"So you risked your life to comfort her? That's a true friend."

"And don't forget it."

"Never."

"Listen, I'll let you go, but call me later and I'll let you know who's going to take her."

"Okay," Dara replied nervously, "just make sure it's someone I like...who loves cats...and is skilled in cat parenting."

"Any other requirements, milady?"

"She's my baby."

"I know. I'll do my best."

"Thanks. Feel better, Reg. Speak to you later."

Dara struggled through the rest of the day. When the house quieted again, she helped her mother to bed. Her niece and nephew were already asleep in Amanda's old bedroom. Dara joined her sister and Andy around the kitchen table with a quart of milk and a plate of homemade chocolate chip cookies from one of their neighbors.

"Remember when Bill made chocolate chip cookies with us and had to put the batter on top of the fridge so we couldn't eat it and get sick?" asked Amanda.

"Yeah, then he caught me climbing up on a chair to try to get at it," said Dara.

"You were relentless," said Amanda.

"Do you think he's here?" asked Dara, suddenly solemn. "I mean, I feel him here so strong, and if I were him, I'd be hanging around the house right about now, checking up on everyone."

"Probably," said Amanda, "knowing him."

"Don't tell me you guys believe in spirits," said Andy.

"Of course, I do," said Dara. "What, you think we just cease to exist after death? That makes no sense whatsoever."

"I don't believe things I can't see and feel," said Andy.

"What about radio waves?" asked Amanda.

"Huh?" he replied.

"Do you believe radio waves exist? You can't see or touch them, but we know they're there."

"Good point," said Dara. "Anyway, you'll see I'm right one day."

"Hopefully not one day soon," added Amanda, putting her hand on her husband's.

"I'm not going anywhere," he assured her.

Dara watched them snuggle, a familiar emptiness in her chest. She recalled watching Bill walk her sister down the aisle years ago. She had been so happy that Amanda had someone to give her away, and she'd hoped that maybe one day he would do the same for her. Now Bill was gone, her company was on the skids, her reputation was in jeopardy, and her love life was in its usual, sorry state of void. A jumble of emotions rose in her chest. She washed them down with the last gulps of milk and glanced at the clock above the sink: ten after one. *God, how did it get so late?* She needed to call Reggie to check on his cat sitter search. Luckily, it was three hours earlier in Los Angeles.

"I'm going upstairs," said Dara, stretching and putting her glass in the dishwasher. "I'll see you in the morning."

When she reached her bedroom, she called Reggie's hospital room.

"Hello?"

"Hi, Reg. How you feeling?"

"I'm good. They're releasing me first thing in the morning."

"Great! Did you guys have any luck?"

"Well, not at first," he hedged. "Just for the record, Maxine spent a good part of the afternoon trying to convince friends of mine whom she's never met to take your cat."

"And?"

"There were no takers. Everyone's got a good excuse, though. I can vouch for that. She wrote them all down for me."

"But you found someone?" she asked with hope.

"I did, and Maxine has already transported your little baby to her new digs with all her food, litter, and toys, and I'm happy to report she's doing just fine."

"Oh, that's a relief!" said Dara. "Who's my new hero?"

"I'm about to tell you, but first I want you to remember three things."

"What?"

"One, I always have your best interests at heart; two, this was the only person I could find to take her; and three, I'm still lying helpless in a hospital room."

"Reggie, who has Mallory?" she asked with growing concern.

"It's someone I became friendly with after you left for Connecticut."

"That was only yesterday."

"It's someone who loves animals and who felt sympathetic for your loss."

"Reggie, I'm really not in the mood to play guessing games when my baby's life is hanging in the balance."

"Her life's not hanging in the balance," he assured her. "It's hanging out over at Nick Wyatt's condo."

"Nick Wyatt?!" she screamed. Then she put her hand over her mouth for fear of waking her mother. "Are you crazy?" she seethed more quietly.

"I told you I became friends with him. He's really a nice guy. I promise."

"What do you mean you became friends with him?"

"Well, if you must know, I saw how genuinely kind he was to you after you found out about Bill, and I realized that he's a good guy—someone I could reason with. Turns out, I think I was right. We went out for a couple of beers last night, and—"

"How could you do something like that behind my back?"

"Come on, behind your back is the only way to do something like that."

"So you have a beer with the guy, and you think it's okay to just drop my baby at his house? He could be an animal abuser for all you know!"

"He loves animals. His dog died recently, he even got choked up about it."

"Oh, well then, by all means hand my daughter over to him."

"Your daughter?"

"Adopted daughter."

"Okay, this conversation is getting really strange. Suffice it to say, she's in good hands, and this could afford us the opportunity to get out of this whole legal jam."

"What makes you think that will happen?"

"Well, he's already considering the resolution I laid on the table."

"Who died and made you my attorney?"

"And it would only involve a small monetary payout—"

"Reggie!—"

"—mainly for his legal bills—"

"—I can't believe—"

"—he's thinking it over."

"—you did this!"

"I know you don't want to hear this, but it's for your own good, and believe it or not, Mallory's, too. I have his phone number, so you can call and check up on her, but it's late, so wait until tomorrow."

"Does Mike Blum know what you did?" she demanded.

"No, and you're not going to tell him. I'm waiting to hear back from Nick, and I'm not going to sabotage things by bringing in the big brass."

Dara was quiet for a moment, letting it all sink in.

"Harri, was your life in shambles before this phone call?"

"What are you talking about?"

"Just answer the question."

"Yes. So?"

"So maybe you've generally been on the wrong track. Why don't you let me take the reins for awhile? If it doesn't improve, I'll hand them back. In the meantime, you need to grieve and be with your family. Your cat is fine, and your business may be soon, too, so stop worrying."

"All right, on one condition."

"What's that?"

"You set Nick up with Skype. I don't trust him, and I want to see for myself that Mallory is being well taken care of."

"Okay, I'll make sure he gets set up tomorrow."

"Good."

"Are you okay now?"

"Of course not. Bill is gone, my mother's a mess, and my baby's in the hands of a money-grubbing jerk."

"I really don't think he's grubbing for money."

"Well, he's still a jerk."

"If you say so."

"I do. Now give me the jerk's phone number."

Twenty-nine

THE NEXT DAY, NICK SAT on his overstuffed couch staring in the direction of his fifty-inch television, which hogged a giant stretch of wall and floor space at the far end of his living room. He wasn't looking at the screen, however, but at the funny feline who sat in front of it, intently watching a fisherman reel a huge striped bass into his Viking boat. Her little furry head tilted slowly from side to side and humorous squeaks emanated from her twitching mouth.

He had to admit, in the last eighteen hours, the little fur ball had proved to be much better company than he'd expected. She cuddled with him in bed, purred when he petted her, played a mean tug of war with a shoe string, and didn't fight him for the remote. It wasn't nearly as bad as he'd imagined when Reggie had called him from the hospital. For a moment, as he listened to the sob story, his mind had conjured up reasons, both real and imagined, why he couldn't take her, but by the end of the plea, he found himself relenting, much to his own surprise and dismay. How could he say no to a man confined to a hospital bed? It wasn't like his calendar—or his home—was too full to accommodate a cat for a week or two. Apparently, they didn't need to be walked; you just put a litter box in your bathroom, and food and water on the kitchen floor twice a day. How lame would he have to be to screw that up?

Nick was secretly glad for the company and very curious to know how Ms. MateSearch reacted to the news. He would have loved to have been a fly on the telephone wire for that. As if on cue, his phone rang. He leaned over the coffee table and checked the caller ID but didn't recognize the number.

"Hello."

"Nick?"

"Yes."

"It's Dara Harrison."

Nick smirked, pivoted, and propped his feet up on the couch.

"Hello. How are you doing?"

"I've been better."

"Sorry again for your loss."

"Thank you," she said. "I'm going to be here a little while longer, but I'll try to get back as soon as I can."

"No emergency. Things are under control."

"How's Mallory?"

"She's fine. She's watching television."

"Has she been eating? Did she sleep okay?"

"Yes and yes. In fact, she slept with me. Every time I woke up during the night she was lying on a different body part."

"What?"

"Sorry, that sounded weird."

"I want to thank you for taking care of her. I had no idea Reggie was actually telling me the truth about being allergic."

"Deathly allergic."

"Evidently. Did he contact you about Skype?"

"About who?"

"Skype. He's going to send someone over later to set you up with tele-conferencing."

"What for?"

"For me and Mallory."

"You're going to teleconference with a cat?"

"It's just a picture phone, so I can see her for myself."

"What, you think I have her bound and gagged in the closet?"

"No. I just miss her."

"Uh-huh," he said suspiciously.

"Oh, by the way, she likes that animal channel," Dara informed him.

"We're watching the Fishing Channel. She likes that, too."

"Fishing?" she said. "We don't like fishing."

"Speak for yourself."

"Oh please," said Dara. "The only thing more boring than fishing is watching it on TV."

"Anyway…" said Nick, now getting irritated and hoping to rush her off the phone.

"Yes, anyway, I wanted to leave you my cell phone number in case of an emergency."

"I have it."

"And give you the number of her vet and the emergency hospital."

"Got those, too. Reggie's very thorough."

"Do you have enough food for her?"

"Uh-huh."

"Dry and wet?"

"Check."

"Okay, then," she said, beginning to relax. "Can I ask you a favor?"

"Another one?"

"Can you put the phone to her ear so I can say hello?"

"Are you kidding me?" he asked.

"No, I'm not kidding," she replied with annoyance.

"All righty then." He walked over to Mallory and held the phone near her right ear. "Okay, she's listening," he shouted while rolling his eyes.

Dara spoke and Nick could hear every word. "Hi, baaaby! It's Mama. I miss you, baby girl. I love you so much." She made smooching noises for a few seconds and he took the phone from the cat who was staring at it curiously.

"She says she loves you, too," he told Dara.

"Well, please take good care of her and I'll Skype you tomorrow."

"Can't wait!" he said.

"Bye."

Nick hung up the phone and shook his head.

Dara had to admit she felt some respite after talking with Nick. He didn't sound like the kind of person who'd be abusive or neglectful of her cat. In fact, she got the impression that he liked Mallory. Perhaps it was the visual in her head of the two of them watching television together—or maybe the note of normalcy and even kindness in his voice. Anyway, she looked forward to Skyping that information for herself.

The rest of the afternoon brought another deluge of visitors offering fond recollections of Bill, as well as platters of deli, baskets of bagels, homemade casseroles, and sugary desserts, none of which the immediate family had the appetite to eat. Dara willed herself to stay strong, even as she watched her mother wither behind a stoic façade while listening to story after story, memory after memory. Although she knew this would help with the process of grief, Dara repeatedly tried to change the subject. It always returned to the reason they were gathered there.

At some point, Uncle Martin, pragmatic though indelicate, asked Jackie what she planned to do with her life. Dara could sense her mother's overwhelming fear and wished she could come to her rescue, whisking her away from pain and death. Instead, she discreetly left the room.

Dara walked through the kitchen and headed for the back door, grabbing a long button-down sweater that hung on a nearby hook. She stepped outside into a backyard bordered by trees and evergreen shrubbery, which offered privacy from the neighbors. The yard's starkness mirrored her current world view. All the potted plants were gone, and the garden furniture was in the garage for the winter. Remnants of snow and ice clung to the barren oak tree. Although she could see her own breath, the air felt good. She inhaled it in gulps. She knew she only had a matter of minutes before someone spotted her from the living room windows and called her back inside out of concern, so she headed for the storage shed, a large, white wooden structure. She opened the door and stepped inside.

The shed smelled of citronella candles. It stored a mishmash of family items, like her niece and nephew's summer toys, a few bicycles, gardening tools, a barbeque, and cartons of Christmas decorations. She closed the door and maneuvered her way to a small step stool, opening it and sitting on the top stair. As she pulled the sweater tightly around her, she remembered when she helped Bill build the shed, hammering nails at his direction and helping him sand rough edges. It had been their summer project, something they'd worked on together every weekend, her mother bringing them limeade on breaks and checking Dara's fingers for splinters.

Bill loved to talk while he worked and share colorful stories from his life, beginning each one with the question, "Did I ever tell you...?" Dara would usually inform him when he was repeating himself—unless she wanted to hear the story again.

Her favorites were about his time as a singer in a fledgling rock band called The Zone. She could tell how passionately he'd loved it. She remembered going to a few of their performances and a recording session in a studio in Manhattan before he quit the band to start a business with her mother. Bill would regale her with tales, like the time they were called in a pinch to be the main act, replacing another bigger band that never showed up. That night The Zone earned its chops, as it had previously been merely an opening band. Dara imagined screaming girls, colored spotlights, blazing guitars, and the excitement of impending fame. She felt so amazed that this steady, sturdy man had once been so cool and exciting.

After Bill left the band, The Zone went on to have a few hit songs and to tour the country. She often wondered why he chose to quit in favor of what she considered a mundane life. She couldn't help but feel some disappointment that he'd given up his dream so easily.

Now Dara wished she could share her troubles with Bill, who had a knack for problem solving. Her mother would always become too flustered and worried to be much help, and the last thing she wanted to do now was upset her even more. She thought about the lawsuit, the *LA Times* article, and her upcoming humiliation on national television, but her despair went deeper than that—much deeper. Although she had denied wanting or needing any romantic attachments, her own common sense told her she couldn't and wouldn't sustain that state of mind forever. Seeing how her mother longed for her husband, and how her sister was comforted by hers, she suddenly felt more alone than she'd ever felt in her life.

"Oh, Bill," she said aloud. "I'm so lost...I wish you were here." Her eyes watered and a shiver went up her spine. She rubbed her arms vigorously and realized her hands were starting to go numb. She blew warm air into her fists, stood up, and looked around once more, letting her eyes travel over the vaulted ceiling with wood planks.

"I'm going to miss you so much," she said, hoping he could still hear her. Then she dashed across the lawn, and back inside the house.

❧ Thirty ❧

NICK FELT LIKE AN IDIOT waiting around his condo for Maxine to arrive. Not that he had any place else to go. It wasn't his day to work at the bike shop. He had no doctor or physical therapy appointments, and he'd already finished his workout. He made himself a turkey and Swiss melt on rye with mayo, sat down on his couch, and took a big bite. He was tempted to turn the television on but he'd promised himself he would cut down before his mind completed its journey to total mush-dom. Mallory was curled up on one of the leather easy chairs. She raised her head and sniffed the air.

"You still have dry food in there," he said to her, tilting his head in the direction of the kitchen. She stood up, stretched, yawned, and jumped from the chair to the couch to investigate further. "Nobody said anything about turkey sandwiches being on your diet."

When she was about a foot away, she sat down politely and just watched him eat. Nick took another bite, trying to ignore her, and a sip of water from a bottle. He glanced at her again. She was still eyeing him with those big baby blues. Nick pulled a piece of turkey from his sandwich. He held it out and only then did she sniff it with interest. After a few moments she decided against eating it and lay down on the couch instead. Nick looked at her with disbelief. "Cats," he said, shaking his head.

A minute later, his buzzer rang. Maxine was at the door with a plastic bag and a smile. He recognized her from his two visits to the MateSearch office—not the most pleasant association.

"Hi, I'm Maxine. We've met."

"Come on in," he told her.

"How's Mallory?" she asked, looking around for her.

"She's fine," he said, wondering if Maxine was doubling as Dara's spy. "See? There she is, relaxing on the sofa, safe and sound," he said, pointing into the living room.

"Hi, Mallory!" Maxine squealed. Mallory stretched and rolled around on the couch. Maxine went to rub her belly. "Wow," she observed, "cats usually aren't this calm when they're away from home. She must like you."

"I guess," Nick replied. *Or maybe she needed a vacation from her crazy owner.*

"Anyway, I brought the equipment," said Maxine, pulling a small round webcam and a headset out of the plastic bag. "Where's your computer?"

Nick led her to the alcove where his computer sat on a small brown desk. Maxine got down to the business at hand, downloading the Skype software and setting up an account. When it was installed, she hooked up the webcam and headset and told him he was all set to try it out.

"Do you know anybody else with an account?" Maxine asked him.

"Can't say I do," Nick replied. "Most of my friends aren't really into all this new computer gadgetry. We're more outdoorsmen," he said, trying not to seem archaic.

"At least you have a computer."

"Well, I'm not from the Stone Age."

"This is what you have to do when Dara calls you." Maxine explained the ins and outs of video conferencing and told him not to shut off the computer because it would disconnect him from his account. "And don't worry," she joked, seeming to read his mind, "she can't see you unless you're online!"

A few minutes later, Maxine kissed Mallory goodbye and thanked Nick again for being so cooperative in Dara's time of need. Nick gave a little smile and a wave as she left. Then he took a dish towel from the kitchen and walked back to his computer, eyeing the strange little webcam that now sat on top of it. *Can't see me unless I'm online, huh?* He flung the towel over the camera just in case.

Dara waited until it was nine-thirty on the West Coast to contact Nick. That was long past Mallory's breakfast time, so she figured Nick should be up. She went into the upstairs den, which Bill had used for an office, and with a lump in her throat, fired up his computer. Luckily, she knew his password by heart, since she had often used his computer when visiting. Her heart pounded as the monitor displayed his wallpaper. It was a family picture they'd taken a few Christmases ago. She closed her eyes and lowered her head. The pain and guilt of missing his last Christmas was so horrific, she swept it from her mind, taking a few deep, cleansing breaths. She plugged in Bill's webcam, and stretched his headphones over her ears. She was proud of how computer savvy he'd been, considering the generation from which he'd hailed. After a minute or two, she reached for the mouse and set Skype in motion.

Nick's computer rang several times before his face finally appeared on her monitor, hastily fitting the headphones into his ears. In spite of his befuddlement, he seemed genuinely amazed at the technology. "Hey, this thing really works," he said with a smile.

"Of course," she answered.

"Pretty cool."

"Where's Mallory?"

"I don't know. Last I saw she was sleeping in my laundry basket."

"Can you find her, please?" Dara asked impatiently.

"Sure," he said, removing the earphones and leaving the computer.

Dara used the opportunity to check out the room behind him. It looked like a warm, comfortable place, your typical bachelor living room— not far from what she had imagined, except for the pictures on the walls. She could make out some framed movie posters with signatures and action photographs of a man, most likely Nick, in various motorcycle shots. She was wondering how many women he'd impressed with the display when Nick entered the room with Mallory perched on his good shoulder like a parrot.

"Careful, she'll fall off," Dara scolded, until she remembered he couldn't hear her yet.

Nick sat down and Mallory, still on his shoulder, stared at Dara on the screen. He could see Dara's stern face morph into a smile when she saw the cat. She motioned him to put on the earphones and he did.

"Is that how you carry her around?" she asked, containing her annoyance.

"Sometimes. Why?"

"She likes to be held like a baby."

"Does she look unhappy to you?" he asked.

Dara ignored the question and asked him to turn his left earpiece outward so the cat might hear her voice. "Hi, Mallory! Can you hear me? Can you see Mama?"

Mallory stepped off his shoulder and onto the desk to more closely inspect the monitor with her twitching nose.

"Hi, sweetie! Do you miss me? How are you doing over there?"

Mallory rubbed her face against Dara's on the monitor, much to Nick's astonishment.

"I miss you too, baby!" Dara cooed. "Mama loves you."

"Hey, she really can see you!"

"Of course she can see me."

Nick stroked the cat's long, silky fur. "So how's it going over there?"

"Okay, I guess. You know…"

"Yeah, I lost my mom when I was eight and my dad a few years ago."

"I'm sorry." There was a moment of silence between them. "Eight years old? That must have been tough."

"It was—and my dad was always on a set, so it was just me, Annie, and Aretha most of the time."

Dara remembered the name Annie from the signature page of his contract and knew she was his sister. "Who's Aretha?"

"My nanny."

"Oh."

"So anyway…" he said, moving the call toward its end.

Dara, however, wasn't ready to disconnect. "So is that you in all those motorcycle pictures?" she asked, pointing behind him.

Nick glanced around as if he needed to check. "That's me," he confirmed.

"Where were they taken?"

"On the set of my show and a couple of movies I worked on."

"I never knew anyone who became a stuntman. What do you need to break into a field like that—besides a death wish?"

Nick laughed. "Well, some vehicle expertise helps. Cars, planes…I was the motorcycle guy. The guy they called in for the big jumps. I've been riding since I was fifteen."

"I see."

"And it helps if you know someone, too. My dad opened the door for me, and I ran through it. There's actually a lot of nepotism in this field."

"I suppose the mentality is passed down by generation."

"Mentality? I don't know why, but that sounds like an insult."

"No, I mean, it's just such a foreign concept to most people's thinking."

"Uh-huh," he replied, dubiously.

"So, besides your father and your obvious love of bikes, what makes someone want to risk his life on a daily basis?"

"Well, first of all, we don't look at it as risking our lives, even when it is. It's a job—a challenging and exciting job. Most people can't say that about what they do every day—except maybe cops and firemen."

"I suppose," she replied, "but they take risks to save lives."

Nick sighed, an uncomfortable look on his face. Dara was willing to bet that it had been a very long time, if ever, that a woman challenged his life's work instead of drooling over the stories.

"Look, I grew up on the set, hung around with some of the best stunt-men, the biggest stars… it was fun and I guess it was the natural course for me. What can I say?" he said, sounding a little defensive. "It's in my blood."

"So are you still riding these days?"

"Haven't been on a bike since my accident," he said quietly.

"Really? Aren't you supposed to climb right back on the horse or something?"

"Not if the doctors tell you not to."

"Oh."

Mallory's attention was clearly waning and she jumped to the floor.

"I guess she's through with the visit," said Nick.

"Okay. Bye, Mallory," yelled Dara with a wave. Nick turned his ear-piece back around to his ear.

"So, you satisfied?" he asked.

"What do you mean, satisfied?"

"You wanted to make sure I was taking good care of her. Can you relax now?"

"I am relaxed," she shot back.

"Glad to hear it."

"What time can I call you tomorrow?"

"Tomorrow? Is this going to be an everyday thing?"

"Is that a problem?"

"Well, I will be going to work tomorrow."

"How are you back at work?" she asked with surprise.

"It's a new job. I'm just helping out a friend at his bike shop."

"Oh. So what time do you get home?"

"I guess around four thirty—unless I stop at the supermarket or the drugstore or something."

"Okay, so I'll call at five and if you're not there, I'll just try you again every fifteen minutes or so," said Dara, having no intention of being brushed off when it came to her baby.

Nick sighed again. "Fine, I guess."

"Hey, it's too bad you can't just leave the connection on all the time so I can peek in and check up on her whenever I want," she said, not completely in jest.

"Yeah," he replied with sardonic enthusiasm, "that would be *awesome!*"

"Okay, I'm signing off," she told him.

Dara closed down the Skype program and stared for a minute at the picture on the desktop: Bill, her mother, Amanda, Andy, the kids, and her in front of their Christmas tree looking pleased as the punch they were drinking. Bill appeared so genuinely happy, so completely content, as if his eyes and smile were saying *I've had a good life. I'm a lucky man.*

Dara scanned the desktop icons, knowing there would be a great deal of important information there and wondering how her mother would ever have the strength to go through it. Bill took care of their finances, insurance policies, important contracts, all the things her mother didn't have the patience to handle.

A folder labeled Important Documents caught her eye. She considered calling her mother in to explore it with her, but decided she'd been through enough that day. Instead, she double-clicked the icon and brought up a list of files that included living wills; last will and testament; mortgage information; house, car, and life insurance policies; and a few other personal files. Did her mother even know there was a life insurance policy? She opened the file and skimmed the legal jargon before locating the amount of coverage he had purchased. Tears welled in her eyes as she realized that even from the grave Bill would manage to take care of the family to which he had devoted his life.

Later that evening Dara slipped on her robe and tiptoed through the hallway. Her mother's light shone from underneath her door, so she knocked.

"Come in," her mother said.

"Hi, Mom, can I talk to you about something?" she said. Jackie was in her nightgown, sitting up in bed. She was not reading and the television wasn't on, so Dara knew she had probably been staring into space, her new pastime. Her ivory comforter was pulled to her chest and a cup of tea cooled on the mahogany night table. Dara walked to the windows. One of the three shades was still partially open. She pulled it down and drew the floral curtains together before turning to her mother with a little smile.

"What is it?" Jackie asked.

Dara climbed into her bed and propped herself up on two pillows. "Did Bill ever talk to you about life insurance?" she asked.

"Probably. You know I always let him take care of that stuff. It was too hard for me to talk about those things."

"I know, but I was on his computer, and I found a file with some important forms."

"Yes?"

"There's a life insurance policy for us, Mom."

"Well, I guess I'm not surprised by that. You know Bill."

"Yeah, but did you know his policy paid out two million dollars?"

"What?" she asked, her face not able to register the news.

"It's true. I know how worried you've been about taking care of the business, the house...everything. I just want you to know that Bill made sure that, financially, you have nothing to worry about."

Jackie slowly began to comprehend the magnitude of the gift. Her expression went from shock to happy surprise to tears. She hugged her daughter and cried into the pink terrycloth of her robe.

Dara held her tightly and rubbed her back. "It's okay, Ma. It's going to be okay. You still have me, Amanda, your grandkids—"

"I miss him so much!" she said, grabbing a tissue and blowing her nose. "Even with the money, I don't know how I'll get by without him."

"But you will," said Dara. "I promise. We'll be there to help you."

"I know you will. You've been so strong for me, Dara Lynn," she said. "I know how much you loved him, and I haven't seen you have a good cry since you've been home. Don't think you have to hide your feelings on my account."

The words hit Dara strangely. Why hadn't she let loose her emotions? Was she just keeping strong in case her mother had another mental breakdown like the one she'd weathered three decades earlier? Or was she still in shock? Numb to the pain? In denial?

"Okay, Mom," she said because she couldn't answer her own questions. "I won't."

Thirty-one

"**I**'M GLAD HARRI'S NOT HERE TO SEE THIS," Reggie told Maxine after reading Amy Landry's article in the *Times*. He threw the newspaper down on Maxine's desk and said, "Burn it."

Maxine looked up at him quizzically. "I think that might be in violation of the fire code."

"I wasn't serious, Maxine. Just dispose of it, and if Harri calls, whatever you do, make no mention of it."

"Of course not," she said, shoving the paper into the pail beneath her desk.

As Reggie continued to his office, he wondered how the story would affect business. Normally, derogatory coverage was bad news all around, but from what he'd been observing in the media lately, any attention was good attention. He tried to talk himself into this particular line of thinking. Especially since only four of their members had shared their disgruntlement. Would it have killed that damned reporter to interview some of the happy clients? The only reference to them was from Dara's quote, and it seemed less than convincing in comparison.

To make matters worse, Shelby Gerard from the *Ophelia Show* had been calling, wondering when Dara would be returning from Connecticut. He had told her about Dara's stepfather's death and she'd expressed her condolences. However, her production deadline for the show loomed.

Reggie knew Dara had released Tony from his role as impending fiancé, but he did not tell Shelby about the end of their relationship. He decided to focus on damage control and make as many public relations calls that week as possible. Maybe by the time Dara returned to L.A., he could offer her a positive spin on the coverage. He was glad the article made no mention of Nick, even obliquely. That should put some of Nick's fears about exposure to rest. He thought about calling him to follow up on their legal discussion but decided that he'd give him some time to get to know Dara (and her trusty feline) on a more personal level first. He smiled with pride at how he had parlayed his brush with death into what could be his most brilliant public relations coup yet.

Dara's cell phone ring pulled her out of a dream about Bill's funeral. In it, she stood in front of the mourners, trying to speak but unable to form coherent words. She reached for her phone on the night table. The clock read two-fifteen, and she couldn't imagine who'd be calling her at this time of the night.

"Hello?" she whispered hoarsely.

"Sorry to wake you, but you said to call if there was anything important."

"Who's this?"

"It's Nick."

"Nick?" she said, willing herself awake. "Is Mallory okay?"

"I don't know. She's been coughing like she's going to vomit or something for the last couple of minutes, and I'm wondering if I should take her to the hospital."

"Put the phone near her and let me hear," said Dara, sitting up. Nick brought the phone near Mallory, and Dara listened intently to her cat hacking away.

"Can you hear it?" he asked nervously.

"Yes. It's probably just a fur ball. Get the Vaseline. It should be with her stuff."

"I was wondering what that was for. I thought you packed it by accident. Hold on."

Dara waited a few seconds until Nick was back on the line.

"Got it," he said. "What should I do?"

"Just take a small dab of it on your finger and spread it over her mouth."

"Are you sure?" he asked. "Is that healthy?"

"Just do it."

Nick followed her orders, and suddenly, Mallory stopped coughing.

"She stopped and she's licking her lips," he reported happily.

"Okay. That'll help ease the fur out of her. She should be okay now."

"She seems to like the stuff."

"She does."

"Learn something new every day. Do all cats do that?"

"I think so. Especially if they have long fur and are obsessed with keeping it clean."

"She does lick herself a lot."

"How is she now?" asked Dara.

"She looks okay. Uh…sorry I woke you."

"Don't be. I told you to call me, didn't I?"

"You did."

"Better than rushing her to the hospital when it wasn't necessary. Cats don't like going to the doctor."

"Who does?" said Nick. "My dog hated the vet, especially once he got really sick."

"Sick? With what?"

"Lymphoma."

"That's terrible. How old?'

"Twelve. He was great. Sometimes I even brought him to the set. One of the PAs watched him while I was shooting. I hated leaving him home alone all the time. The dog walker didn't spend enough time with him." Nick sighed before continuing. "You know they once used him as a stunt dog because the one they hired wasn't a strong enough swimmer. Grady swam like a fish, so we took him to a shoot in Malibu, and a star was born."

"What'd he have to do?"

"Basic stuff. Retrieve some floating clothes, solve the case, you know."

"That's so cute! I hope he got paid."

"Sure, got scale," Nick said. "Took it out in dog bones."

"That's a good thing about dogs. They can partake in your life outside the house. Cats don't like that kind of excitement. They're homebodies, but they sure are nice to come home to. I've only had Mallory for three years, but I'm pretty attached."

"Ya think?" he said. "I never thought that cats were as good pets because they seemed to just sleep all the time and didn't care if you were around or not."

"That's so not true! They play, they cuddle, and Mallory loves when I come home. You should see how she greets me at the door."

"I know, she greets me, too—and sleeps with me every night."

"Really?" she said with surprise.

"Yeah, and she likes to play and you can train her."

"Train her?" asked Dara with disdain.

"Yeah, I didn't know you could train a cat, but you should see how she retrieves her toys now. I taught her."

"She what?"

"I throw the toys and she brings them back in her mouth."

"She does not!"

"Oh, really? She also rolls over on command. I'll prove it to you tomorrow on Skype," he said.

"You trained my cat?" she said, aghast. "You're not supposed to train cats. Part of their charm is that they don't do anything you say."

"Well, Mallory does. You have to have more faith in her," Nick said, egging her on.

"Faith in her? Of course I have faith in her!" she said defensively. "I let her do reiki on me for God sakes!"

"Do what?"

Dara was sorry the words had slipped from her mouth, but now she had to acknowledge them.

"Reiki. Energy healing?"

"Come again?"

"That's right. My cat has healing paws. Didn't she ever put them on you and you could feel heat coming out?"

"So her paws are warm. What does that have to do with healing?"

"She can make migraine headaches go away faster than my prescription drugs can. That's what."

"And you think it's because she's doing…reiki?" Nick began to laugh.

"That's right. She's got a gift and I'm not afraid to admit it," she said, although she clearly was.

Nick continued laughing. In fact, he laughed for over a minute, wavering from chuckles to hysterics as Dara held the phone away from her ear and pursed her lips.

"It's not funny. I can prove it! Just ask my neighbor, Jesse," she said, knowing that doing such a thing would hardly help her case.

Nick was still laughing as Dara tapped the phone with her fingernails. "Excuse me. I think I'd like to get back to sleep now if that's all right with you."

"Sure," he said, trying to catch his breath. "Sorry. Couldn't help it."

"Please give Mallory a kiss good night," she said, eager to bring the humiliation to end, but as she hung up, she could still hear him laughing.

❧ *Thirty-two* ❧

J ACKIE HAD BEEN SAYING FOR DAYS that she needed to go to their hardware store to "tie up some loose ends." Amanda and Dara had kept her from the task knowing it would most likely prove upsetting. Her mother's persistence eventually won out and Dara agreed to accompany her the day before the store would open for business again.

Dara drove while her mother, strapped into the passenger seat, stared out the window. Dara sensed that although her mother's eyes were directed at the world around them, she was not taking in the view. Her focus remained inward, her thoughts clouding her vision as they had since Bill's death. When they arrived, Dara pulled into one of the spots close to the back entrance.

"Okay, Mom," she said, "let's do this."

The two women, wrapped in their winter coats, climbed out of the car. Jackie fumbled in her purse for the keys and unlocked the door. Inside, darkness surrounded them until Jackie flipped on the lights. While taking in the room, a wave of depression engulfed Dara. She half expected to find Bill tapping into the cash register or on a step stool fetching merchandise for his customers. She wondered where exactly he had keeled over and died, and then was glad she'd never asked. She really didn't want to know.

Jackie walked haltingly through the store, tears filling her eyes.

"What is it you needed to do?" asked Dara. Jackie only shook her head and ran her hand over Bill's desk, tucked away in the back corner. She picked up a picture frame that sat atop it and held it close to her heart. She squeezed her eyes shut, but tears escaped, trickling down her cheeks.

"I knew this was a bad idea," said Dara, walking to her side.

"No," her mother said, shaking her head. "I needed to come."

"But why now? It's only been a week."

"If I didn't come now, I don't know if I'd be able to come back at all."

"If that's the way you feel, maybe you shouldn't. You wanted to sell the store...Amanda and I could take care of that for you."

"Oh, Bill," her mother cried. "What am I supposed to do now?" Jackie collapsed into her daughter's arms. Dara held her, her own pain so acute she could not find any more words to comfort her mother. Instead, she guided her out of the store, turning off the lights behind them.

That night, after Amanda and her family had returned to their home, Dara brought her mother a melatonin and some hot chamomile tea. She escorted her to bed very early, hoping a good night's sleep might help her face the day ahead with a bit more fortitude. Afterward, Dara poured herself a glass of Cabernet and went upstairs. She sat in front of Bill's computer, placed the headset over her head, took a hefty swallow of wine, and rang Nick. She knew that her cat's little furry face might be the only thing to cheer her up.

Nick arrived at his condo, threw down his gym bag, and grabbed a bottle of cold water from the fridge as his computer began to ring. He walked to the desk, sat down, and pulled on his earphones.

"Hi. How are you doing?" he asked, seeing the exhaustion on her face.

"I've been better," she replied.

He thought about inquiring further but didn't want to pry. "I'll go get Mallory," he said.

"Okay, thanks."

A moment later, Nick was back with Mallory in his arms. He sat down, placed her on his lap and refitted his headset, one earphone turned outward. Mallory stretched her arms down over his knee and purred.

"She was playing with her feather toy in the bedroom."

"She loves that toy," said Dara, her expression lightening. "Hi Mallory!" she called with a wave. "You look like you've been working out," she said to Nick.

"Yeah."

"How's that going?"

"I do everything the doctors tell me to do, but as of my last appointment, I'm still in sorry shape. It may be wishful thinking, but I've been feeling stronger lately. Had a great workout today, and I've been sleeping better too," he added, realizing he hadn't had his nightmare all week.

Mallory stood up and lifted her paw to touch the screen.

"Awww, cutie! Remember me? Your Mama? How's she been doing?"

"Fine. She slept on my pillow last night, on my legs the night before. She seems right at home now."

"Well, she better not get too used to it!"

"You're telling me," he said.

"I was hoping to come back in a few days, but I may have to stay a little longer."

"Is something wrong?"

"My Mom. She's not doing well."

"Sorry," he said. "I remember how hard my dad took it when my mom died," he said, stroking Mallory's back.

"Can I ask you something?" said Dara.

"Sure."

242

"How long did it take for him to...pull himself together?"

Nick leaned back in his chair. "I'm not sure, I was pretty young. I remember it was a while, but his work helped him deal with it. Kept him busy, and he had his buddies around all the time."

"Unfortunately, that won't help my mother. She worked with Bill. In fact, we went to their store today, and she just...lost it."

"That's a tough one."

"I'm thinking maybe she should sell the place."

"Can she afford to?"

"Yes. They were planning on it in the next year or so anyway."

"And then what?"

Dara took a gulp of her wine. "That's the sixty-four-thousand dollar question—actually, a bit more," she muttered.

"How are you holding up?"

Dara shrugged. "It's really hard. I'm glad I'm not eight years old like you were."

Nick nodded.

"But that doesn't mean I don't sometimes feel that way," she added.

"I was a mess for a while," said Nick. "Even stopped talking, or so my sister tells me, but I guess I managed to block out the pain."

"Stopped talking?"

"Yeah."

"For how long?"

"I think around a month."

"Wow."

"Aretha got me really busy with schoolwork, sports, friends... and I came back to myself. In fact, after a few years, a lot of doors began opening for me—like God was trying to make up for what he took away."

"What kind of doors?"

"I don't know...everything I guess. Things I wanted just came easy," he said. "When I was sixteen, I was playing football, dating Gina Brooks, learning stunts, riding my Harleys...and later, when I started working, I had a good life—a lot fun, you know? I started performing some really advanced stunts and pretty soon, I got job offers all over the place. I was the guy they called in when nobody else thought they could handle it."

"So you really do have a death wish."

"That's why I earned the big bucks," he said with a humorous swagger.

"Well, money or not, I think it's crazy to risk your life like that."

"I was doing pretty damn good—until my luck ran out," he said, his smile beginning to fade.

"You survived a horrendous motorcycle crash and came out in surprisingly good shape. That may have been your luckiest day yet."

He shrugged. "Accidents will happen."

"How did this one happen?"

Nick drew in a breath before speaking. "Well, the jury's out on that one. I think the crew screwed up. They probably think I did. Either way, it happened, and I'm out of work."

"Hmm," she commented.

"What?"

"So oftentimes it happens that we live our lives in chains, and we never even know we had the key."

"Huh?"

"Profound, isn't it?"

"Where have I heard that before?"

"The Eagles, 'Already Gone.'"

"Yeah, that's it. Why are you reciting lyrics to me?"

"I don't know. They just came to me. Must be apropos. Happens sometimes."

"I was hardly living in chains! Are you kidding? I had a great life. People would kill for the life I had."

"And some might involuntarily die from it. Did you ever think that playing games with your safety was a desperate cry for help?"

"First of all, Madame Freud," he said, his voice growing stern, "I wasn't playing games, I was working, and second of all, why would I need to be helped out of a great life?"

"Why?" she asked as Mallory yawned and jumped off Nick's lap. "Well, first of all, you were clearly being used for your reckless nature."

"Reckless?"

"And second, what masqueraded as good fortune was more likely a shallow, empty existence. Hasn't anyone ever suggested that to you before?"

"Only jealous people."

"Don't be defensive."

"Do you really think I somehow wanted my life to turn into what it is now? Do you think watching TV, going to the doctor, cat sitting, and talking to you makes for an awesome life? Don't even answer. I know what you think. You said it in your deposition. I've become—what was it?—oh, yeah, a dour man looking to bring others down to my level."

Dara was quiet for a moment. "I'm sorry," she said.

"Why are you psychoanalyzing me?" asked Nick.

"I don't know. Probably because I don't want to confront my own quandaries, so I like to unravel everybody else's."

Nick welcomed Dara's sudden candor, a refreshing glimpse into this complicated woman.

"And another thing," he said.

"Yes?"

"Why do you talk so funny?"

"What do you mean?"

"You know, fancy words all the time. It's very…"

"Discombobulating?" Dara asked with a taunting smile.

"Annoying," he corrected with some irritation.

"Maybe you should brush up on your vocabulary," she suggested.

"Maybe you should talk like a normal person instead of a dictionary."

"I do—a normal, intelligent person."

"Anyway," he said, ignoring the implied slight, "I'm going to get in the shower."

"Okay, I'll speak to you tomorrow. Bye, my little Mallomar!" she called before the screen went blank.

About half an hour later, Dara's cell phone rang. It was Jesse. She pressed the talk button. "Hi, Jess," she said, her voice laced with fatigue.

"Dara Doll, I called your office and Reggie told me everything. I'm so-o-o-o sorry," he said, his voice brimming with sympathy.

"Thanks, Jesse. Are you back from your trip?"

"Yes, I got back this afternoon. Why didn't you call me on my cell? I'd have come back sooner to see you and take care of Mallory."

"I didn't want to ruin your vacation. You so rarely take them."

"But I feel terrible I wasn't there for you. How are you holding up?"

"I'm hanging in there. It's just such a shock."

"I know, honey. How's your mom?"

"Not good."

"Oh dear," he said, fretting. "Well, I suppose something this tragic is going to take some time to digest."

"How was your trip?" she said, trying to change the heavy mood.

"Oh, silly, I don't want to talk about that now. All I care about is that my best friend in the world is hurting. Do you want me to come out there to be with you?"

"No, no, I'll be coming back soon enough."

"Well, I can certainly pick Mallory up from that Nick guy. When Reggie told me he took her there, I almost died! *Our* Mallory, alone with that fortune-hunting brute! You must have been beside yourself when you found out!"

"It's actually not too bad, Jess. He's really good with her, believe it or not. I've been Skyping him every day."

"Really? I'm shocked!"

Dara laughed and said, "I know. Me, too."

"Well it's really no trouble—"

"I know, and I appreciate it. I know how much you and Mal love each other, but I don't want to disrupt her again until I come back and get her."

"Okay," Jesse said skeptically. "If you're sure that's the right thing to do."

"Yeah, thanks, though," Dara said, surprising herself. A few days ago, she'd have sent Jesse over to rescue Mallory as fast as his car would take him. Now she felt strangely at peace with the arrangement.

❧ Thirty-three ❧

REGGIE DREADED CHECKING HIS EMAIL lately. He'd been receiving more and more complaints from members who felt they'd been slighted or unjustly reviewed by other members. He was sure the *Times* article had spurred this new slew of grievances, and he had recently arranged for the company's most diplomatic employee, a young woman named Freda, to counsel such members. He instructed her to gently remind them of why they'd joined MateSeach in the first place.

A wave of relief washed through Reggie each time he confirmed that a disgruntled member had, in fact, signed his or her own contract and thus, had no legal recourse. Unfortunately, they could still resign from the service after six months, spread the bad word, and even talk to the press themselves. This left him with an uneasy feeling about the future of the business that he couldn't yet share with his grieving partner.

As Reggie sipped his diet Dr. Pepper from an ice-filled beer mug, he contemplated ways to quell the "troop uprising" before the taping of Ophelia's follow-up show. Now that Dara was coming up empty-handed on the romance front, he had to make sure the other challengers overshadowed her failure with their own blissful relationships, courtesy of MateSearch. Two of the couples seemed all set, but he was concerned about Serena. He wondered if she and Tony were still dating—or if there was someone new in her life? He decided he'd better find out.

The hours Nick worked at the motorcycle shop passed swiftly. It felt great to be back in his element. His colleagues were affable guys who shared his love for bikes and riding. They often joked, shared stories of rallies, and spoke reverently about life's discoveries during soul-seeking trips to places like Alaska or through the historical towns of Europe. Nick reveled in it all.

The restoration area where he worked was clean and bright, and he chose the music he liked best: his favorite Southland classic rock station. As Nick affixed custom ape hanger handlebars onto a Harley Fat Boy, the sounds of Led Zeppelin's "Over the Hills and Far Away" echoed off the tiled walls.

After finishing, he glanced at the clock, something he'd done several times that day. Usually he lost all sense of time while working on his bikes. In fact, he almost felt guilty taking a paycheck for it. But today, for some reason, he was itching to be on his way by the four o'clock quitting time.

Nick drove up Santa Monica Boulevard, happy he'd opted for an early visit to the gym that morning. With each workout, his cardio and weight training abilities improved, leaving him feeling stronger and more energized. As he rounded the corner of his street, he finally realized why he was so eager to get home. Was he going crazy? Was his social life so pathetic that the highlight of his day was a Skype connection with the woman who had helped demean him in front of a sizable portion of Los Angeles? He shuddered. But over the past week he had seen her vulnerable side and had gotten to understand a little bit about the woman behind the tough façade. He suspected Reggie was right. She wasn't a monster after all.

They'd spoken via Skype many more times, usually late into the East Coast night. Mallory would grow weary from their lengthy visits and curl up on a nearby chair or in Nick's lap. The discussions ranged from their pets to current events to favorite movies—but when their chat veered into personal relationships, he got a firsthand glimpse inside her heart.

"Of course I've been in love, hasn't everyone?" she remarked.

"Not everyone. So who was he?"

"A guy from college. Zach."

"Together long?"

"A year."

"So what happened?"

Dara sighed uncomfortably. "I guess he wasn't ready to settle down. I mean, we were pretty young."

"But *you* were ready?"

"I thought so."

"Were you devastated?"

"It was for the best," she said.

"Usually is," he replied, playing along. "Hey, I have a confession to make. I caught you on Ophelia."

"Really? Didn't know you were a fan," she teased.

"Yeah, sure," he replied dryly. "So am I allowed to ask about your…dating progress?"

"No."

"I didn't think so. Top secret, huh?"

"You'll have to watch the follow-up show like the rest of America," she said. "So I have a confession, too."

"Oh?"

"I know you used to date Adriana Norris."

"And how do you know that?"

"A little birdie told me."

"A little tabloid birdie?"

"Maybe."

"Don't you know that stuff is mostly gossip?"

"Gossip is usually based in fact. Are you telling me you two weren't an item?"

"I didn't say that."

"Aha!" she replied triumphantly. "So what happened between you?"

Nick sighed, wondering how to answer. "She wasn't the woman for me."

"When did you figure that out?"

"After she slept with my director while I was in the hospital," he offered matter-of-factly. "I guess I shouldn't have been surprised."

"Why not?"

Nick grunted. "You don't know Adriana."

"Actually, I kind of do."

"What's that supposed to mean?" he asked warily.

"I did a little research," she admitted.

"Research?"

"Curiosity got the best of me."

"And what did you find out?"

"Just that she seems to have a thing for *Stormcats* men. She dated Matt Everhart before you, right?"

Nick was uncharacteristically quiet. After a few moments he answered, his voice softer. "Yeah."

"Didn't that bother you?"

Nick didn't respond.

"Nick?"

"Matt was my friend."

"Your friend? Really? Is that why he handed his girlfriend over to you?"

"You know, you got a big mouth for a little girl," Nick said, suddenly turning angry.

"What are you getting so upset about?" she asked, genuinely surprised. "I figured you'd be used to all the tawdry Hollywood drama by now."

"Well, since you already think the worst of me, you might as well know. Adriana and I got together before she ended it with Matt. There. Have I confirmed all your sleazy thoughts about me?"

"You stole her away?" she said, digesting the news. "Well it's not like that doesn't happen all the time," she said, "especially in Hollywood."

"Yeah, right," said Nick bitterly. Suddenly, the memories of that time flooded back and forced the words from his lips. "But it shouldn't have happened to a good guy like Matt, who didn't know it was all a fucking game, who couldn't tell the difference between lust and love—and who decided it was worth shooting himself in the goddamn head over it."

Dara sat stunned, staring at Nick. "What are you talking about?" she finally asked. "It was an accident. It was a prop gun with blanks. Why would anybody—"

"Matt knew all about prop guns and blanks. We talked about stuff like that all the time. He was depressed. I knew it, and I ignored it for months because I didn't want to know. I didn't want to feel the guilt."

"But—"

"He knew the damage a blank could inflict at close range," Nick said with resignation. "He knew."

"God," Dara said, speechless.

Nick's eyes drifted from the monitor and into the empty air beyond it. "It was my fault," he said, somehow relieved to finally admit it aloud. "The way I was living my life…I guess it finally caught up with me."

Dara put her hand to her mouth. "That's why you crashed," she said, as if the pieces of the puzzle were finally coming together.

"People crash all the time."

"Not you. Not like that," said Dara.

He pursed his lips. "I was distracted."

"It's more than that," she said shaking her head. "You were punishing yourself, weren't you?" she asked hesitantly.

Nick looked at her, the acknowledgment on his face. "It's been a long day. I'm going to go now, okay?" he said.

Dara nodded. "Okay."

Before he could remove his earphones, he heard her voice again.

"Hey, Nick?"

"Yeah?"

"When you asked before…if I was devastated about Zach?"

"Yeah?"

"I was," she admitted, looking into his eyes before her screen went black.

Still thinking about that conversation, Nick walked into his condo. He had been astonished at having bared his soul to her, of all people. A purring Mallory greeted him, and he fixed them both a snack. Then he waited for the familiar beep of the Skype connection. When Dara didn't call by five, he turned on the television and ran through the cable channels. Nothing drew his attention, so he ran through them again, finally settling on an old sixties western. He wondered if it was one his father had worked on. The thought brought a sudden pang of loneliness.

Thirty-four

TAKING HER MOTHER OUT TO DINNER proved to be a bad idea. Although Dara chose a restaurant Jackie and Bill had never tried, the food was mediocre and the conversation one-sided. Jackie didn't speak and barely ate. When they got home, Dara took one look at her mother's exhausted face and helped her upstairs to bed. Then she took a hot shower, letting the stream rush over her neck and shoulders, hoping to relax the knots of tension. Afterward, she pulled on a pair of flannel pajamas and a robe. She was about to head into Bill's office to call Nick when she heard footsteps in the hallway and the familiar squeak of the hallway stairs. She slid her feet into slippers and padded after her mother.

"Hi, Mom," she said as she entered the kitchen, careful not to startle her.

"Hi," her mother said, glancing up as she poured milk into a small pot on the stove. She, too, was wrapped in a robe, her eyes red and puffy.

"You okay?"

"Couldn't sleep. I thought warm milk might help. Want some?"

"Does it really work or is that just movie mythology?"

"I guess we'll see."

"Add some for me if you've got hot chocolate."

"In the pantry," she replied. She added more milk to the pot and reached into the cabinet for another mug.

"Maybe you should have taken melatonin again," Dara said as she placed the cocoa on the counter. Her mother didn't respond. Dara opened the breadbox and found some chocolate Stella D'Oro Breakfast Treats. "It's almost ten P.M. Are we allowed to eat these?" she said, making a feeble stab at humor.

"None for me," her mother said, missing the joke.

The milk began to boil and Jackie filled the mugs, took hers to the kitchen table and sat down, while Dara scooped chocolate powder into hers and stirred. Then she joined her mother.

"If you need me to stay longer than next week, I'll call Reggie and work it out."

"No," her mother replied, now becoming more lucid. "You have a business to run. I know what that means. Besides, Amanda's only a few minutes away if I need anything."

"I don't like the thought of you here alone."

Tears welled in Jackie's eyes. "I keep hoping I'll wake up soon."

"I know. Me, too."

"I never thought I'd be alone again. At least not while I was ambulatory," she joked. "I always hoped I'd go first."

"Mom."

"It's true. When Bill came into our lives, I knew how lucky we were. You were so young, you didn't realize how hard things were for me."

"Yes, I did."

Jackie looked her daughter in the eye. "Maybe you had an idea, but he was...my savior."

"I know."

"I couldn't believe how my luck had turned. He was such a good man. I loved him, he loved me, and he loved my girls, too—more than you know."

Dara nodded.

"I only wanted the same for you and Amanda. I got my wish with her, but I'm worried about you," Jackie told her, knitting her brows together.

"You don't have to worry about me. I'm fine," Dara assured her, giving her mother's hand a squeeze.

"Fine isn't the goal in life. Great is the goal. *Love* is the goal," she said. "Bill wanted the same thing for you—the happiness we had. He was just more...subtle about it."

"What do you mean?"

"He may not have talked about your love life with you, but he put away money for your wedding."

"He what?" Dara asked.

"He even had something to give you on your wedding day."

"Really? What?"

"I'll show you," Jackie said. "Wait here." She returned a minute later with a small box and placed it on the table in front of her daughter. Dara looked at her and back down at the box before opening it. Inside was a lovely heart-shaped ruby and diamond pin.

"It belonged to his great-grandmother. His mother left it to him."

"It's beautiful," she said, lifting it out of the box and admiring how it sparkled.

"He thought it could be your something old. He told me it gains value with age like a woman does," she said, smiling at the recollection. She gave a little chuckle. "He said by the time you get married, you should both be worth a fortune."

That sounded just like Bill. Even as Dara smiled, tears began to fill her eyes. She blinked them away before her mother could notice. "He may have had a small point there."

Jackie looked directly at her daughter. "You know, Dara Lynn, there was nothing I could do to stop your father from leaving us."

"I know that! Why are you even bringing that up now?"

"Because things shouldn't be swept under the rug. Feelings shouldn't be swept under the rug. They only fester there."

Dara took a deep, labored breath. "I don't blame my father for what's happened or what hasn't happened in my life."

"I'm not suggesting that you blame him, but I don't think you've ever moved on from the pain. I think it's still affecting your life."

"Mom, lots of people are single at my age. It's practically an epidemic. Why do you think MateSearch caught on so quickly? Not to mention the fact that some people are perfectly happy being alone."

"Maybe. Or maybe they just think they are because they've never known true love and don't think it exists," she said. "When your father left, I was one of those people, but Bill proved to me that I was wrong. He tried so hard to prove it to you, too, but maybe you need your own Mr. Right to do that."

Dara looked down at her cup as if wanting to crawl inside it.

"Bill thought he could take away yours and Amanda's pain by adopting you, but he realized even that wouldn't heal you."

"Adopting us? What are you talking about?"

"Don't you remember?"

"Remember what?"

"Dara Lynn, we told you about it the first summer Amanda went to camp. You went hysterical."

"I what? I don't remember."

"You told me that if he became your father, your real father might never come back. You cried all night until we came into your room and told you he wouldn't pursue the adoption anymore."

It was coming back to her now. How could she have blocked out something as important as that? "Oh, my God, Mom. I completely forgot."

"It was traumatic for you. You weren't ready, and then we were afraid to broach the subject again."

As the momentousness of the event began to register, Dara shivered. "He must have felt awful. He must have felt so rejected," she said as tears slid down her cheeks. "How could I do something so horrible and not even remember it?"

"You were a child. He knew that. He still loved you. Why do you think he left the band when they went on tour?"

"To go into business with you."

Jackie shook her head. "No. He did it because he wanted you to see that he wasn't going to leave you, that he was here for the long haul, that he was going to love you like a real father—or in your case, better than a real father."

The wave of emotion rose so quickly inside her that Dara couldn't stifle it. She began to release sounds of anguish she didn't recognize as her own. Jackie jumped to her feet and bent down next to her daughter, holding her quaking body in her arms.

Nick lay atop the blue plaid comforter on his bed, fully dressed but barefoot. He turned his head and glanced at the digital clock on his night table for the umpteenth time—8:10. He was actually growing worried about Dara. She'd called every day for almost two weeks, and suddenly, nothing. He stared up at the ceiling, debating whether or not it was too late to try her cell. Mallory leapt onto the bed, climbed onto Nick's stomach, and sat down. He petted her while absentmindedly gazing into her eyes, and suddenly the answer dawned on him. He would call under the guise of another inquiry about his furry little roommate—although exactly what he'd yet to figure out.

Ten minutes later, he scooped Mallory off of his torso and reached for his phone.

Dara, already floating in the alpha state, barely heard the ringing. The two melatonin and one valerian root she'd downed an hour earlier to calm herself had taken full effect. By the fourth ring, fumbling in the dark, she found the source of the noise. She pressed the talk button and spoke groggily.

"Hello?" she said. Her nose was still stuffed.

"It's Nick. I woke you, didn't I?"

"Mmm."

"I have a question about Mallory."

"Is she okay?" Dara asked, fighting to become more alert.

"Yeah, yeah, she's fine. It's just that she...got into my turkey sandwich when I wasn't looking. It's okay for her to eat turkey, right?"

"She doesn't even like turkey."

"Ahh...maybe it was the mayonnaise she liked. That's not dangerous to cats, is it?"

"Not that I know of. Is she acting sick?"

"No. I just thought I should find out, you know, just in case."

Dara sighed, wondering why she was having this inane conversation in the middle of her herbal-infused stupor.

"Are you okay?" asked Nick.

"Why?"

"You didn't call today. That's a first for you."

"I had a rough night."

"You sound like you've been crying."

Dara couldn't reply.

"Want to talk about it?" Nick asked.

Dara, now pulled mostly from her funk, thought about what had happened that evening and suddenly felt sick to her stomach. Her eyes watered, but she found Nick's voice on the other end of the line soothing.

That someone seemed concerned for her state of mind and eager to listen comforted her more than she could admit. She needed a friend now—although she never would have imagined it would be Nick Wyatt.

As the tears flowed again, she sniffed and reached for a tissue.

"You *are* crying. What is it?"

"I guess it's just all hitting me today. I had a talk with my mother and she told me things...things I didn't know about Bill, things I didn't remember."

"Bad things?"

"Good things."

She blew into the tissue and dried her eyes, but they quickly filled again.

"I loved him so much—and I never really...let him in. He did everything for us. I know you don't consider me normal," she said, "but if it weren't for Bill, believe me, I'd be a whole lot worse." She took a shaky breath. "He loved us more than anything, and I could never appreciate that...and I don't know why that is, but I feel so horrible about it, and now it's too late," she said, breaking down again.

Nick waited quietly.

"Can you believe I forgot that he wanted to adopt me?"

"You forgot?"

"I was eight. My mother said I threw a tantrum because I thought if he did, my father would never come back," she said between sobs. Dara shuddered after blurting this out, remembering that the phone number and address of her birth father was still stuffed deep inside her purse. "I had it all right in front of me, and I was so damned stupid, I couldn't even see it! Bill was the best father I could have asked for, the only father I ever really knew, and I never told him how much I love him. I wouldn't even call him Dad. Oh, my God!" she wailed. "I never even called him Dad!"

260

Some time later, Nick sat on his bed staring at the telephone receiver he'd just set into its cradle. He wished he could take Dara in his arms, this crazy, vulnerable woman he'd come to know, and the thought jarred him to his core. He had searched for the right words to comfort her. None had come, so he'd listened as hers became a jumble of emotion—listened, as her heart spilled out across the miles. It wasn't until he heard her soft breathing on the other end of the line that he realized she'd fallen back to sleep, and he'd finally hung up. Nick walked across his bedroom. He scooped Mallory up off the armchair where she'd been sleeping, cradled her in his arms, and kissed her furry head.

Dara was cloaked in a cocoon of warmth when she felt someone stroking her hair. The motion gently woke her.

"Morning, sweetie, are you okay?"

"Hmm?" she responded without opening her eyes.

"It's almost noon. You must have been up all night."

"Noon?" she mumbled, her surprise evident through her sleepy haze. She stretched her arms and looked up at her mother through heavy lids. "Had a rough night."

"I know. I didn't mean to upset you, you know."

"I know."

"I've been thinking all morning about when you were little, how happy and peaceful I felt watching you with Bill—riding bicycles, building things, even just doing your homework. You had a wonderful relationship with him, closer than most."

"But I never told him how I felt," she said, her eyes growing glassy.

Jackie pushed a lock of hair out of Dara's eyes. "Bill was a very wise man. Just because you didn't say it doesn't mean he didn't know. Of course he knew, Dara Lynn. Love is palpable. He knew how much you and Amanda loved him, just like he knew I did."

"You really think so?" she said, wiping tears from the sides of her face with her palms.

Jackie nodded. She took her daughter's hand. "Your father caused you so much heartache. If you hadn't come back to me that time in college," she said, recalling her daughter's suicide attempt with an anguished face, "I never would have forgiven him. One thing I know is that Bill would never want to be the cause of any more pain for you."

Dara reached her arms around her mother's neck. Jackie hugged her, then pulled away to look her in the eyes. "And now, my darling, I think it's time you called the airlines and went home."

A few minutes later, after her mother had left the room, Dara climbed out of bed and retrieved her big black Coach purse. Unzipping the top, she fumbled through the contents until she found the fax that Claire had sent. She pulled out the folded up page and stared at it. Then, with absolute assurance, she ripped it to shreds.

Thirty-five

D ARA COLLECTED HER BAGS from the conveyer belt at LAX. It was almost eleven P.M., but Reggie was there to greet her with a smile and outstretched arms. She fell into them.

"I missed you, Harri!"

"I missed you, too. Thanks for coming out so late to get me, and thanks for taking care of everything. It really means a lot."

"Of course. What are partners for? How was your flight?" he said grabbing her large suitcase.

"I worked on some ideas for the newsletter. It felt good to get my mind on work again." She felt a warm breeze drift in through the automatic doors. "Good to get out of that dreary Connecticut weather, too."

Later, they circled to the airport exit in Reggie's Mercedes convertible, the top closed despite the mild L.A. winter weather, and found Sepulveda Boulevard. Deciding it was too late to catch up on work issues, they agreed to a complete debriefing the following morning at the office.

"So how'd Nick take to your daily calls?" asked Reggie nonchalantly, although he was clearly bursting to know if a friendship of sorts might be developing between them.

"Fine," she said.

"That's it? Just fine?"

"What are you angling for, Reginald?" she asked suspiciously.

"Nothing, just curious if he's still your arch nemesis."

"He took care of my baby, I can't exactly hate him anymore," she said, giving a modest assessment of their improved relations.

"Did you have long talks or just quick checkup calls to make sure Mallory was still alive and kicking?"

"We spoke for a while sometimes," she admitted.

"Really? About what?"

"Lots of things. Why do you care?"

"Well, considering my company is being sued by the man, can you blame me for being curious?"

She looked over at him and narrowed her eyes, knowing there was more to it than that, but she responded with a shrug. "I guess not."

"So?" he asked.

"So what?"

"Harri! What did you guys talk about? Personal stuff? Work? The lawsuit? Give it up, woman."

"Fine. We talked about Mallory, our families, his new job…life, I guess."

"Life, you guess?" he repeated as he glanced at her.

Dara remembered how she'd broken down the night of her revelation about Bill. She couldn't bring herself to admit just how much she'd come to value her talks with Nick, how their relationship had been transformed, not even to Reggie—not even aloud. She had to sort out what had happened between them. Was it the relative safety of three thousand miles and an electronic connection that made it possible? Her fragile state of mind? Or something else?

"Yeah, life," she said. "And death."

Reggie nodded as he turned onto the Marina Freeway.

"Did you discuss the case?"

"No."

"Really?"

"Really."

"Hmm," said Reggie. "That may actually be a good sign."

"Reggie…"

"I'm just wondering which way he's leaning."

"I don't know, and right now I really can't think about it."

"Well, he seems to have let the blustering wind out of your sails, any-way. I just hope you did the same for him."

She glared at him but decided to let the comment go.

"On another note, have you spoken to Tony lately?" he asked.

"No," she said with some surprise. "Why?"

"Just wondering. I checked, and he and Serena are still dating," he said, glancing over at her to gauge her expression.

"Really? Well, that's nice," she said.

"You're okay with it?"

"Of course. I wouldn't begrudge him a good time, but he is on the re-bound."

"And what if they make it onto Ophelia?" asked Reggie.

The question spurred a sudden twist in her gut; she smiled in spite of it. Besides, she knew that even if Tony stayed with Serena long enough to make it onto the show, they'd be broken up within a few months. She almost felt sorry for Serena. She probably had no idea she was dating a man who had once equated marriage to driving off a cliff.

"Well, the publicity might help his boat company. That'd be good," she replied.

Reggie shrugged his shoulders and pulled up to her condominium complex. He helped her upstairs with her bags, and stood outside her door as she unlocked it.

"Are you going to be all right tonight? You can always grab an over-night bag and sleep at my place."

"Don't worry. I'll be fine," she said. "I'm picking up Mallory first thing tomorrow, so I'll be into the office around ten."

"Sounds good," Reggie said, giving her a kiss on the cheek. "Glad to have you back, Harri," he said as he headed for the elevator.

Butterflies danced in Dara's stomach as she drove her car toward Nick's home the next morning. She recalled all the personal things they'd shared long distance, the confessions, the pain, and the tears. She felt embarrassed for having bared her soul to him. How would it feel to see him in the flesh again?

Dara found his apartment and knocked twice. Nick answered it clad in a black Harley T-shirt, worn light blue jeans, and no shoes. He smiled.

"Good morning," she said, looking up at him.

"Morning," he replied, motioning her in. "How was your trip back?"

"Fine, thanks," she replied as she looked around the apartment. Mallory, hearing her voice, came running in from the bedroom. "Mallory!" she exclaimed, running toward the cat with a big smile. Dara picked her up, furiously kissing her fuzzy face. "I missed you so much! How are you, baby girl?" she said, rubbing her face into her long, silky fur. Mallory purred. Nick stood back and watched them.

"Hey, I keep forgetting to show you," he said.

"What?"

"Put Mallory down for a minute."

Dara reluctantly placed the cat on the carpet.

"Mallory?" Nick called, getting the cat's full attention. "Roll over!" he said, gesturing with a winding motion of his arm. The cat immediately lay down and rolled from her left side to her right, revealing the long swirl of fur on her tummy. Dara realized her jaw had dropped when Nick began to laugh.

"Told ya," he said with a big smile.

266

"Oh, my God, you turned her into a dog!"

"You want to see her fetch?" he asked.

"No!"

"How about sit up and beg."

Dara's jaw dropped again.

"Just kidding about the begging!" Nick assured her with a wink. "Hey, can I get you anything to drink? There's coffee—"

"No thanks, I've got to get to work," said Dara, still looking curiously at Mallory. She glanced around the apartment that up until now had been merely an image on her computer monitor. It was cozier and more appealing than she expected. Mallory had probably felt right at home.

"I better pack up her stuff," said Dara.

"All done," he said, pointing to two large plastic bags on his kitchen floor. "That's the food, the dishes, and her toys. That's the litter box and litter, and her carrier is over there," he added pointing near the door.

"Couldn't wait to be off duty, huh?" she joked.

"No," he said with sudden seriousness. "I just wanted to have everything ready for you. Oh, almost forgot one more thing." Nick walked to his computer, picked up a bag and handed it to Dara. "It's the web camera and the headset," he told her. "I think my Skyping days are over."

"Thanks," she said, taking it.

Their eyes met in a shy glance as Dara's felt the butterflies twirling again. She picked up Mallory and put her in the carrier.

"I'll walk you down," Nick told her, slipping into flip flops and grabbing the two plastic bags.

They walked down the corridor in silence. Outside the building, the cool, dewy air sent a light shiver up Dara's spine. She put the carrier on the floor of the passenger seat and opened the trunk for Nick to deposit the bags.

"Thank you again for everything," she said as Nick slammed the trunk closed. "I'm...we're..." she said hesitantly, "in your debt."

He brushed off the idea and walked to the passenger side of the car. "Bye, Mallory," he said. He bent down and stuck his finger between the grates of the carrier. "It was nice knowing you."

Dara watched him. The coolness of his words didn't conceal the warmth of his tone. The big brute had grown attached to la femme feline. She found this knowledge surprisingly endearing.

Nick closed the passenger door gently as Dara walked to the driver's side.

"Bye," she said with a little wave as she got inside. She could feel him watching her as she strapped herself in and started the engine. After backing out Dara glanced in the rearview mirror to see Nick turn and walk back toward his condo.

Later that day, Nick was ushered in to his doctor's examining room by a nurse named Ginger. He visited the orthopedist monthly and was getting tired of hearing the same assessment time after time. His progress had been slow, incredibly slow, and neither of them knew why. Nick did everything he was supposed to do. Physical therapy, vitamin regimen, rest, but nothing much changed. Needless to say, his appointments had become a source of anxiety and disappointment. The longer he was relegated to the sidelines of life, the more frustrated he became.

After weighing him and taking his blood pressure, Ginger, a soft-spoken young woman with a cheerful disposition, told him the doctor would be right with him. Nick sat down on the crinkly, white paper that covered the examining table. He wasn't sure if he had been imagining it, but he'd been feeling stronger, more limber, and in less pain than usual. He hoped against hope that the doctor's examination might reveal some good news this time.

Dr. Lou Crawford knocked on the door and entered the room.

"Hey, Doc," said Nick.

"Hi there. How we doing this month?" The doctor took a seat across from Nick and placed his clipboard on the counter. He was a tall, gangly man with a balding head, wide-set eyes, a prominent nose, very long fingers—and a reputation as one of the top orthopedists on the West Side.

"Pretty good, I think," Nick replied. "I've been feeling a lot stronger."

"Well, that's good to hear. Let's take a look."

The doctor went through his usual examination, testing Nick's muscle strength, pain levels, and reflexes. When he'd finished, he folded his arms and stood over Nick, one eyebrow raised. "So what have we been doing differently this month?" he asked curiously.

"Differently?" Nick parroted. "I don't know. I've been working out more the last couple of weeks. Oh, and I started restoring motorcycles at my friend's shop. Don't worry, I'm not riding them—yet."

"Uh-huh, and what else?"

"What do you mean what else?"

"Nick," said the doctor, unfolding his arms and looking keenly at his patient, "the range of motion in your shoulder has drastically improved since your last appointment, and the swelling in your knee is almost nonexistent. Have you been taking some sort of new supplements I should know about?"

"No. Except for what you told me, maybe two Advil once in a while, that's really been it," he said, feeling new hope.

The doctor grabbed the clipboard and scribbled a few notes onto Nick's chart. Then he looked up. "It's just very rare to see such nominal improvements for so many months, and then such radical change in a few weeks, but I guess you must have turned a corner this month. I'm happy to say that it looks like you're finally on the mend, Mr. Wyatt," he said, squeezing Nick's good arm. "Whatever you're doing, keep it up, and I'll see you next month."

The doctor's words echoed in Nick's mind as he drove home. Was he really, finally turning a corner? What could account for the dramatic improvement? He considered the events of the last month: the lawsuit, meeting Gary again, his job at the showroom, the joys of cat sitting, and getting to know Dara in a whole new light. He was living life again. Maybe that was it. Maybe that was why he was finally on the upswing.

As he pulled into his spot in his garage, he eyed the tarp-covered mass against the cement wall in front of him. It had become so familiar that he barely noticed it anymore, but today it captured his attention. He got out and stared at it for a moment, his hand on his hip. Then he lifted the tarp to look at the turquoise and white Harley Davidson with custom-painted gas tanks and a shiny chrome frame. He dropped the tarp to the floor and ran his hand along one of the pipes. He felt a mix of longing and apprehension, excitement and dread. After a moment, he straddled the seat, his arms stretched onto the handle bars. He recalled the wind whipping through his hair, the roar of the motor, the liberated feeling he had always treasured. Inevitably his thoughts returned to that last day on the set, the horror of knowing he was completely out of control and headed for disaster. He climbed off, grabbed the tarp, and pulled it back over the bike once more.

Nick entered his apartment, and looked around for Mallory. His heart sank when he remembered that she was no longer there and he was all alone again. As stoic as he'd pretended to be about cat sitting, losing his new little friend had reopened the wound that Grady's death had caused. He hated the thought of having his bed to himself again; he'd been sleeping so well. Then he realized that since Mallory had come to stay with him, he hadn't dreamt about the accident—not once.

Nick sighed. He walked over to his computer and touched the spot where the Skype camera had sat, wishing it was still last week—wishing he could turn on his monitor and see Dara's face again. Suddenly, he knew exactly what he had to do.

❧ *Thirty-six* ❧

BEING BACK AT WORK HELPED clear Dara's mind of all the sorrow—at least for a few precious hours. She found the warmth and concern of her employees touching; many of them stopped in to pay their respects and offer their sympathies.

During an almost two-hour meeting, Reggie caught her up on pressing MateSearch business and finally informed her of the unfavorable *Times* article and the resulting rash of member complaints. Surprisingly, she was barely fazed, at least not the way she would have been before her trip home. Of course, Reggie helped soften the news with some new public relations successes, including two morning show appearances, an article in *Cosmopolitan* magazine, and a feature in none other than *LA Entertains*. It gave her a special kind of satisfaction that The Beast would know how she'd bounced back even bigger and better.

Dara made herself a cup of Chai tea, topped it off with a dash of milk, and headed back to her office. Reggie had done an amazing job of not letting too much work pile up. The last thing she needed right now was a paper avalanche. Sorting through her messages, she decided which calls needed to be made immediately, which could wait, and which were probably moot by now. Shelby Gerard had called several times, but Reggie said he'd given her an enthusiastic update on two of the challengers. He also finally broke the news that Dara was no longer seeing Al, who, quite conveniently, had moved on to the third challenger, Serena. While pondering the best way to deal with the pushy segment producer, Dara was startled by her phone's buzzer. She pressed the intercom button and heard Maxine's sunny voice.

"Hi, Dara. Mike Blum is on two for you. He says it's important."

"Thanks, Maxine. Can you please ask Reggie to come into my office?"

"Sure."

"Hi, Mike," said Dara after pushing the second button on her phone.

"Hi. How are you doing?" he said.

"I'm hanging in, thanks—and thanks for the flowers. That was very thoughtful."

"No problem. I know you just got back, but I have some good news."

"Well, that's always welcome," she said. Reggie entered her office and sat down. "I'm putting you on speaker, Reggie's here."

"Okay."

"Hey, Mike," he said.

"Hi, Reggie. I just got a call from Drew Johnson. He told me Nick wants to set up a settlement meeting as soon as possible."

"That's great!" said Reggie. "See, I know how to handle things," he whispered to Dara, who smiled back.

"I have no idea how we got so lucky," continued Mike, "and I don't think Drew knows either, but we better take advantage of this opportunity immediately."

"Of course," said Dara. "Set it up. I have nothing pressing in the next few days. You, Reg?"

"Are you kidding? Anytime, anyplace!" he said excitedly.

"I guess seeing you in distress at the deposition changed things," Mike speculated.

"Yeah, that was it," said Reggie, shooting Dara a conspiratorial look.

"Now, I don't know how much he's going to ask for, but just the fact that he's willing to settle means things should start calming down, so let's all approach the meeting with a healthy dose of good will, okay?"

Dara knew the comment was aimed at her. "Of course. Thanks, Mike. Let us know when and where."

"Will do."

As they disconnected, Reggie leaned back in his chair wearing a Cheshire cat grin. He propped his legs, one at a time, on Dara's desk, his fingers pressed together like a tent at his chest. "So how do you like the way Reggie handles things?" he said.

"Oh, great, so now you're going to get all bigheaded on me?" she said. "And get your filthy feet off my desk," she added with a smile.

"Harri, you're back!" he said. "Believe it or not, I missed you."

At eight that evening, Dara knocked on Jesse's door. She could hear the muffled musical stylings of Don Ho before Jesse opened it. He was barefoot and wearing a grass skirt, a coconut shell-inspired bathing suit top, a yellow lei around his neck, and a string of purple orchids encircling his head. He held up a pink lei necklace and Dara bent her head so he could place it around her neck.

"Aloha, Dara Doll!" he exclaimed, giving her a welcoming hug.

"Hey, Jess! I knew you were cooking Hawaiian, but I had no idea it was the theme of the night. I'd have dressed up."

"That's okay, honey. I wanted you to be comfortable. I just dressed to set the mood—and because I'm the hostess," he said, ushering her inside. "Besides, when the Gidget goes Hawaiian, she goes Hawaiian all the way," he sang, doing a little hula dance.

"I can see that! Mmm, something smells great! What's cooking?"

"Prepare yourself for a feast! Dinner is huli huli shrimp, coconut rice, and aloha sweet potatoes!" he said, licking his lips.

"That sounds awesome! I wish I was creative in the kitchen. I guess you have to step into the kitchen for that to happen," she said.

Jesse's apartment was a mirror version of hers; the similarities pretty much stopped there. While hers was calm and subdued in decor, his was kitschy and bursting with color. Several shades of purple, pink, yellow, and green splashed across the living room in the form of an elegant, old-fashioned chaise lounge, a high-backed couch with oversized pillows, two huge armchairs featuring embroidered art, a modern art-inspired coffee table, and large, colorful pop-art pictures in the vein of Warhol and Lichtenstein.

Dara followed Jesse to the couch. On the coffee table sat a tray with a pitcher and two blue and pink tropical glasses. Jesse poured the thick, white icy liquid from the pitcher into the glasses.

"This piña colada recipe is to die for," said Jesse, handing her one of the glasses and carefully clinking his against it. "To best friends."

"Cheers," added Dara.

They both took a sip.

"That's yummy!" said Dara.

"Sinful, isn't it? Stick with me," Jesse said with a wink. He put his glass down on a mango coaster, faced her, and gave her a solemn look. "I missed you, girlfriend! How have you been holding up?"

"I'm doing okay. It's a process—grief, I mean."

"I know, honey, and anytime you need a shoulder or a hug, I'm two steps away. Never forget that!"

"Thanks, Jess. Let's not talk about it right now. Let's talk about something more cheerful," she said as she placed her glass on a pineapple coaster.

"Of course. Well, I know I'm not supposed to share details with you yet, but if you haven't already guessed, my trip to Hawaii was amazing!

Luaus, Diamond Head, snorkeling, volcanoes, sun, fun...paradise! That about sums it up!"

"I'm so glad you had a great time."

"Yeah, Sal told me—" Jesse began and then gasped at the disclosure, covering his mouth with both hands. "Sorry, it slipped out."

"That's okay," Dara said calmly. "I'm just glad you both had a fabulous time and that you're getting along so well. That's all I need to know. I just want you to be happy," she told him, and abruptly her eyes filled with tears.

"I know you do, honey," he said as he put his arm around her shoulders. "You thinking of Bill?"

Dara shrugged. It hadn't been Bill in her thoughts. At that moment, she was feeling envious of Jesse—of his excitement, contentment, hopefulness—and that even he had managed to find someone special. Ashamed of her feelings, she swallowed them like a bitter pill and focused on the positive. "I really am happy for you, Jess."

"I know, and I want the best for you, too. Are you still seeing Al? He seemed nice."

"No, it didn't really work out."

"Oh, that's okay," said Jesse as he placed his hand on hers. "You'll meet someone else. Someone as endearing and wonderful as you could never stay single for too long."

"Unless you call a decade and a half too long. My mother does."

"Nonsense. Everyone finds who and what they need in their own good time. Look at me!" he said, pointing to himself with both hands.

"You're right," she said, wiping a tear from her cheek. "Here's to you and Sal!" she said with a smile.

"And here's to you and your Mr. Right—whoever he is!"

Thirty-seven

THREE DAYS LATER, AT DREW JOHNSON'S office on Wilshire Boulevard, Dara, Reggie, and Mike checked in with the receptionist, just as Nick exited the elevator and pulled open one of the double doors of the office. Nick and Dara immediately locked eyes. She gave him a Mona Lisa smile, almost involuntarily, and he nodded his head. Then he shook hands with Mike and Reggie, and the receptionist led them all into the conference room down the hall.

Drew entered holding a file and welcomed the group. Nick and Reggie took seats on the opposite side of the shiny wooden table from Dara and Mike. Drew sat at the head, opened his file, and clicked his pen. "So, it's nice to see everyone again," said Drew. "Dara, again, I'm very sorry for your loss."

"Thank you," she replied.

"And I hope this meeting will be a lot more productive than the last one," he said, glancing around the table.

"I think we all do," added Mike with a smile.

"If we can just let cooler heads prevail, I'm sure we can work something out that all parties will find amenable," said Drew with special attention to Dara and Nick. "So let's get started. My client has three items that are especially important to him, given his line of work and public persona. First and foremost, we request a retraction that sets the record straight on the lies Ms. James has perpetrated against Mr. Wyatt—a retraction that will be emailed to all MateSearch members. Second, we request his legal fees be paid in full by MateSearch, and third—"

Dara closed her eyes, hoping the sum of money would be in the realm of reasonable when, to her surprise, Drew turned in another direction.

"—we are requesting that MateSearch either do away with its Rate-a-Mate policy, or put in place a mechanism to ensure that lies about other members cannot and will not be tolerated, and that those who do blatantly lie will be exposed and forced to forfeit their memberships altogether. Now I know the details of such a policy may be difficult to work out, but if we see that Ms. Harrison and Mr. Dayton are making a good faith effort in this regard, we will give them a three-month deadline to implement the changes."

The room was quiet for a moment as Reggie, Mike, and Dara digested Drew's words with some confusion.

"Is that everything?" asked Mike.

Drew nodded as if he were a little surprised himself.

"So you're not seeking damages?"

Drew shook his head and looked at Nick, who leaned back in his chair.

"Okay," said Mike, perking up. "May I have a few minutes to consult with my clients privately?"

"Of course," Drew told him. He motioned for Nick to follow him out of the room, and they closed the door behind them.

Mike took a deep breath and looked at Dara. "I don't know what's gotten into Mr. Wyatt, but if you don't take this deal, I won't be held responsible for the consequences."

"Don't worry, Mike," said Reggie. "We'll take it! We'll take it!" He looked over at Dara nervously and said, "Right?"

Both men watched as Dara sat back and began twisting her chair back and forth.

"Right, Dara?" asked Mike.

"Well, I'm not happy about an outsider dictating internal policy to me," she said.

"Rate-a-Mate has been the source of practically all of our MateSearch headaches," said Reggie. "I'm all for figuring out a way to soften it up."

"It's also the reason why we're famous," she replied.

Reggie winced, afraid she might actually decline the deal.

"But…I suppose we can tweak things a bit so we never have to go through this nightmare again." Dara leaned forward and placed her arms on the table. "Of course I'll take the deal. I'm not *that* crazy!"

Reggie's wince turned into a smile, and Mike breathed a sigh of relief. "Okay, let's let them know," said Mike. He opened the door and asked the receptionist to send Drew and Nick back. A few seconds later, they entered and took their seats again.

Mike addressed the two men with a smile. "Mr. Wyatt, Mr. Johnson—looks like we have a deal!"

Nick glanced across the table at Dara, and she gazed back at him. They broke into simultaneous smiles as everyone else stood up and shook hands.

Dara had just bid Reggie and Mike goodbye in the parking lot and was unlocking her car door when she saw Nick walking briskly toward her. She wasn't sure why he seemed in such a hurry until he called her name. She pulled her car door open and stood waiting for him as a cool wind mussed her hair.

"Hi," he said.

"Hi. Is everything…copacetic?"

Nick chuckled. "That means okay, right? Yeah, sure."

"That's good. I was afraid you'd changed your mind or something," she joked.

"Nope," he assured her, sticking his hands in his pockets. "Just something I wanted to ask you."

"Oh, okay," she said.

Nick froze for a moment before speaking. "How does Mallory like being back home?"

"She's getting readjusted. I hate to admit it, but I think she may miss you."

"No kidding?"

Dara shrugged as if she couldn't imagine why.

"So listen," Nick said, getting to the point. "Now that this legal mess is coming to an end, I was wondering if...I could take you to dinner?"

"Dinner?" she asked, her stomach flipping over.

"Yeah, dinner," he said, looking down at her with a smile.

"Um, when?"

"I don't know, Friday night?" he suggested. "I know it's short notice, and you probably have plans—"

"Actually, I haven't had a chance to make many plans yet this week."

"So then..."

Dara took a deep breath to steady her nerves. "Yes, sure," she said, pushing the hair away from her eyes. "Let's have dinner."

"Great!"

They both stood there for an awkward moment.

"I'd ask for your number, but I already have it," he finally said with a wink.

Dara smiled.

"So I'll call you later?" he asked.

"Okay."

Nick nodded and turned to walk away. Then he suddenly turned back. "Hey, do you like Italian?"

"Sure. Who doesn't like Italian?"

"Right. Talk to you later," he said, unable to contain a burgeoning smile.

"Okay," she replied again, her heart racing.

As she watched him walk off, she slid into the driver's seat, shut her door, and released the breath she'd been holding.

For the next couple of days, Dara teetered between tempered excitement and abject fear. She could barely eat or sleep and was on edge at work. By Friday, Reggie had done enough tiptoeing around her. He walked into her office, closed the door, and folded his arms across his broad chest. Dara was in her chair, elbows fixed on her desk, and palms supporting her cheeks. Her work productivity had ebbed to a near stop as she stared blankly at her monitor, unable to focus on her contributions to this month's newsletter. She lifted her head and looked at Reggie. "What?" she asked, perplexed by his sudden appearance.

"No, that's my question."

"Huh?"

"I've seen you up, I've seen you down, and I've seen you nutty. I just can't figure what's going on with you the last couple of days."

"Nothing. What'd I do?"

"You've been distracted, timid, nervous—these are not your usual traits, Harri."

Dara had weighed the pros and cons of telling Reggie about her upcoming date with Nick but had decided against it. Now, however, she could no longer contain her feelings. She took a breath, closed her eyes, and blurted it out.

"I have a date with Nick tonight."

"You what?" Reggie said. He dropped his arms to his sides and took a seat in her guest chair.

"You heard me."

"And when were you planning to tell me this?"

Dara shrugged.

"I can't believe you've been holding out on me."

"He only asked me a couple of days ago."

"No wonder you've been such a wreck. This is huge!"

"Don't make me more nervous than I already am, please."

"Sorry."

"I'm scared to death."

"For you, that's a good sign."

"Why?"

"Because it means you like him—a lot."

"Well, I'm thinking of calling in sick."

"When?"

"Tonight."

"For your date? Are you crazy? You call in sick for work, not for a date with a hottie."

"I don't know if I can go through with it."

Reggie leaned toward her with a stern expression. "You can, and you will. You hear me?"

"Why do you care?"

"Because you're my friend, and I know what's best for you. You can't run forever."

Dara looked down at her hands, which now rested in her lap. "I'm having Zach flashbacks."

"I know he looks a little like him, but you can't hold that against him. It ain't his fault."

"It's not just his appearance, it's the Hollywood thing. I can't compete."

"Who's asking you to? He doesn't even do stunts anymore, right? He refurbishes motorcycles."

"Yeah, I guess."

"And the man's forty not twenty. I'm sure he's more stable than Zach."

"He's single, gorgeous, and a former Hollywood stuntman. How stable could he possibly be?"

"Okay, so he's had an exciting life. He's lived. At least he won't feel like he's never sowed his oats. He'll appreciate you."

"I'm no Adriana Norris."

"Come on. You're just as pretty."

Dara looked up at him dubiously and tilted her head to one side.

"Well *I* think so," Reggie assured her.

"That why I love you, Reg."

"So where's he taking you?"

"A restaurant his friend owns in Malibu."

"That sounds cozy. And what are you wearing?"

"I haven't decided for sure if I'm even going yet."

Reggie gave her a disapproving look.

Dara sighed and leaned back. "I've got three outfits laid out on my bed. Hopefully, they won't be covered in cat fur when I get home."

Reggie smiled. "That's my girl."

"I need a sedative."

"It'll make you too sleepy. Just have one glass of wine while you're getting ready. It'll take the edge off."

"Okay," she said, taking an uneven breath.

"And stop worrying. I know you don't remember, but dating can be fun if you're with the right person. God, I sound like a 1950s educational film."

Dara cracked a smile and reached for Reggie's hand. He stood up, walked around her desk, and lifted her up for a bear hug instead.

Thirty-eight

THE SOUND OF THE BUZZER startled her, making her spill some chardonnay on her vanity table. "Shit," she said as she grabbed a tissue and mopped it up. She had already checked and rechecked her hair and makeup several times. Now she hurried to her front door, glass in hand, and buzzed Nick in.

"Bottoms up," she whispered before guzzling the rest of the wine, wiping her mouth, and popping a mint. Then she paced in a small circle, repeating the mantra she'd devised that afternoon as her new coping mechanism: *No big deal, it's just a date. No big deal, it's just a date. No big deal, it's just a date.*

His sturdy knock catapulted her out of her trance, causing her to jump, her hand flying to her chest. She walked to the door, took a deep breath, and opened it.

"Don't you ask who it is before you buzz someone in?" he said with a smile.

"Why, are you dangerous?" she asked, ushering him in.

"You never know," he answered devilishly. "Nice place," he said, looking around at the spotless French country décor. He caught sight of Mallory sitting under a dining room chair.

"Hey, Mal!" he said, bending down. The cat trotted over and rubbed her head against his knee. He scratched her head and smiled at her. "I've missed you."

Dara bent down to give Mallory a head rub, too.

"Where are her toys?" asked Nick.

"Around. Why?"

"I want to show you how she fetches."

"Oh, please," Dara said. "How many times do I have to tell you cats don't fetch."

"I can prove it."

"Not necessary," she said, ending the discussion flat. When she stood back up, she felt lightheaded for a moment but was thankful for the glass of wine. It seemed to have stopped her hands from trembling.

"You look great," he said, taking in her black jodhpurs, high heeled boots, and emerald silk top.

"Thanks," she replied, her eyes discreetly roaming over him. He wore dark gray slacks and an elegant button-down shirt. She thought about offering him a glass of wine, but that would mean more alone time in her apartment, something she couldn't handle just yet. He seemed to read her unspoken sentiments.

"So, you ready to go?"

"Sure," she said, grabbing a fitted blazer and her Chanel evening purse.

"Bye, Mal," he said to the cat.

"See you later, baby," Dara added as they left.

Awkward silence filled the car for most of the drive to the restaurant, interrupted only by Nick's attempts at breaking the ice, and a Tom Petty CD playing over the car's speakers. Dara glanced over at him a few times, noting the differences between his and Zachary's facial features. Nick's nose was a bit sharper, his eyes larger, and his lips fuller. His hair was loose waves, not the curlier texture she remembered of Zach's. She almost hated to acknowledge it: Nick was actually better looking than Zachary.

No big deal, it's just a date. Her heart pounded a bit faster as they drove up the Pacific Coast Highway. She drank in the ocean breeze, hoping it might calm her. Ten minutes later, Nick turned left down a sandy beach road and pulled his car into a lot alongside a small, residential-looking building. They emerged from the car, and Dara could make out a sign that read Positano.

"I've never heard of this place."

"Best-kept secret in Malibu. They've been around since I was a kid. My dad used to take us here for special occasions," he said as he walked her toward the front door. The sun was beginning to set over the ocean.

"Beautiful, isn't it?" she commented.

"Yeah," he replied.

They stopped to take in the view, but soon she sensed that his focus had shifted to her. She looked up to meet his eyes and was surprised when her knees quivered ever so slightly.

"Shall we?" he said, pointing his head toward the restaurant.

Dara nodded, and together they walked toward the front door.

"Nicky boy, how are you? It's been ages!" said a stout, balding man in a dark gray suit as they entered. "You look terrific! Back to your old self again, eh?"

"Getting there."

"Johnny and Viola will be in later. I'll send them over to say hello," he said, his smile warm and genuine. "And who is this lovely lady?"

Nick introduced Dara to Charlie, the restaurant's longtime manager, who escorted them through a small, crowded bar to a corner table with a large window overlooking the beach and the crashing Pacific.

As they took their seats, Charlie removed the reserved plaque and handed them menus and a wine list. Then he looked at his watch and said,

"By my calculations, you have about another twenty minutes to enjoy the view. So what can I get you to drink?"

"Red wine sound good to you?" Nick asked Dara.

"Sure," she replied.

"I'll give you a couple of minutes to look that over," said Charlie as he left the table and headed back to the front of the restaurant.

Dara took a quick glance around the modestly sized room. Every table was either full or being set up for another party. Beautiful gold moldings decorated the ceiling, and small crystal chandeliers emitted a dim, romantic glow. Lovely paintings of European resort beach towns adorned the walls. She smiled and looked back at the man across the table who was now perusing the wine list.

"They have a really good Pinot noir from Oregon I once had, or if you like Cabs there's a bunch from Napa I like. I'm not up on the foreign labels."

"Either sounds fine to me," she said as a slender, olive-skinned man approached their table.

"Good evening," he said graciously, "my name is Adolfo. I'll be serving you this evening. Are you ready to order some wine?"

"Yes," said Nick. "We'll have a bottle of the Argyle Pinot noir."

"Right away, sir," said the waiter, taking the wine menu from Nick and heading off.

"When was the last time you were here?" Dara asked.

"A few months before the accident, when Annie was visiting. We usually come here when she's in town."

Dara wondered if Adriana had been part of the dinner party. She swept the thought from her head as she opened her menu and began to read.

"They're known for their gnocchi, but everything is great," Nick informed her.

A busboy came by and laid a basket of warm Italian bread on the table along with a small plate of salami slices, olives, ricotta salata, and shaved Parmesan. Nick lifted the long thin bottle of olive oil that sat on the table.

"Want some?" he asked.

Dara nodded, and he poured a small puddle of it onto her bread plate and then onto his own. Dara pulled a piece of the bread from the basket, ripped it in half, placed a bit of cheese inside and dipped it in the olive oil. She took small bites while gazing out the window at pink streaks over a darkening ocean. Nick folded some salami and cheese into his bread and took a hefty bite.

"I could live on this stuff," he said with a cheek full of food.

The waiter appeared again, placing two large wineglasses in front of them and presenting the bottle to Nick, who nodded his approval. The waiter uncorked it and poured him a sample. Nick took a sip and nodded again. Then the waiter poured for Dara and topped off Nick's glass.

Nick lifted his glass for a toast. Dara followed.

"Here's to...new friends."

Dara smiled and tapped his glass before they both drank.

"Good?" he asked.

"Very."

After they discussed the menu for a few minutes, Nick motioned the waiter over and ordered a Caesar salad for them to share, gnocchi in a pesto sauce for Dara, and chicken parmesan for himself.

Dara took another swallow of wine. "I'm glad to see you're feeling so much better. You're not favoring your leg anymore."

"I know. It's unbelievable that it finally seems to have healed. I couldn't get over that last hump for so long. It was driving me crazy. My doctor's amazed at the change from last month to this one. He can't figure it out."

Dara listened while nibbling on some more cheese. Then she looked at Nick. "Well, I can. That's easy."

"Oh, yeah? Why?"

"Mallory."

"Huh?"

"Mallory. I told you about her…gift. You thought I was crazy."

Nick smiled and gave a little laugh. "Yeah, right."

"Still don't believe me?"

Nick looked askance at her.

"Okay, I guess it's just a miracle," she said, her eyes widened in jest.

Nick considered the idea for the first time. Then he shook it off as ludicrous. "Did you ever think that maybe physical therapy had something to do with it?"

"Really? Then why didn't it work last month or the month before…or the month before that?"

"Things take time."

"If you say so."

Nick shook his head and smiled. "You're funny."

They fell silent as the waiter served their salad and refilled their wine glasses before moving on to the next table.

"So I was wondering, how come you don't have any tattoos?" Dara asked, out of the blue. "I thought all bikers had tattoos."

"Nice to stereotype, but I guess you're right. I don't like the way they look as they age. Kind of just become blue blotchy things. Besides, as a stunt man, I'd have to worry about covering them up when I double. Who needs the hassle?" he said, taking a gulp of wine to wash down the Romaine.

"Makes sense."

By the time their entrées were served, Dara had finished her second glass of Pinot. The knots in her neck muscles were beginning to unclench, and the nonstop worry machine in her head seemed to finally have taken a coffee break. Nick regaled her with some stories about Johnny and Viola,

Positano's owners, who had moved from New York's Little Italy to Malibu back in the seventies. She heard about the first time a movie star, Steve McQueen, had come to Positano on a busy Saturday night. Johnny had no idea who he was and told him to call ahead for a reservation in the future. He told her how Viola's entire family had moved West, one by one, and at one time accounted for the entire restaurant staff, from cooks to busboys. She also heard about their boys, whom they named Brian, Carl, and Dennis after the Beach Boys, the objects of Viola's musical obsession and the main reason for their move to Malibu.

"So what are their daughters' names? Rhonda and Barbara Ann?"

"Funny," he replied. "No daughters. The boys used to ride with me sometimes. Good guys."

Dara lapped up the stories while stuffing herself full of the most delicious gnocchi she'd ever tasted and helping him finish the bottle of wine. Soon, Nick looked over at the entrance to the restaurant and smiled.

"Speak of the devils."

A short, pudgy man with a mustache and thinning hair walked in with a slightly taller woman who had short dark hair and wore dramatic makeup. They were greeted by Charlie and continued on to the bar. Nick stood up.

"Excuse me for a minute. I have to say hello."

"Sure," she said, watching him stride across the dining area and into the bar while admiring his firm back end.

Nick was met with smiles and grand hugs from the couple. He pointed at Dara and they all turned their attention her way. She smiled and raised her hand in a little wave as Nick led them to her table.

"Lovely to meet you, Dara," said Viola.

"Welcome to Positano," added Johnny. "First time here?"

"Yes, and everything's delicious."

"Glad you enjoyed it, and thanks for getting Nicky out again. I was beginning to think he was becoming a hermit," said Johnny.

"Not quite," said Nick.

"You two must join us for dessert," said Viola. "Carl and Brian are meeting us here. Brian's been up north for the last month on a project."

"I don't want to intrude..." Nick started with a glance toward Dara. He seemed to be trying to gauge her thoughts on the matter.

"We insist," said Johnny. "It's been too long."

"We'd love to," Dara interjected, surprising herself and causing Nick to smile.

"Wonderful," said Viola. "Charlie's setting up a table for us right now."

Fifteen minutes later, Dara and Nick were sitting at a large round table with Johnny, Viola, Carl, and Carl's wife, Elena, when Brian entered with his children, a girl of four and a boy of six. Nick gave him a hug, then introduced Dara.

"These are my little monsters, Cammie and Jordan," said Brian.

"I'm not a monster!" said Cammie.

"I meant it affectionately, sweetie," said Brian, tugging on her long, sun-kissed braid. "Notice *he's* not denying it," he added as he tousled Jordan's fine, blond hair.

"Come here," said Nick to the kids. "The last time I saw you, you were fighting over a rattle or something. I can't believe how grown up you guys are," he said, hugging them one at a time.

"A rattle? That's for babies," said Cammie.

"Okay, so maybe it was a stuffed animal," Nick said.

"Was it Loopy the Elephant?" asked Jordan.

"I don't know, maybe," Nick said, lifting Jordan onto his right leg.

"I wouldn't fight over Loopy," said Cammie. "Maybe it was Cindy, my tiger."

"You have a tiger named Cindy?" asked Nick.

Cammie nodded.

"Come here, you little squirt," he said.

Nick lifted her onto his left leg and Dara suddenly felt an enormous pang rip through her heart. She quickly blinked away the tears as Nick cuddled the children.

"Hey, what about Gramma?" said Viola, holding out her hands.

The kids leapt off Nick's knees and ran to hug Viola.

"Fickle kids," Nick joked. He glanced at Dara and seemed to notice something wasn't quite right. "You okay?" he whispered to her.

"Uh-huh," she said, nodding.

"Having a good time?" he whispered.

"Yes," she said with a smile. "Very good."

A waiter balancing a tray on his shoulder approached their table and began placing a dazzling array of desserts in front of them, everything from tiramisu to cannolis, tartufo to Napoleons, and more. He took their coffee and espresso orders and left a bottle of sambuca and a bottle of Frangelico on the table.

Dara couldn't believe how completely at home she felt among this family. She found herself laughing and joking with them as if they'd known each other forever. They continued reminiscing about old times with Nick, but somehow she didn't feel left out. Their memories brought Nick's father and Annie to life for her, and she found herself discovering a whole other dimension to him—one that captivated her.

Sometime after her third bite of tiramisu, Nick took her hand under the table and squeezed it. For a moment, she lost her breath. How long had it been since she'd connected this way with a man? Had she ever?

No big deal, it's just a date, she reminded herself. *No big deal...yeah, right.*

Dara didn't have to wait long to see him again. After walking her to her door, he told her he was meeting his friend, Gary, and Gary's new girlfriend for lunch the following day. He asked if she wanted to join them. She hoped her smile didn't reveal her relief.

"Sounds good," she said.

"I had fun with you tonight," he said.

"Me, too. Thanks for taking me. They're great people."

"They liked you, too."

"How do you know?"

"I just know," he said, moving closer to her.

"Are you going to kiss me good night now?" she asked.

"Where did you get that idea?" he said, sweeping a lock of hair off her face as he gazed into her eyes.

"Just a wild guess."

His lips were warm and soft against hers and his body firm and strong. Her knees wobbled again, and she steadied herself with a hand on her door. He pulled away, leaving her breathless and wanting more. She looked up at him, and his eyes bored into hers.

"Want to come in for a minute?" she found herself saying, much to her own surprise.

"Yes...but no," he replied, slowly stroking her hair.

She nodded, understanding. "Where's the diner?"

"Hollywood."

"Why don't I meet you at your place tomorrow, so you don't have to drive so far out of your way."

"I don't mind."

"No really, it's silly. So what time should I pick you up?"

"I guess come by at around eleven."

She nodded again, her eyes sleepy, her smile tired but happy.

"G'night," she said, unlocking her door.

"'Night," he whispered as he watched her step inside and close it behind her.

Thirty-nine

"GOOD MORNING, REGGIE," Dara said. Her eyes were still closed while she held the receiver. "You have the patience of a fly."

"You're lucky I didn't call last night. I've been on pins and needles."

"What for?"

"What for? Remember, I was the guy who had to talk you out of calling in sick last night."

"Yes, I remember, and thank you. I had a great time."

"Yeah?" he asked excitedly. "That's a relief!"

Dara chortled. "You're such a worry wart."

"Me? You were practically catatonic in your office yesterday."

Dara opened her eyes for the purpose of rolling them and propped herself against her backboard. "A gross exaggeration."

"You really like him, don't you?"

"Reggie—"

"You can tell me."

"Sure I can. You'll have us sitting in a tree, k-i-s-s-i-n-g any minute."

Reggie laughed. "Okay, just the highlights. I deserve that much, don't I?"

"Okay, okay," she said, placating him with a synopsis of the evening from sunset view to family reunion.

"Did he kiss you good night, I hope?"

"Yes, he did."

"Did he stop there?"

"Of course he stopped there. What do you think I am, a slut?"

"Slut? You're practically a virgin again."

"Shut up."

"So when are you going to see him next?"

Dara glanced over at the clock. "In about two hours."

"You're kidding! That's great! Where's he taking you?"

"To meet a friend of his at some retro diner in Hollywood."

"Must be that place with the motorcycle on top of it. Cool. Wish I could come."

"Don't you dare!"

"Call me later, 'kay?"

"Okay, Reggie. You can finish interrogating me then," she teased.

Dara arrived at Nick's condominium and pulled her car into a guest spot. Nick met her downstairs, and together they walked to his car in the underground lot. Dara wore jeans, cowboy boots, and a sleeveless top. She carried a white cable sweater just in case. Nick was in jeans, boots, and a Harley T-shirt. As they approached his car, she noticed the tarp-covered motorcycle.

"So you kept one," she said.

"Yup," he replied, opening the passenger door for her.

"Can I take a peek?"

"Now?"

"Why not?"

"Okay," he said, sliding the tarp off the front end. "How's that?"

Dara moved in closer to get a better look. "Pretty hot," she said as she fingered one side of the gas tank. It was adorned with a lightning bolt and the word *Stormcats*.

"Yeah," he said with a smile, watching her.

"Are you allowed to ride her yet?"

"Yup. The doctor said it should be fine as long as I take it easy. Just haven't done it yet."

"What are you waiting for?"

Nick folded his arms across his chest and became thoughtful. After a moment he looked at Dara. "I don't know."

"How many helmets do you have?"

"Two."

"So…"

"What are you trying to say, blondie?"

Dara smiled and put her hands on her hips. "Why don't we take the bike to lunch today?" she said, spelling it out.

"Hmm."

"Come on, the longer you wait, the harder it is."

Nick rubbed his shoulder reflexively and tipped his head from side to side.

"It's a short ride, isn't it?" she asked.

"Yeah."

"So let's do it."

Nick ran his hand through his hair while staring down the length of the motorcycle. After a moment, he looked over at Dara who sported a childlike look of excitement on her face. "I'll run upstairs and get the keys and stuff."

"Okay," she replied happily.

While he was gone, Dara removed the rest of the tarp so she could get a complete view of the bike. Soon after, Nick returned holding two leather jackets and two helmets. He held the smaller jacket out for her. She took it and inspected it.

"So whose jacket am I borrowing?" she asked a bit suspiciously.

"My sister's. She keeps it here for when she's in town."

Dara put on the black jacket, lined with fringe. She had a little trouble closing it up. Nick came to her rescue, zipping it for her like a mother sending a child off to school. He stood back to admire his new motorcycle chick.

"Cute," he said, staring down at her admiringly.

She lifted her head and smiled.

"So when was the last time *you* were on a motorcycle?" he asked, folding the tarp and putting it in his car's trunk.

"Me? Oh...never."

He looked over at her with surprise. "Never?"

She shrugged her shoulders.

"So this'll be an experience for both of us, huh?"

"I reckon. Just please, no wheelies or anything, okay?"

He laughed again while locking his car, walked to the motorcycle, and climbed onto the seat. She watched as he ran his hands along the handlebars and got his bearings. He lifted the kickstand and slowly backed the bike out of its spot, rolling it into position for driving. "Let's fire this thing up," he said, turning the key and kick-starting the bike. The motor roared to life.

"Come here," he said.

Dara walked over to him, and he placed a white helmet on her head, fastening it under her chin. Then he put on his blue one.

"Ready?" he asked. "Climb on."

Dara lifted her left leg over the large seat. She snuggled up behind him and gingerly positioned her arms around his waist, waiting for him to check his mirrors. He turned his head and shouted over the thundering motor, "Here goes nothing."

The door opened automatically as they approached, letting a stream of sunlight shoot across the garage. Nick checked for oncoming traffic before driving out into the California breeze.

Despite the fact that she had to close her eyes in terror every time he turned a corner, Dara found the motorcycle ride invigorating. Of course the man she was straddling may have had something to do with that. She felt a special satisfaction in being a motivating factor in what was clearly an important moment in his life. She leaned her chin against his back and peeked around his shoulder for a view of what lay ahead. Traffic, luckily, was light on Santa Monica Boulevard, and Nick drove responsibly, using hand signals and not splitting lanes. Every once in a while, when they stopped for a red light, he'd reach back to touch her leg and say something clever like, "Oh, good, you're still there."

Dara sensed Nick's exhilaration—his inner wild child breaking free. They pulled into the diner's parking lot and she spied the motorcycle prop atop the building that Reggie had described. Nick pulled alongside another Harley and killed his motor.

"You come here often?" she asked.

"It's a big biker meeting place." He pointed to the bike next to them, "That's Gary's." He removed his helmet and turned around with a big grin. Dara released her arms from around his waist and took off her helmet, too. "My baby rides nice, huh?" he said.

"Yes," she enthusiastically concurred, climbing off and handing him the helmet. He kicked down the stand and climbed off, too. Then he locked the helmets in his saddle bag and they walked into the diner.

Nick spotted Gary waving at him from a booth about halfway down the aisle.

"Hey, we saw you pull up. I knew you couldn't hold out much longer! It's about time, dude!" Gary called.

Sitting next to him was a slender and pretty young woman in her twenties with short red hair, whom Gary introduced as Lily. She wore a black cut out top, and a big silver cross around her neck. Dara was sure she had had a boob job, as her breasts appeared to defy gravity and were disproportionate to her extremely tiny frame.

"Nice to meet you. This is Dara," Nick said as he and Dara slid onto the bench seat across from them. They ordered coffee from the waitress who appeared with more menus.

"So what finally did it?" asked Gary.

Nick pointed his thumb at Dara and said, "This one twisted my arm."

"Whaddaya mean?" asked Gary. "I've been twisting it for months now with no results, but I guess I'm not an adorable blonde."

"No, I can vouch for that," said Nick with a little smirk, tilting the metal milk container into the coffee the waitress had just poured.

Dara smiled at the compliment and opened her menu.

"They have great burgers here," Gary announced.

"I didn't have breakfast yet. I think I'm going for an omelet," said Dara.

"Me, too," said Nick.

As they ordered, Dara caught Lily stealing glances at Nick. It made her stomach twitch. Maybe she's just impressed with the whole Hollywood thing, she thought, giving her the benefit of the doubt. The men didn't seem to notice anyway.

"Lily and I saw a great show last night," said Gary. "Did either of you see *Love Over Easy?*"

"No, but I heard it was good," said Dara. She remembered that one of the challengers had taken a date there, and that Shelby was annoyed that the theater wouldn't let her film crew follow.

"So I heard you own a dating service," said Lily.

"Yes."

"Is that where you met?" she asked.

"Kind of," said Nick. He threw an awkward glance in Dara's direction.

"It's a long story. Next time," added Dara, unsure whether she wanted to share those details with this particular person.

"We met at Ruby's," Gary interjected, putting his arm around Lily. "It's a dance club."

"No one calls them dance clubs anymore, Gary. It's a club."

"Excuse me. It's a club—where people dance—mostly young people," he added with a laugh.

"So how's business?" Gary asked Dara.

"Great!" she said automatically. As she went into some detail, Lily began talking to Nick about his stunt career. It was hard to keep a conversation going with Gary while monitoring a parallel one, but she was determined. When Lily's polite curiosity turned to giggles and flirtation, she wrapped up the dialogue with Gary and redirected her attention to Nick. He was now sharing some of the highlights of his stunt career.

It was a look only a woman would recognize in another woman—the coyness of her smile, the way she tilted her head, fondled her coffee cup—and it made Dara's cheeks burn. Lily was coming on to Nick, and she wasn't afraid to do it in front of her, or even her own man! This was what she had dreaded about dating a man like Nick. Reggie would have told her to stand her ground—to put this little nymph in her place. She never wanted to be one of those women who fought over men. It reminded her of those horrid daytime shows where trashy exhibitionists forfeited any semblance of decency or privacy for a brief shot at fame. She wanted a man who wanted her, cherished her, just like she had advocated to the women of Los Angeles in her column for all those years.

Dara watched as Nick spoke about how much he loved working with Gary, handling the bikes and employing his creativity again. Nothing in his voice or expression should have fed her growing insecurity, but it didn't matter. Men like Nick were too in demand. Every woman wanted one, and in L.A., hot women were a dime a dozen. This was what she would have to contend with regularly. She didn't have it in her. She felt her high hopes about Nick begin to drain out of her faster than bathwater from a tub.

When lunch was over and Gary and Lily had driven off on Gary's bike, Nick turned to Dara.

"So, Graumann's is just a couple blocks from here. Want to take a walk of fame?"

Dara, having succeeded in depressing herself with self-manufactured problems, was less than enthusiastic but agreed anyway. They walked the first block, mostly in silence, and by the time they reached the second, Nick turned to her.

"Something wrong?" he asked.

"No," she lied.

"Yes, there is. I noticed it at the diner. Did someone say something to upset you?"

"I think Gary's very nice," she assured him.

"It was Lily, wasn't it?"

"What do you mean?"

"Let's just say I'm hoping Gary ain't in love," said Nick.

"Oh? Why would you say that?"

Nick stopped walking, took her hand, and pulled her in front of a souvenir shop. "I think you know why."

"Because she's too young for him?"

"That's one reason."

"Because she treats him shabbily?"

"That's two."

Dara folded her arms across her chest and eyed the Marilyn Monroe statuettes in the window behind his head.

"Because she came on to you?"

"That's the one I was looking for."

"You didn't seem to mind."

"Whoa. I was being polite. That's all. If you were paying such close attention, you'd know I wasn't flirting back."

"It's none of my business anyway."

"You're my date. Of course it's your business, and just for the record, even if she wasn't my friend's girl, and I'd never met you, I'd still have no interest in her."

Dara unfolded her arms and shifted her weight from one foot to the other. "Really?" she asked like a hopeful child.

"Really," he said as he watched the blood flow back into her face. "I'm happy you came with me today," he added.

"Me, too," she replied.

He took her hand again and they began to walk, but this time, he didn't let go. They walked over the star-shaped blocks that lined the sidewalk, glancing down at such names as Bud Abbott, Pat Boone, and Lionel Barrymore.

"And one more thing," said Nick.

Dara glanced over at him.

"Thanks for getting me back on my bike."

Dara said nothing, just squeezed his hand a little tighter.

Forty

S
HELBY GERARD HAD BEEN LEAVING MESSAGES for Dara
every couple of days. Now that she had added "Urgent" to her last
one, Dara knew she could no longer put her off. As soon as she got
to her office Monday morning, she shut the door, sat down at her desk and
called her. She still hadn't decided what to tell her, but one thing she
planned to omit was her budding relationship with Nick Wyatt. All she
needed was for Shelby to coax them under her lights for some awkward
and embarrassing video moments guaranteed to scare Nick off and ruin
any chance they had of developing a natural relationship.

"Dara!" Shelby said into the phone. "Thank God!"

"I'm so sorry I haven't gotten back to you, it's just that—"

"I know. I'm very sorry about your stepfather. Horrible news."

"Thank you. Things have been—"

"I completely understand. I hope you're on the mend now."

"Yes, I think so."

"Wonderful, because my producer is freaking!"

"Why? What's wrong?"

"Well, I've got plenty of footage in the can of the other challengers—
and by the way, I'm sorry things didn't work out for you and Al."

"That's okay. I hear he's been doing pretty well with Serena."

"Yes. I think we have our third success story there. But you, my dear, what are we going to do about you?"

Dara leaned her elbows on her desk and put her head in her hand. "I'm just happy things are working out so well for everybody else."

"But you're the one America is really curious about—the pretty, single owner of the hottest dating service in the West? They want to see *you* find love! And since you've agreed to take your own challenge, people are going to be riveted!"

"Shelby, I've just been through a lot. I'm sure America will understand that sometimes life gets in the way of romance."

"So tell me, have you checked your profile lately? Any new men hoping to meet you?"

"Actually, no," she replied. "I just haven't had the head for it."

"Do me a favor, honey. Do yourself and your company a favor, too. Get back in the game. You only have a couple of months to make this thing happen! Do you really want to go on the most-watched talk show in the nation and come up empty-handed?"

"Okay, Shelby. I'll do what I can."

"That's a girl! I'll be in touch."

After they disconnected, Dara thought about Nick. She couldn't rush things with him because of a television show and knew that even if she tried it would most likely backfire. So what could she do? Appease Shelby with some more phony MateSearch dates? Admit to the country that she was living proof her own service did not work for everyone? A few months ago, she would have done practically anything to save her company's face, but things weren't so cut and dried anymore. She had other important considerations now—one in particular.

Over the next few weeks, Nick and Dara spent much of their free time together. He took her swimming in Malibu, up the coast to Santa Barbara for horseback riding, biking on the beach path, out for elegant dinners at The Palm and to Michael's for Valentine's Day. They also took leisurely trips up and down the coast on his Harley, which helped Nick to feel more like his old self again.

The two became romantic and affectionate with each other, often ending their dates with a fully clothed make-out session; however, neither made any overtly sexual moves and, remarkably, both seemed perfectly content with that choice. They had discussed the importance of moving slowly, and had both agreed on it. With each date, Dara was surprised at how well she and Nick were getting on. It was as if a less uptight, more fun-loving version of herself had taken over her body, determined that her previous persona not screw things up. Whoever this calm, agreeable new woman was, she was grateful to know her.

Although she had balked when Reggie suggested that it wasn't too late for her to meet the MateSearch Challenge with Nick, she secretly entertained the notion, and still held out hope. She invited Nick for a home-cooked gourmet meal on Saturday night, under the pretense of finally expressing thanks for his stint as cat sitter. She enlisted the culinary aid of neighbor and top chef, Jesse, who by now was aware of her budding romance and had forgiven Nick his trespasses against her. Jesse had planned a sumptuous meal that featured a fine Bordeaux and a chocolate soufflé for dessert. He supervised her every move, but Dara prepared, cooked, and baked everything with her own two hands so she could, in good conscience, take credit when her guest offered his compliments.

They began preparing the meal at noon in order to allow for any unfortunate mistakes or forgotten ingredients and to leave her plenty of time to primp. By the time the clock struck five-thirty, she was in the shower. By six-forty-five, she was dressed comfortably in a sleeveless sheath dress with a delicate floral print and elegant slip-on sandals. She pulled a lacy, light blue negligee out of her closet and flirted with the idea of later excusing herself to "slip into something more comfortable," but reminded herself that she wasn't living in a Doris Day movie. She put the negligee back and closed the closet door.

Makeup done, hair blown into soft waves, and perfume strategically sprayed, she left the bedroom. In the kitchen, she set the oven alarm for eight-thirty as a reminder to bake the soufflé, and set the dining room table with a bouquet of flowers Jesse had picked out. She poured herself a glass of wine from the already opened bottle (at Jesse's suggestion, it had been breathing for the last hour) and took a sip. He was right, it had opened beautifully. She slipped a Sinatra CD into the stereo and sat down on the couch.

At five after seven, the buzzer rang. Dara took a deep breath, put down her glass, and walked to the intercom.

"Who is it?" she asked, remembering how he'd chided her for buzzing him in without question.

"It's your dinner guest."

"Can you be more specific?"

"Nick."

"I know three Nicks."

"You think you're cute, don't you?"

"What's the password?"

"You're gonna get it."

"No, that's not it. Want to try again?"

"Dara!"

She giggled while buzzing him in, and left the door ajar while she went to check on her hors d'oeuvres.

A minute later, Nick pushed the door open. He was wearing crisp-looking jeans and a black golf shirt, which revealed his now tanned and muscular arms. In his left hand was a videotape. In his right, a small box of Godiva chocolates.

"Do you just leave your door open for anyone?"

"Do you really want to bait me again?" she said as she walked over and gave him a peck on his lips. "Mmm, you smell good," she said. "Like mango or something."

"Mango? Must be my shampoo."

"Chocolates? For moi?" she said, taking the box with a big hungry smile.

"Oh and here, I told you I had it on video," he said, handing her the tape. "I inherited my dad's film library."

She took it and looked at the jacket cover. "*Now, Voyager.* You remembered," she said with a smile, referring to their Skype conversation about their favorite films.

"I figured we could watch it after dinner if you want. I never saw it."

"Sure," she said, placing the video and chocolates on a nearby table.

"Whatever's cooking in there smells fantastic," he said.

She smiled. "Thanks. I just hope it tastes as good as it smells."

She poured a glass of wine and handed it to him. Then they walked into the living room and sat down on the couch as Old Blue Eyes crooned about a "Summer Wind."

Nick sipped the wine, questioning if he should really be drinking. It had been an eventful and somewhat stressful day for him, so he'd swallowed a Xanax around four o'clock. When he still felt uneasy, he'd swallowed one more just before leaving his condo. In fact, he'd been feeling inordinately anxious ever since Dara had invited him for dinner. It was an invitation he had highly coveted, so he never expected this sudden bout of angst; it was so unlike him. He wondered nervously if there was something wrong with him. Why would any man feel apprehensive about getting closer to a beautiful woman who made him this happy?

Mallory trotted in from the bedroom. "She was sound asleep in the linen closet," said Dara. "Must have heard your voice."

"Hey there, stranger!" he called. She jumped up on the couch and sat down next to him. He put his glass down and lifted her onto his lap. He scratched under her chin, and she lifted her face to accommodate him, purring loudly.

"So what did you do today?" asked Dara.

"Well, this morning I played some basketball with a neighbor of mine who's been inviting me since I moved in. I finally felt up to it."

"Good. How'd you do?"

"Not too bad, considering," he said. "And this afternoon, Gary pulled me into his office."

"Uh-oh."

"He wants to open up another store—this one in Hollywood."

"Really? I guess he's doing well."

"Oh, yeah, and he wants me to run it and be half owner."

Dara put down her glass and looked at him. "You're kidding! That's great! Are you going to do it?"

"Well, obviously I haven't had much time to think about it, but it sounds like a pretty great deal."

"Fabulous!" she said as she grabbed the stem of her glass and held it up to him. "To your own business," she said.

"Wait a minute. I didn't say I was doing it yet."

"Okay, then…to a great business offer. How's that?"

Nick tapped his glass against hers. "That, I can drink to," he replied with a smile.

"So when do you think you'll be making a decision?"

Nick laughed. "You're excited about this, huh?"

"Of course. Aren't you?"

"Actually, I am. We're meeting Tuesday night to discuss the details. Then I'll have more concrete info to base a decision on."

Nick took a sip of wine and leaned back. "So you mentioned that you spoke with that woman from the *Ophelia Show*."

"Yeah."

"What happened?"

"The usual. She hounded me to get out on some dates and let her tag along."

"Does she know about me?"

Dara shook her head.

"Thanks for not subjecting me—us—to that whole circus. I think I've been through enough humiliation for a while." Nick caught himself. "Not that I'd be humiliated to be with you, of course. I meant the whole national television spectacle."

Dara sipped her wine and nodded half heartedly. "I know," she said softly.

"Hey, this is really good!" Nick said with some surprise after swallowing a mouthful of seafood risotto.

"Well, don't sound so shocked."

"I didn't know you could cook."

"Neither did I," she mumbled.

"Huh?"

"Okay, I admit it. I had some supervision, but I did all the work by my-self."

"What kind of supervision?"

"Jesse, next door. He's a gourmet cook."

"Ah, so you had a secret weapon!" he teased.

"Maybe, but I do everything else for myself. I just never liked cooking for one. It seemed like such a waste of time for a woman on the go."

Nick smiled. "It's okay," he told her. "I'm just glad I didn't have to choke some horrific creation down my throat while pretending to love it." He scooped up another forkful but before eating it he confessed, "You know, I found your MateSearch profile."

"What do you mean, found it?"

"I printed it out before you ended my membership. I thought it might come in handy sometime."

Dara put down her fork. "Really? For what, pray tell?"

"At the time, I was thinking for the case."

"You sneak," she joked.

"I never thought it'd be of interest to me…personally," he said, taking a drink of wine. "You know, you could learn a lot about a person from their MateSearch profile."

"Well, duh. That is the idea," she said as she lifted her wineglass to her lips. "So what revelations did you have?"

"Revelations? Let's see. Well, first of all, I had no idea I was dating a woman who could build bookshelves and install ceiling moldings. You'll be handy to have around."

Dara lifted her hands with a flourish, as if to take a bow.

"Oh, and you get extra points for copping to the fact that you once shoplifted a candy jaw breaker."

"I was seven, so I figured the statute of limitations must have run out on that crime by now."

"And as of yet, I don't think I've experienced one of your PMS breakdowns, so that was a surprise," added Nick.

"I've been careful to medicate."

"Thank you."

"You're welcome."

"I found it a lot more interesting to read all that stuff after getting to know you."

"Understandable. You have a frame of reference now."

"Yeah...so I could really use a breadbox for my kitchen. Your profile says that's your specialty."

"Yes, breadboxes are my forte. After dinner I'll show you mine."

"Ooh, that sounds naughty."

Dara giggled before turning the tables on him. "So I couldn't help but notice that *your* profile was a little nebulous."

"Uh-oh, here come the big words again. Do you mind translating?"

"Vague, you were very vague."

"That's because Annie wrote most of it, and she knew I'd kill her if she exposed too much."

"You mean your profile was filled out by proxy?"

Nick shrugged. "It's too late to penalize me, right?"

"Well, I guess I could let you off the hook if you fess up to something juicy I don't yet know about you."

"What do you mean something juicy?"

"You know, admit to some uncontrollable neurosis or something. Wait, you're not sciurophobic, are you?" she asked with concern

"What the hell is that?"

"Never mind. So?"

Nick put down his fork and took a sip of wine while pondering her question. "I hate to disappoint you, but I can't think of anything."

"Really?" she asked. "You have no irrational fears? No idiosyncrasies? No obsessions or compulsions?"

"Not that I know of," he said, scooping the rest of the risotto into his mouth.

"If you say so," said Dara dubiously, finishing the wine in her glass and pouring them both some more.

"Well, don't be disappointed. Don't you want a man who's neurosis-free?"

"Honey, there is no such animal."

"Such a skeptic," he said, chuckling. "That's one of the things I like about you, though."

Dara caught his eyes coyly. "Oh yeah? What else do you like?"

Nick leaned forward and smiled. "Let's see, I like that you're smart, funny, and deep down, a good person."

"What do you mean deep down?"

Nick laughed.

"Anything else?" she asked, fishing.

"You mean beautiful and sexy?"

"Jackpot—thank you."

They both laughed.

"I never knew what it meant when a friend told me his girlfriend was really his friend, too, someone he could talk to, feel comfortable with. I always thought it sounded kind of hokey, you know?"

Dara tilted her head slightly, listening.

"It's not," he continued. "It's nice."

She put down her glass and took his hand in the middle of the table. "It is nice."

It was obvious to Dara that her meal was a hit, just as Jesse had promised. If her own taste buds had deceived her, the proof was in Nick finishing two hefty portions. At her suggestion, he was now lounging on the couch, shoes off, Mallory on his lap. She finished clearing the table just as the kitchen timer went off, and she carefully placed the chocolate soufflé in the oven. Then she set the timer again and headed back into the living room. Nick had slipped his video into the VCR and was cuing up the movie as she sat down next to him.

By the time Bette Davis had morphed from frumpy, insecure spinster to lovely leading lady, Nick was lying sideways on the couch, spooning

Dara, who lay in front of him. His arm rested around her waist, and his body cocooned her in warmth. She felt perfectly content, a feeling so foreign to her when it came to men that she decided to allow herself the luxury of reveling in it.

She got off the couch only once during the movie in order to remove the soufflé from the oven. She put it on the counter and decided to serve it when the movie ended. Sometime later, after Bette uttered the iconic last line of the movie, "Oh Jerry, don't let's ask for the moon. We have the stars," Dara wiped away a tear that was winding down her nose and gently squeezed Nick's hand. "I know, kind of a chick flick," she said. "Thanks for watching it with me."

Nick didn't respond, so she carefully maneuvered a one-eighty-degree turn on the narrow couch and saw that he was fast asleep.

"I guess I should have picked an action film, huh?" she whispered to Mallory who lay curled on the couch back. Dara lay with him for a few minutes before rolling off the couch and heading for the bathroom. She brushed her hair and teeth, and wiped away the smudges of mascara from under her eyes. She went back to see if Nick had awakened yet. There were no signs of life, so she lay down next to him, figuring the movement might bring him to—no luck. His breathing was slow and deep, but happily he didn't snore. She began to stroke his hair—no response. She kissed him lightly, first on the cheek, then on his mouth—nothing.

"Nick?" she whispered. "Nick?"

She'd never known such a deep sleeper. It couldn't have been the one bottle of wine they'd shared. Dara lifted her head and stared curiously at his face. Was this really happening to her? She felt insulted. How could he fall asleep on her tonight of all nights?

"Nick?" she said, now using her full voice and stroking his face.

He wiggled his nose and turned on his back, but he did not awaken. This move forced Dara off the couch. She stood up and crossed her arms, staring at his sleeping figure. Then she lifted his arm about a foot off the couch and let it drop—still nothing.

Dara sighed. "Come on, Mal. It's just you and me," she said.

Mallory didn't budge.

"You missed him, huh? Okay, keep him company. I can handle two rejections in one night."

Dara pulled a summer blanket from the linen closet, which she spread over Nick's slumbering body. Then she covered the untouched soufflé in tin foil, before moping her way to the bedroom.

Mallory's leap onto Dara's bed woke her from a dream in which she was late for her own wedding. She opened one eye and spotted her cat walking toward her while licking what would be her lips, if cats had lips. She stopped when she got near the pillow, sat down, and began to wash her face with her right paw. Dara glanced over at her clock, which read eight fifteen. Thoughts of the evening flooded back and she remembered she had a guest passed out in the living room. Her door was still mostly shut, the way she'd left it. She sat up and rubbed the sleep from her eyes, sprang out of bed, and headed into her bathroom.

Since she hadn't removed her makeup the night before, raccoon eyes stared at her from the mirror. She removed the remnants with a cotton ball, washed her face, and quickly reapplied some light makeup to cover the early morning circles under her eyes and to give her cheeks a healthy-looking glow. She brushed and fluffed her hair, dabbed a bit of Vaseline over her lips, and slipped on her long, silky robe.

She slowly walked down the hall to the living room. Her stomach dropped when she saw the blanket, now nicely folded at the edge of the couch. She turned to check the kitchen, but she already sensed it in her bones. Nick was gone.

The emptiness hit her in the pit of her stomach. How could he just up and leave? Wouldn't a man who seemed as interested in her as Nick did, have knocked on her bedroom door? Whispered her name? Or even climbed into bed beside her for a morning cuddle? Was he that intent on avoiding any chance of physical intimacy? And if so, why? Could it be there was some truth in Palulah's assertions? She couldn't remember a time when a budding sexual encounter had been impeded by anyone but herself.

Suddenly, her thoughts turned angry. After all the toiling to prepare her gourmet dinner and the buildup of expectations, what Nick had done was just plain rude. *That's what you get when you pin your hopes on a man,* she thought. She felt the protective iron wall begin to rise over her heart again.

Dara walked into the kitchen. She scooped some vanilla coffee into her drip maker, added a bottle of water, and pressed the start button. She ran her hands through her hair—and then her eyes locked on the little table beside her front door. There lay the Godiva chocolates and beside them, a scrawled-on envelope. She picked it up and read:

Dara,

So sorry I conked out on you last night. My loss. Dinner was amazing and I liked what I saw of the movie. I woke up early and didn't want to wake you so I'm going home to shower and shave. I'll call you later.

Love, Nick

P.S. I fed Mallory breakfast for old time's sake.

Relief tinged with guilt flooded her body. The words, *ye of little faith,* darted through her mind. She smiled and reread the note. Then she lifted the top off the box of chocolates, fished out a round truffle, and popped it in her mouth. The chocolate ganache filling and dark outer shell melted on her tongue. She savored it for as long as possible before swallowing. A tingly feeling rose inside her, replacing the dread of a minute earlier and shifting her mood in a much more agreeable direction. She stepped into the kitchen and poured the coffee into a large, brightly-colored ceramic mug, humming a tune that—thanks to Frankie—had been in her head all night: *I've got you under my skin.*

❧ *Forty-one* ❧

"**S**O TELL ME AGAIN WHY you still haven't slept with him?" asked Reggie in disbelief, his elbow on the conference room table, chin in the palm of his hand.

It was time for their weekly catch-up meeting, which was supposed to be about MateSearch business but often veered into other more personal subjects, thanks to Reggie. Dara poked her chopsticks into one of the white boxes on the table and gingerly retrieved another helping of lo mein.

"The time hasn't been perfectly right, yet. That's all."

"You've been seeing him for what, like six weeks? And on a regular basis! It's just weird already. How long you going to make the man wait?"

"He doesn't seem to mind," said Dara, lifting her chin and slowly winding the Chinese pasta into her mouth. She just couldn't bring herself to admit she'd tried and failed to consummate their budding relationship.

Reggie furrowed his eyebrows while looking at his partner. He forked some egg foo young into his mouth and began to chew. "And you don't think that's weird?" he finally said after swallowing.

"Of course not," she said unconvincingly. "We both want to take things slow. There's no rush."

"You've been celibate for over a year. You told me he has, too. At this point, I don't imagine anyone besides the Amish would consider it rushing."

317

"Can we please talk about business?" asked Dara with annoyance. She poured two packets of sugar into her Chinese tea and took a sip. "This subject is getting very boring."

"Sex is never boring, unless, of course, you're not doing it."

"Business, please?"

"Okay, okay," he said. "First order of business—I think the fixes you made to the Rate-a-Mate component are excellent. Nick will be pleased we took his suggestions."

"Thank you. I hope the public doesn't think we're wimping out."

"We're going to implement the changes at the beginning of next week—and, don't worry, we'll still have an edge, we just won't have a lot of grumpy people calling us."

Dara nodded.

"And second—I hate to say it, but I think we need to discuss the Ophelia matter."

Dara finished chewing some spicy eggplant and sighed. "I know."

"Are you still against asking Nick to participate?"

"Yes."

"Why? Do you think he'll say no?"

"I think he'll probably decline the offer," she said uneasily. "Besides, I don't want to take any chances. Things have been going really well. The guy's been through a lot. He has a modicum of fame, a public reputation. I don't want to risk things by making him uncomfortable."

"I understand, but it's just too perfect. You're actually dating a MateSearch member, and it's going well!"

"Former member."

"Still, it's such a waste for MateSearch not to capitalize on the situation. Think how awesome it would be if the single owner of the hottest dating service around actually found love in her own backyard."

Dara rolled her eyes at the cornball sentiment, but deep down, she knew he was right.

"I know, I know. I'm seeing it all as a public relations victory," said Reggie. "It's not that I don't want things to work out for you guys, it's just that...well, like I said, I hate to see a perfect situation go to waste."

"Sorry. It's just off the table, so let's explore our other options."

Reggie gulped down some water. "Okay. Well, Shelby knows about your stepdad. We just have to let everyone know his death has affected you so deeply that you just aren't ready to date again yet."

"That's not fair. I'm not going to blame Bill. As upset as I am over losing him, it actually helped bring me and Nick closer. I can't in good conscience use Bill as an excuse."

Reggie pursed his lips. "All right, any other ideas?"

"Maybe I could just tell the truth. That I'm seeing somebody who's...camera shy."

"That sounds like a copout. Everyone else on the show is exposing their personal lives for all the world to see. You can't hold yourself above them. People will be pissed if there's a different set of rules for you."

"I guess."

"You know, Harri, you may just have to take your lumps."

"Meaning?"

"Just say you lost the MateSearch Challenge. Two—or possibly three—success stories are pretty damn good."

Dara put down her chopsticks and stared off into space dejectedly.

"It won't be the end of the world."

"I'll lose credibility."

"We can handle it. We're surviving Jesse and—what did you say his name was?"

"Sal."

"Yeah. Still can't believe it. I'm dying to look the guy up."

"Don't. I told you if we don't know anything for sure, we don't have to address the issue."

"Or we could just start a gay MateSearch offshoot."

"I've got enough on my plate right now."

"I hear you."

"Look, I put every dime I had into this company—not to mention my blood, sweat, and tears," she said.

"I know."

"What makes you so sure we can take the hit?"

"Not everyone watches Ophelia," he said, trying to sound convincing.

"Yeah, and the people who don't will probably get to read the magazine articles that will pick up on the story."

"I think you're suffering from delusions of grandeur. There are lots of things going on in the world that trump a story about the co-owner of a dating service, you know: wars, famines, terrorists, lewd political scandals."

"Just give me a few more days to exhaust all possibilities before I relent, okay?"

Nick's meeting with Gary went even better than expected. They talked for three hours over a Tex-Mex dinner, discussing money, location, business arrangements, and a host of other salient topics. By eleven o'clock, all the plans and figures were swimming in Nick's head, but one thing was clear: Bikers' Heaven was a great opportunity and he couldn't pass it up. He accepted Gary's offer and they toasted it with margaritas on the rocks.

Nick drove home tired but excited. He couldn't wait to tell Dara. He saw how happy she'd seemed at even the prospect. He got home, lifted his phone, and plopped down with it on his couch. She answered on the second ring.

"So?" she said. There was a smile in her voice.

"I hope you're free Saturday night because we're celebrating at the most expensive restaurant I know."

Carolina was a top-notch restaurant and dance club that was just as hot that Saturday night as it had been every weekend of the ten years since it had opened. Dara had read about the place in magazines but had never ventured there, because it conjured up visions of velvet ropes, long lines, and almost certain humiliation. Reggie was the only person she knew who had seen the inside of the place, and even he was cowed by it. He made sure Dara was adorned in the most up-to-the-minute fashions from head to toe before inadvertently bidding her good luck instead of goodbye. By that time, her excitement had turned to trepidation.

Tonight she would get a taste of what it was like to be part of the Hollywood "It" crowd, as she sailed to the front of the line on the arm of a Hollywood stuntman. Nick admitted that the place was one of his former haunts when he had worked on *Stormcats*. Some of the cast and crew had wrap parties and other celebrations there, usually on the studio's tab. Although his glamorous life had been on hiatus, the bouncer remembered him and clearly still held him in reverence, escorting the couple swiftly through the tall mahogany doors.

Once inside, it was like old home week. The manager, waiters, busboys, and coat check lady all greeted him like a long lost friend, some asking where he'd been, and a few who knew about the accident, inquiring about his recovery. They were led up a curved stairway to the top level, which featured a magnificent, elegant restaurant. It had high ceilings, long, diaphanous white curtains, archways and moldings, all reminiscent of the old Hollywood glamour and charm of the twenties and thirties. Dara shivered slightly, silently thanking Reggie for his fashion prowess. Her crystal-embellished, modified flapper dress perfectly coordinated with the décor. The place was already filled with beautiful people in impeccable dress, clinking champagne glasses, and spooning caviar onto blinis with dollops of crème fraiche. Dara and Nick sat at a table for two against a wall lined with gilded mirrors. The hostess handed them menus and then left them alone.

"You look amazing," said Nick appreciatively.

"Thank you. I didn't realize how beloved you are by the staff."

Nick laughed. "They get paid to kiss your ass here."

"If you don't get tossed out on it first. That's some security detail."

"Look around and you'll see why."

Dara gazed around the room and did a double take when she spotted Julia Roberts and her husband at a table across the aisle. She looked back at Nick with wide eyes; he smiled. Then he nodded his head discreetly toward a round table behind Dara. She nonchalantly turned her head to see Rob Reiner, Billy Crystal, and some friends laughing as a waiter poured them wine.

"Holy shit," she whispered to Nick.

He laughed. "Don't tell me you're still star-struck after all these years in L.A."

"Are you kidding? Of course I am. These are biggies! I was expecting some super hot teeny boppers I've never heard of from some television show I never watch."

"You'll get those here, too. I'd point them out, but I'm as clueless as you. I'm almost afraid to tell you this. We passed Ben Affleck when you were checking your wrap."

"What? No way!" she said, staring longingly toward the staircase.

"Too late, he was leaving," Nick replied.

"Blimey!"

Nick laughed as the waiter brought them a bottle of sparkling water and poured some of it into their glasses. Dara took a sip and opened her menu. When she spotted the prices, she nearly choked.

"Told ya," Nick said half under his breath as he scanned his own menu.

"How much did you say you have in savings?"

"At least enough to cover dinner," he replied with a wink.

"Awesome," she said, eyeing the smoked salmon and Ossetra caviar appetizer.

When the waiter returned, Nick ordered a bottle of Cristal champagne and the appetizer Dara coveted, for two. Then, out of the corner of his eye, Nick caught sight of a tall, burly man and an athletic-looking young brunette being escorted to a nearby table.

"Holy crap. T.J.'s here."

"Who?"

"A friend of mine from the set."

"Oh," Dara said, her stomach tightening. She seemed to have a visceral reaction at even the mention of the show. Thoughts of Adriana Norris and a bevy of other anonymous beauties darted through her head. *Stormcats* was a hazy but intimidating world to her.

"Excuse me a minute, will you?" he said as he pushed his chair out and put his napkin on the table.

"Sure."

Nick ambled over to T.J.'s table and put out his arms. T.J. looked up with surprise. He laughed as he sprang to his feet and hugged Nick, patting him on the back. She could just make out their boisterous greetings. T.J. had dark hair, brawny arms, a broad chest, and stood about six foot two. He pointed to his date and Nick shook her hand. Dara sipped her sparkling water as she watched them talk for a couple of minutes. Nick arrived back at their table just as the waiter approached with champagne and a free-standing ice bucket. He sat down and the waiter dropped the napkin back in his lap.

"Looks like you had a nice chat," said Dara.

"Yeah, they're going to stop by after dinner. He wants to meet you, and another friend of ours is downstairs, too. We'll have to say hi later."

"Sure."

The waiter uncorked the bottle, poured the bubbling liquid into old-fashioned champagne coupes, and placed the bottle back in the ice bucket. Dara held up her glass.

"Here's to your new life as business owner extraordinaire."

Nick held up his glass and she touched it with her own, careful not to spill any of the champagne over the sides of the shallow glass. A minute later, the caviar and smoked salmon platter arrived and they dug in eagerly. Dara piled chopped egg on top of the caviar and topped it off with crème fraiche. She gingerly maneuvered the blini into her mouth and closed her eyes, savoring it on her tongue.

"Mmm."

Nick eyed her intently. "Good, huh?" he asked with a lascivious look on his face.

She smiled with delight. "So what did your friend have to say?"

"Teej? Just shootin' the breeze. He asked me if I was coming back to work."

"And what did you say?"

"What do you think? I told him about the store."

"Oh," she said, trying not to look relieved.

"I think I shocked him."

"Why?"

Nick laughed. "I mentioned the rep I have in the business to you, didn't I? I was known as Mr. Adrenaline, because I'd come up with some really wild stunt ideas that nobody would do but me."

"Why's that?"

"I guess nobody else had the cojones. That's how I made a name for myself; why I was always in demand. I guess you could say it was my calling card."

Dara nodded as she wondered how much of that daredevil was still alive and well and yearning to break free from wherever Nick had banished him. The thought unsettled her, and she took a gulp of champagne.

As if sensing her unease, Nick took her hand on top of the table and smiled at her. "However crazy I was in the past, I'm only crazy about you now."

The words caught her by surprise. She lifted her chin, looked into his eyes, and smiled.

Blue velvet couches, overstuffed chairs and glass coffee tables decorated the downstairs lounge. Although situated on the far end of the bottom floor, away from the dance floor and the band, the area still buzzed with excitement. After dinner, Dara and Nick decided to take their coffee and cordials there so they could visit with T.J. and his date, Joanie, and Ralph and his date, a beautiful auburn-haired woman named Colette who had delicate features and what Dara immediately deemed a perfect body. The band played at a volume that required leaning toward each other's ears in order to be heard. The group drank cappuccinos, espressos, and sambuca-filled snifters garnished with coffee beans.

As the men talked shop, Dara made efforts to join in the women's conversation, which so far had confirmed Dara's immediate presumption that both of them were actresses. Joanie was presently a stand-in for a few of the female characters on *Stormcats,* where she had met T.J. Colette had been a body double for several famous stars and was up for a supporting role in a new series, something that intensely excited her. Neither of the women asked Dara about her own line of work once they established she was not in theirs, something Dara found even more curious than she did rude. As it turned out, she was not in the mood to discuss her business that night. Instead, she just listened and offered a stray comment or question as the women compared notes and exchanged verbal résumés. Occasionally, Dara stole a glance at her dashing date.

Nearby, Nick was getting caught up on the show's business and gossip, including the rumor that Adriana and her latest *Stormcats* flame were currently on the rocks, something that left Nick with an unexpectedly pleasant feeling. To his even greater satisfaction, both T.J. and Ralph spoke of the many replacements for Nick who had come and gone over the last year. It seemed Kenny, their stunt coordinator, had been spoiled by Nick's creativity and derring-do, and had proclaimed on more than a few occasions how much he missed him. He had also said he wished that Nick would drop his lawsuit against the studio so he could return to the set. Since Nick had done so, soon after settling the case with MateSearch, that wasn't a factor anymore.

Hearing this put to rest one of Nick's most fervent concerns: to what extent his professional reputation had been harmed by the accident and its aftermath. The men urged him to contact Kenny and let him know how well he was doing, in spite of his change in career plans. Who knew what could happen in the future? As good as it felt to have his ego stroked, all the information his *Stormcats* buddies shared with Nick was also stirring unexpected feelings of conflict. He began to wonder for the first time if his decision to open his own Bikers' Heaven had been hasty—or even worse, the result of the fears and insecurities that had emerged since the accident. Had he given up the stunt life too easily? Was he about to make a giant mistake about his future?

Nick looked over at Dara. He knew she was not in her element. He appreciated the way she made the best of the situation, and thought about how much he yearned to be closer to her in spite of his unusual apprehension. Then it struck him. He had let fear take over. Fear—something he'd never really met until the day of the crash—yet it had conquered not only his professional life, but his personal life, as well. An overwhelming feeling of shame rose up in him. He imagined what his father would say. Would he think him a coward? Would he feel he was dishonoring the Wyatt name? Nick took a sip of espresso and placed the cup back in its saucer. One thing was clear: He had an awful lot of thinking to do.

Dara felt ill at ease as Nick drove her home that night. It wasn't anything blatant that she sensed about him but rather a certain worrying distract-edness. The polite distance between them at that moment kept her from asking if he'd like to stay over again—this time in her bed. Once again, something wasn't quite right. She looked over at him again as he stared out into the night through the car's windshield.

"So how was it, seeing your old friends?" she asked, hoping he'd reveal some of the thoughts that seemed to be consuming him.

"Huh?" he said, snapping out of his trance. "Oh, nice. Kind of weird, but nice. Thanks for being such a good sport. I know it was supposed to be our celebration."

"Well, life is serendipitous."

Nick glanced over at her with a smile.

"That's some vocabulary you got, Professor."

Dara smirked at him. He turned his attention back to the road and to his thoughts. She decided not to probe further, figuring that when he was ready to share, he would. A few minutes later they walked to her door. All set to excuse herself due to fatigue, she was surprised and dismayed when he excused himself first for the same reason.

"Sure, I'm tired too," she told him. "Champagne crash, I guess."

"I'll call you tomorrow," he said, kissing her softly on the lips.

"'Kay," she replied, and went inside.

It was the first restless night of sleep that Nick had had in many weeks. He stared up at his bedroom ceiling, recalling the evening's events, and letting his mind travel back to the good times he remembered on the *Stormcats* set. He, Kenny, and the assistant coordinator Jimmy would dream up some breathtaking stunts over beers after the day's shoot had wrapped. With Nick's input, they'd come up with some of the show's most memorable action scenes, including a hair-raising jump off the Golden Gate Bridge, a motorcycle race around the steep, winding path of the Pacific Coast Highway, and an amazing scene where a cyclist and his bike precariously dangled from a Cessna. The team always knew they could count on Nick's expertise, his follow-through, and his nerve. He was damned good at what he did; he'd proven that to everybody. So maybe he had been too quick to bury his inner daredevil, as if he'd been killed off in that nasty accident last year instead of living to tell the tale.

Nick entertained the idea of sharing his thoughts with Dara, but he knew she wouldn't be able to give him objective advice. He was well aware of how threatened she felt by his past. Groggy and confused, he retrieved his old address book from his night table as soon as the sun came up, flipping the pages until he found Kenny's phone numbers. He left the book open to that page on top of the table, then turned over in his bed to salvage a few hours of sleep.

"Hey, Kenny, Nick Wyatt."

"Nick Wyatt?" the man at the other end of the phone line replied with surprise.

"Yeah, what's the matter? You forget me already?" Nick joked.

"No, didn't forget you, I'm just surprised to hear from you, that's all! How ya doing, buddy?"

"I'm doing good. I'm doing real good."

"Glad to hear it."

"I ran into T.J. and Ralph last night at Carolina. We were talking old times, and of course, your name came up."

"I'd be insulted if it didn't."

"So I wanted to give you a call, see how things were going."

"Things are going great. You know, I was just telling some of the guys how I hoped you'd be feeling better soon, so we could bribe you to come back."

"Bribe me? Really? With what?" Nick asked with a laugh.

"I don't know. Didn't get that far. After the accident, I wasn't sure what to expect. Man, I'm so glad you're doing better. It's a miracle, ya know?"

"Yeah, I'm the miracle man," Nick said.

"No, I mean it," he said seriously. "You don't witness a freak thing like that every day."

"Witness? Try being the victim!"

"You know what I mean."

"Yeah."

"Hey, it's so good to hear your voice. Whatcha been up to?"

Nick refrained from discussing his situation at Bikers' Heaven and spoke instead about his quiet life, his move, and his new girlfriend. Kenny offered up some *Stormcats* news, some of which Nick had already heard from T.J. After a few minutes of catching up, Kenny asked what Nick assumed had been on his mind for the entire conversation.

"So, you thinking about coming back at all?"

"I don't know," Nick hedged.

"'Cause I could really use you. These guys they're sending in don't have your expertise...or your balls, ya know?"

"Yeah."

"And did you hear? Adriana's a free agent again."

"Let's not go there."

"She asked me a few weeks ago if I'd heard from you."

"You're kidding."

"Nope," he said. "Anyway, Jimmy and I have some freaking great ideas—we're working on one in particular, but there ain't nobody we think can pull it off."

"Oh, yeah?"

"Am I piquing your interest yet?"

"Maybe."

"Sounds like Mr. Adrenaline may make a comeback."

"We'll see."

"Give it some thought. I got a budget increase. The studio finally figured out that the audience tunes in for the action, not the damn story."

"What story?"

"Exactly. So like I said, give it some thought, come down to the set. We'll do lunch," he said with a chuckle. "Talk things over."

"Okay, man. Thanks. Great to talk to you, Ken."

"Yeah, you too."

As he hung up the phone, Nick felt the familiar pounding of his heart.

❧ *Forty-two* ❧

NICK BARELY REMEMBERED DRIVING to work at Bikers'
Heaven Wednesday morning. His mind was so cluttered with
thoughts of how his conversation with Gary might go. He felt
terrible backing out of the deal after his friend had given him such a vote
of confidence; however, he couldn't deny the excitement he'd begun to feel
about getting back to his old life—especially now that he knew how
welcome he was.

Meeting Ken for lunch had cemented those feelings. Driving through
the gates of the studio and strolling around the set again revivified Nick.
This was where he belonged. This was what he knew. Now he realized
that being away from it all for so long had fed his insecurities. He'd only
given up on Hollywood because he'd assumed Hollywood had given up
on him.

Ken and Nick ate lunch at the commissary and discussed the current situation on the show. Ken told him that they had upcoming
shoots in Italy, France, and Spain the following season. Although
thoughts of leaving Dara for so long gave him pause, he didn't reveal his
concern. The show wanted him back, and he wanted back in. After
lunch, the two dropped by the set, and Ken urged Nick to get back on
one of the bikes to get the feel of it all again. Nick practiced some small
jumps and other minor stunts, thrilled to see that his skills and abilities

had never left him. He believed that with a little time, he'd be able to prove his expertise all over again, and felt amazed that he had no tightness, pain, or discomfort of any kind. It really was a miracle.

Nick managed to avoid seeing Adriana by keeping away from the soundstage on which she was shooting. Of course, if he came back to work, he'd have to face her some time. He thought about the last day he'd seen her. She'd come to visit him in the hospital, but had been too much of a coward to tell him she was already sleeping with their director. He'd found that out sometime after being released a few weeks later. His fickle ex had called and asked him to "be strong and please understand that these things happen," and "we really need to be adult about it."

Baffled and distraught, he'd hung up after assuring her he would accommodate her wishes. It wasn't until the next morning that he realized her affair must have been going on for some time behind his back, the way theirs had gone on behind Matt's. He never spoke to her again—and perhaps more surprisingly, except for the sex, he never really missed her.

Nick entered the Bikers' Heaven showroom feeling like a dog with his tail between his legs. He immediately told Gary he needed to meet with him as soon as possible, then buried himself in his current work project. At around ten-thirty, Gary called him into his office. It went better than he expected. Gary was clearly disappointed, but expressed relief that it happened before plans had gone any further. Nick apologized for leaving him, and told him he would do what he could do to help him find a replacement in the coming weeks.

Guilt plagued Nick the rest of the day, not just because of Gary, but because he'd been too uncomfortable to even discuss this sudden change in plans with Dara. He'd never consulted anyone about any decisions he'd made in the past, especially those related to his career. It felt too strange to suddenly start now—or maybe it was that he knew Dara had the power to alter his thinking and he didn't want to give her the chance.

Nick spent the rest of the day contemplating the best way to break the news to her. By the time he arrived home, he had his answer. He called and invited her over for an impromptu dinner. He knew privacy was called for with such a delicate matter. This, he hoped, would also give him the opportunity to advance their relationship to the next level. Dara would be upset, but he would explain how important she was to him, admit the depth of his feelings, and finally make love to the woman who'd helped bring him back to life.

Dara knew that Nick's request to have dinner at his home was actually a thinly veiled invitation to finally spend the night together—and this time in the same bed. She left extra food out for Mallory and packed a small overnight bag with toothbrush, nightie, some toiletries, and a change of clothing for the morning. Not wanting to let on to Nick, she left the bag in her trunk. When she got off the elevator on his floor and walked to his place, he was already waiting for her with a big smile, his door wide open. He grabbed her around the waist and kissed her, which surprised and delighted her.

"I missed you," he said, escorting her into his home.

"You did?" she replied with a demure smile as she removed her sweater and slung it over a dining room chair. "Me, too."

"Want some wine?"

"Sure," she replied. "What's cooking?"

"I confess, I only make, like, three things, and you're about to taste one of them," he said as he stepped into his kitchen and poured them each a glass of Syrah.

"And what would that be?" she asked, taking a seat on the living room couch.

"I grilled up some spice-rubbed shrimp on the barbie," he called to her, invoking his best Australian accent, "and I've got rice and mixed vegetables."

"Sounds great," she called back.

He walked into the living room and sat down next to her, handing her a glass.

"Any update on when the store might be opening?" she asked, taking a sip.

Nick looked down at his glass. "Uh, no," he replied uncomfortably.

"I guess it's kind of early for that, huh?"

He shrugged and took a drink.

"Anyway," she continued, "I'd like to take you up on your invitation to see Gary's store. At least then I'll have an idea what yours will be like."

When he didn't acknowledge her request she examined his face more closely.

"Nick? Something wrong?"

He sighed and offered a slight smile. "A lot's been going on this week."

"Really? Like what?"

"Well, I didn't want to get into it over the phone."

Dara instantly shifted to high alert. She put her glass down on the coffee table and took a breath. This didn't sound good.

"What is it?" she asked, growing defensive.

"Don't look so worried," he said, aware of the change in her. He lifted his hand to stroke her hair. "It's about the store."

"Oh," she said with surprise and relief. "Is there a problem?"

"You could...say that."

"I'm sorry. What happened?"

"I told Gary I couldn't go through with the partnership."

"What? Why?"

"I don't think it's the right move for me."

"But you seemed so excited."

"Did I?"

"You did to me."

"I've been thinking. I want to go back to my stunt work again."

Dara's heart dropped and the breath caught in her throat. "Are you kidding?"

He shook his head.

"I thought you were done with that."

"I did, too. I mean, I didn't expect to be feeling so good after feeling like crap for so long. It's kind of giving me a new lease on what I can handle."

"You haven't done stunts in over a year. What makes you think you can just jump right back in?"

"The knowledge and expertise is up here," he said, pointing to his head. "I've been practicing all week down at the set, too."

Dara stared at him, trying to process the news.

"You okay?" he asked.

"Practicing? Why didn't you tell me?"

"I wasn't sure how."

"I didn't think you wanted to go back. You never let on."

"I didn't know myself."

"What made you change your mind?" she asked, although she had an inkling.

"I guess it started to really gel when we ran into T.J. and Ralph."

"Nick, that was only a week ago. Are you sure you're not being impulsive about this?"

"I don't think so."

"It kind of sounds that way to me."

"Maybe going into business was the impulsive decision. It's not like I've ever done anything like that before."

Dara thought about it and then shook her head. "No," she demurred. "The store was a great opportunity."

"Look, I realized something important this week. I think I was leaning toward the business for the wrong reasons. My accident, what happened to Matt, they did a real number on my head and I was…anxious about going back—but stunts are in my blood. I don't want to wake up one day and realize I let fear stop me from doing what I do best."

Dara folded her arms around herself. "I see," she said quietly. "Are you going back to *Stormcats*?"

Nick nodded. "I met with the coordinator for lunch this week. He offered me my job back. The only bad thing is I'll have to travel to Europe for part of the season."

Dara closed her eyes and let her head drop.

"What is it that bothers you so much about this? I don't get the feeling it's about my safety," he said, attempting to lighten the mood with a joke.

Dara stared into her lap.

"Is this about Adriana? Because if it is, you have nothing to worry about."

Dara looked up at him, doubt in her eyes.

"I mean it, Dara," he said, leaning forward and touching her face. "I'm not interested anymore. I'm happy with you."

"It's not just that, it's that whole world. I don't feel comfortable knowing you're a part of it. It isn't just a job, it's a lifestyle, and not one that's conducive to having a normal relationship."

"You know, I think you're making blind judgments here."

"It's such a volatile way to live. Industry people are always working odd hours, traveling on location…playing musical sex mates. Sorry, I don't want to be home alone in bed wondering where you are and what you're doing. I'm too old and exhausted for that. What I want now is some stability. Relationships out of the Hollywood scene are hard enough, but on a TV set, with all the gorgeous starlets and giant egos, the deck is really stacked against you."

"Just 'cause I work there, doesn't mean I have to be a part of all that."

"Doesn't it?"

"Come on, Dara! Are you telling me I can't have the job I want and the woman I want at the same time? That's just crazy."

She sighed. "Apparently you've made up your mind, so there's nothing for me to say."

Nick took a deep breath and stared at one of the motorcycle photos hanging on the wall. After a minute, he spoke again. "I don't know what to say either. You know, I was hoping tonight was going to be...special. I was hoping you'd stay over—that we'd finally be together."

Dara felt a wave of emotion rise in her. She felt so conflicted, so frightened. Tears brimmed in her eyes. "I'm sorry. I just can't live that way."

"What way?"

"Not knowing...not knowing..." she said. She got up from the couch and walked quickly to get her sweater, about to fall apart and not wanting to do it in front of him.

"Not knowing what?" he called to her in frustration.

She couldn't bring herself to say it before she left, but she thought it just the same. *Not knowing when—or for whom—he might leave her.*

Dara sat stunned behind the wheel of her car. The raw emotion she felt offered her a spontaneous out-of-body-like experience. She probably shouldn't have been driving at a time like this, but the alternative, staying and talking it through, was beyond her current capabilities.

She drove past Reggie's home but couldn't bring herself to stop. She couldn't tolerate a lecture, although she knew on some level that she deserved one. Her cell phone rang in her purse; she ignored it, and headed west and then south. Soon, she pulled into her own garage, her hands still shaky, her face stained with tears and mascara.

When she walked into her condo, her phone machine blinked furiously at her. She unplugged the phone, shut off her cell, stripped down to her panties, and threw on a nightshirt. She wandered into the bathroom, rummaged through her stash of medication, and prepared an herbal sedative cocktail, which she washed down with water slurped from her cupped palm. Wincing from the taste, she wiped her mouth and headed straight for bed, where her trusty cat was waiting to comfort her. Tonight, though, even Mallory didn't stand a chance.

Nick left two messages on her machine and three on her cell. At about three o'clock the following day, she finally called him back. Afterward, she chided herself for doing so. Nothing had changed from the evening before. The conversation simply served to rub salt in a fresh wound.

"Why do you have so little trust in me? Have I done anything to warrant that? I admit I had my wild days, but since I've been dating you, haven't I been good?"

"Yes."

"Then why are you so freaked out about this?"

"I don't know."

"Well, maybe you just need to give it a little time, so you can see there's nothing to worry about."

She didn't respond.

"Dara, I know you're the one who's usually psychoanalyzing me, but you don't have to be Freud to see what's going on here. How do you expect to ever find a guy and be happy if you're always waiting for the other shoe to drop?"

"I don't know. I just know I can't go through it all again. I promised myself."

Nick sighed deeply.

"I'm sorry, Nick."

"Me, too," he said as he reluctantly hung up.

To add insult to injury, Dara's weekly meeting with Reggie set her even further off kilter. She had filled Reggie in by phone on the depressing goings-on of the weekend, but when he'd pressed her to find out how she could give up on the best relationship of her life so easily, she'd brought the conversation to an abrupt halt. Now she sat across from him again in the conference room. Both sipped coffee from mugs.

"Okay, so now that I have you captive, I need to get some answers," Reggie said.

Dara offered an annoyed sigh.

"Have you talked to him again?"

"No."

"Why not?"

"Because there's nothing left to say."

"You're clearly miserable, so something's not right with the world. You know, you're your own worst enemy, Harri."

"Reggie, we have something bigger to worry about."

"What?"

"Me making a fool of myself and this dating service on Ophelia," she said.

"We'll be fine. We have three great success stories."

"Three? You mean—"

"Yeah, I was going to tell you. I just got off the phone with Serena. Tony, I mean Al, is coming on the show with her."

"You're kidding. She got him to come on? I'm impressed. Well, I guess that solves one of our problems."

"There's more news," he said almost ominously.

"What?"

"Harri," he said, taking her hand.

"Yes?" she asked looking down at his hand, and then up at his face.

"They're engaged."

A huge lump formed in Dara's throat, rendering her speechless. She swallowed so she could form words again. "Are you sure?"

He nodded.

"Tony? Engaged? For real?"

"I know it's hard to grasp."

"I'm—"

"I know, I was, too."

"—stunned. So you're telling me he actually went out to a jewelry store—deliberately—and plunked down a few thou for a diamond? Tony?"

"I'm guessing."

"Holy shit!"

"It's a good thing, right? We have three success stories in six months. I didn't think we'd do it!"

She didn't seem to hear him.

"Harri?"

She stared off into space, trying to absorb the shock.

"Harri? You okay?"

She shook her head.

"I know it's hard to take, but think of how great MateSearch is going to look," Reggie said, trying to comfort her.

"It's not MateSearch I'm thinking about...it's me," she said. "What does it say about me, the woman with all the answers? I'm basically proving to the world that I'm a fraud, that my long-held and long-preached philosophies on love don't always work—or worse, that they work for others, but not for pathetic little me."

"Come on…"

"I'll be mocked."

"You don't know that. You're being very melodramatic, Harri," he said.

"It's so ironic, you know?"

"What is?"

"That my professional success has become contingent on my personal success."

"Yeah, it is when you think about it," he agreed.

"It's like somebody up there is trying to make a point or something," she said, indicating the ceiling.

"Like what?"

"Maybe that the last fifteen years of my life have been a sham."

"Have not. You had a successful career as a columnist, and now you're proving to be a smashing success as an entrepreneur. Every challenger has won the MateSearch Challenge! That's pretty amazing if you ask me."

"It won't spare me my own humiliation. Until recently, I bore that particular failure in private. Now it'll be on display for all of America to see."

"Actually, Ophelia runs overseas, too."

"Reggie!" she cried in reproach.

"Sorry."

She pushed her chair away from the table and walked to the door.

"Where you going?" he called to her.

She didn't answer as she left the room and fled to the privacy of her office. She closed and locked the door, sat behind her desk, and let the tears flow.

Tony is going to beat me to the altar? Was this some sort of cosmic joke? How could I possibly join three blissful couples under the glare of television lights and international media exposure?

It was more than she could bear. She grabbed a large bunch of tissues and held them to her face, hoping to mask the sounds of her sobs. She cried about Tony. She cried about Nick. Most of all, she cried for the little girl who, once again, found herself alone.

❦ *Forty-three* ❦

T HE SHRIEK OF HIS ALARM AT SIX was a welcome intrusion
for Nick. For the third time in as many nights he'd found himself
in the grip of the nightmare he thought he'd finally vanquished
from his subconscious. He had enjoyed two months of peaceful slumber
until now, and had largely attributed this respite to finally getting back on
his motorcycle and facing the open road again. Thinking back, he realized
the dreams had ceased before then. In fact, their ending had coincided
with Mallory's visit—the time he'd forged a surprising friendship with the
woman he'd previously yearned to strangle.

Now he just wanted to shake her—shake all the insecurities and fears
free from her mind. It had been two weeks since her bizarre exit from his
life, but he still couldn't fathom it. A person doesn't break up with someone over a job decision. It wasn't like he'd decided to become a stripper or
a male escort, was it?

Deep down, Nick really wasn't too surprised. He may have dated
scores of women, but that didn't mean he'd ever understand them. He
hated to admit it, but after his previous breakups, the only thing he'd really
missed was the sex, so forgetting Dara should be easy, right? Only somehow, since she'd gone, he'd experienced loss on a level of which he didn't
think he was capable.

After quieting the alarm, he leaned back on his headboard to collect
his thoughts. It was his first day back on the set and he could feel nervous

343

twinges in his gut. *It's just that damned dream,* he told himself as he threw the covers off and jumped out of bed.

Later, while weaving his car through the winding canyon roads that led into the valley, he found himself thinking about Gary and hoping he'd find someone to partner with on the new store. Gary had been so remarkably understanding over the last two weeks, which had made Nick feel even more guilt about his sudden change in plans.

As he drove through the gates of the studio, his body filled with anticipation. Seeing the scene backdrops, the busy executives, the production crews hard at work made him smile. He pulled into a designated parking spot and got out of his car. Then he took a deep breath and went to find Kenny.

Depression could be murder on creativity, or so Dara found out as she sat wrapped in her bathrobe at her home computer, attempting to produce a coherent column for the MateSearch newsletter. In recent months, she'd tackled the subjects of "Dating Decorum," "Broadening Your Dating Horizons," "Relationship Rx," and "Donning the Right Attitude." It was no coincidence that this month's topic was "Letting Go of the Wrong Love." Dara hoped that through the writing process, she might glean some useful self insight; however, it had been close to two hours of fits and starts with no real progress. She looked glumly at Mallory, who lay on the desk watching her. The *Ophelia Show* taping was only a week away, and it weighed heavily on her mind. With a thought to that, she decided to take a short break and make a long put-off phone call. She lifted the receiver, leaned back in her chair, and punched in the familiar digits.

"Hey, Tony, it's me."

There was a short pause before he responded. "Hey, stranger."

"How are you?"

"I'm good, I'm good."

"I'm sorry I haven't been in touch. I just wanted to congratulate you on your engagement. That's wonderful news."

Another pause. "Thank you," he said. "You must have been in shock, huh?"

"Who, me?"

"I know it's kind of quick, but—"

"Hey, when things are right, they're right. Right?" she said forcing enthusiasm.

He laughed. "Right. Serena's a great girl. We really hit it off."

"I told you I had a knack for this."

"You do, you do. Funny how things work out, huh?"

"Yeah," she said, trying not to sound gloomy. "You tell her about us?"

"She thinks we just dated a few times through the service."

"Thanks," she said with relief. "That's best."

"I figured."

"You okay with doing the show?"

"I got used to the idea. Shelby said I could plug my business if I do it discreetly."

"Said the magic words, huh?"

"Yeah," he replied with a chuckle. "So what about you?"

"Me?" she asked, trying to stall.

"Did you meet The Challenge?"

"No. No, I didn't."

"Oh. That's okay, not everything can be done on a schedule, you know."

"I know."

"Someday it'll be right, watch and see."

Tears formed in her eyes. If there was one thing she couldn't stand right now, it was pity from Tony. "Anyway, I just wanted to say congrats, and I'll see you in a week, 'kay?" she said, her voice beginning to crack.

"Sure, sure. Hey, thanks for calling."

She couldn't answer for fear he'd hear her break. Instead, she hung up and hung her head to cry. After a few minutes of feeling sorry for herself, she wiped her face with a tissue, dried her eyes, and returned to her computer.

"Work, damn it. Work!" she commanded herself.

She forced out a few more inane sentences and printed the page she'd written. She lifted it out of the printer and began to read, hoping to find some lucid ideas among the mix, but she knew in her heart it was just dressed-up muck. She angrily crumpled up the piece of paper and threw it across the room. Suddenly, Mallory sprung up and flew after it. She picked it up in her mouth and in a second was back, the bunched up paper clenched between her tiny fangs. She dropped it at her slipper-clad feet and looked up at her expectantly, as Dara watched in astonishment.

It only took a few hours before Nick was right back in the thick of things, and by the end of his third day, he had dived off a building headfirst and jumped a bike from a dock onto an ocean freighter. But it was the stunt that Kenny had been so vociferously promoting on the phone that Nick had been intently chewing over. He had to admit it was an awesome idea and his old fervor instinctively kicked in. Kenny had sold him on the idea his first day back. The plan was to have him leap out of a helicopter while on a bike, flip over in the air and land on the rooftop of a posh hotel, where a "bad guy" would have already poured gasoline and set it on fire. Nick would then go up in flames as he and his bike careened off the rooftop and into the hotel's luxurious pool, sixteen flights below.

Every detail had been planned out for months, thanks to Kenny, and Nick spent many hours going over them with a fine-toothed comb, shoving any fears or doubts to the back of his mind and focusing like a laser on the execution of the stunt. Now that he'd been given his life back, he needed to prove he was worthy of it.

Sitting alone in the stunt trailer, he was studying the storyboard when he heard a knock on the door.

"Door's open," he called, but whoever it was didn't seem to hear. He opened the door to find Adriana Norris standing before him with a big welcoming smile. She had long wavy dark hair, sultry, almond-shaped eyes, and the body of a *Baywatch* babe. She wore tight jeans, a sleeveless pink top sans bra, and silver flip flops. Seeing her again, he remembered why he'd felt so drawn to her. She was one of the sexiest and most gorgeous women he'd ever seen in his life. Apparently he wasn't the only one who thought so.

"You can't avoid me forever, you know," she told him, one hand on her waist.

"Who says I was avoiding you?"

"It's been three days. I'd have thought you'd come to say hello."

"I've been busy."

"I'm just teasing," she said. "Can I come in?"

"I'm kind of in the middle of—"

"I'll just stay a sec," she said, stepping up into the trailer before he could stop her. "You look really good, Nick," she said, giving him a twice over. "Nice to see you back in one piece."

His jaw tightened as he nodded, trying not to notice how her nipples protruded through the silky fabric of her shirt.

"Things have been kind of tiresome around here without you," she told him.

"I don't know. I hear you've been keeping pretty stimulated."

"I meant professionally. Nobody seems to have your grit. You made the rest of the stunt crew look like mere mortals."

Nick raised one eyebrow at her attempted flirtation.

"You impressed everyone. I know you impressed me," she continued.

"Look, Adriana—"

"It's all right. I can see you're still holding a little grudge. That's okay. You're a big boy, you'll get over it."

"I am over it, Adriana. Have been for a long time."

Her eyes seared through him. "Glad to hear it," she said. "Maybe we can start over fresh, you know?" she said, stepping closer to him and flipping her hair over one shoulder.

"Don't tell me you're recycling your conquests already," he said. "There must be some fresh meat around here somewhere. Have you tried the craft service cart?"

"You really are still sore at me, Nicky, and I'm sorry. We had a good thing," she said, eyeing his body again. It angered him that he felt a familiar fluttering in his jeans. He flashed back to her nude body, he'd never seemed to get enough of it while they were together and she knew it. From the look in her eyes, she still believed that to be true.

"I don't know what we had Adriana, but whatever it was, it's over."

"Never say never, sweetie," she said with a wink.

"Look, I need to get back to work. Thanks for stopping by."

"Sure," she replied, walking toward the door. He watched as she stepped out, her rear end swinging in a last attempt to taunt him. After she was gone, he blew air from his pursed lips and turned back to his boards.

The next day, Nick got to the heliport extra early to help set up the long-planned spectacular feat. He consulted with Kenny and Jim, the other stuntmen, and crew members who were involved in the planning and execution. Each one assured him they'd done their job and didn't expect any glitches. They slapped his back, egged him on, and looked at him with the same reverence that he had thrived on over the years—the same reverence his father had garnered during his long, illustrious career.

Nick pored over every detail several times, but still felt a nagging in his gut, a foreign sensation to the man once known as Mr. Adrenaline. He chalked it up to the crash, which had brought the realization that he wasn't infallible. Until then, he had never let such thoughts even enter his imagination.

By ten-thirty, everything was in place. The helicopter was parked in the area that had been cordoned off for the production crew. Nick, dressed in a fire retardant suit, warmed up by riding his bike around in circles while running each component of the stunt over and over in his head.

By eleven o'clock, the crew had loaded a custom Honda 900rr, one of Nick's favorite stunt bikes, onto the helicopter. Ten minutes later, the pilot fired up the helicopter and its blades began to whirl. Kenny, holding a clipboard, ran over the process again with Nick for the umpteenth time, but Nick couldn't hear a word he was saying. It wasn't due to the noisy chopper. Something peculiar was occurring deep inside of him. It was a feeling that was as intense as it was unexpected.

"That sound okay to you?" asked Kenny.

Nick didn't answer; he seemed mesmerized by the spinning blades. He was thinking about Dara—how she'd expertly summed up his old life. His need to impress was just a way to appease his insecurities. He had taken inordinate risks to prove himself worthy—but of what? He thirsted for admiration, but it was always short-lived: he was only as awesome as his last stunt.

"Nick?"

"Yeah," he replied, still far away.

"You better get on the chopper," said Kenny.

Nick spied the pilot motioning him through the cockpit window. He became aware of the intensity in Kenny's eyes, a look that told him pulling off this stunt was the most important thing in the world to him, and that Nick was only a means to that end. It made him shudder.

"Hey, Nick?" said Kenny as he touched his arm and cocked his head toward the helicopter.

Nick stood transfixed by his own thoughts. His whole outlook on life had transformed, propelled by his powerful new feelings for Dara. The realization sent endorphins shooting through his body. He was no longer an empty drum.

By now Kenny was clearly nervous. There had been no mention of the crash since their first phone call and he'd probably assumed it was a nonissue—or at least hoped as much, especially since Nick had seemed so eager to perform.

"You're not nervous, are you, man?"

"No."

"Then what is it?"

"I just realized something."

"What, did we forget something?" Kenny asked anxiously

"No. I just realized…I don't want to do this," he answered matter-of-factly.

"Huh? Why?" Kenny asked with alarm.

"I just don't need to do this anymore," he replied calmly, removing his helmet. He knew Kenny could never begin to understand the reasons even if he tried to explain them. Nick took a deep breath and let it out, his face brightening as Kenny's darkened.

"It's the crash, isn't it? You're thinking about the crash," said Kenny.

"No…not in the way you think, anyway."

"Nick, don't talk in riddles. This is a big deal, a big expensive, fucking deal. I thought you were as pumped about it as me."

"I'm sorry, Kenny. I shouldn't have come back. I thought I was coming home," he said looking around, "but this ain't my home anymore."

Forty-four

I T WAS THE DAY DARA HAD AGONIZED over for six long months and now that it was here, she couldn't wait to get it over with. She thanked God for Reggie, who provided her the support and guidance that would help to get her through it. He sat with her in the green room, whispering a pep talk in her ear as she watched the three challengers and their significant others across the large room, mingling, sipping Orangina, and nibbling an assortment of tiny sandwiches and pastries. She had greeted Tony warmly, and he her, but watching him with his fiancée, who was sporting a modest pear-shaped diamond on her left ring finger, only contributed to her anxious state.

Dara had spent the better part of the previous week's sleep time pondering the spiel she would offer Ophelia when confronted with the obvious questions about her failure to meet the MateSearch Challenge. She finally decided on a game plan: she would paint herself as a mother hen looking after her chicks. She'd claim that her intense focus on the success of others' relationships, including the other challengers, was her first priority, even if it meant less time to concentrate on herself. She would tell of all the wonderful men she'd met at MateSearch and describe how proud she was of her superior clientele, while professing her desire to focus on her own love life in the near future. The best part, though, was that she had talked Shelby out of using any footage of her embarrassing dates. Reggie

351

had agreed that her strategy was probably the best way to handle this sticky situation, all things considered.

"So who else did you invite besides the office gang?" asked Reggie, attempting to distract Dara from her thoughts.

"Just Jesse. I got him and Sal front row seats. I'm finally going to get to meet his mystery lover. Do you think I should act surprised by his sexual preference?"

"I don't know. I just hope the cameras don't hit them. What if they tell everyone they met on MateSearch? We didn't prepare a response to that."

"I made him promise not to say a word and to try to dress conservatively to call less attention to himself."

"Jesse? Yeah, right."

A harried young woman with an earpiece and a clipboard swung open the door to the room. The buzz quieted as she gave the guests their five minute warning. Two of the women squealed with anticipation, and Reggie squeezed Dara's hand to calm her as she tapped her left Manolo Blahnik pump in a rapid beat.

"Relax, you're going to do great," he whispered.

"You promise?"

"Just take a deep breath and be yourself!"

Dara stood up and straightened the skirt of her blue Prada suit. "Ironic, isn't it?" she said as he walked her out the door and toward the stage.

"What?"

"Right now I'd rather be anyone else."

"And we're back with Dara Harrison, co-owner of MateSearch, still Los Angeles's hottest dating service," said Ophelia excitedly as the audience applauded. "You've met two happy couples, are you guys ready to meet the third challenger and see how well she made out?"

The audience shouted out variations of "Yeah!"

"Eddie, please roll the tape," said Ophelia.

A moment later, a montage of video clips began to play featuring Serena on two less-than-successful dates and then a series of promising dates with "Al." The audience watched as the couple dined in fine restaurants, listened to jazz, biked in the park, and sailed on a rented yacht. It was on that luxury boat that the footage caught him kissing Serena passionately on the lips just before bending down on one knee to offer her a ring.

Dara watched, the lump in her throat re-forming. She didn't know the engagement had been caught on tape. Of course, knowing Shelby, she shouldn't have been surprised. Despite her less than passionate feelings for Tony, watching him fall in love with someone else left her despondent. When the tape ended, the lights came up and Ophelia brought Serena and Al onto the stage.

Dara forced a smile and applauded along with the rest of the studio audience as the couple took their seats between her and Ophelia.

"Congratulations, guys!" said Ophelia. "So we have three success stories, Dara. How do you feel about that?"

"Wonderful, of course," Dara replied. "They make a great couple, don't they?"

"Absolutely, and I'm glad there are no hard feelings between you and Al."

"Of course not," said Dara and Al in unison.

"Let me explain to the audience and the folks at home. Al was one of Dara's MateSearch matches. In fact, they went out several times. Can you tell us why things didn't work out?"

Tony and Dara looked at each other uncomfortably for a moment. Then Dara spoke softly.

"Just wasn't meant to be, I guess."

"Dara's a great lady," Tony told Ophelia.

"But Serena is clearly the one for him," said Dara.

Ophelia asked the couple a few more questions. By then, Dara was approaching emotional overload and began to zone out, until something caught her eye in the front row. Despite the glaring lights, she could just make out Jesse, dressed in a floral wrap-around dress, furiously blowing kisses at her with his right hand, as his left held the hand of someone in a suit and tie with short red hair. Dara squinted in an attempt to finally get a gander at the man her friend was so excited about. Instead the delicate features of an attractive woman came into focus.

Holy moly! she thought, as the show went to commercial. Before the shock could register, Tony and Serena were bidding her goodbye and she was instructed to move into the seat next to Ophelia, who was now shooting her odd but affable glances. Dara wondered if this was her way of showing empathy for her sorry state after encountering so much adoration and excitement among the six previous guests. She took a deep breath and ran over her spiel again in her head, as a makeup artist touched up Ophelia's face and patted hers with some light powder.

The cameras went live again and Ophelia sprang into action. "We're back, people, and ready for the moment you've all been waiting for! We're going to find out how Dara Harrison herself fared on *my* challenge to *her*!"

God, did she have to play it all up for such a huge letdown? This was just cruel— especially because Ophelia had been informed about the unfortunate facts of her case days ago.

"Now I know y'all are going to be disappointed that we don't have a film to show you for Dara," Ophelia explained. "At her request, we decided not to use it for a very special reason. Dara, would you like to explain why?"

Dara felt her face flush. It was time to break the humiliating news, and she found herself choked up for a moment. "Well, I'm sorry to disappoint everyone, but things worked out a little differently for me," she began apologetically. "As it turns out—"

"As it turns out, people, the creator of this amazing dating service didn't just match up three lucky members of my audience, she even managed to make herself a match, too!" Ophelia shouted at the audience with exhilaration as they began to applaud.

Dara shot her a look of panic. Did Shelby forget to inform the show's host of her plight? Would a blabbermouth like Shelby ever forget something as critical as that?

"Ophelia, I don't think—"

"That's right, we have four success stories! This lovely matchmaker has found love, too!"

The audience exploded in an uproar as Dara frantically tried to get Ophelia's attention.

"Now...now," Ophelia said, quieting the room, "Dara doesn't know her special man is here today, just waiting in the wings to come out and meet us."

Dara shot frenzied looks to either side of the stage until she caught Reggie standing just beyond the curtain smiling big, his arms folded over his chest. He winked at her and her jaw dropped. Reggie was going to try to convince the world they were an item! Had he gone mad? Or was this his craziest publicity stunt yet? She wanted to flee the set and catch the first plane out of LAX to Siberia. They may not have heard of Ophelia there.

"The reason she doesn't know," Ophelia continued, "is because she's been keeping him a secret!"

The audience gasped and laughed as Dara closed her eyes and willed herself to disappear.

"Do you want to tell us why, Dara?"

Dara opened her eyes wide and shook her head.

Ophelia laughed. "Well, then, I guess I'll explain. You see, Dara is such an amazing lady that she was willing to come on our show and admit to falling short of meeting the MateSearch Challenge in order to respect a wish for privacy from her man—but guess what?"

"What?" Dara frantically asked along with the hyped-up audience.

"What she doesn't know is that just today, he contacted the show to say he changed his mind and wants to be here for her! Isn't that romantic, people?"

The audience cheered and applauded.

"So please welcome..." Ophelia shouted as Dara stared at a surprisingly calm Reggie, "...Dara's handsome new beau, a man she met through her very own dating service, Nick Wyatt!"

Dara's mouth fell open again as Nick emerged from behind Reggie. He wore dark slacks and an elegant, cobalt blue collared shirt. His eyes sparkled as he walked toward her. She stood up, her knees wobbly, her mind so in shock she didn't know how to respond. The expression he wore was serious and contrite, as if trying to gauge her reaction. When he saw her break into a relieved and happy smile, he moved more swiftly, grabbing her around her waist and planting a fiery kiss on her lips as the audience stood for an ovation. When the room settled down, the couple took their seats near Ophelia. Dara couldn't stop staring at Nick, wondering what, how, why he was sitting next to her at this moment.

"So tell us, Nick, what made you suddenly change your mind?" asked Ophelia.

"Well," he began, "I realized I was being selfish. I was concerned about my reputation and didn't want to be here because I didn't want the publicity."

"The publicity?" asked Ophelia, riveted. "What is it that you do?"

"Well, I used to be a Hollywood stuntman," he said, turning to Dara who looked at him with so many questions in her eyes.

"Sounds dangerous!" said Ophelia.

"It can be," admitted Nick, still looking at Dara, "but I'm ready to stop taking so many chances with my life—especially now that you're in it. I thought going back meant I was facing my fears—then I realized something."

"What?" asked Dara, looking into his eyes.

"The only thing I'm afraid of is being without you."

Dara's eyes watered and her heart thumped wildly. Nick's voice was solid as he uttered the words he had evaded his whole life.

"I love you."

Forty-five

THE REST OF THE DAY WAS A HAPPY BLUR. After the taping, they went out for an impromptu celebration with Reggie and his boyfriend, Cole, and Jesse and his girlfriend, Sal, formerly known as Sally, at a Santa Monica joint called Garrett's. Throughout dinner, Nick repeatedly touched her, held her hand, and stroked her hair. Dara's thoughts sailed to a new dimension. She tried to discern the unusual, new feelings inside her and midway through her entrée, they crystallized. She belonged somewhere. She belonged here, sitting next to the man who had entered her life like a lightning bolt and won her over in spite of herself. Faults, fears, neuroses—none of them really mattered if you loved someone. She of all people should have known that.

She dipped a forkful of salmon into the puddle of dill sauce on her plate and brought it to her mouth just as Nick leaned over and whispered in her ear.

"Hurry and finish. I've got plans for you."

Dara emerged from her bathroom in a black, baby doll negligée that she'd owned for three years and from which she'd finally cut the tags. Already in bed, the covers pulled to his waist, Nick crossed his brawny arms behind his head when he saw her, a grin climbing across his face.

"Wow," he said as she twirled around. "Get over here."

As she walked seductively toward the bed, Mallory scampered out of the room, as if offering them privacy. Nick pulled the covers back for her to climb in. She stood there for a moment, gazing at his nude body for the first time.

"What's the matter?" he asked.

"Just thinking about something," she said, smiling.

"What?" he asked, lifting himself up onto one elbow.

"I'm thinking how glad I am that we settled out of court."

Nick laughed in surprise. "Why's that?"

She let her eyes travel slowly down his body, a little smirk on her face. "'Cause I definitely would have lost that lawsuit."

Acknowledgments

To the man who made this book possible, Mitchell Silbowitz, my husband, my friend, my partner, my love. Thank you for your innovative spirit, your enduring faith in my talent, and for sharing your business acumen with a stubborn, right-brained, business dummy like me.

To my exceptionally wonderful parents, Harry and Marilyn Trachtenberg, for always being a steady, loving presence in my life, and for counseling me through more than my share of neurotic relationships. You deserve Purple Hearts! I love you both forever.

To Victoria Skurnick, your belief in me and this book means more than you can imagine. Thank you for your friendship, your dedication, your efforts, and so much more.

To Laura Grace Montaruli, for coming to the rescue with your beautiful cover illustration on very short notice.

To Nancy Doherty, for your brilliant, eleventh hour makeover. You are an editor extraordinaire.

To Jen Harrison, my favorite cheerleader and buddy, for your encouragement, talent, and unceasing enthusiasm.

To Linn B. Halton and all my talented colleagues at LoveaHappyEnding.com, for your support, generosity, kindness, and camaraderie. I am blessed to be a part of such a wonderful crew.

To all my buddies in the Come Back to Me group, for opening your minds, your hearts, and your blogs to me! You are extraordinary individuals, stellar promoters, and best of all, cherished friends.

With special thanks to international bestselling author and creator of the World Literary Café, Melissa Foster, for your generosity, inspiration, wisdom, and friendship. Thank you for teaching me, and so many other authors, what success really means.

About the Author

Bonnie Trachtenberg is the award-winning, bestselling author of *Wedlocked: A Novel*. She writes a monthly relationship and advice column for LoveaHappyEnding.com. She was senior writer and copy chief at Book-of-the-Month Club and has written seven children's book adaptations. Trachtenberg lives on Long Island with her husband, four cats and a dog. *Neurotically Yours* is her second novel.

You can learn more about Bonnie Trachtenberg and read her blog at http://www.BonnieTrachtenberg.com

Read her relationship column: http://loveahappyending.com/editor-bonnie-trachtenberg

Find her on Facebook: http://www.Facebook.com/BonnieTrachtenberg

Follow her on Twitter at http://twitter.com/#!/writebrainedny

www.ingramcontent.com/pod-product-compliance
Lightning Source LLC
Chambersburg PA
CBHW050908250626
47155CB00001B/153